DAVID EBSWORTH is the pen name of writer Dave McCall, a former negotiator for Britain's Transport & s born in Liverpool but has lived in W e Ann since 1981.

Following his retirement, Da n in 2009 and has subsequently pul rs dealing with the 1745 Jacobite re r, the Battle of Waterloo, warlord rivalry in sixth century Britain, and the Spanish Civil War. His sixth book, *Until the Curtain Falls* returns to that same Spanish conflict, following the story of journalist Jack Telford, and is published in Spanish under the title *Hasta Que Caiga el Telón*. Jack Telford, as it happens, is also the main protagonist in a separate novella, *The Lisbon Labyrinth*.

Each of Dave's novels has been critically acclaimed by the Historical Novel Society and been awarded the coveted BRAG Medallion for independent authors.

This seventh novel, *The Doubtful Diaries of Wicked Mistress Yale*, is the first in a trilogy about the life of nabob philanthropist (and slave-trader) Elihu Yale, told through the eyes of his much-maligned and largely forgotten wife, Catherine.

For more information on the author and his work, visit his website at www.davidebsworth.com.

Also by David Ebsworth

The Jacobites' Apprentice
A story of the 1745 Rebellion. Finalist in the Historical Novel Society's 2014
Indie Award. This has been out of print pending publication of a second
edition. Updates about the book and its availability can be found at
www.davidebsworth.com

The Jack Telford Series
Political thrillers set towards the end of the Spanish Civil War.
The first of these is *The Assassin's Mark*.
"This is not a novel you will be able to put down."
–Rachel Malone, Historical Novel Society

The sequel is the much-acclaimed *Until the Curtain Falls*, published in Spanish
as *Hasta Que Caiga el Telón*. Telford also features in the e-book novella,
The Lisbon Labyrinth, which follows Jack's later misadventures during the
Portuguese Revolution of April 1974.

The Kraals of Ulundi: A Novel of the Zulu War
Picks up the story of the Zulu War where Michael Caine left off.
"An accomplished, rich, beautifully produced and very rewarding read that
brings a lesser-known era of history to life."
–Cristoph Fischer, Historical Novel Society

The Last Campaign of Marianne Tambour: A Novel of Waterloo
Action and intrigue based on the real-life exploits of two women who
fought, in their own right, within Napoleon's army.
"Superb! David Ebsworth has really brought these dramatic events to life.
His description of the fighting is particularly vivid and compelling."
–Andrew W. Field, author of *Waterloo: The French Perspective* and the
companion volume, *Prelude to Waterloo, Quatre Bras*

The Song-Sayer's Lament
"A rich, glorious, intricate tapestry of the time we know of as the Dark Ages.
With echoes of Rosemary Sutcliff's magnificent *Sword at Sunset* and Mary
Stewart's, *Crystal Cave* series, this is at once a fast, fierce tale of the old gods
versus the new, of old politics and honour replaced by venal expediency –
and of humanity in the face of implacable disease as the first great plague
swept through. It's steeped in authenticity and heart. I loved it!"
–Manda Scott, author of the bestselling *Boudica* series and *Into the Fire*

To Phil

The
DOUBTFUL
DIARIES
OF
Wicked Mistress Yale

Hope you enjoy!

DAVID EBSWORTH

Dave

SilverWood

Published in 2019 by SilverWood Books

SilverWood Books Ltd
14 Small Street, Bristol, BS1 1DE, United Kingdom
www.silverwoodbooks.co.uk

ISBN 978-1-78132-855-2 (paperback)
ISBN 978-1-78132-856-9 (ebook)

British Library Cataloguing in Publication Data
A CIP catalogue record for this book is available from the British Library

Page design and typesetting by SilverWood Books
Printed on responsibly sourced paper

Dedicated to the memory of Marilyn Cronyn

Author's Note

This is, of course, a work of fiction, though very firmly rooted in the history of Catherine and Elihu Yale. Research has been time-consuming but, as always, enjoyable – though it posed a few problems. The first of these was the dating of Catherine's diary entries. These are written as they would have been at the time and as seen in the personal correspondence of Elihu Yale and other real-life characters from the story, as well as the records of the English East India Company. Under the old Julian Calendar, then in use, the new year officially began in April of one year and ended in March of the next (although the 'calendar year' still began on 1st January, of course), so that February would, for example be dated as 1674/5, while May three months later would simply be dated as 1675.

Second, I have tried to limit the use of now obsolete vocabulary but, in places, it has been necessary in building the period's character. Hopefully, the glossary that appears at the end of the book will help if any of that vocabulary is troublesome. However, I have made no real attempt to include place names in the list, particularly for the locations in India. The contemporary documents are confusing in this regard, often with several entirely different spellings or identities for the same place, so that I have settled on names that keep the geography as simple as possible. Similarly, I have tried, where I was able, to use Tamil versions, or something approximately like Tamil, for words of local southeast Indian dialect. But, as always, all errors in any of this are entirely my own.

To my wicked wife…

That is what he wrote. Despicable fellow. His last will and testament, this Schedule in his own decaying, detestable hand that I should have known anywhere after all these decades. He did not even afford me my name. No *Catherine* even. Well, the curtness of phrase stands testimony to the man, says far more about Elihu Yale himself than any infamy it would ever cast upon one of my advanced years. Yet, beyond the phrase, there is nothing. A blank section upon the page. It cut me, and it angered me at the same time.

'Is this intended as some form of irony?' I said to the attorney. 'Some attempt at dark humour? He bequeaths me nothing, after all he owed me, and he symbolises the fact in this distasteful manner?'

There was rain whispering darkly at the small windows, a funereal gloom casting shadows upon the mysterious mounds of scrolls and documents piled ceiling-high around his establishment.

'Mistress Yale,' Mister Lloyd-Hughes attempted to correct me, 'I believe the Governor may simply have paused in the drafting.' It has always struck me as strange, that so many folk should continue to style my estranged husband as *the Governor* when he rescinded that title twenty years ago. At Fort St. George. Madras. But that is Elihu Yale for you. A long reach even in death. 'Never completed the task,' said the lawyer. 'Other clauses the same. Incomplete. Including your daughters.'

'At least he troubled to list our daughters' names,' I said. 'Yet my only surviving son,' I went on, 'warrants not even a mention.'

'But this? Well, I must allow I never saw its likes before. This…'

He stabbed a finger at the offending line.

'A wicked wife?' I said. 'My husband was a pecksniff, sirrah. You

1

had your own dealings with him. Well? Did you not?'

'Speak as you find, I always say. Or show me his friends and I'll tell you the man. All he's done for the town. For the church. You'll find few around here, madam, with a bad word for Elihu Yale.'

But plenty for me, I suppose. A wicked wife? Is this what was in his mind? Was this what fed those deathbed words of his? My fight for them all these years? Or was it Benjamin's court case? Or the way I hated him for each of their deaths. Five of them wasted, gone. My poor boys. Is hate too strong a word? Everybody needs someone to love, they say, and I suppose that I did love him. At times. In my fashion. But I think it is true that every one of us also needs an object for our hate – and how bizarre that, in Elihu, I seem to have found both in the one man.

Yet, if it were any of those, they were minor sins, though part of the reason that brings me here today, to set matters straight. To see him buried. But those other matters, of which I can barely write – oh, of those issues, he could hardly have known the half. The blood on my hands. The Poison Nut seeds. The traitors I have sent to the gallows. My revenge upon Elihu himself. And for those you should need to return to the beginning.

To the very beginning.

Fifty years ago, when I was still a young bride. Though not, of course, Elihu's bride. Not then.

Volume One

Fort St. George, Madras Patnam

Yesterday I met a most objectionable fellow.

The southwest monsoon has brought in yet another vessel to our Coromandel Coast, and there we stood, on the palm-fringed strand, so early in the forenoon, to watch the deep-bellied *masula* surf-boats ferrying their passengers ashore. She is anchored in the roadstead, half a mile distant, and I could hear the boatmen, even above the raging surf, as they paddled and steered their way across that treacherous bar, singing their mystic rhythms.

'They'll catch a soaking today,' Joseph sighed, as some of the Gentues began to leap overboard in their fashion and, with difficulty, communicated to our European brothers that they should clamber onto their shoulders to be carried to dry land. It is never an easy task since the arrivals are invariably so encumbered and also twice the bulk of their porters – even after the inevitable weight loss from their six-month voyage on scant rations. And, on a day such as this, there are apt to be accidents. It was therefore difficult not to be moderately amused as first one, and then another, took a tumble or became soaked by rogue breakers.

'*Illai, illai!*' I yelled. No, no. And I flapped my parasol at the native boys running forward to offer limes and coconuts to the newcomers, as they struggled through the last of the waves. 'Accept their gifts at your peril,' I cried to our drenched recruits. 'Or they will consider themselves forever contracted to your service.'

'Better if they had arrived yesterday,' said Joseph. 'Or perhaps on the morrow. But now…'

'It is *karma*, I suppose.'

'What, this matter of *sati* and the girl too?'

One of the merchant captains, Mister Goulding, had died. A fever. And he, like our friend Matthew Parrish and many another, had kept a *bibi*. But this one young, little more than a child. Kalai. How young? Thirteen? Fourteen?

'Perhaps we worry unnecessarily.' I tried to reassure him, though he simply rewarded me with a scornful glance.

'Well, nobody of importance among them, at least,' he said. 'Judging by their ages.' One of those moments when I have to remind myself about the difference between us, ten years, though you would hardly know it from the laughter in his eyes, the lightness of his step, the slightness of his tall frame. And these recruits did, indeed, seem especially young. Writers, most of them. Junior clerks. And a couple of calico sorters. Not one of them much older than myself.

'Fie upon it, ma'am!' said a fellow who seemed better dressed than the others. 'If I'd known the place had such a stench, I should have asked to be dropped at the Comoros.'

My first impressions of him were that he was bovine, a bubble. Rakish and rapacious. In short, ambiguous.

'I am certain the Gentues would be happy to take you back, sir,' I snapped at him. Impertinent. The truth is that I have become somewhat proprietorial about our little home here, despite its many shortcomings. And, personally, I could smell nothing except the smoke from the cooking fires, the spices and incense from Black Town.

'The river, I'm afraid,' Joseph told him, and pointed away to our right, past the boatmen's shacks. There came the bloodcurdling curlew's cry from the same direction, from the brackish stream beyond the line of trees and the Half-Moon bastion at our back. 'Can't really see it from here. A little in spate, too, with the recent rains. Though it generally doesn't trouble us inside the gates. But you've arrived in time for prayers, at least. And how we need them today.'

A quizzical look from the fellow, the beginning of a question, and I determined to head off any premature discussion of our woes.

'Compulsory on Sundays and Wednesdays,' I said, my tone sharper than I intended. 'Governor Langhorn is scrupulous about such things. No dueling. No blasphemy. No gaming. No taverns after eight o' the clock.'

'You take me, madam, for a man who would indulge such vices?'

He slapped at a mosquito upon his neck.

'My wife has recently delivered me a fine son,' said Joseph. 'I fear she's not entirely recovered her usually jocose nature.'

Jocose? Is that what my husband thinks of me? Heavens, I do not recall ever considering myself jocose, even before the children came along. Baby Richard, peacefully asleep in his crib as I write these lines in the wake of that dreadful evening, and Joseph Junior, left playing happily on his rug with the fist-sized wooden elephant, which Akbar carved for him and has served him so well while he began cutting his teeth. But the impertinent incomer who had been so concerned about the odours had the grace, at least, to congratulate us.

'Then give you both joy of your new arrival, Mister...'

'Hynmers, sir. Joseph Hynmers. Second-of-Council at our fine establishment.' Joseph addressed himself now to the new writers collectively. 'My only regret, gentlemen, is that Governor Langhorn could not be here to greet you in person. Otherwise engaged, I fear.' Oh, indeed he was! 'But allow me to name my wife, Catherine, and...' Yet that was when the heavens opened once more. Bullets of water. 'Make haste, gentlemen. Make haste.'

Joseph, as was his wont, jumped to help another of the clerks struggling with his dunnage, and I found myself almost accosted by that crass fellow. To my astonishment, he seized hold of my parasol, held it above my head in what, I assume, he imagined might pass for an act of chivalry. Indeed, I was so shocked that words failed me though, naturally, he did not scruple to fill the silence.

'My pardon, ma'am,' he yelled through the downpour, and steered me towards the Sea Gate. 'If it ain't too fro'ward, perhaps you might allow me to introduce myself?'

'If you insist,' I told him, though it was a matter of indifference to me.

'Yale,' he said. 'Elihu Yale.'

An astonishing thing! That the vessel bringing this Yale person will sail again shortly and proceed to the Company's new factory at Taiwan. We have been trading there for years, but now a factory, complete with an entire mission of godowns.

And, Elihu Yale aside, the ship brings such treasure. Some distraction, at least, from the cloud hanging over us.

A letter from Mama, which I turn over and over in my hands, hold it to my nose and lips, hoping it may have retained some of her essence. Yet how could it be so? Written six months ago – no, seven. Before last Christmas. And in response to that which I had penned a twelve-month earlier again. All that time in a sack within the vessel's stinking hold. Even so, there is something. A sense of her proximity.

The weather here, daughter, she writes, after her opening endearments. *The rain – it has not stopped for weeks. And now there is snow. Great drifts of snow.*

It makes me laugh and cry, both at the same time. For the musket balls hammering upon our roof here are raindrops such as Mama could hardly imagine. In England, precipitation is tedious. Here, a terror.

And Baby Joseph, she writes. *Do I not, at least, deserve an image of him? Is there nobody of your acquaintance capable of portraiture? Your husband, I recall, has a certain talent in that regard.*

Indeed he does. A true gift. The house here almost awash with his sketchings. So I am determined that he should produce an exact likeness to accompany my own letter back to England. And not just Joseph, as she requests, but my little pudding Richard too – of whom she knows absolutely nothing, of course. Privately, I hope, she may appreciate the gesture, though she would never acknowledge it. Or… Perhaps I am reading her note incorrectly. For I now perceive a series of stains upon the page that I had not observed in my own excitement. Tear stains, I realise. And it shocks me. Saddens me. Rare indeed for her to so plainly exhibit her emotions.

Such an image, she continues, *might perhaps provide some solace. For I have suffered another mis-birth, and I fear that one more might kill me. It may be God's will that I should do my husband's bidding, but I do not believe the Almighty would wish to see me dead in the process.*

Poor Mama. Forty-one, and still bearing children, though there is not a word about my discordant younger brothers. This her third, perhaps fourth, mis-birth, though she is never one to dwell on misfortune, always keen to report on more impersonal matters of the outside world. So what would she think, I wonder, about young Kalai? How I wish I could talk to her about it all. Yet there are merely a few additional words about her health, and then this:

Yet you would wish to know, I think, that momentous news has reached us.

Thomas Fairfax has died. Poor Fairfax. Retired these eleven years past but surely the great parliamentarian of his age. Respected for his part in winning the civil wars. Respected equally for his part in securing the restoration of the monarchy. A man who understood that, often, simply being right, having morality on one's side, is not enough to secure victory. I saw him last at my father's funeral. Perhaps you will recall him too, for he was much taken by your presence.

No thanks to you, though, Mama! I was seven when Grandfather died, and threw such a foul humour when, at first, I was told I might not attend his burial. Mama and Papa finally, and untypically, surrendered to my mood, claiming that his stubborn streak was plainly strong in me, also. And yes, I remember Sir Thomas, the way he set me down and spoke to me, as though I were an equal, about his own respect for Mama's sire. Richard Chambers – London alderman for Walbrook Ward – stood against the tyrant king, thirty years ago now, led a troop of horse against him, but then, with Parliament victorious, refused to attend the public proclamation of the Commonwealth. Stripped of his positions as a result, imprisoned too. And though he was eventually pardoned and released, he never received the relief to which he should have been entitled.

'Your grand-sire,' Sir Thomas Fairfax had told me, 'was a just and honourable man, imprisoned and broken by a Commonwealth that was, itself, also inherently just and honourable. Such is, at times, the irony of life.'

In truth, I cannot be certain whether the words of Sir Thomas stayed with me or whether they remain in my memory through the frequency with which Mama repeated the anecdote as I was growing. But Fairfax dead. Gracious, the end of an era.

Meanwhile, your father's affairs, Mama informs me, *still flourish, and thus we are able to send the few tokens, which I trust may arrive safely.*

And yes, indeed they did! A carefully packaged crate. Four yards of the most elegant stuff – simple Irish linen, and it would have seemed like coals to Newcastle, yet scarlet! Heaven alone knows the value of the *cochinilla* involved in the dyeing, and presently being so admired by our *ayah* and several of her associates, though they seem less intrigued by the twenty yards of French satin. All the same, a dozen pairs of silk stockings, the lengths of ribbon – all worth their weight in gold.

Treasure! A second crate, specifically for Joseph – though she would never admit that this was her intention. But why else should she send me ten gross of long clay pipes, sixty pounds of fine tobacco and three beaver hats, unless they are to be gifted to my husband?

He smiled when he saw them, though I know his thoughts were somewhere else entirely.

'How could she know?' he said. 'The number of times I have succeeded in sitting upon my pipe.'

'I fear, sweet Joseph,' I replied, hoping to distract him from the ominous chanting we could hear, even then, from beyond the walls, 'that it is a tendency you share with my father. A common risk, the very least of perils, shared by gentlemen in this little stateless world of ours.' The world of the merchant adventurer, the world in which our men, our women, our children are all engaged through the peculation, the pursuit, the chance of trade that is far more than the simple accumulation of wealth itself.

The church bell had been ringing for an age, though my *ayah* refused to be hurried in her preparations.

'Must look good, *memsahib*, for your Yesu Kiristu.'

Her usual Sunday morning admonition, and she had laid out my finest white satin. Sleeve panels slashed and lined in my favourite pink, a match to my petticoats. Elegant, and in the expected fashion – at least, the fashion from two years ago – but how I envied her cool cotton *saree*. And how difficult it is to look good when the glass reflects so little of note, my eminently plain features, those entirely unremarkable mousey locks.

'Quickly, Tanani,' I gasped as she tightened the last of my lacings and I set my modesty cap carefully atop my curls. 'And my fan,' I pouted, 'where did I set the thing?'

I found it precisely where I had left it, naturally, and I needed it too, as I joined Joseph on our terrace walk. The rain had stopped and the earth, between our corner of Middle Street and the Fort House, which a half-hour earlier had been ankle-deep in mud, was now set solid once more. So I was just planting a final kiss on Richie's cherubic little cheeks and passing him to *ayah* Tanani when I became sensible that we were not alone.

'Ah, Mister Yale,' said Joseph, and I turned around to see the fellow there, one expensively buckled shoe set upon our lowest step, and his hand gripping the *veranda* post. They were chalk and cheese, this Yale fellow stocky and solid, to Joseph's slender and ethereal.

'The strangest thing,' he said. 'I cannot stop my legs from trembling. And it seems as though the very earth is pitching like the ship's deck.'

'So much time at sea,' my husband explained. 'A common complaint. Yet I trust you find your quarters comfortable.'

Yale looked over his shoulder to the blockhouse, which rose like a keep from the open square, fashioned from the same baked earth as the terrain itself.

'Somewhat in need of repair, Mister Hynmers, do you not find? And the whole thing eaten alive by white ants, is it not?'

'In danger of falling down,' Joseph laughed, 'though we have some workmen about to add buttresses. A few pillars here and there. That should help to keep it up.'

'A matter of some urgency, I would have imagined.' Mister Yale looked at my husband askance. 'With the Dutch threatening the warpath again?'

'Rather our own fault,' I said. 'Would you not say, sirrah? The Hollanders theoretically our allies, yet we plot with France against them.'

'A bold statement, madam, if you will forgive me saying so, especially with those savages baying at the gates.'

'The whole thing makes us all somewhat peevish,' said Joseph, while a beating drum announced the imminent arrival of the Governor's bodyguard. 'But you mustn't be concerned, sir. There are those among us with a peculiar gift for vigilance. Those with certain contacts. Keeping watch upon the Hollanders. The locals too. That sort of thing.'

'Spies?'

'God's Hooks, Mister Yale,' Joseph exclaimed, feigning distaste. 'A less than elegant word, I fear. No, in truth simply the upright uniformed gentleman yonder, so busy assembling a section of his company for church-parade.'

'Professional soldier?' said Yale. 'The garrison strong, at least.'

I laughed.

'Matthew would be delighted to hear you say so,' I told him. 'But the practice here is rather that the garrison's two companies are each commanded by a merchant captain.'

'Parrish,' said Joseph. 'Matthew Parrish. A man of considerable talent. For commerce. For poetry. And for the military.'

Matthew, like a young Alexander, was jostling his pikemen and musketeers into some semblance of disciplined order, yelling instructions.

'Two companies hardly seem adequate either, Mister Hynmers. Even for a poet. That would be – how many men would that be, precisely? And Europeans, I hope?'

'As it happens,' said Joseph, 'they are. Two companies, eighty in each. Quite an army! But the local auxiliaries are steadfast fellows too, in the main.'

Steadfast, I thought, *and far less trouble*. For the incidence of unruly behaviour among the English, Scots, Irish, French, Swedish and Portuguese recruits has so frequently been a cause for serious concern. But then, as if to lend the lie to my husband's words, Sir William's bodyguard marched – or, rather, shambled – into sight, around the corner from the Sea Gate.

'Great heavens.' Mister Yale was plainly taken aback. 'Do they serve any purpose above the ornamental?'

Indians. Portuguese. And a mix of both bloods. Colourful. Spiked helmets and mail. Stamping feet. The clash and chime of shields and weaponry that would have seemed ancient a hundred years ago.

'They rather grace the town, I find,' I said, wafting a cool breeze across my face from the peacock-feather fan.

'A very fine settlement it seems too,' Yale replied, and he looked along the length of Middle Street. 'Apart from...' He could not resist a wary glance towards Black Town. Still, at least he did not seem troubled by the heat, though he swatted another mosquito, then slid a finger inside the edge of his cravat, loosened it from his sweating neck.

'Fine,' Joseph smiled. 'If you ignore the ants, the flies, this climate that rots everything in sight, and the regular threat that we might all be murdered in our beds. The occasional noxious odour, too, of course.' He sniffed at the air. 'As you noted earlier. You should try the local attire too, Mister Yale. More fitting to the climate, we find.'

My husband looked very elegant. A simple white *kurta* tunic. Alluring, I thought, for he shares some characteristics with a certain class among the locals, those with sharp and noble features, I should say.

'I shall consider it, sirrah. Yet the streets so clean. And lined with – what? Fruit trees?'

'Pomegranate.' I pointed, recalling the *granados* from my Spanish childhood so well. 'And those are plum, of course. And there, a mango tree.'

'And that, with the palm fronds. Are those...?'

A flock of our local emerald parakeets swooped and screeched between the houses, almost drowned out the clamour from Black Town.

'Banana tree,' said Joseph. 'Not strictly a tree at all, of course. And sacred to the Gentues here. The fruit a rare delight. The leaves medicinal, as well as answering very well in place of tableware. A pious tree, they say, which symbolises their Lord Vishnu.'

'They have not been brought to the Bible, sir?'

'They appear to have survived passably well without it, Mister Yale. And it is not the Company's policy that we should interfere with their beliefs.'

'All the same, does that riotous assembly beyond the walls not signify?'

'Perhaps we might speak more of this another time, Mister Yale. You see? It is time for us to attend to our own devotions. The service about to begin. But if you should care to see our humble abode at closer quarters, you might join us for a small social gathering? This evening?'

'Poor fellow,' I said, almost without thinking, and watching Governor Langhorn take his seat within the modest Fort House dining room that served as our chapel. So much to occupy him.' Joseph glanced at me, reproachful. My sarcasm. For there had been murmurings among the good-wives of Madras Patnam that the Governor might have been supplementing his lawful income with a not inconsiderable quantity of illicit private trading.

'The French, you mean?' Joseph asked me.

'The French. The Dutch. And then this matter of *sati*.'

'It is the talk of the Fort House, sirrah,' said Yale, who had chosen to sit alongside us. 'And upon my word, I have my views. If we brought them to God's love, we should not have this problem. And if they do not wish to accept the true faith, we should perhaps not trouble ourselves to interfere.'

'You think,' I snapped, 'that we should allow that young woman to immolate herself from spite that she has different beliefs to our own.'

The impudence of the man. Here five minutes!

'Not spite, Mistress. No. But I do not believe we can face in both directions at once. We either intervene in their traditions, demonstrate a better way. Or we do not. Naturally, I should prefer the former, as everybody else has done. If the Dutch, the French and the Portuguese have no qualms about prohibiting this vile practice in their own settlements, and no qualms either about employing missionaries to bring them the Word of God, even in the form of Papism, well— '

'Because it is not the policy of our Company,' said Joseph. 'Yet this is a special case, I believe. One thing where the wife of a higher-caste Gentue determines to throw herself on her husband's funeral pyre. But here? The *bibi* of a white factor? A young girl? Goulding already buried. And she announcing to the whole of Black Town that she will perform *sati* in his honour.'

Two days ago. A great procession of Gentues parading the girl, Kalai, just outside the Choultry Gate. Drums. Chanting.

'*Maha Sati!*' they had sung. '*Maha Sati!*' What a devoted wife!

'Something of an irony that it was Parrish sent to rescue her,' said John Nicks, a rising star of the garrison, seated just behind us.

'Why?' I asked him. 'Because he has a *bibi* too? You all have short memories, Mister Nicks. Francis Day chose this place to establish our fort simply because his own *bibi* was here. But what a momentous decision that turned out to be.'

'Forty years ago, Mistress,' said Yale. 'This is a very different age. A modern age.'

Matthew had taken a section of his military company, under instruction of Governor Langhorn, and snatched the girl despite her own protestations and those of the angry crowd. Shots had been fired, into the air, the mob dispersed. For a while, at least. The tradition of *sati* required Kalai to fast until the moment she was fed to the flames, but the Governor had instructed her confined within the Fort House and, from then, there had been a very different procession – of those trying to persuade Kalai to either relent or eat: the Governor himself; Reverend Warner, the Company's official chaplain; Matthew; and, for good measure, Matthew's *bibi*, Sathiri. But all to no avail.

'Well, Gentue or no,' I said, 'we can still pray for her.'

We did so, the chaplain giving Kalai special mention in the list of

14

those for whom he sought God's Mercy at the service's close, yet he had barely mentioned her name when there was a great commotion outside the Fort House, reaching us even there.

'What on earth…?' said Joseph.

Drums again. Muffled chanting. Matthew in uniform, urging us to be calm while he and Governor Sir William Langhorn went to investigate.

'The children…' I murmured, suddenly very afraid for them. My husband had Joseph Junior by the hand, and I had baby Richard in my arms.

'Here,' he said. 'You must take this brave soldier too.' And he gave Joseph's two year old fingers into my free hand. The little fellow had his other fist jammed into his mouth, as he was wont to do when he was fearful. My husband had gone in rapid pursuit of Matthew and the Governor. He was Second, after all, and took his responsibility seriously.

In the passage that led from the mess hall chapel to the outer gate of the Fort House, members of the congregation were pressing together, some shouting. With the gate now flung open, the chanting outside was clear, loud, even over the rhythmic pounding of the drums.

'*Maha Sati! Maha Sati!*'

I could see the Governor, attempting to reason, though to no avail, with those in the front ranks of the protestors, who had breached all rules by swarming into the compound. And there were women among us screaming now.

'Heaven protect us! We shall all be murdered!'

Mister Yale was by my side, and I saw that he had fetched a pistol from his quarters.

'Fear not,' he said. 'I shall protect you. And your beloved sons.'

'You think it appropriate?' I asked him, aghast at this sacrilege, despite my terror. 'To fetch such a weapon into the House of God?'

'Please, ladies,' Reverend Warner was remonstrating. 'These are our neighbours. And you will frighten the children. Please, calm yourselves.'

'I only thought…' Yale muttered, then he too was gone to join Sir William at the gate.

The Governor was looking frantically over his shoulder, chaos now both in front and behind. Then he turned to the crowd once more, made some gesture to pacify them, shouting something in his own fractured Tamil that I could not quite catch. Matthew close beside him, shaking his head violently, even while the Governor upbraided him, pointed repeatedly back down the passage until, at last, our friend began to push his way through our masses.

'What is it?' I cried to him as he came close.

'Do not ask, Catherine,' he said. 'Too monstrous.' But then he was gone. The women around me were in a state of great confusion.

'They want the girl,' somebody was saying. 'Why don't we just give them the girl?'

The cry was taken up by others, though they fell silent when Matthew Parrish returned, shame-faced, leading Kalai by her slender brown arm, a look of absolute triumph alight in her eyes.

We could hear the celebrations from Black Town all through the afternoon and past sunset. Malice menacing the air. The devil still in the distance but creeping ever closer, stretching his fearsome fingers out to caress my shoulders. Sunday, but none of our customary company with any interest in the normal amusements, the men all out on the *veranda*, the Dutch tobacco smoke from their pipes normally lending such a pleasing and manly aroma to the house but, this evening, a strange prelude to the thing about to happen.

'We should never have surrendered her,' I could hear Matthew Parrish arguing.

But I could see Mister Yale from the corner of my eye. He alone among the men-folk had remained inside.

'What else could we do, ladies?' he said. 'With those barbarians within our own gates.'

The ladies, it seemed, agreed with him. But then there was Mister Nicks, his shrill cry.

'Great heaven,' he yelled. 'They've lit the fire.' And we all crowded out then onto the terrace walk. A glow in the sky, inland and to our right.

'The North River islands,' said Joseph. The Gentues' funeral ground at the bend in the river a half-mile west of Black Town. Beyond the gardens laid out for our collective pleasure. The word gardens perhaps conjures a particular image but these, here, have little formal structure.

16

A few simple paths and shrubs, and well inside the limited boundaries within which we are permitted to venture from the fort itself. They occasionally serve, of course, as the location for various improper liaisons. Or for private inebriation. Tonight, however, Satan himself would stroll there, seeking his own amusement with the girl, Kalai.

'How can those heathens glean such joy from a thing like this?' said Mister Yale.

Joseph adopted the tone he sometimes reserves for Joseph Junior when he tries to explain something he feels should be self-evident even to a small child.

'I remember as a boy,' he said. 'In Porto. The Inquisition was burning three men, guilty of who-knows-what. And the sheer delight on the faces of those civilised God-fearing folk who had turned out to enjoy the spectacle. Yes, enjoy, Elihu. That is the very word.'

'Papists, sirrah.'

'And is it so long,' said Matthew, 'since our own Church was burning those same Papists? Sixty years, no more, since the last man was burned alive in England. To great acclaim. Wightman the Anabaptist. The dark side of humanity is not restrained by race, colour or creed, Mister Yale. Sadly not.'

The thought seemed to stir him and, without a word, Matthew jumped from the *veranda* steps and strode off towards the Choultry Gate.

'Matthew!' Joseph cried, then turned to me, desperation carved into his features. 'My dearest…'

'Go,' I said. 'If you must.'

Of course he must, though I was terrified for him. Joseph always must.

'Do they mean to intercede?' Mister Yale stammered. And then he, too, hurried to catch them.

There followed some of the most anxious moments of my life, with the light of the not-too-distant fire brightening ever more of the sky, and the raucous rumble of ritual growing to fever pitch. Time crawled, and so did my flesh, imagining every horrendous outcome until, at last, there was a great shout. Almost immediately after, the shouting pierced by a shot. I was sure it was a shot. A single shot. Momentary silence. But then the chanting, the drumming, the crashing of cymbals began afresh. The women gathered around me, our fears shared. But then my beloved

Joseph came staggering back across the compound, Matthew and Mister Yale supporting him, helping him along.

'Sweet Jesu,' I cried, 'what has happened to him? '

'He's fine,' Matthew assured me. 'Shaken only.' I saw tears on my husband's cheeks.

'What?' I said.

'The heathens had dug an enormous fire pit,' said Yale. 'Enormous. Heat like a furnace. Hotter than hell itself, begging your pardon, Mistress.'

Yes, an objectionable fellow, though by the end of that terrible evening – and as I now satisfy my obsession with recording as many of the confused details as I am able in my journal – perhaps marginally less so.

'The girl?' I said, almost unable to contain the dreadful images that filled my head.

'Changed her mind,' Matthew grimaced, 'when she felt the flames.'

'She's safe? We heard a shot. At least...'

'She tried her best to run,' Joseph sobbed. 'To us, my dear. And there was the *sadhu*. You remember him? The holy man?' How could I not, strange creature. Old as the hills. Great masses of lank white hair and beard. His face and shoulders daubed in dried mud. Otherwise naked except for a cloth around his meager loins. 'He began to preach at us. Something about Madari. And *sati*.'

'Some lines from the *Mahabharata*,' said Matthew. He had been working on a translation of the thing, for he admired it greatly. The longest epic poem ever written. Longer even than the *Iliad*. Possibly even older. Part mythology. Part ancient history. Part philosophical treatise. The Four Goals of Life, he had once explained to us. 'The verses,' he said, 'that praise Madari herself for committing *sati*.'

'He cursed me, my dear,' said Joseph. 'The damn'd creature cursed me. And the crowd took back the girl, flung her into the flames. Her screams. Oh, sweet heaven...'

'Then...?' I said, chilled by the threat of the *sadhu*'s curse, horrified at the image of the child's immolation.

'Joseph,' said Matthew, 'had the presence of mind to seize a musket from one of the guards at the gate.'

'I had to do it,' wept my husband. 'Could not bear to see her suffer a second longer.'

It has not been the easiest of years, the writers and factors kept hard at their work or dispatched hither and thither upon trading missions. So, little time, even during periods of festivity for excessive social intercourse. And then the constant threat of yet another conflict with the Hollanders, everybody so timorous that, barely two days since, one of the guards on the Choultry Gate shot and killed a Portuguese captain of our auxiliary troops. Mistook him for a Dutchie.

Yet our garrison and complement at Fort St. George now seems all reunited again, that unfortunate incident with the Portuguese captain forgotten and this day of celebration for most here. Oak Apple Day, commemoration of the king's birthing and, of course, the anniversary of his return to England with the monarchy's restoration. Thirteen years ago now. He had been thirty, I had been nine, and my poor Papa at his wits' end, ranting that all we sacrificed to rid ourselves of those pariahs had been for nothing. Thus it is my wont to avoid the Cavalier faction's Oak Apple Day festivities whenever possible though, this year, after this morning's official parade and church service, Joseph was persuaded by Matthew Parrish to hold a more informal gathering that, he felt, would help him fathom which of the newer writers sat on the respective sides of the political fence.

Thus, Mister Yale and several other guests arrived punctually though, by then, it was impossible for them to gain access to our terrace walk, our *veranda*. We had returned from church to find a familiar scene. Upwards of twenty of the Gentue women from Black Town, squatting on their haunches, each demanding to be heard at the same time, the normal musical lilt of their Tamil turned to sheer cacophony, the words spat out along with the streams of red juice from the betel nut, which they all chew so incessantly.

'Usual problem?' said Matthew Parrish, dressed in his more customary attire, a rare blend of Gentue and European garb. He recited one of his own witty couplets, about not being able to touch the same flowing water twice.

'I fear so,' Joseph smiled, then engaged the women in their own tongue, which rewarded him with screams of laughter, the ladies almost choking on the crimson spit dribbling through the many gaps in their teeth.

'They make jest of you, sirrah?' Mister Yale demanded to know.

'A shared jest, perhaps,' said Joseph. 'They simply seek justice. Part of my role here, after all, as you well know. As though being Mintmaster and Second was not enough. You must have seen this already, the number of times these untouchable women are denied access to the Black Town wells. And the village council, the *punchayet*, unwilling to resolve the matter. I've explained to them that this is our festive day but that I'll pursue the issue on the morrow. They seem to find something hilarious about my promise. But – ah, here comes Akbar. That should tide them over.'

Our head steward Akbar had brought several goatskins of fresh water, distributed them among the women, who had soon vacated the *veranda* and headed off back towards the Choultry Gate, allowing our guests to file through the house and into our dining room. A dozen of us for dinner. Joseph and myself. Matthew. The garrison's purchasing officer, Steward John Barker and his precocious daughter, Katherine. The Widow Keeble – now, with the recent death of her husband, licensee of the *Golden Pheasant* tavern. Mister Yale and one of his fellow writers, Vincent Seaton. John Nicks, the Council's Secretary, keeper of the Diary and Consultation Book. And three of the new writers, only arrived last week. Twelve, though we were outnumbered, of course, by the servants. So many of them that I can scarce remember all their names. All men, naturally.

'Ah,' said Mister Yale, as the first drinks were served, 'a refreshing breeze.' It emanated from the large cloth fan suspended above the table and, this early in the meal, still swinging energetically with the *pankah* boy's first burst of enthusiasm, a wish to impress that I knew from experience would not last long.

'Now, Mister Hynmers,' said one of the very newest arrivals, 'you said that the women were untouchables. In what way, sirrah – untouchable?'

Mister Yale guffawed at the question, winked at the young fellow and slapped him on the back. What was that all about? Some salacious intent? Yale a licentious libertine? He might pass for one, certainly. Elegant canions of embroidered brocade above his silk stockings, a fashion from a former age, I thought. Such a foppish waistcoat, too. Deep mustard, gold thread embroidery. But Joseph chose to ignore him.

And what else may I say about Mister Yale, a year after his arrival? He has mettle, of course, as he demonstrated on that terrible evening of the girl's *sati*. But I have noted that it is rather his habit to prefer female companionship to that of his fellows. He smokes only in moderation, seems to drink wine or ale purely on occasion, and – unlike every other writer and clerk in Fort St. George – never engages in games of chance, I am told. Eating appears his only vice. That and a roving affection for women. Joseph, of course had taken a dim view of this aspect within Elihu's character, though he likes him well enough apart from that. 'I fear he has taken a shine to you, my sweet,' Joseph would say. And I, in turn, would scold him for his foolishness. In truth, I have my fantasies, as I collect all women must do. Fantasies that wake me in the night. Hot and damp. But I swear that Elihu Yale has never featured once within those fancies.

'The caste system here among the Gentues,' Joseph was explaining in his normal, colourful way. How, according to their own sacred texts, the first people sprang from a clay body fashioned by Brahma. The most valued, the Brahmans, from the mouth; the next, the Kshatriyas, from the arms; the third, the Vaishyas, from the thighs; and, the lowliest, the Shudras, from the feet. Among these Shudras were all the groups considered as having occupations that might somehow pollute the castes above them, and therefore considered untouchable. Those who might be in contact with dead creatures, such as leatherworkers or butchers, or with human wastes, even sweat, and thus including washerwomen or servants.

'Barbaric,' said milk-faced and freckled Mister Seaton, Yale's friend, as we took our places. 'Un-Christian.'

'You say so?' Matthew Parrish admonished him. 'Is life not the same for those in the lowest levels of society at home?'

'Surely you cannot compare such a system with our own civilisation?' Mister Yale replied.

Oh, I thought, *must we have this conversation each time we are sent yet another batch of these young men?* And Joseph was plainly just as bored. It was the main reason, of course, that I so rarely felt able to invite Matthew's *bibi* to our gathering, even though Sathiri is my closest friend. It would not have been proper in most circumstances but certainly not with strangers in our midst. They could not have understood. Not yet.

'Forgive me, gentlemen,' said Joseph. 'But this does feels a little like *déja vu*. Have you learned nothing in the months some of you have been here? It would serve you well to remember that Indian civilisation pre-dates our own by a considerable period. While we were still struggling through our own Dark Ages, the local Pallavas, Pandyas and Cholas were building temples that put the best of our cathedrals, even now, to shame. Visit the pagodas here in Black Town. Or you can see more astonishing examples not far from here. At Mylapore. At Thiruvalikkeni. Perhaps an excursion might be in order. Ah, but here comes the food.'

'But heathens, Mister Hynmers,' said Seaton, who also had the excited manner of speaking sometimes displayed by a frolic, a madcap. 'We are not required to fill them with the Lord's spirit?' Joseph explained to him, as he had done several times previously while, for my part, I introduced the newcomers to the *thattu* being served to each of our guests, a banana leaf for each place setting, heaped with a central mound of rice, and the rice surrounded by separate dishes: spiced lentils and bell pepper; spinach with onion; okra and wax gourd; eggplant and goat's cheese; and pieces of that flaky flatbread we now call *parota*. All the garish colours that, for me, are emblematic of all things Indian.

'What about you, Matthew?' I'd heard John Nicks murmur, then thump Parrish on the arm. 'Fill them with the Lord's spirit? That it, eh?'

Matthew knocked his arm aside, choosing instead to answer a simultaneous query from another newcomer about whether there were poisonous insects or serpents that posed any danger here in Madras Patnam.

'You will find, sirrah,' said Matthew, scooping some of the lentils into a fold of bread, while regarding Nicks most frigidly, 'that there are all manner of venomous creatures here at Fort St. George.'

'I was telling these young fellows, ma'am,' Yale was saying to the Widow Keeble, 'how much I give Mistress Hynmers joy of this fine house. Indeed, the whole town. Not exactly what they'd expected. Nor myself, when I landed. Such fine mansions. Brick and stone. Elaborate porticos. Nor expected this excellent food either.'

'But gracious,' said one of the youngsters, 'it is fiery, is it not?'

Widow Keeble assured the youth that these were among our mildest offerings. Yet the town? Yes, she agreed with Mister Yale. Commodious, for a garrison. And how she loved the scent of jasmine that filled the air in so many places.

'Some small solace,' she said, 'for this strange world in which we live.' The world of the foreign merchant, she elucidated. 'No roots, see? Roving folk. Or driven to the roving life. Danger and disease on every hand. But we're like gamblers, I reckons. Always that chance just around the corner. The fortune to be made.'

'And little better whenever we return,' I said. 'The roving in our blood. We long for England's green and pleasant lands – and as soon as we get there, we can't wait to be at sea again. Strangers in a strange land, wherever we happen to be.'

'Still,' said swarthy Katherine Barker, 'how I should love to see London. Lord! How rum that should be.' Her father patted her forearm, gazed at her with devotion as he munched upon the meal.

'Perhaps one day,' said Nicks, 'we might see it together, Katherine.'

He was infatuated with her, though I did not understand his affection, nor the father's worship of his half-Portuguese daughter, and I had only invited them at Joseph's insistence. To provide some balance in the company, he had said. Yet Katherine Barker is a mere chit, something of a drab, a reputation that follows her like the stench of foul fish after the boats have come in. Rumours that she will offer her favours to any man foolish enough to show an interest in her.

'That is exceptionally fro'ward,' she snapped at John Nicks. 'But we might have news of that great city, perhaps? Mister Yale?' I saw the sickly smile she offered him. 'You were born there, sir?'

'No, indeed,' Yale told her. 'Boston, in fact. Massachusetts. My father had wanted to make his fortune in the colonies. I was born on the same day that news of the king's trial and execution arrived there. God bless his soul. Fifth day of April. The year of our Lord, 1649.'

'You take the Cavalier side then?' I said. He was falling further in my estimation with almost every sentence, for there had been little opportunity to gauge him fully during our rencounters this past year. But I still had my guests to attend. 'Akbar!' I shouted. 'Please fill the glasses.'

It brought another flurry of activity from the servants: rose waters, *panch*, coconut arrack, Brunswick mum or that refreshing concoction that our Gentues call *maththu*, a sweet mix of fermented milk and mango.

'The King is anointed by God, Mistress,' Yale replied. 'Regardless of the faults. Regicide is a sin against the Almighty himself. Though my father owed a certain debt to Cromwell too. The religious intolerance in Massachusetts – well, it drove him back to England. Cromwell, the Commonwealth, had made it clear that the country was now well disposed towards independent and enterprising traders. Besides, he had come into inheritance. Family property. In Denbighshire. Plas Grono. You see, miss?' He beamed at Katherine Barker. 'My people descended from the Lords of Iâl, princes of Wales.'

'Then,' said Katherine Barker, as though she would dismiss him, 'not London.' Her accent held the soft sibilance of her mother's tongue though her features were more homely than exotic.

'Ah, no, Miss Barker. You misunderstand. I have spent most of my life in London. Dugard's School for a while and then...' He paused, as though absorbed by some painful memory, a shadow passing across his eyes. 'And then St. Paul's.'

'Fortunate,' said Joseph. 'My own father didn't consider a public school appropriate for a son destined for the counting house and foreign fields so I was sent to Turberville of Kensington – French, Italian, Greek, Latin, music and mathematicks. But he, too, had enough connections to secure me a post at Leadenhall Street. Of course, by the time you started, Mister Yale, Catherine and myself were already in Madras. I came out as Fourth, but promotion's quick here.'

'Give you joy of that also, sir,' said Yale. 'But I count myself fortunate that I had returned to London in time to see Cromwell disinterred, tried for his sins even in death, the decaying body sent to the gibbet, the head spiked on London Bridge.'

'Perhaps a little more delicacy while we eat?' I suggested, as the manservants removed the remains of the *thattu* and brought fresh dishes, goat's meat cooked in a rich, red *kari* sauce. More rice.

'Your pardon, ma'am,' said the verbose Mister Yale. 'Though heavens above, such aromas. I thought I should miss good English cooking. But these colours. The flavours. Exquisite. I am grown insatiably fond of them. What say you, Vincent?' he cried, as he encouraged one of the servants to heap his bowl of goat a little higher.

'Always a little rich for my taste,' Seaton replied. He was sweating profusely and I signaled to the *pankah* boy to renew his efforts. 'Cannot get used to it, I fear.'

'You say so?' Yale smiled, studied his bowl appreciatively a moment before picking up his narrative again. 'In any case, my father fell ill during the Great Plague. He survived, though sadly one of my younger brothers did not. In the following year, the Great Fire took our home. Cripplegate. But I worked in my father's counting house a while too. He had good links within John Company.' He said it so pointedly, as though to underline his seniority over the younger writers – the older hand referring to our employer in that informal way, for they would never have heard the term John Company used in Leadenhall Street itself, that was certain. 'By coincidence,' he went on, 'or perhaps not, it was the father of a friend from Dugard's. Sir John Moore. A Director, you may collect. Anyway, Sir John secured me a post as a writer. Three years ago. Imagine, Miss Barker. Leadenhall Street. Working there every day. Passing beneath that fabulous façade. Like the high stern of a sleek caravel. Then this opportunity arose. India. The Company needed twenty young men. My father had to sign a bond, of course. Five hundred pounds against my good conduct. As a writer.'

And then that interminable part of the meal in which we had to endure the tale's versions as told respectively by Seaton, Nicks and the three newcomers. Yale and Nicks, we had already discovered, were also acquainted. The same school, though John Nicks a few years senior to our Welsh Massachusetts peacock.

'And you, Mister Hynmers,' said Seaton. 'Born in England, did you say?'

'Were any of us?' Joseph laughed. 'No, I in Amsterdam. My father traded there.'

'And a famous translator,' I added, proud of his heritage.

'Hardly famous,' said my husband. 'But he turned Blaeu's epistle on maritime navigation into English. *The Sea Beacon*. And my goodly wife? Born in Alicante. It's how we met. In those days, you may recall, the western Mediterranean had become a paradise for interloper merchants like my father. Good trade to be had in Málaga, Genoa, Alicante and Leghorn. Woollen cloth, pepper, lead and herrings going out. Oranges, raisins and wine coming back. Ah, those Alicantes. You've tasted *Fondillón*, I trust, gentlemen?' They had not, and Joseph shook his head in feigned dismay. 'My father was a partner to Johannes Lakeman, along with Moscoso. By the year sixty, Lakeman and my father had become part of the English colony in Porto, the Factory House there, bringing in dried cod, *bacalhau*, and shipping back red wines. White *alvarinho* too. A few years later I had been twice here to India. As a Cape merchant. Then a rare return visit to London. A joint gathering of our respective families. And there – well, my Catherine. And the Honourable English East India Company recruiting for Fort St. George.'

It brought back memories, naturally. Not all of them pleasant. My initial dismay at the prospect of marrying a man ten years older than me. It seemed such a difference. Not uncommon at all but hardly what I had imagined for myself. But then Joseph had that ability to make his years fall away whenever we were in each other's company and I soon realised that good fortune had placed us together. And now he was busy slapping Vincent Seaton upon the back. The fellow seemed to be choking on a piece of goat, coughing and spluttering.

'But tell me, gentlemen,' I said to the new writers. 'Your quarters, how do you find them?'

'The offices, ma'am,' one of them replied, 'the reception rooms and the mess hall all seem adequate. No dedicated chapel, of course...'

Seaton was trying to say something between gulps of rose water and failing miserably.

'A mess hall also serving as chapel does no credit to the glory of God,' said Elihu Yale. 'I have said so many times. Why, we are even outshone by the Papists' own church.'

I thought I saw Seaton flinch at Mister Yale's words, but that may simply have been my imagination. Or perhaps it was a reaction to the spices, with which he was plainly struggling. The Portuguese cook in the Fort House kitchen serves much simpler fare.

'It was established somewhat earlier than our own,' Matthew explained to the youngsters. 'And it is located outside the walls. In Black Town, gentlemen. Among the heathens.'

'Hardly surprising, sirrah,' said Yale. 'And I suspect that none of you young fellows shall be spending much time in your own quarters. Down in the bowels of the building. Each an oven in which, you will find, we all stifle.'

'A deliberate policy of the Company,' Joseph smiled at the youngsters. 'It encourages dedication to duty. The prospect of promotion. The morning gun shall wake you each day at sunrise and then it's noses to the grindstone, I fear.'

'Yet,' said Katherine Barker, 'might we not know how Mistress Hynmers herself came to be born in Alicante?'

I cannot recall anybody ever asking before, and it took me some time to gather my wits. Being half-Portuguese herself, I suppose, might have prompted the girl's curiosity, but Joseph was nodding at me, encouragingly.

'Where to begin?' I said. 'With my father, I suppose. Walter Elford. A Turkey merchant, working for the Levant Company. A factor, in Smyrna. But his sympathies publicly Parliamentarian. And once news of the Revolution's beginning reached Turkey, my father was imprisoned for treason against the king by Sir Sackville Crow, then our Ambassador at Constantinople. At the same time, English merchants in Smyrna had petitioned Sir Sackville to remove the Quaker missionaries who had begun arriving there.'

'Your father a Quaker, Mistress?' Yale seemed astounded.

'We have a certain talent for Dissenting, Mister Yale. A family custom. Though I don't believe my father ever actually joined the Society of Friends. He was more, you might say, a fellow traveller. But he spent thirty months in prison. Terrible conditions. In the same year that you, sir, were engrossed with Cromwell's disinterment, my father was still petitioning Parliament for compensation. Meanwhile, he had also found fresh trade in Alicante, far from the reach of the Levant Company. And I was born there. Only returned to London with my mother when I was twelve. Papa eventually opened a coffee house, though that, too, was lost during the Great Fire. My little sister as well.'

'I am sorry,' said Yale, 'about your sister. Yet such a collection of languages you all possess. The Indian tongues. Dutch. Portuguese. Spanish.' And he looked at me with open admiration. It was perfectly disquieting. 'I am doing my best to emulate your fine example, ma'am.'

'Essential,' said Joseph. 'How else to understand our rivals in trade? The Portuguese may no longer be a force in Coromandel, begging your pardon, Miss Barker, but many individual merchants and settlers now confined to Madras or Porto Novo. Limited trade with Sumatra and Siam. The Dutchies with their main base at Batavia, and their local factory at Pulicat. Jan Company!' He laughed at his use of the sobriquet for the Dutchies' own East India venture. 'The Danes, mostly an irrelevance for us, but a small garrison still at Dansborg. And then there are the French. We tend to see the Hollanders as our main problem. Tradition, I suppose. But it's the French that worry me. They seized San Thomé from the Golconda authorities so readily. And no sign of the Dutch and Golconda armies doing anything about it. The Dutch more worried by us, it seems. Yet the French have established themselves a mighty base, at Pondicherry.'

I missed much of the ensuing debate – glad to do so, for all this talk of our enemies unsettled me – and went upstairs to check on the children, found them playing happily with *ayah* Tanani. When I returned I took the side door that leads out onto the red-tiled *veranda* so that I did not need to make my excuses to our guests and there I found Matthew Parrish, enjoying a pipe of tobacco.

'Oh, Matthew,' I said. 'I fear I must apologise. Those jibes from Mister Nicks.'

'I've a thick skin, Catherine. And Nicks is a harmless little scrub. Holding forth just now on his views about how we should strike the French before they grow too strong. Your Mister Yale suggesting I should use my talents to undertake some spying upon their enterprise.'

'*My* Mister Yale?'

'Clearly besotted by you.'

Inside, the table had been cleared and, as was Joseph's wont, festive afternoons have become an occasion for music. Singing. Though, even then, the performances seemed to be dominated by that same Mister Yale. A rousing rendition of *Ho, Cavaliers*. I might have guessed. And then joined by the Barker girl for a raucous version of *Brandy-Nosed Moll*. Equally appropriate.

'This again,' I said. 'What stuff, sirrah! Besotted indeed,' I scoffed, almost offended at the suggestion, keen to change the subject. 'But shall you? Spy upon the French, I mean.'

'I have enough such duties here,' he said, and then plainly regretted his words.

'Here, Matthew?'

Was I shocked? I suppose not. Something of Eden about this place that I have always known could not last. The most perfect of petals must perish.

'Instructions,' said Matthew. 'Orders. From London. They arrived with the new youngsters. And I thought – well, I wondered whether I might discuss the thing with you. At some stage. A chance to strike a blow of which your father might approve.'

Truly? I wonder what he intends and, as the candle flickers upon my writing slope, I cannot help recalling the times that Papa's political views have landed him in a stew.

I suffered badly during the nine months of my pregnancy. Sickness almost without end. Fear for the baby. Bleeding that could not be explained by the collective knowledge of the garrison's mothers in general, nor that of Mistress Crouch the garrison midwife specifically, nor that of the two garrison chirurgeons, Sherman and Heathfield, in particular. Frustration that my movements were so often impeded. And the pain. Our Lord Jesu protect and save me. As though my bones were being broken and ground, one each hour through every day of my torment, flensing through my stomach, my hips, my spine.

Thus I have given little or no time to those tasks I have been undertaking this past year on Matthew's behalf and, of course, with Joseph's agreement. To put no finer point on the thing, he has been charged with providing reports to the Company about any evidence of possible corruption here – financial corruption for the most part, though there have been concerns, too, about other alleged breaches of Company policy. Matters, as he put it so gently, that might also offend our Dissenter principles. I was initially disgusted by the suggestion that I might have a part to play in his underhand activities though, as it happens, I quickly came to realise how often I was a party, albeit an innocent one, to quite a considerable amount of dishonourable dealing, discussed openly at times within the scandal-broth gossip of the settlement's women, and some of those matters I did, indeed, choose to bring to Joseph's attention and for Matthew's consideration. My mother's influence, I think. That one can be as guilty of misdeeds as the perpetrators by witnessing them and doing naught.

Joseph, of course, had balked at my complicity in Matthew's investigation where it specifically concerned Sir William's activities.

'What might be thought?' he had said frequently. 'If the Governor is removed and I am required to replace him, even temporarily, and it being known that my own wife had been in part responsible for his removal?'

It makes no sense, of course. For how could anybody know that? But now I sought a very different form of private consultation – with Matthew's *bibi*, for she is also the most renowned *dai* in all Madras Patnam, and the examination was thorough. Very thorough.

'Well, Sathiri?' I said, when it was all done, and she squatted against the wall of my bedchamber to gather her thoughts. She is one of the most beautiful women I have ever seen, and Matthew told me once that her name, Sathiri, means *Beautiful One* in the Tamil tongue spoken by the Gentues here. Yes, beautiful, though I suspect she is nearer my mother's age than my own. Older than Matthew too, therefore. Yet she was unlike most of the other *bibis* within the compound. But the others, whether Gentue or Moor, are respected among their own communities for devotion to their white *sahibs* as though they had been formally well-wedded according to their respective customs – whereas Sathiri has always rather rejected the role of doting house-keeper, of abiding strictly to her own home. No confinement to the *bibikhana* for Sathiri. Of course, within our European ranks, such arrangements are always viewed as highly irregular, not prohibited by the Company, though rarely to be mentioned openly in polite society.

'Catherine,' she replied, 'I can find nothing wrong.' She is the only Gentue, I think, who has ever called me by name. And her English impeccable. It is the unspoken additional role of the *bibi* to help her *sahib* learn the local languages and customs though, in this case, she must have received as much reciprocal knowledge from Matthew himself. 'But tell me, the other little ones. The thing was difficult?'

'Not at all. Incredibly easy.'

She smiled.

'And since then? Two years. How many of the white women here have lost their children while giving birth, or died themselves?'

I counted them off. Three infants still-born within Fort St. George alone. Two mothers consumed by birthing fevers.

'But what has that to do with me, Sathiri?'

'My people believe that, sometimes, our spirit can be possessed by a devil, a demon – and such a demon can spring from that which we have seen or experienced around us. To put it more simply, we see pain and death, and our fears create in us the unshakeable belief that we will suffer the same fate. It is not a conscious thing. It happens deep and unbidden in our soul, our *jiva*. But the effect is the same. We forget our *karma*. Forget that all is written. We begin to exhibit the outward signs of those things we have seen. We must rid you of your demon, Catherine.'

I feared she would suggest one of those endless drumming and chanting rituals I had seen practiced at times in Black Town, but she taught me, instead, to reach deep within myself, to focus upon the pain and subdue it. There were other elements, naturally. The healing amulets, the sacred ash, and the blessed intoxication of the drink she called *soma* – so that, within a se'nnight, I was all but cured and Joseph remarking upon my recovery, claiming he had never seen me so in looks, though I kept carefully mumchance about the *soma*, to which I fear I may have become somewhat addicted.

And this other addiction, my journals. I find myself writing more and more, feel as though I have some talent for the thing, a better way to fill the many solitary hours while Joseph attends to his duties than my simple embroidery alone. My father always kept with him a treasured copy of those *Meditations* by Marcus Aurelius and I often wonder why we do not see more diaries published by the great thinkers of our own modern age. Not that I consider myself a great thinker, naturally, but perhaps one day somebody shall find interest in my scribblings. Yet, now, this is a private passion, something I would nor share even with my husband.

Meanwhile, all passed well, therefore, until several weeks before my full-term. I knew that something was wrong. Felt wrong. Looked wrong.

'Oh, my dear,' said Midwife Crouch. 'The infant's head is upwards. But never fear, it will turn in the coming weeks.'

Never fear? How could I not fear at such news?

'And if it doesn't, Mistress Crouch?'

'I have delivered little ones successfully in that way, Catherine. Once or twice.' But she sounded doubtful, caused all the old terrors, the pain, to return, despite Sathiri's *mantras*.

'I wish Sathiri to deliver the child,' I told Joseph that night, as I set aside my needlework, unable to give it my full attention, but he was less than happy.

'Personally, I would wish for nothing more,' he said. 'But you must know the way the *dais* are viewed by everybody else. I will admit that I have seen some wholly unsavoury practices among a few of them. But I could say the same of several European women who style themselves midwives. It will simply not answer, my sweet. If anything went wrong...'

And so we settled on Mistress Crouch. After all, she is licensed by the Church to practice her arts. Mistress Crouch had taken her Oath, had she not? So that, when my pains began in earnest and I knew the birthing to be imminent, the baby's position still the same, Joseph went a-nidgeting to fetch her while *ayah* Tanani tried her best to still my abject panic and miseries, for I was certain I would not survive.

'Yes, *memsahib*, I will care for boys,' she assured me. 'But all will be good. You will see.'

And then she, Joseph Junior and little Rich were swept away from me by the tide of women following in Mistress Crouch's wake. John Barker's Portuguese wife and their awful chit of a daughter. A half-dozen others that I can scarce now even remember, except the Widow Keeble bringing the required caudle of warmed and spiced ale.

'The best Brunswick mum that the *Golden Pheasant* has to offer,' she said.

My bedchamber became, literally, a hive of activity. The bed itself and my chests pushed aside to allow more space, the linen all carefully folded and set away, the shutters closed and candles lit. My rugs lifted and sawdust scattered deep in their stead, mingling its resinous odours with those of the melting beeswax. The birthing stool brought. It was some small irony, and a minor comfort, that it was Matthew who had fashioned and carved the thing. A talent, he has always insisted, that he inherited from his father. But the whole construction far more ornate than its purpose deserves. I now think that, in the ensuing endless hours of my agonies, it was only the touch of those twining mahogany vines, the intricately rendered fruits, the spread wings of its exotic birds, which kept me sane. Though, every now and then, I would recoil at the touch of the serpents' heads hidden within the chisel-work and, oh, so carefully concealed.

I could hear Joseph out on the *veranda*, the gossip of men who should have been about their duties, yet glad of any excuse to escape the sullen heat of the Fort House for a while. Matthew with him, of course. And the sonorous tones of Mister Yale, drowning out most of the others with some tale about his mother's tribulations in Boston, giving birth to their first child, Elizabeth. They both survived, however, he was saying. Yet, afterwards, the tragedy of baby Elizabeth living only a matter of weeks. But, by then, I was stripped to my shift and Mistress Crouch was pressing me into the chair.

'We must turn the child,' she was shouting, pressing her hands against my abdomen, trying to manipulate the baby's form. Pushing and heaving for such a time, until I could feel the hurt of the bruising almost more than the contractions and spasms.

'Perhaps *senhor* Hynmers, he help…' Mistress Barker suggested.

'A drop more of the caunce…' said Widow Keeble.

But no, I must be walked about the room until I could walk no further. Then more of the midwife's manipulations, or her fingers probing inside me.

'Perhaps…' she was saying. The proposed remedies seemed to last half the day. The additional herbs in the caunce. The emetics. The ergot of rye. By that time, the pain was relentless and I was beyond reason – until I saw her reach into her bag and produce a pair of hooks. Now, in my more rational moments, I realise that she simply removed them to find something else in the depths of that leather satchel. But then—

'Enough!' I screamed. 'You will fetch the *dai*, Sathiri.'

'Be patient, my dear,' said the midwife. 'A little delirium is to be expected,' she explained to the other women.

'Delirium be damn'd,' I told her. 'Send for Sathiri. Ask Matthew…'

'Mistress Hynmers – Catherine. It is part of my Oath that if I know any woman practicing these arts unlawfully, I am obliged to report the matter to the appropriate authorities, in this case, the Governor.'

'Report whate'er you wish. But fetch her.'

'Even among her own, that woman is considered unclean.'

'And will I not also be considered unclean by the Church, after bringing my baby into the world? Will I not have to undergo the rites of purification at the next service I attend?'

'Yes, you will. And you are required to have your midwife in attendance for the churching. Shall you do that, Catherine? Take that Gentue woman into our Christian chapel?'

I yelled and bellowed until Joseph insisted on being allowed to see me, his poor handsome face lined with woe. It gave me some modicum of relief to see him and he readily agreed to fetch Sathiri, called Matthew to do his bidding while, at my further insistence, he cleared the room as diplomatically as he was able, silenced the midwife's howls of protest moderately with the small pouch, a dozen diamonds, that he had been keeping for her reward. And once the chamber was cleared, I found myself able to remember Sathiri's teachings, to reach my inner self once more, reciting the words she had taught me. Of course, when she arrived, there was more sacred ash. *Soma* too, the Lord be praised.

'Why is it, do you think, Catherine,' she said, once my foul humours had somewhat abated, 'that animal babies may be born with active bodies but with heads and brains small enough for their birthing to be quick and easy? But human babies are born with helpless bodies, though bigger brains, eyes open, ears listening. Our babies born when their heads, their brains, have grown almost too large for them to be allowed passage, our hips too narrow for the process. Yet, if our hips were wide enough for our babies' heads, we would not be able to walk. I must ask our holy man to explain it.'

'The baby must be turned?'

'No. We will deliver this little monster buttocks first.'

'But how can it take so long?'

'A simple thing. The child's buttocks are softer than its head. It exerts less pressure. Takes longer. Besides, you allowed the demon back into your body. Your fears. Those women. All that noise. Do you not feel the pain slipping away with the stillness?'

She was correct. It was indeed slipping away. Though perhaps that was the *soma*.

Her fingers were gentle, warm, as she carefully searched for the baby.

'There?' I said, knowing the answer.

'Yes. I can feel them now.' My waters broke in that moment. 'Now, stand. Come, I will help. You must push only when you feel the urge to do so. Not before.' There was more walking. Some squatting. But, in the end, it was onto my hands and knees, bathing in the sawdust smells, a *soma* haze muddling my head until, at last, that first relief as the baby's buttocks and body came free. 'A boy,' she said. 'I think it is a boy.'

'Walter,' I gasped. 'For my father.'

'A good name. But now we must wait. For the head. Patience now. Be ready.'

'How can he breathe? Like that?'

'It is normal. When they are born this way. Just wait... There!'

It was done. The cord pulled clear to help deliver the afterbirth. Sathiri placing the placenta over the baby's head, telling me it would prevent infection of the little one's eyes. A dozen other suggestions, too, about how we might utilise the placenta – all of which I chose to quickly ignore. The cord cut and tied. The child swaddled, at my insistence, to protect him from evil until he could be baptised. Joseph granted admittance once the carnage of battle had been cleared, and my period of lying-in begun.

So, yesterday. Another Sunday and almost time for my churching. And for baby Walter's baptism. The parade of the Governor's bodyguard and a show of strength among the garrison. Mistress Crouch had been persuaded, grudgingly, to stand in her role as midwife while I was churched, cleansed after the degradation of childbirth. After all, she had taken the diamonds, Joseph reasoned with her. And did her Oath not confirm that she might accept a gift only where she had fulfilled her duty. Besides, Joseph had bribed her further with a promise that she might also sponsor baby Walter, act as godmother, present the little fellow at his baptism, swear to take responsibility for his religious well-being. I saw the light in her eyes then. The belief that she might wipe out the hazard of Sathiri's heathen involvement in his birth through this proffered gesture. Yet, with the service at its end, the baptism ceremony about to begin, Reverend Warner fell into a swoon. He had seemed unwell all through the service thus far, but now it was plain that he could not continue, my churching complete but the baptism needing to be postponed.

It troubled me, for there was suddenly some foolish recollection of the *sadhu*'s curse in my mind, though it was quickly dismissed as we emerged again into the sunlight, where the soldiers and the Governor's bodyguard were being dismissed.

'If the Dutchies only knew that this was all that stands between us and them.' Mister Yale, of course. Come with several friends, including John Nicks, to escort us back across the square.

'Still three months until our ships come in,' said Joseph. 'Things should have settled down by then, Elihu.' Cargoes arriving, we hoped, of woollens and broadcloth, sword blades, looking glasses, guns, knives, gold and silver bullion. The value of gold and silver higher here in India than in Europe. Returning vessels would carry spices, precious stones, Chinese porcelains, Japanese screens and fine cotton cloth. The trade around which our whole universe revolves. 'But the French...'

They now have a small camp, almost on our doorstep. Triplicane, a mere half-mile away, this side of their base at San Thomé.

'The Dutch almost as close,' said Yale. 'An hour's march will bring them to Caldera Point.'

The fearsome threat of war once more.

'Then we should thank heaven the Governor has seen fit to invest in the additional guns,' Joseph told him.

We now boasted seventy cannons around the ramparts though, privately, Joseph had explained that some of them would be more dangerous to the defenders firing them than to any onslaught. Yet the threat of attack by a hostile Dutch fleet once more. War broken out again – the third time with the Hollanders – and I cannot help feeling fearful for my family as a result.

I can scarce write these lines, my diary flung aside so often for many weeks past. I had not the strength to face it all. I wished simply to hide from the memories, to fold them into some chest and slam the lid, lock them away in the hope that the pain might be sequestered too. Yet I know that if I do not set down my recollections, they will be lost to me. And baby Walter lost along with them. The precious few weeks I had with him. Sathiri, of course, tries to console me with quiet words about *karma*, assuring me that what is written is written – and that recording all of this in my journal, every detail that I can remember, will be part of the process to help me heal some of the hurt.

But where to begin? Innocuously, I suppose. With Mister Yale's good fortune. Two pieces of good fortune perhaps.

Early last month, a week earlier than expected, our ships did indeed come in. They brought with them the usual consignment of young hopefuls, new writers to help cope with the growing trade. And they brought something more besides. Dispatches. Authority from the Company for our people here to ignore those clauses within their signed covenants that have previously forbidden them from private trade. A complete reversal. Private trade now encouraged. At least, in those goods for which the Company has no real interest. Nutmeg, cinnamon and cloves. Neck-cloths. Sapphires, rubies, diamonds and pearls. Our salaries can now be enhanced by our private trade in any of those. But never in calicoes, pepper, tin, silk or saltpeter. None of these items. It caused Joseph to smile when he read the directive – though that, I think, was the last time I saw him smile. More than a month. This awful month.

And I wondered how it would affect Matthew's investigations, my own small part in them. He had come to visit just as I was about to take the children for a stroll around the gardens, and he begged to accompany us. Quite a procession, myself and Matthew, Akbar to carry the roundel, two more servants with the baby suspended between them in his wicker basket, *ayah* Tanani leading the other two boys, the children's first outing for many days since each of them had been confined to the house with mild fevers. Yet I considered they were now sufficiently recovered. Everything seemed so perfectly safe. Then. It seemed safe.

'It never ceases to offend me,' I said, as we passed among the heaving and colourful masses of Black Town's Market Lane, which stretches west from the Shambles to Caldera Point. 'How a mere one hundred paces can take us out through the Choultry Gate, away from our fine houses and into this other world.'

The dwellings here of the Gentues in this quarter, the Moors and Mussulmen beyond. And so many of the poorer Jews beyond that again. Yet all the same. All mean. All mud and dirt and thatch. Tethered beasts, goats and chickens, and those that roamed the lanes at will. Sullen glances, too, at times. I had rarely experienced anything of this kind in our early days here but they were now more frequent within these dark waves of humanity since the night of the immolation, even though that was two years ago. But Gentues, it seems, like their elephants, have long memories. However, the headman of the village council, the *punchayet*, still showed unreserved civility, the palms of his hands pressed together and bowing low to us as we passed the wood-built Catholic chapel.

'Time to worry, Catherine, when it *does* cease to offend. *Be to the dispossessed always kind, be to injustice never blind.*' Lines from his best-known poem, of course, *A Fable of England*. 'Mister Yale might say, I suppose,' he went on, 'that their condition would be yet more desperate still, were we not here to share at least a modest portion of our wealth.'

'And why, pray, do you name Mister Yale, sirrah?'

He laughed, brushed some dust from the long Gentue tunic that he, like so many others at the fort, were wont to wear.

'No reason whatsoever. Only...'

I could have guessed what he might say, though he was interrupted by the chapel door being thrust open and Father Ephraim stepping around the goats tethered outside, to greet us, remorse written in his eyes.

'*Monsieur* Parrish. *Chère madame.* My deepest apologies. God give you joy of your new arrival. I was down in San Thomé.'

'I would have thought you had seen enough of the place, Father,' said Matthew.

Father Ephraim de Nevers has been here at Fort St. George for more than three decades. Finally received permission from Rome to build his chapel here, to act as missionary within Black Town. But the Portuguese priests at San Thomé rather resented his activities, arranged for him to be kidnapped. The Inquisition incarcerated him for nearly three years, though they were finally forced to release him.

'*Eh bien*, most of my years in prison were passed at Goa, my friend. So I have no resentment towards San Thomé. Only a stone's throw away. But I should have preferred to be here. And since my return...'

'Always so much to do, Father,' said Matthew.

It was strange how little it mattered that Father Ephraim might be a Papist priest, as though his profound and evident goodness lifted him above any such consideration.

'And is it true,' I asked him, 'that you plan to build your chapel anew?'

He reached inside his cassock, drew out a rolled parchment.

'*D'accord, madame.* You see? My authority. A stone church. To the glory of God and St. Antony.' He crossed himself. '*Magnifique.* We begin work next month. But if you are going, up there, I urge you to take care.'

'Up there?' I said.

'The Gentues' burial ground,' he replied. He seemed surprised. 'Forgive me, *madame*, you have not heard. The old *sadhu* is back in town. People say they have seen the spirit of the girl, Kalai, dancing in the fire pit. I thought...'

I assured him that we would, of course, heed his advice. We had the children with us, after all. Then we bade him farewell.

'That will certainly set the fox inside the hen-house,' laughed Matthew. 'New church for the Papists and we still stifling within the Fort House chapel. It will be amusing to see what happens next.'

To be honest, it was not the main thing on my mind and I was surprised that Matthew had so entirely ignored this news of the *sadhu*. In any case, we had reached the end of the lane, and I realised that Tanani was no longer at our side. She and Akbar, the other servants, had stopped some distance behind and I walked back towards them.

'What is it, *ayah*?' I said, seeing the fear in her face.

'The shade of Kalai, *memsahib*. We should not go there. With little ones.'

'Stay then,' I told her. 'But Akbar must come with us.' He looked astounded. Yet it would have been entirely inappropriate for me to continue unaccompanied with Matthew, and I was now somewhat set on visiting the site of Kalai's terrible death rather than a simple stroll around the gardens. Though I must admit to sharing some of their fear. I could almost feel the girl's spectre lurking in the shadows.

'But who will keep sun from children?' he cried, and waved the roundel parasol in the air.

'Give it to one of the others, Akbar. They can manage.'

He did so reluctantly, then followed in our footsteps like an old hound as we turned the corner of the bastion and came in view of the river. It was full and fast-flowing from the monsoon rains again, of course. But we turned north there, past our own burial ground, then west along the edge of the guava plantation until we came to the North River again, to the pair of islands on this nearer side of which lies the Gentues' sacred site – and the pit. The heat from the regular funeral pyres must be terrible for, while the hole itself was still half-full with charred timbers, thick with ash, the ground for many yards around was blackened too.

'Is she still…?' I began, pointing at the ash.

'Normally,' said Matthew, 'after each funeral the ashes are collected by family or friends, then scattered upon the waters. But with Kalai? I have no idea. After Joseph made the shot – and thank the Lord he had the courage to do so – it was all a matter of getting back to the gate as soon as we were able. Even Mister Yale, though he insisted on protecting our rear during the retreat. Unnecessary, as it transpired. But appreciated, Catherine. But come, there's nothing more to see here.'

No ghosts at least.

So we began to retrace our own steps.

'And Mister Yale now rewarded with this authority to trade privately.'

'He and everybody else, of course. It makes sense too, the basic salaries being so poor.'

'And how does this affect your investigation?'

'I sent my last report under private seal when the ships were heading back to England last November. With your inestimable help, of course.'

It had been Sawcer's death that had finally persuaded me. Lawrence Sawcer, one of those young calico sorters who had arrived on the same day as Yale and the others, two years ago. And made no secret of the fact that, within months, he had written to the Company with allegations of irregularities, and especially of what he described as Governor Langhorn's fraternisation with the French and with the local popish priests, Father Ephraim included. And then, suddenly, Sawcer was dead. A mysterious drowning accident.

'It makes me feel like a scrub, all the same,' I said.

'But we are bound by our oaths, my dear. By our duty to God Almighty that we should not let the corrupt go unpunished. And there was considerable evidence against the Governor. Nicks too. A couple of the others. But now this change of policy. And no further instruction for me. What am I to make of it all? Most of their then–illicit dealings now permitted after all. Apart from the calicoes, of course.'

We were back in Market Lane by then, back among the heaving, rowdy legions of Black Town's society, all the rainbow colours of their clothing and the exotic pungency of their spices. I looked for the children, was pleased to see them precisely on the spot where we had left them. Only they were not alone with the servants any more. And the servants were in a state of some turmoil, openly fearful. Tanani had gathered them into a tight defensive group for, squatting in front of them, there was the *sadhu*, chanting at them in his high-pitched wail. I broke into a run, placed myself between him and my babies, until Matthew joined us.

'Nothing to fear,' he said. 'I believe the old fellow is largely harmless.' Then he cocked his head on one side, trying to interpret the ancient words being intoned by the holy man.

'Harmless?' I snapped, as I pressed our party around the old devil. 'Did he not set a curse upon my husband?'

How I wish now, in the midst of my grief, that I had simply taken the little ones that day and fled somewhere far from the *sadhu*'s curse. But I did not. And it was largely Mister Yale's fault for, that same evening, with the rains upon us once more, there was a gathering at our house to discuss the fellow's second piece of good fortune. Governor Langhorn would normally have hosted the meeting, though his own mansion was then undergoing some major renovation work – Matthew Parrish had his own views about how this might have been financed, of course – and the Governor had asked Joseph, as Second, as Mintmaster, and as Justice to the Choultry Court and Customs House, to furnish some light supper for the occasion.

'Parrish told me all about it,' said Mister Yale, while we were still arranging their capes and periwigs to drip and hopefully dry a little on the *veranda*. 'But you have no need to trouble yourself about his heathen superstitions.' He constantly fingered his own cropped hair, for many of those who favour the peruke remain prone to considering it a social stigma when they are deprived in public of the accouterment – though heaven alone knows how any man can bear the things in this heat. 'Neither for yourself,' he went on, 'nor your delightful children. Why, if the scoundrel troubles you further, we shall have him flogged from the town.'

He was loudly supported by Joseph's guests, even by Governor Langhorn who, Matthew's suspicions aside, is the least provincial or narrow-minded of men, a great advocate on behalf of the Gentues and their beliefs. Though there was no comment from my husband who had considerably drawn within himself since the events of April. Far worse now, of course.

Even so, with the gentlemen seated at table, my children retired to their beds, the baby in his crib within my own bedchamber, *ayah* Tanani watching over him, I settled in the withdrawing room, along with Winifred Bridger who had come to keep me company, or herself from boredom perhaps, each of us with our embroidery to occupy us, while her husband John attended the meeting. Bridger has been here two years longer than we have, though lost his first wife almost immediately. John remains junior to my husband – Third, to Joseph's position as Second. But they are both justices and John, as Warehouse Keeper, is Elihu Yale's chief. Well, I was curious, and though Winifred kept up a light chatter in her gentle Portuguese accent, I tried my best to pick up snatches of conversation from the dining room also.

'A singular honour, Mister Yale,' the Governor was saying. 'The Khan of Gingee is highly influential. A potentially important ally. For him to invite the Company to dispatch a representative in this way is singular, sirrah. Singular.'

Gingee, so far as my geography tells me, lies a hundred miles south and west of us here. It sits just across the border within the neighbouring Sultanate of Bijapur, while we pay our annual tribute to the Sultan of Golconda, as well as to the Sultan's governor, or *naik*, for this province of Chingleput – our one hundred and twenty-mile stretch of the Coromandel coast. Each of these, of course, is a Mahometan lord, the Sultans ruling over their own independent kingdoms but, ultimately, owing suzerainty to the Mahometan Mughal Emperor himself. Always at each other's throats though. For the Emperor Aurangzeb belongs to the Sunni stamp among the Mussulmen, while the Sultans are Shia. I cannot now quite recall the difference between these two factions, though Sathiri has explained it to me countless times. Yet she says that it must be as mysterious to me as the division between Catholic and Protestant is to her.

'And the Khan wishes us to propose a new factory there?' said Yale. 'But why me, sir, if I am allowed to ask?'

'Forsooth! You look this gift horse in the mouth, sir?'

'I believe, Governor,' I heard Joseph murmur, 'that Elihu simply wishes to avoid appearing excessively fro'ward among his fellows. But there is no favouritism in this, Mister Yale. The Council was unequivocal in its choice. You have been diligent in your study of the local languages, and we have every faith in your ability to negotiate with the Khan.'

'Besides,' laughed John Bridger, always one to lighten the mood, 'you have the best set of clothes in the whole of Fort St. George, Elihu. The Khan is apparently an exceptionally elegant fellow and we could think of none other who might answer.'

'Then I am your servant in this endeavor, sirs. Constant as the Northern Star.'

'*Julius Caesar*?' said my husband. 'Was Shakespeare not implying that Caesar saw himself as uniquely equipped to rule? That a man is known by the power he wields. Is that your belief too, Elihu?'

'Bravo, Joseph!' the Governor roared. 'I think you may be ditched with that quotation, Mister Yale.'

It made me smile to hear the fellow put down so neatly, but I paid the price for my lack of charity, pricked myself with the needle, while Mistress Bridger continued with tales of the village in which she had been born and I tried my best to nod and agree in all the correct places.

'In truth, sir,' Yale replied, 'that is indeed one of my beliefs. For what is a man without power, gentlemen? How does he show his worth? His quality.'

'I am not certain,' Joseph told him, 'that we ever truly have that opportunity. Master Shakespeare had another line, did he not? About us only being remembered for the evil that we do, the good going with us into the grave.'

It was typical of the morbid manner in which poor Joseph had begun to view life. And perhaps he was correct. But there was a break in the business.

'Prithee, Joseph,' I heard the Governor murmur, 'might I avail myself of the Oliver?'

Akbar was duly summoned, with chamber pot and cloth. Mistress Bridger and myself making polite pretense at not hearing the subsequent gush and gasp of relief from within the dining room screen, while Joseph and Mister Yale continued to dicker about the finer points of Shakespeare's verse.

'Yet, in the end,' said Mister Yale, 'is it not the *goods* that are oft interred with our bones?' He plainly considered this a fine jest, chortling a long while before he went on. 'Trade is all, gentlemen, don't you know? What else should our restless merchant souls desire, except trade?'

I could hear the Governor passing the piss-pot back to Akbar, the latter's gracious thanks to the *sahib*.

'You see, Mister Yale?' said the Governor, scraping his chair back into place across my beautifully polished dark-wood floor. 'Precisely the reason for dispatching you to the Khan. The very fellow. And unless I am much mistook, we will see you raised to factor in no time at all.'

Mistress Bridger allowed herself a slight conspiratorial smile, the first indication that she, too, had been following their conversation. She set down the whitework baby bonnet that she had just completed.

'*Pobre coitado*,' she whispered. Poor man. 'A bubble, I fear. Is that what you say?'

'A harmless hoodwink, perhaps,' I replied, for we all understood the Khan of Gingee's rather exotic taste in young men, the price he so often exacted for an exchange of trade. But then I raised my voice to its normal pitch. 'And did you hear?' I said. 'That the Papists are about to build a new chapel? I had the thing direct from Father Ephraim. Heavens, I fear that if we do not soon set our own house in order, the Almighty may entirely forsake us.'

But then I could have no idea how quickly He might do so.

Yet, before that, another treasure. A further letter from Mama, which I had decided to read afresh as soon as Joseph's guests had departed, out into the rain once more, and I could settle in the withdrawing room alone so that I might not disturb the baby. And oh, how I now wish that I had been less diligent.

Of course, I had written to her in November, with news of Joseph Junior and Richard, sketches of them enclosed, executed by my husband – Joseph Junior the image of his father, handsome and slender, Richie more my father's build, stocky and robust. Word too that I was, once again, with child. And with summary of the most significant events in the life of Fort St. George during the twelve months since my previous correspondence. Remarkably little of note, truth be told. And Mama's own letter, scripted at Christmas and dispatched aboard one of the Company's outbound vessels in January, so that our respective missives will have passed each other in mid-ocean. Where? I always wonder. Somewhere along the western coast of Africa, or at the Cape of Good Hope, I collect, where we travel together for that brief spell as, perhaps, our ships pass in the night. And you might think from the content that we inhabit universes each entirely separate from the other. I suppose that we do. For her own is so full of fears.

Your father, she writes, *finally received due recompense for his unlawful detention and determined that he should see the coffee house built anew. Of course, we should not have suffered the ruination from his imprisonment had he been more circumspect about his beliefs. A little more careful with his tongue. After all, no matter the circumstance, any age will only allow a given amount of truth to be told.* A harsh judgement. Papa had previously leased premises in Exchange Lane, and it had become a well-known meeting place for Turkey and Levant merchants like himself until, as I had previously told Mister Yale, it was lost during the Great Fire. *But it is all ill-news of late and I pass each night without sleep, fearing for the fate of yourself, of Joseph and the boys. Lord Almighty! Our fleet, and that of the French, defeated by the Dutch, time and time again. And those defeats here, in our home waters, where we should be at our*

46

most secure. So what must be happening there, my dear, a world away, where you must surely be at their mercy? There! The true tragedy. That she imagines us beset by the Dutch when, in fact, they have so far posed no problem at all for Fort St. George, while the true disaster – the entirely unthinkable, which slices through me like a thousand blades, which fills my heart and soul with ice and agony – has struck us down, here in our own dwelling. Oh, Mama. You cannot imagine how sleepless a night can be.

But there was so much more in her letter. And though we may be a world apart, I can sense the stirrings of yet more upheaval in England that may certainly touch us here, as well. The Company too.

You would wish to know, she says, *that Parliament has passed new legislation. The Test Act, they call it. By which all senior post-holders, civil and military, are required to take an oath, renouncing the doctrines and practices of the Roman Church, and to receive the Eucharist under the auspices of the Church of England. It has been no surprise to many of us that the Duke of York has refused the oath. Refused, my dear! The king's own brother. Heir to the throne indeed. James Stuart. Now forced to resign as Lord High Admiral – not that he has distinguished himself greatly in that role, as you will understand from our defeats at the hands of those Hollanders. And the broadsheets now replete with revelation about his no longer so secret conversion to Papism. Yet I suppose it is some small mercy that the king has ensured that James's daughters, at least, are raised under the care of our own Church.*

More in the same vein. Fears of a Catholic resurgence. Then a few anecdotes to illustrate that my younger brothers are no better behaved than previously. Her account of Elkanah Settle's new play, *The Empress of Morocco*, at the Dorset Garden Theatre, which she says made her think of me yet again.

Then the scream. Tanani's scream.

'What, in the name of heaven…?' I heard Joseph cry. He was still out upon the terrace walk, enjoying his final pipe of the evening. But by then I had hoisted my skirts and was racing up the stairs, along the darkened upper hallway and flung open the door to my bedchamber.

'No, *memsahib*,' Tanani hissed at me in a tremulous whisper, and I saw by the candlelight that she was standing at the rocker she favoured so much, her elbows tucked into her sides and the palms of her hands flattened towards me, at the sides of her face, in a gesture of surrender

– but the hands shaking violently and her eyes wide with terror. 'I should not scream, *memsahib*. I fall asleep. And when I wake…'

I looked around but could see nothing untoward. Though the window shutter was, unusually, open a few inches. Yet the little one was snuffling in his crib as normal, the netting draped all around to keep any malignant insects at bay.

Joseph's urgent footsteps pounding on the hallway's flooring boards, general commotion below and outside as the servants roused themselves in their small compound, a torch flame flickering somewhere beyond that gap in the shutter, and my eyes adjusting to the meager light.

'What is it, *ayah*?' said Joseph, joining me just inside the room.

'Oh, *sahib*. I fall asleep. Then…' She pointed a quaking finger towards the crib. 'No, *sahib*!' she cried, as he took a step towards the baby. '*Nalla pambu*. I hear him, see him. When I wake.'

Joseph stopped in his tracks, lifted a protective arm to hold me back.

'Here? In the room?' He peered into the gloom that filled each corner.

'*Nalla pambu*?' I said, searching for the meaning yet already cold with fear.

'The Tamil name…' Joseph began. 'My dear, you must be brave, now. It is the name they give to the serpent.' I know that I jammed my fist into my mouth to stifle my own scream. 'To the cobra. But, *ayah*, where in the room? Do you know?'

'I tell you, *sahib*. There!' And she stabbed her finger towards the crib once more. 'With baby.'

I clutched Joseph's arm then, some awful contraction within my head, the silent scream clawing inside my brain.

'Calm, Catherine. Be calm, I beg you.' He edged towards the crib, towards my baby, gently reached for the hem of the gauze netting. He lifted it an inch. Slowly. Ever so slowly. Another inch. And every nerve in my body shuddered, urging me to throw myself upon the crib. Slowly, Joseph lifted the gauze, until he could attach the hem to the hook, by which the net was hung from the ceiling.

There it lay, coiled upon the linen gown in which my baby was so peacefully at rest. So helpless. So unaware.

'If we make no sudden moves,' I said, though all I wanted to do was to snatch my baby away. 'Perhaps…'

'And you, *ayah*,' said Joseph. 'Go below. Tell Akbar. Ask him to come up. He will know what we need.'

Tanani was well pleased, I think, at least in part, to be out of the room. And then there was the waiting. Moments that felt like hours. All I could think about was the time this was all taking. Where *was* Akbar? I felt sick to the pit of my stomach. Cold. Alone. Rejected Joseph's every attempt to comfort and calm me. How could sweet Lord Jesus desert me so. But then I remembered that interruption to the little fellow's baptism; Reverend Warner afterwards suffering from a fever; our decision that we would wait until he was fully recovered before completing the ceremony; and, of course, there was the *sadhu*'s curse.

'Perhaps...' I said again, but Joseph did not allow me to finish.

'They say that the cobra is a thinking snake,' he said. 'That it will not harm anybody unless it is deliberately attacked. No snake will maliciously bite other creatures. Why? Because no animal except man will maliciously attack a snake.'

We had not even heard Akbar climb the stairs, but he spoke then, caused us both to start. He was in the doorway, holding a long and slender rod, a fine cord and noose attached to its upper end.

'But man,' said Akbar, 'will see a snake and say: "I must kill that snake." Even when the snake threatens no harm. Of course, the snake does not think like that. But this is only true of *nalla pambu* if the serpent has not, itself, been enchanted, and sent to harm humans.'

What was it that made Akbar say that?

Yet something, in that instant, stirred the child from his slumbers. He opened his little mouth and wailed. Just once. Then began to flap his harmless, innocent arms. And the serpent awoke too, its eyes suddenly like two pieces of sparkling obsidian. It lifted itself, its head, a foot or more into the air, spread that ugly hood, its back dark but those spectacle markings as light as its evil pale belly. The forked tongue flicked at the air, again and again, as Akbar advanced upon it.

'Gently,' I murmured. 'Oh, gently. And Sweet Jesu protect my child.'

The cobra was swaying now, baby Walter wriggling beneath its coils. And the noose was almost there, almost above the serpent's head.

But then the baby opened his mouth again, screamed with all the power in his tiny ill-fated lungs, thrashed with his arms just once, so that the cobra struck, buried its fangs in his beautiful face.

Yet this was merely the beginning of my horror.

Within an hour, my infant boy was pronounced dead. Within a day, buried in his tiny coffin. In our English Golgotha, there at the north-western corner of Black Town, at the edge of the guava garden that stretches away down the slope and into the distance. It stood witness, that cloistered settlement of the dead, to the mortality rates among our White Town citizens, for it had long outgrown its original and extensive limits, the latest tombs and headstones cascading in layers down the open margent of the plantation. And thus we mourners stood somewhat protected from the monsoon's measured miseries by the vaulted roofing while the heavens drummed a death march rhythm upon the domes above our heads, and the Gentue untouchables fought their battle against the open elements, against the rising waters within the small grave they had dug, setting weighting stones upon the lid of Walt's casket. Now, of course, he has his coverlet to protect him, the quarried grey and ochre Pallavaram, carefully carved with its Latin inscriptions, the date of his pitiable loss. *Mensis Julii 9° An 1674.* But then...

There had been no saving him, it seemed. Neither the chirurgeons, Sherman and Heathfield, nor Doctor Fryer, nor Sathiri's infusions of leaf and herb, nor the prayers of countless desperate well-wishers, nor those of Father Ephraim, nor even those of Reverend Warner, finally summoned for the ministration of a belated private baptism. Guilt, of course, that if we had been more diligent about the little one receiving the blessing of Christ earlier, perhaps – well, perhaps. Yet we had joined now in the Lord's Prayer before the prescribed Collects were intoned and, all that time, I watched the fang marks redden and swell, the vomiting begin, eruptions of the milk with which I had so carefully suckled him such little time before. It was Matthew, I think, who named him, as my baby's tiny lungs began to labour against the venom's invasion of his blood.

'Walter I baptise thee,' Reverend Warner had said, 'in the name of the Father, and of the Son, and of the Holy Spirit.' Then he did his best to pour the blessed water carefully upon the babe's head but, by then, the little one was convulsing in my arms and, before we could all be admonished to do our sacred duties, to protect the child from Satan's evils, he had fallen still, lifeless.

That night, thirty-seven days ago now, I stood upon the *veranda* with Joseph, each of us lifeless, empty of any words between us. In truth, he had spoken not a word all day, all through the burial, for each of his attempts to do so had merely dragged from him great racking sobs. But where were my own tears? I did not know. Not then. And I still do not know these thirty-seven days later, each of them an interminable struggle, each of them feeling like a se'nnight and only the other boys to drag me through the endless, empty hours. There has been a red rage that burns silently within me seeking blame wherever I can apportion it, and the heat of that anger must surely have dried up any lachrimosity within me.

'What happens?' I said. 'In heaven – to babies, I mean. Who cares for them?'

'"*For of such is the Kingdom of Heaven.*" Is that not what the gospels teach us?' He spoke the words with bitterness. 'That we shall not enter unless we do so with the innocence of children?'

'We must be rid of her,' I said. 'Tanani. The shutters.'

Yet I knew that this was foolishness, for we still had no idea how the serpent had even reached the room. Akbar, of course, had refused to kill the creature, despite my demands to the contrary, and had presumably set the evil thing free somewhere far away from the house. At least I hoped so.

'What good are recriminations against the servants?' said Joseph. 'There is only myself to blame. The *sadhu*'s curse. And Heaven, my dear? I cannot bear the thought. I prefer the Gentues' vision. That the little fellow will be re-born. Perhaps over and over again. Each life a chance to improve on the previous. Many lifetimes until, at last, he finds union with the divine. Akbar tells me that some of his people believe we may be fated to marry the same person in several lives.'

'That he will be re-born to us? You believe so?'

'Better than all those platitudes about life having to go on. Though it must, naturally. For Joseph Junior and Richard, if for nothing else. Though I wonder...'

'About our life here?'

'It has begun to suffocate me, I fear. Even before this.'

'Hold me, dearest?' I said, and I peered out into the curtain of rain.

But then I heard a cry, saw a figure stumbling through the downpour. The voice of Elihu Yale.

'Quickly!' he was shouting. 'Oh, Sweet Jesus, quickly.' He had lost his hat, water cascading down the sides of his periwig onto his cape that was sodden with mud. In fact, his whole attire, his boots, dripping with wet clay. And he was carrying something within his cloak. A small bundle. I couldn't make it out, but Joseph had run down the steps, helped him the final few paces onto the terrace walk. 'I went back,' Mister Yale was saying. 'To the burial ground. God blind me, I went back. Something drew me there. And the rain. It had washed away the very earth. Then... I heard—'

He drew aside the cape's folds, and there was our child, still wrapped in his tiny shroud, though also covered in filth. I screamed, and Joseph wrapped his arms about me, but I struggled free, threw myself down upon Walter's poor bedraggled form, snatched him from Yale's arms.

'What have you done sirrah?' said Joseph, his face stricken with horror. 'In God's name, what have you done?'

'I heard the child cry, sir,' Yale whimpered. 'I swear it. The casket was uncovered, the earth washed away. I could hear...'

Was there warmth still in the tiny body? I thought so. But perhaps just an illusion. A desperate illusion. Yet no breath. No other sign of life. Oh, how I prayed and begged God for the miracle.

'You opened it?' Joseph demanded, and he knelt to embrace me again, sobbing once more. 'The casket?'

'With my dagger. Lifted the lid. Lifted it at last. But, by then... There was nobody to help. Nobody!'

Nobody. And now I shall never know. But we made a pledge to each other that night, myself, my sweet, distraught husband, and Mister Yale. A pledge that, apart from Reverend Warner – who quietly arranged for the burial to privately take place again at dawn the following morning – this thing should be kept between us. This was the most intimate of matters and, between us, we kept a silent vigil until first light, assured ourselves that the babe was truly gone. With Tanani's help, I fashioned a clean shroud, and I know the load would have been too great for our society as a whole, for the unbearable nightmares have tormented me each of these past weeks. I know they will do so for the rest of my life.

More than two years. And still the nightmares persist. That recurring dream that I am trapped in the coffin with the babe, each of us clawing at the lid and screeching until our throats are raw. Though, this morning, there was the visit from Matthew Parrish to distract me. Our chairs out upon the *veranda*, which now served as a constant reminder of that night, yet the gloom lightened today by little Rich's gales of childish laughter as he played with Tanani, and our latest arrival asleep in his crib. Yes, she is still our *ayah*.

'You seriously believe they may have killed the Major?' I said.

'One. Perhaps both. We need to look at the facts, my dear. Puckle arrives in July last year with a brief, arising from my reports. Our reports, I should say.' He gave me that slightly conspiratorial look of which he is so fond. 'To investigate conditions not only here but at all our other factories in India besides.'

I have long since ceased to concern myself about the part I play on Matthew's behalf. No, that is not correct. I act the informant on my own behalf, not his. Fort St. George is, after all, a small imitation of society back in England. Divided, as it has been these decades past. Riven down the middle. We Dissenters, Presbyterians, Levellers, Covenanters, Puritans on the one side. We who still call the internecine conflicts of the Forties and Fifties our Great Revolution. On the other side, devout Royalists and High Church Anglicans, Cavaliers – so many merely one step away from the Church of Rome's idolatries. Men who see those conflicts not as a struggle for tolerance and liberties, but as a seditious Great Rebellion. In England, they have the upper hand, this Cavalier faction, the Crown party, control Parliament entirely. But here things are a little different. Divisions within our divisions, naturally, but that is broadly the way of things. Yet the ladies tend to see themselves as above such matters, united by the role that we, ourselves, must perform. For our men. For our children. And thus we gossip, exchange intimacies about our husbands' activities, while I remember the cavalier injustice done to my father by those enemies of Parliament. To the father whose family name my new baby now carries. Elford. To those many other victims, also, who shared my family's Dissenter beliefs. I remember, I make notes, and I stoke my own animosities, here within these pages.

'But Major Puckle's brief was indeed to investigate conditions, Matthew. Conditions.'

'Simply a euphemism. Puckle was very clear when we spoke. He shared our beliefs, Catherine. A strong follower of Cromwell, treated badly at the Restoration and forced to find new employment. With the Company. I furnished him with our latest intelligence. About the Governor. Other matters. And, so far as I know, he took some of our evidence with him when he travelled north.'

'With Mister Yale and Mister Seaton.'

'Puckle chose them on the Governor's recommendation. Perhaps not the wisest decision, in the circumstances. Granted, the Governor has great faith in Mister Yale's talents. Apart even,' he laughed here, 'from those he must have employed that time with the Khan of Gingee. You remember?' I did, indeed. I had wondered about it many times. 'Yet,' Matthew continued, 'it is more difficult to discern why he would have recommended Seaton. A rum devil, at the best of times.'

'Wait,' I said, incredulous. 'You imply that Governor Langhorn may have sent Seaton deliberately to act the assassin's part?'

'Impossible to know, my dear. But Puckle? Hale and hearty when he left. And then, not long after, he's dead.'

Five weeks ago, the middle of October, and news just reached us by fast sloop from the Bay.

'Hardly unusual out here,' I said, and could not help casting a glance in the direction of the burial ground, a stab of burning anguish piercing my heart.

'I'm sorry,' said Matthew. 'The wound still raw, I imagine.'

'This world that we inhabit keeps it so. I wrote to Mama just after – well, you know when. Informed her about Walter's death. Though when her own letter arrived in the July following, she had still not received my own, sought news of her latest grandson. She knows now, of course. And my latest will have informed her, I hope, that I was then once again with child, her anxieties presumably therefore at their highest while I, here in Madras, have been enjoying the blessing of little Elford's presence all these months. It seems so cruel.'

'That is the life we live, my dear. As you say, cruel. Think of poor Puckle.'

'He made enemies,' I said, recalling Joseph's description of that acerbic meeting of the Council. When was that? February, I think. Major Puckle had spent several months digging and probing, then confronted the Governor and Council members. Why no official register of vessels mooring at Fort St. George? No details of whence they came, nor whither they were outward bound. If no register, how could the Company be assured that all transactions involving those vessels were legitimate? Why no official record of all those dwelling in White Town and not employed by the Company, whether English or Portuguese, though seemingly paying no rent nor accounting for their activities? Why have we allowed the presence of two Romish churches in Black Town, and even a Jewish temple, several heathen pagodas, when we of the English Church have only our crumbling dining room within the Fort House? Serious implications towards a lack of due diligence – or something far worse.

'Enemies, Catherine? You know barely the half of it. He shared confidences with me about bribes and inducements he could prove have been taken purely for the Governor's personal gain. He may be an amenable fellow but...'

'You will send word to the Company? About these latest suspicions?'

'I shall do so. And encrypt them too.'

'Gracious, you are become a spy in truth,' I laughed. 'But you are certain? About Mister Yale. I find it hard to believe that he would in any way be a party to Major Puckle's death.'

'Again, I fear we must examine the facts. Puckle takes Yale and Seaton off with him on his expedition to the north. He gets as far as Masulipatnam and, quite suddenly, he is struck down with a calenture. He dies there. How convenient. And when his two companions return, they do so with a quantity of booty and some tale about having come across an auction for the worldly goods of two nameless deceased fellow Englishmen.'

'You know that Mister Yale attempted to regale me with some lengths of ribbon and a very fine bone fan when they returned?'

I stopped myself. I was about to remark that it had become Mister Yale's wont, attempting to ingratiate himself still further with my family, with myself in particular, since that night. But despite our friendship and close association with Matthew, even he had been excluded from our secret. Mister Yale, however, had tried to speak of it to me many times, though always rebuked for doing so. Yet I knew that the same questions must haunt him as trouble myself and Joseph too. Akbar had finally been persuaded to confess that, yes, he had heard of cases. Far away cases. In which the bite of *nalla pambu* had induced the very appearance of death, only for the victim to awaken again later. I shudder at the very thought, my nightmares now filling my waking hours also. But no, *memsahib*, this could not be such a case. The baby, *memsahib*, had indeed left this life. But once that Pandora's Box has been opened, it can never again be closed. An evil that gnaws at us and must, also, gnaw at Mister Yale. Did he truly hear baby Walt cry in his coffin? If so, could he have acted more quickly in opening the lid before whatever remained of the air inside the casket was exhausted? Or was it simply some trick of the breeze, some phantom sound upon the monsoon's wind? How can we ever know?

'I have said before, my dear. He admires you greatly, I think. And do I sense some reciprocal sympathy? Did you accept his gift?'

'Impertinent, sirrah. And no, I did not. It was an exquisite fan but I do not believe he would have flaunted it so if it could be shown to have any connection with Major Puckle. He may be a bluff cove, Matthew, a little naïve – those absurd clenches and quibbles he practices against us, annoying more than amusing – yet he is no fool. I cannot quite see him as an enemy to our beliefs. As though he sits somewhere in the neutral ground between our Independent sympathies and those of the closet Cavaliers. Certainly no murderer. Nor yet a murderer's accomplice.'

'But Seaton?'

'Seaton I perceive less plainly. As you say, something of the devil in him. Outwardly still the madcap, yet there are times when he regards me that I sense – well, it is difficult to explain. But if you think there is evidence, you should present it. My only question is whether it will be taken seriously.'

'I sense that the Company may presently be more willing to act. They could hardly risk further divisions here with the Hollanders still threatening. But now…' It was Major Puckle and the Company's dispatches, several broadsheets, that had brought us that news too. In truth, we have been at peace with the Dutch for almost two years, though unaware until the Major's arrival. The Treaty of Westminster, each country making concessions to the other.

'Mister Yale claimed that his gifts were intended to give me joy of the latest news from the Colonies. He has the rare belief that this New York will one day eclipse even London.'

'Fanciful,' said Matthew, 'even for Mister Yale. Still, I was working on a couplet, something about this being a town that needed naming twice. Though I do not quite have it yet. Anyway, we need to be able to hold it this time.'

Matthew's poetry has helped to keep me sane, I think. And that distant colonial township? It has changed hands so many times already. First settled by the Dutch as New Amsterdam. Captured by our own forces and renamed New York. Then the Hollanders again, New Orange. Now New York for the second time. Whatever next?

'Always important. That we are able to retain that which we hold dear.' Perhaps I may have inadvertently glanced towards the crib, where the babe still slept, for Matthew perceived my meaning at once.

'There seems to be naught amiss with Richard,' he smiled, as the child crashed into his outstretched shanks yet again. 'And little Elford,' he followed my gaze towards the crib, 'must be the most contented babe in all Coromandel. While young Joseph – well, a sharp boy, is he not? Like his father.'

They certainly share a gift for mathematicks. Six now, and this morning confined to the withdrawing room for more lessons on that very subject with our schoolmaster, Mister Ord.

'Your point, Matthew?'

'That the child you lost…'

'Walter,' I snapped. 'He was named Walter. We must always remember.'

'Forgive me. That what happened to Walter was a tragic accident. No indication that anything untoward will happen to this little one.'

'The curse?'

'If it ever existed, the *sadhu* is long gone. Any curse gone with him. He will not trouble you now.'

His eyes grew hard and cold as he spoke the words and I wondered, not for the first time, about the *sadhu*'s fate. Simply never seen again in Black Town nor, so far as I could gather, anywhere else.

'It is an outrage,' cried Mister Yale. 'A blatant outrage. Who could have invented such a thing?'

We had a full table for dinner and Joseph could not look me in the eye though, for my part, I did not experience even the smallest sensation of guilt. Well, very little anyway. I merely observed how much things had changed, how much Matthew Parrish had set the trend, Mister Yale's attire still more stylish than the rest, but each of them now having adopted Matthew's custom of more comfortable, half-Gentue clothing.

'How can we ever know?' said the Governor, while John Barker's wife patted his arm sympathetically. 'Some unperceived rivalry, perhaps. Simple malice.'

'But they have presented allegations?' said John Nicks. 'Charges to be answered? A chance for you to refute their concerns?'

'You plainly do not understand John Company, Mister Nicks. I provided response to each of the concerns raised by Major Puckle. Even the church. Great heavens, the Catholic church. Was it truly such a crime? To have the guns fired in salute at the consecration. We are all Christians here, after all. Awash in a sea of heathens.'

I am still uncertain from whence came the original proposal though I am fairly sure it was Joseph who first talked openly about the project. Governor Langhorn has subsequently claimed credit, saying that Major Puckle was correct. A disgrace that the Catholics now had their original wooden church, as well as the newer stone-built structure – their shrine to St. Antony – both in Black Town, while we had simply that meager place of worship across the square. So, subscriptions had begun among our Protestant community. This had been not long after we lost baby Walter, and Joseph had certainly been the very first to make a contribution.

'Can we afford so much?' I had said to him.

'Thirty-two pounds,' he had replied. It was a full one-third of his official annual salary. 'I should think it a pittance if it helps to counter the curse. To bring us back within God's Mercy.'

Yet the guilt had run deep and it was Mister Yale's subscription that had raised eyebrows. His own salary at that time a mere ten pounds per annum – and six of those pounds he had donated to the cause. A sure sign that he was being rewarded handsomely by his private enterprises.

'It is a great wonder,' said Elihu now, helping himself to another portion of fish *philoorie*, 'to see our very own St. Mary's rising week by week from the ground.'

Just across the square from us, as it happens. There has been a great deal of dust, to my annoyance, from the stonemasons' work.

'And I am correct, am I not?' said John Nicks. 'That this will be the finest English church built anywhere east of Accra?'

Mister Yale snorted into his food.

'Sirrah, it will be the *only* English church east of Accra. The first ever built. How could it possibly be anything other than our finest? Indeed, do we have a church in Accra at all?'

There was a deal of table thumping and merriment, especially from that jade, Katherine Barker. It had been almost impossible to disentangle her from Mister Yale's arm as I tried to seat everybody for dinner and now she was clapping her dainty hands together in adoration for the fellow.

'I do not believe,' said Nicks, glowering directly at the girl – some jealousy there, I had cause to collect – 'that any of this is a laughing matter. We have the Governor to defend, after all. At least we might all pen our own affidavits, attesting to the falsehoods in these accusations.'

'Already done, John,' said Yale. 'Though difficult to refute allegations when the Governor himself does not know their nature.'

Yet I could see that it was not righteous indignation that fed the eyes of John Nicks but fear. Matthew had been clear on the matter – that Nicks was concerned about his own possible exposure, and especially his future without benefit of Governor Langhorn's patronage and favour. After all, Nicks was Secretary to the Agency Council, responsible for the books, and it had been another of Major Puckle's criticisms – that, all too frequently, there were gaps in the records. Suspicious gaps.

'You have all been kind,' said the Governor, and he seemed to look at me in particular, so that now I *did* feel guilty, felt my cheeks colour. 'But I fear that no amount of affidavits will change the Company's mind. They should see it, I suspect, as a case of protesting too much. No, I shall simply leave behind my book collection and sail into the sunset. My successor is already appointed in any case.'

Yes, I thought, *sail into the sunset with the residue of your ill-gotten gains*. Matthew's intelligence tells him – and has therefore informed the Company – that the Governor's bribes and sweeteners from local Gentue merchants alone has amounted to some twenty thousand pagodas each year. Seven thousand pounds. And while the Company may have lifted the restriction on limited private trade, the cap on gains from such enterprise remains at a relatively modest three hundred pounds. Sir William is already the benefactor of a considerable inheritance, so I doubt he will starve. Yet I know that there is some mild disappointment on Joseph's part. Disappointment that, with the new Agent, Mister Streynsham Master, already named as Sir William's successor, Joseph himself would not have the chance for advancement even on a temporary basis. But he made a favourable impression on us both when he landed here briefly, back in July, on his way north to the Bay.

'And where is your successor at this moment, Governor?' said Joseph. 'Do we know?'

'Completing the Company's business on the Hoogli River, I believe,' the Governor replied. 'He is a dedicated fellow, as you all know. Here and in post early in January.'

Mister Master – I shall never get used to naming him so – has a certain reputation as one of the Company's pathfinders here in India, of course. And to be fair, he had been named as next Agent for Madras Patnam long before any hint of impropriety on Sir William Langhorn's part. Simply normal good form. For Agents and Governors are as prone to sudden demise as everybody else here, so it is reasonable business practice to always have a replacement waiting in the wings.

'Well,' said Mister Yale, 'I trust that when he arrives we shall not all find ourselves thrown into the Tower for some fault as unjustified as your own, Sir William.' The subject of the Tower seems to have been on the fellow's mind since the previous year's news arrived with the new Governor in July, including that of the skeletons, two children, discovered within the White Tower, the Tower of London. *"'The tyrannous and bloody deed is done,'"* Elihu began to quote, not for the first time. *"'The most arch act of piteous massacre, That ever yet this land was guilty of.'"* Sirrah, it should not surprise me were we accused of poor Puckle's murther.'

I am certain that something passed, at that moment, between the Governor and whey-faced Vincent Seaton, though I cannot be certain. I wish that Matthew could have been there to see it, but he was far up-country on some secretive endeavor. In any case, this talk of the children weighed heavily upon me.

'I doubt,' said Governor Langhorn, 'that any of us may share the fate of the young princes.' *At least,* I thought, *the king intends to see those poor boys buried afresh in the Abbey.* Some small consolation perhaps for the evil done to them by their crook-backed uncle. Yet that small thought cut through me like a knife, and it must have showed. 'Why, my dear lady,' the Governor said to me, 'have I spoke something to disturb you?'

I exchanged a glance with my husband, saw his own sadness, a match to mine.

'No, Sir William,' I replied. 'Of course you have not. It was simply – well, I have been struggling with the question of whether we may, in the next few years, have to think about sending the oldest boys home. Joseph Junior and Richard. When they would, I suppose, be almost the age of those same princes. Almost.'

'But nothing is yet settled,' Joseph reminded me, firmly. 'No such decision yet made. And far too early to even contemplate such a thing.'

This was no place for growing boys. And Mama has promised to see them educated. But the hazard! Yet the conversation had meanwhile returned to the new Governor.

'It simply seems a madness,' said John Nicks. 'To change one's Chief when we have these savages on our very threshold.'

The Gentue, Shivaji, had set out seven years ago to build his own Maratha Empire, to champion Gentue values and conquer the Mahometan Moghuls, as well as to take whatever he was able from the foreigners in his way. Since then, Shivaji has slowly consolidated his territory, clashing frequently with the Moghuls and striking down as far as Bijapur where, in June, he had captured Gingee, pillaged Porto Novo, and was now besieging Vellore, a hundred miles inland.

'The gifts we gave him in May,' Sir William replied, 'should have been enough to keep him from our door. At least they gave us the chance to strengthen our defences. And Streynsham Master knows Shivaji's tricks of old. You need have no fears in that direction.'

'And Agent Master's politics, his persuasion,' said Vincent Seaton. 'Do we know anything of that? I heard tell that he may be another damn'd Quaker. A heretic. Is that correct? Sirrah, just when the Lord has rid us of their chief ranter.'

There it is again, the division in our society. Always in the background. More of last year's news. That Gerrard Winstanley has died. That great reformer respected so much by my father. An acquaintance of the family. Yet heretic seemed such a strange way to attack Agent Master.

'Perhaps, Vincent,' said Mister Yale, 'a little moderation might be in order. And where do you find these fancies? We both met the fellow up-country and he seemed perfectly orthodox in his opinions. Certainly no Quaker by the way he sports his weapons. Besides Mistress Yale's father is himself, I collect, of that same persuasion.'

'Really, ma'am?' Seaton looked at me aghast, though he had plainly forgotten our earlier conversation on this very subject.

'I assure you, Mister Seaton,' I told him, quite enraged, 'that it is no affliction. And I have said before that my father was – perhaps still is – an admirer of the Quakers, though not of their fellowship. Mister Winstanley, on the other hand, has often been in Papa's company. Had he been born a little earlier, I believe he would have joined that gallant band upon St. Georges Hill. My father is a True Leveller in spirit if not in fact. He shares Winstanley's dream of turning a corrupt world upside down, I think.'

The table fell silent momentarily as the servants moved in to clear the empty bowls and I feared I had revealed too much of myself. There had been great speculation. About who, among our number, might have been spreading accusations, feeding them to the Company's ever-suspicious Directors. For the charges always seemed to be directed towards those of the Cavalier faction.

Joseph to the rescue.

'But such is the value of our own community here,' he said. 'That we are at least free of such family feuds. Such utopian dreamers. Here, Catherine's greatest concern is how to manage twenty servants when, in London, we should need no more than two or three.'

'Lord!' I trilled a good-wife's merry laugh feigned in response. 'How true, my dear.' But I could see in his eyes that he knew he would pay dearly for his remark once we were alone again.

The siege is lifted. To be precise, it was lifted ten days ago, on the very day that the new Governor's sails came over the horizon to the north and east. Not a hugely complex siege, naturally. For that same attribute, which makes Fort St. George so eminently defensible – that our strip of land is protected on three sides by the two inland rivers and by the sea – also means that it only needs a blockade on the northern roads to seal us off entirely from all but maritime relief. And, even there, that rogue Lingappa, Mahometan Governor, *naik* of Poonamallee, had set enough vessels offshore to prevent our succour from anything but the East India Company's own fighting ships.

And so we spent a sparse Christmas-tide. No great hardship for myself and Joseph for we each remarked that it reminded us of our youth, when the Puritans and Cromwellians had banned all celebration of our Lord's birth except for appropriately devout worship. But the almost popish idolatry that has become so much the custom, the excuse for profit-making established as such an obsession across the nation, all of that had gone. For a while at least. And our Dissenter beliefs, in part, longed for those simpler times to be restored once more. Well, this year, our wish was granted. The siege had made it so.

Yet we all knew that Lingappa would return, again demanding tribute for Poonamallee, his neighbouring town to the west, perhaps fifteen miles away. And after Poonamallee it would be each of the other local towns, dozens of them. Bad enough that we should pay such tribute to the *naik* of Chingleput Province, and to the Sultan of the Golconda kingdom. But the Fort's Council had decided that there the drain on the Company's finances must stop.

So, today, Agent Master has convened a meeting, a private meeting, in my house, in my withdrawing room, with Joseph as Second, and with Matthew Parrish. Sir William had, of course, sailed away on the same ships that had brought the new Governor to our rescue. Streynsham Master had landed somewhat to the north and been met by Matthew's company of buff-coated pikes and muskets, as well as those Council members fit enough to stand, and when the procession reached the Great Pagoda in Black Town, all the guns of the Fort had fired a deafening salute. There had, according to my husband, been a terse and brief examination of the Fort's accounts, the official hand-over of the Consultation Books, the most formal of farewells and thereafter Sir William was carried out to the bar, deposited in a large *masula* surf-boat and ferried out to the *Bengal Merchant*.

Good riddance to him, I thought, as Tanani and myself settled once more on the terrace walk to the entertainment of young Richie. He will be six this year and was having to be restrained from chasing the flock of rose-ringed parakeets that insisted on swooping before him, squawking and tormenting. Joseph Junior, on the other hand, will be eight. And the infant Elford will see his second birthing day very soon. He has that curious waking ability to resemble his father, those innocent smiling eyes set in a lugubrious face yet when he sleeps my husband tells me that he is all his mama – my pouting lips, he says, the nose, cheeks and chin settling into my more rounded features. Elford is a joy, yet I am now reconciled to the fact that the eldest two should be sent home at an appropriate juncture, though it will break my heart to do so. All the same, my husband and I have at least arrived at some consensus. A postponement of any decision until Joseph Junior has turned ten.

Poor Walt would have been four in the next few months, of course. But I shook that thought away from me, trying to catch the conversation from within, which was almost drowned out by the construction work across the street, elephants and their *pahans* hauling timber to the new church.

'You were there when Major Puckle died?' Matthew was asking the Governor.

'It was unlike any other fever I've ever seen before. The poor fellow, twelve days a-dying. His diary disappeared too – though his son Samuel inherited his periwig and tongue scraper.'

'A poor inheritance,' said my husband.

'His investigation,' said Agent Master, 'lacked teeth. Another poor inheritance. But we shall set that to rights. I've studied my subject, Mister Hynmers. I laid before the Company Court a paper of proposals, each of them endorsed wholeheartedly. About the keeping of accounts; the trade in European goods; and our contracting arrangements.'

Joseph had been surprised by the speed with which change has been introduced. New rules posted in the Fort House mess room. The Council now to meet every Monday and Thursday without fail. The Governor to keep the cash and cashbook himself, personally. The writers to have duplicates of all their books, and have them permanently ready to be sent to England for auditing. More repairs to the Fort. All admirable proposals, I believe, that bode well for our futures under this new governorship.

'And Lingappa?' said Matthew.

'He will be back. And unless I miss my guess, he will go straight to the Sultan of Golconda and complain that he has been slighted, demand that the old man sends his warriors to help him. To teach us a lesson. It's clear the dog knew I was coming. But we shall have to deal with him. Send a clear message to all these fellows that there is now a new order here.'

I simply hoped that the Sultan would not see this new order as a challenge, agree to Lingappa's demands and dispatch his savages to slaughter us in our beds. An elephant bellowed, made me turn sharply, recalling the occasion when one of the beasts, in its male rutting season, its *musth*, had turned upon its keeper before my very eyes, crushing the poor boy in an instant.

'Tanani,' I said, 'let us make sure that Richard remains here on the *veranda*.' She set herself between Richie and the steps, squatting before him and emptying out his box of wooden animals, knowing that he could not resist them while, for my part, I settled myself into my chair and picked up the copy of Donne's book that has been amusing me. I admire Mister Donne's poetry but this I find especially entertaining. *Ignatius His Conclave*, a beautifully vindictive satire against the Jesuits. Yet today it was hard to distract my thoughts from the conversation within.

'You have a plan, sirrah?' I heard Joseph ask.

'Perhaps,' said the Governor. 'Shivaji, my old adversary, may provide a solution.'

It was something of a legend. That, at the start of his campaign of conquest, Shivaji had reached the Company's factory at Surat to find it defended by a somewhat younger Streynsham Master and a force of just thirty men. Together, they held off Shivaji's hordes until they simply tired of the game and moved on. Well, that gives me some comfort at least, that Governor Master may similarly protect us from the threat.

'The Gentues claim he has already been here,' said Matthew. 'To Fort St. George, last October. In disguise, of course.'

'Why, the devil! You reported this to Council, Mister Parrish?'

'We had no evidence, I'm afraid. Just rumours.' That he had received from Sathiri, naturally. She had been full of the news, believed she had seen Shivaji entering our renowned Kalikambal Temple, to worship his goddess, Bhavani. The man's beauty and elegance themselves also a legend. And she had described in infinite detail the precision with which his raven-black beard was trimmed, the graceful curve of his nose, the sandalwood sheen of his features – images that had fed my dreaming fantasies on more than one occasion.

'Oh yes, Catherine,' Sathiri had laughed. 'Without mistake. The most beautiful of men.'

'And before we could chase the rumours,' said Matthew, 'he had vanished again. If he was ever here at all, of course. Back to his armies. But an alliance? You think that possible, sir?'

'Shivaji would make an unreliable friend,' Governor Master replied. 'Especially now he's allied himself to Golconda, despite the Sultan being a Mussulman. So we can never predict who might hold the upper hand when the fighting's over. No, I believe this may be a case of holding with the hare and running with the hounds. If we could find some way of offering Shivaji a tempting morsel that would avert his eyes from Madras, that might suffice. Suggestions, gentlemen?'

There was some discussion that I could not catch. The elephants again, the cries of their *pahans*, the yells of the near-naked workers unchaining their loads of timber. And there was, of course, the ever-present stench of dung whenever the beasts were upon the streets. But I picked up the conversation again with Joseph's insistent proposal.

'Perhaps,' he said, 'open a different door for him within Bijapur.'

'Vellore?' said Matthew.

'Why not? We owe Vellore nothing and Shivaji has held the place under siege for six months now. If we could gain intelligence about the disposition of their armies, find some weakness in their defences, arrange for that intelligence to reach Shivaji…'

Richie was stamping his own small wooden elephant against my toes.

'You would undertake this mission, Mister Parrish?' the Governor asked.

'I believe,' said Joseph, 'that we might have a more suitable candidate. Mister Yale is already – how should I put this? – trusted by the *naik*. Old acquaintances. We can easily persuade him that we have heard rumours of possible aggression from that quarter. Once he returns with the intelligence, it will be a simple enough task to relay the details to Shivaji.'

I gave Richard my best tiger's roar imitation, then smiled, of course, recalling Mistress Bridger's view of Yale, my own too, as something of a bubble.

'Yale?' Agent Master laughed. 'I cannot take to the fellow. All he's done since I arrived is complain about the additional work I've inflicted upon him. And then had the nerve to enquire about his own advancement.'

'He works diligently enough,' Joseph explained. 'Not the most likeable of the writers, but diligent. And he has worked hard to grasp the languages. He's very good at several tongues. At one point I even thought we might be able to dispense with the services of that cove, Veranna.'

Kasi Veranna has been our resident native merchant here since before my husband and I arrived. An institution of Fort St. George, entrusted to lead many of our negotiations with local suppliers, though always viewed with suspicion even by those who, I am certain, are guilty of far worse violations of Company procedures. He is a Gentue of the Vaishya caste, according to Matthew.

'I agree with Mister Hynmers,' Matthew now added. 'Yale is not exactly to my taste, but he would be eminently suitable for this venture, sir. And advancement? Might that not be the answer?'

'Offer him promotion to factor?' said Agent Master. 'Allow him to sign new bonds upon successful completion of the mission. From the little I know of him, I suspect the offer would at least prevent him asking too many questions. Very well, gentlemen, let me think on it. But your assistance has been invaluable, as always.' There was that dreadful scraping of chairs on my floors again. Oh, how I wish those men would take more care. 'No, I beg you,' said the Governor, 'please keep your seats. I shall show myself out.'

And a moment later, he had joined us on the *veranda*. He is a handsome man, fine-featured. Almost forty but all the appearance of being younger, despite having spent most of his years here in India. His father, I know, was once a strong supporter of Parliament but later sided with the Royalists, though Streynsham Master himself seems to have tended more towards the Commonwealth faction.

'Mistress Hynmers.' He bowed graciously as I set down my book. Then he straightened quickly. 'Great heavens,' he said, 'those creatures smell less than sweet, do they not?'

'I am certain you must be accustomed to the less than savoury odours we sometimes have to tolerate here, Governor.'

'Indeed, ma'am,' he smiled. 'And I thank you for your inestimable hospitality. But I only learned yesterday about the loss of your little one.'

'That is kind of you, sir,' I replied, as Richard threw himself into my arms, timid in the presence of this tall stranger. 'Yet I think we must both have suffered our respective losses at about the same time.'

'My wife?' His entire face darkened with sadness. 'Diana. Her name was Diana. And I? Wed and widowed in the same twelve-month. The worst of misfortunes – apart, I collect, from the loss of one's child. But this one,' he tousled Richie's curls, 'seems a tough little fellow. And if you might not mind, Mistress Hynmers, you seem like a lady with an eye for details. So perhaps you might not object to giving me your honest views. About Mister Yale?'

Two months still before the new babe is born and I am already lumbering about like the proverbial elephant. It must be another boy. I know it. If so, we have settled on Benjamin for his name. I must needs tolerate Midwife Crouch's ministrations yet again, of course, but I have spoken quietly with Sathiri to ensure that she is also close at hand.

Meanwhile, all the talk here has turned to Shivaji Maharaj once more. Indeed, he has scarce been far from our thoughts all year. Mister Yale was dispatched to Vellore as my husband and Matthew had proposed and returned with the necessary information: local *khans* susceptible to bribery; weaknesses in the fort's dispositions; and such like. Matthew had used whatever networks he possessed to relay the intelligence under provision that Fort St. George should be immune to Shivaji's ravages. Terms accepted, and within weeks Shivaji had taken Vellore, ending the siege that had cost him so dear for almost a year. We could only now hope and pray that Shivaji would honour his debt to us.

Mister Yale himself has been rewarded, signing new bonds for his promotion to factor. He listed his father as security, a liability of two thousand pounds. And Governor Master, still no more amenable to the fellow – perhaps because of the reservations I, myself, had expressed about him – reluctantly, at Joseph's recommendation, agreed to backdate the appointment to the previous June. His salary thus doubled, to twenty pounds per annum.

'After all,' my husband had admonished me, 'what is a factory without excellent factors to take possession of our outbound goods on consignment, to record and store them in our godowns, ensure their safe transfer to our vessels, and to make profitable sales on any inbound consignments the Company has authorised for trading purposes. And Mister Yale, my dear, regardless of your own doubts, or our shared history with the man, will make an excellent factor.'

But this evening I was forced to endure my doubts and much more. A gentle excursion, Joseph had promised me. An invitation to see progress on the new Garden House – the pavilion that Governor Langhorn had perceived, and Governor Master has set in train this past Lady Day, for the comfort, accommodation and delight of visiting dignitaries.

So we gathered across the square, outside the fast-expanding church, cleverly designed by our Master Gunner, Mister Dixon, and to which his engineers, their teams of local stonecutters, have committed such energy. Two more years, Dixon estimates, before completion for consecration. The tower and steeple some time longer but the church itself shall be roofed within two years.

'I promise you, my dear,' said Joseph, 'that you shall not have to waddle far.' His idea of a jest. 'Caldera Point and no more. The boats will carry us the rest of the way.'

'All of us? Great heavens, I never thought there would be so many.'

Tanani had been left in charge of little Elford, but Akbar was with us, the older boys in tow, delighting them with tales of tigers and the warrior myths of his people as we passed under the arch of the Choultry Gate and turned onto the Market Lane. It heaved with life as it always does at this time of day, a sheer riot of colour: pinks and yellows of the garland makers' produce; white-hot flames of the iron-forgers' furnaces; blues and greens and scarlets of the fruit vendors' *sarees*; cinnamon shades of brown and beige in every variety of skin tone; and everywhere the forehead *pottu* marks of deep vermilion or magenta – the Gentues' third eye, as Sathiri has taught me, the sixth *chakra*. All of this overlaid against the background cacophony cries of hawker and higgler and huckster alike, all ringing around the dried mud walls, the crumbling timbers and threadbare roofing.

'I like this place less with every month that passes.' Elihu Yale panted as he sped to catch us, Katherine Barker upon his arm, almost running to keep up. 'The odours! God blind me.'

'It strikes me,' I said, 'that these may be poor dwellings but not more so than the plague-infested, overcrowded tenements, garrets and open sewers I have seen so often in St. Giles and other parts of London.'

Or Alicante, I thought. Or Porto, for that matter. My father is fond of reminding me about the huge portion of English society that lives in terrible poverty and I doubt that the overall wealth, the rich and the poor combined, could be greatly different here in India than, say, in Spain or England. Perhaps some small differences in the way that wealth is distributed but Black Town's poor seem to me very much the same as those of Blackwall. Yet, perhaps this difference. That these folk of Madras Patnam are somehow more indomitable. Happier, I suppose.

'Yet we live in such a green and pleasant land at home.' He seemed surprised when I did not readily agree. 'You should see my father's estate, ma'am. Plas Grono.'

'I am certain. Mister Yale, that the Khan of Gingee's son might be able to show me parts of his own father's lands that would astound me with their beauty. Yet that was not quite my point.'

'My dear,' said Joseph quietly, 'I fear that Mister Yale has already had a trying day. We should not tax him more, I think.'

Indeed? I said to myself. Did we owe him that amount of consideration? By then we had reached the reed-fringed river, where the boats were indeed waiting: the largest of the *musolas*, yet each now furnished with a poop deck and canopy, adorned with chains of flowers, a dozen chairs on each, the broad-beamed, deep-bellied craft as steady as dry land here upon these gently flowing waters.

'Ah, I wished to discuss that, Mister Hynmers,' said Yale. 'Would it trouble you greatly if Mistress Barker and myself took seats upon your barge?'

I tightened my grip upon Joseph's arm, my attempt to dissuade him.

'We promised to reserve space for Matthew,' I reminded him. 'And Sathiri.'

Yale laughed.

'Sirrah,' he said. 'I assume you won't expect your manservant to be seated?' He glanced at Akbar.

'And surely Mister Parrish would expect nothing better for his *bibi*,' Katherine Barker laughed. 'You see, Mistress Catherine? No shortage of chairs.'

It was insulting, hurtful, but I bit my tongue as we were all handed aboard our allotted *musola*, where we were soon joined by Matthew, Sathiri, John Nicks, Vincent Seaton and our local Indian merchant, Kasi Veranna.

'If the devil had cast his nets,' murmured Matthew as he bent the knee and kissed my hand. He looked very fine this night. An emerald silken coat that would have graced a sultan, his periwig lightly powdered, and Sathiri in a *saree* that matched his own colours. Akbar greeted her with particular deference and I saw that she had added a further marking to her forehead, above the magenta *pottu*, at the parting in her exquisite blue-black hair. This marking was vermilion, and I know it is the sign of a married woman, to bring good fortune upon her husband. I think that is the meaning. For, in the eyes of her own people, at least, she and Matthew are indeed a wedded couple. And her husband insisted that she be seated, though she chose, I noted, to pull her seat across and assist Akbar in entertaining the boys – or perhaps to frighten those upon the boat who so plainly despised her presence.

'Let me tell you, boys,' she cried, 'about the exploits of the Chatrapati Shivaji Maharaj and the miracle of his escape from Agra.'

'Where is the fellow anyhow?' said Mister Yale.

'Gone,' Matthew replied with evident satisfaction. Shivaji's promise to leave Madras in peace in exchange for the intelligence brought by Yale, his easy capture of Vellore, had proved apparently worthless. For, two weeks ago, word had reached us that he was encamped no more than forty miles away, his horsemen sweeping through the countryside in preparation for an attack upon Fort St. George. I could hardly bear to think about what that would mean – for my husband, for my boys, for me. 'It seems,' Matthew continued, giving an almost imperceptible nod of acknowledgement towards Elihu, 'that he was about to move against us when news came to him that the Mughal Emperor had launched a surprise attack on his own territories. I understand that the Governor will give a full report at tomorrow's Council meeting.'

'As soon as one trouble disappears,' said Kasi Veranna, in that strange, swaying way that he has, 'another comes to take its place. I could have known it, *sahib*, that Chatrapati Shivaji is gone. Because, today, Lingappa Naik is back. He send his *Avaldar* to me.'

'Another demand for tribute?' Joseph asked.

'Oh yes, *sahib*. But I send him away. I strike him with my sandal. I knock the turban from his head. Very angry. Yet he is gone.'

Sathiri gasped with shock. It was a heinous insult and bound to bring more trouble upon us.

'And is this reliable information?' demanded whey-faced Vincent Seaton, oblivious to the implication of Veranna's actions. 'About Shivaji?' The relief among the others was palpable but there was always resentment that Matthew, not himself a member of the Council at all, should so frequently possess such knowledge before those with seats at the table.

'Oh, entirely accurate,' Matthew smiled, and I guessed that his spies would have had some part to play in the Mughal Emperor's decision to move against Shivaji at such a precisely convenient moment.

'So there, Mister Yale,' said Joseph. 'I am certain the threat from Shivaji must have added to your pressures. But the news should provide some relief, I collect. Or was there something else you wished to discuss? Ah, there! At last, we're moving.'

The grinning, saffron-robed oarsmen steered us carefully out into the stream, and our vessel took its place in the procession of five other *masulas* moving gracefully inland and sending a succession of white cattle egrets screeching into the blazing skies ahead of us, becoming silhouettes against the sinking, shimmering crimson sun. The sight seemed to drive all thought of his workload from Mister Yale's mind. Indeed, he seemed not to have heard my husband's words at all. He was staring at me strangely.

'"*The barge she sat in,*"' he quoted, '"*like a burnish'd throne, burned on the water.*"'

I could feel the heat rise in my cheeks.

'Very apt, Mister Yale.' Joseph laughed. 'My wife once played Cleopatra, did you know? Our first year here. Our modest attempt at a theatrical production.'

'I was incapable of remembering the lines,' I said, relieved at the diversion he had created from my embarrassment.

'I remember it,' said Katherine Barker. 'I was only a child, of course. But it quite put me to sleep.'

'That surprises me,' Seaton sneered. 'I should have thought Mistress Hynmers to be an excellent actress.'

Wretched fellow. Always so wary in my company. Though there are times when I catch him staring at me with something wholly unsavoury in his eyes. We have no evidence against him, of course. About Major Puckle. Yet that has not been the only strange incident in which he may have been involved. Only a week ago there had been celebrations aboard one of the ships ready to sail for the Bay. Celebrations between those friends who were travelling north, and those who must remain here. The departure delayed by the reveries until long past dark, by which time the surf was running high and one of the *musolas* had capsized, one of our number drowned. Only troublesome Kendal, the jeweler, whose passing nobody at Fort St. George would mourn. And perhaps no more than coincidence that, among his many quarrels, one of the worst had been with Seaton. A dispute about diamonds, it seems. And Vincent Seaton had, of course, been on board the same *musola*. He and all the others had seemingly escaped with ease. But not Nathaniel Kendal.

'An excellent actress indeed, Mister Seaton.' Joseph fixed him with a cold eye. 'She could have rivaled Witty Nell, I believe. On the stage, that is.'

'Mistress Gwynn has retired from that profession now, I hear,' said Matthew. 'Yet still busy in all her other enterprises.'

How he kept his face straight on such occasions I do not know. But it is a favourite diversion, taunting the Cavalier faction, casting discreet aspersions about the king's favourite harlot, and the by-blows she seems so fond of delivering for him.

'That reminds me, Parrish,' said Seaton. 'Have you heard? Those traitorous coves sent to the Tower for their imputations against the Crown?'

Well, of course we had heard. Four great lords – Shaftesbury, Buckingham, Wharton and Salisbury – imprisoned last year for having the temerity to so openly express their fears of a Catholic succession through the king's brother. We had heard, and we wonder how far this backlash against loyal Protestants might reach.

'It seems,' my husband said, gazing down at the flowing waters, 'that we have succeeded in preventing Papists from holding high office, yet not from holding the highest in the land. But perhaps there is hope for us, after all. This marriage to Orange.'

The king's brother, the Duke of York, popish to the core. Almost certain to become James the Second of England, the Seventh of Scotland. Yet his daughter, Mary, now married to staunchly Protestant William of Orange. But what this all means for our futures, none of us can yet discern.

'Sirrah,' said Mister Yale, 'you mention Orange and see what we have.' He pointed to our left, across the Island, that wide expanse of ground trapped between the arms of the twin rivers, the North River – the Elambore – and the Triplicane. 'Are those not themselves young oranges?'

The trees were growing on the open land, just this side of a freshly planted and new guava garden. And it seemed that Mister Yale was right, for they were heavy with small flame-coloured berries. But Sathiri laughed.

'They have fruited early this year,' she said. 'Our deadly *yettikottai*. How do you call them in English, Catherine? Poison Nut? Your Cleopatra, Yale *sahib*, would have died more quickly by chewing the seeds of the *yettikottai*.'

'And perhaps better,' Matthew laughed, 'had we all swallowed some, rather than send Lingappa's *Avaldar* back to him with such an ill-considered response.'

'But *sahib*,' protested Veranna, 'Lingappa is no real consequence. What is Poonamallee, after all?'

'Part of the Sultanate of Golconda, of course,' snapped Mister Yale. 'And no point losing the threat from Shivaji, only to face a new one from the Sultan. And if we break faith with Golconda…'

'I know, *sahib*,' said Veranna, and wrung his hands. 'The diamonds.'

I caught Elihu Yale staring at me once more, and then he launched into another soliloquy.

'*"My Crown is in my heart, not on my head:*
Not deck'd with Diamonds, and Indian stones:
Nor to be seen: my Crown is call'd Content,
A Crown it is, that seldom Kings enjoy."'

'Content, sirrah?' said John Nicks. He had been so quiet I had almost forgotten his presence but he had, of course, spent most of the time watching black-eyed Katherine Barker, envy etched upon his features, while she, in turn, had eyes for none but Mister Yale. 'What, now you are made factor and have your own horse and groom. Assistant to the Warehouse Keeper. Eighth in Council. Is that the limit of ambition?'

'Great reward requires great ambition,' said Mister Yale, still regarding me from the periphery of his vision.

'I'm certain,' said Katherine Barker, 'that even the finest contentment could be sharpened by diamonds. And are we not fortunate? Lord! Here, and only here in the entire world.' Well, that was true enough and I have heard tales of the time she spends in company with the Jewish diamond merchants of Black Town. She would know, as we all do, that the only known diamond mines in the world are here in India. Thirty-eight of them, Joseph had once told me. And twenty-three of those in Golconda. 'Imagine,' she went on, 'if we could have got our hands on the Babur, or any of the Mughal Emperor's other great stones – that we might have had the chance to trade them?'

I had recently sent a small packet of Joseph's gems home to Mama as we had done in previous years. It helped to compensate her for the luxuries she dispatched to us on the inbound vessels, and we always ensured that some of them be designated towards our eventual return to England. Our investment in the future, the boys' future. In the four years since the restriction on our ability to trade privately had been lifted, Joseph had used the facility wisely. Pearls, for the most part. Cloves and nutmeg. But diamonds too. And only the other day, he had shared with me the balances of his particular accompts.

'You see, my dear?' he had proudly announced. 'We have exceeded the line of my expectation. Ten thousand pagodas. Four thousand pounds. Perhaps this will now ensure our long and healthy existence.'

'At least a different one,' I had replied, happy that the gloom which sometimes oppressed him seemed lifted.

And now, upon the *musola*, he had taken out his small notebook, almost the twin of the one in which I write this entry, and begun to make some rapid line drawings of the scene, the outline of the Garden House, the orchard beyond, now close to us, above the Island's low margent.

'Imagine, Miss Barker,' he said, using that most modern of honorifics, 'if the Honourable Company chose to extend its own enterprise to include the trade in diamonds. How quickly we might have completed this very fine pavilion.'

'Oh yes,' she replied, 'I have already made those calculations, Mister Hynmers. Believe me, I have.'

She made the comment as though it had some hugely profound significance but, by then, the first of the boats had reached the specially constructed wharf and Agent Master was leading his party ashore while, from somewhere within the gathering darkness, the violin, bass viol and harp of the Fort St. George musicians. Lawes, sadly. His *Great Consort*, I think. Well, Lawes had paid for his Royalist sympathies during Cromwell's great siege of Chester – yes, I am certain it was Chester – though I happen to have some affection for the piece. One of Mama's favourites. Besides, it was almost immediately drowned by the pyrotechnical contrivances that soon lit the sky, filled it with their thunderous explosions, with shell bursts of scarlet, orange, green and yellow.

It is therefore difficult, now, to calculate the precise point when I began to realise that something was amiss. The quivering sensation I quickly put down to the firework vibrations. The trembling in my legs to the time we had spent under the influence of the *musola*'s motion. The slight sense of nausea to the occasional effects of the babe growing within me. The sudden scattering of all the Island's birdlife to the unaccustomed cacophony created by this celebration. Yet when my entire being seemed turned to jelly, everything around me too, as though there was no longer any ground beneath my feet, earth and air suddenly become liquid in form, I knew that I had experienced this once before. Another earthquake.

Yesterday evening, a further earthquake, less serious than that of last August but, to my family and friends, creating far more devastation.

The previous tremors had left those of us celebrating at the Garden House unharmed but had destroyed an entire street of Black Town's dwellings – all, apparently, in the Moorish quarter and attributed by Sathiri to divine retribution against the Mahometans, some sign that her gods, Shiva the Destroyer, and Ganapati, the Remover of Obstacles, had at last turned their faces towards the Gentues of Madras Patnam, or Chenna Patnam, as she preferred to style it, for the town's village district in which she had been born.

'Perhaps,' she said, 'towards my people as a whole. Good fortune to Chatrapati Shivaji Maharaj for his wars in the north. And may his *karma* keep him there.'

Rewards and retributions. For, if she was correct, did the same divine intervention contribute to the damage inflicted upon the construction work at our church? Worse, what did it presage for the injury done within our guava garden burial ground, the cracks appearing in so many of the memorial stones? And particularly that sad little slab, which marked Walter's resting place.

Evil enough. Yet today, when I carried baby Benjamin to that place, to visit his vanished brother, we found the cracks opened wide, the whole stone now broken asunder and I wept to see it.

It should have been a memorable day, my first outing with the babe since his baptism and my churching. For the poor child has suffered so. A weakly infant despite the ease with which he was delivered into the world. Midwife Crouch declared that she had rarely witnessed such a simple birth, and we had imagined that our troubles were now past.

Yet, within a week, he was ailing, struggling for breath, has continued to ail ever since, until this past week.

Sathiri came, bringing with her a holy man, a garlanded *guru*, who gave Benjamin a blessing, parts of which she translated for me.

'"*I worship the lotus feet of Ganesha, the son of Uma, the destroyer of all sorrows, who is served by the host of gods and elementals.*"'

'Might he try to do something about the behaviour of the others?' I said, hoping not to sound excessively disrespectful. 'But Joseph Junior in particular is so frequently beyond my powers to control. Why, I have caught him many times pulling the wings from butterflies, and when I reproach him he seems hardly to understand the sin.'

Sathiri touched my arm apologetically.

'Catherine, show me a young boy who swears he's never inflicted needless cruelty on one of the Lord Brahma's lesser creatures and I will show you a liar by disposition.'

So yes, this should have been a day of bounties, with Benjamin now an entire se'nnight without distress and taking his milk as he should.

'We will have a fresh one carved,' said Joseph, when he had returned from his work and we felt the first flurries of the monsoon come beating at our corner house from the northeast. 'A new stone.'

'At what cost, my dear?'

'We have enjoyed an exceptional year. The godowns all full and then not nearly enough space. Almost three thousand bales. Fifty grades of cloth. Their value more than a hundred thousand pagodas. We will all share in the profit, sweet girl.'

I unexpectedly thought of Mister Yale. Some pang of fellow-feeling. All those invoices. The bills of lading to be prepared before the goods could be stowed aboard the ships now being readied out in the roads for their return to England. All those grades of cloth to be separated – the salampores from the betelles, the ginghams from the dyapers.

'I did not intend to signify the financial cost,' I told him. 'Perhaps there is some meaning in this that we do not comprehend. Better, perhaps, to let the little one lie in peace?'

'You still suffer the nightmares?'

'You know that I do. And you, husband?'

'Perhaps a different kind. Of being trapped here forever. Shrouded permanently in disease and danger. So very often in dishonesty.'

'Do I understand from your mien that you refer to my work with Matthew Parrish? I should do so if only to protect our own integrity. To help expose the corrupt and thus make it clear that the miscreants are a rare bubo upon our body corporate here. But to strike a blow, at the same time, against these erstwhile Cavaliers. You would wish me to desist?'

'I would not, my dear. That is a vital role. No, I intended to say simply that I now fear my wanderlust is spent. That these chicaneries, bickerings, inveiglements, chaffers, hagglings and inducements – the substance of our trade – have all become as tarnished as St. Audrey's Lace.' Then he paused, grimaced. 'Well,' he said, 'perhaps our nightmares are not so very different after all.'

This evening I could think of no worse fate than complying with the invitation to join in celebrating the birthday of that worthless wench, Katherine Barker. Something of the Puritan in me screamed that such celebrations are merely immodest acts of self-exaltation and only morally justified if we use them to thank God for his gift of life. But that was not entirely the reason for my reluctance.

'Must we really do this?' I complained.

'Really, Catherine, you must not keep smothering the boys this way. They will be quite safe.'

'But shall you, my love? With that chit casting longing glances at everything in breeches.'

'I have no idea, sweet girl, why you have taken so against the child.' It is a mere short step down to Points Street from my own home, but I fear I may have been dragging my feet a little, making just too much pretense at surprise when one of the Gentues' holy cattle came wandering across our path.

'Perhaps simply that. A constant reminder of my own salad days. Four children already – five, I should say. Of course, five. Oh, poor Walter, how I miss him. But that hoity toity harlot. She might be no beauty yet still without a blemish to her flesh.'

'To me, my dear, you are more in looks than a dozen Katherine Barkers. Or does that no longer answer? Do I no longer stay your needs?'

I took his hand and squeezed it tight, tried my best to inflict some small agony upon him for his foolishness. For, in my fantasies, I might favour many men of my acquaintance but, in the flesh, there could never be another such as Hynmers.

'I suppose you must suffice, husband.'

'Besides,' he said, 'here I am, Deputy Governor at last. How should it seem if I failed in my duty to attend? Her father our Purchasing Officer, our trusty Steward.'

'Is he indeed? Trusty, I mean.' I brushed some of the street's dust from my skirts, as though to dismiss Mister Barker, and Joseph gave me a look of such disdain. For, now that Agent Master has sailed north to inspect our factories in the Bay, left Joseph in command, in truth he suddenly seems daunted by the task.

'I have enough to trouble me, Catherine, without your own and Matthew's conspiracies.'

Such a reproach! And then, who should be there to meet us, on the steps of John Barker's Italianate portico, but Mister Yale.

'Hynmers! Thank heaven. You must do something about Veranna.'

He ushered us up through the greetings, an effusive welcome from John Barker himself, and past the flowing chain of dancers in his cleared dining room. They were, I recall, performing a somewhat inebriated version of *Upon a Summer's Day*, to the equally discordant strains of the Fort musicians.

'Shall I remain here while you conduct the Deputy Governor's business?' I said.

'Indeed you shall not, lady,' Joseph whispered. 'I fear I may need some assistance.'

'Here,' said Mister Yale. 'In the garden.'

The Barkers enjoyed a small court at the rear of their house, where a brace of citrus trees grew, and there we found our Indian merchant in a state of great agitation remonstrating with John Bridger while, beyond the wall, among the trees, monkeys were screeching.

'Action must be taken, *sahib*,' he was shouting, waving a parchment in John's face. 'Send soldiers. Teach these men a lesson.'

'I thank you, Mister Yale,' said my husband. 'But I believe we should keep our discussion with Mister Veranna between members of the Council.'

'Oh, Hynmers *sahib*,' shouted Veranna. 'You are here.'

Elihu looked crestfallen. Cast aside. Angered. And I should so much have enjoyed reminding him that he owes his advancement to factor purely on the recommendation of Joseph and Matthew Parrish, Governor Master's opinion of the fellow still as low as it has always been. But I have noted that he is also one of those men who might fall into a midden yet still arise smelling of violets. So I have no doubt that he will one day be elevated to the Council, but he is not there yet – and so plainly resents it.

'Then perhaps I should escort Mistress Hynmers to the entertainment?' he suggested, brightening somewhat. 'Perhaps take a step or two upon the dance floor?'

'Mistress Hynmers,' snapped Joseph, no doubt seeing the look of dismay on my face, 'may go or stay precisely as she pleases.' And, of course, I chose to stay while, as Mister Yale's petulant person stormed back into the house, Kasi Veranna unfolded his complaint once more.

'I have the papers, *sahib*. A lease.'

An elaborately turbaned servant came bowing with a tray of drinks but was promptly dismissed.

'For San Thomé,' said my husband, glancing at the document. 'Yes, I know about this.'

So did we all. Last year, the French had simply abandoned their two bases literally upon our doorstep, at Triplicane and San Thomé. Both of them had been taken almost without protest from the Sultan of Golconda but, after they were abandoned, the king seized them back. Yet, almost immediately afterwards, our inscrutable Indian merchant – by reputation wealthier than all of us combined – had succeeded in completing an agreement with Golconda to lease San Thomé for thirteen hundred pagodas per annum.

'And I have invested a small fortune, *sahib*. Brought new people to the place. Turned it into a true town.'

Joseph had spoken of it frequently, though with some disdain.

'And these new people,' said Joseph. 'Citizens or slaves?'

John Bridger looked at him with alarm.

'I believe that Mister Hynmers intends…' he began.

'I intended, John, no more nor no less than I spoke. I think Mister Veranna understood my meaning well enough. It seems to me that when Lingappa Naik sent his *Avaldar* here with a demand for tribute, it was correct to send him away empty-handed. But a polite refusal would have sufficed, to be followed by our own appeal to the Sultan at Golconda Fort. But to deliberately insult the fellow? Lingappa will have sent his own demand for retribution to the Sultan, and the latter will have inflicted this small punishment upon our Indian merchant for his temerity. We shall be fortunate indeed if this is the extent of the Sultan's reckoning against us. Besides, San Thomé is not, nor ever has been, part of our Honourable English East India Company's responsibility. Or am I mistaken, Mister Veranna?'

'But I Iynmers *sahib*, what would your Yesu Kiristu say, if we left the tomb of his apostle in the hands of this Lingappa?'

The legend, of course. St. Thomas the Apostle martyred there, and the Portuguese building their popish church over his remains more than a hundred years ago.

'I am certain,' Joseph replied, 'that Our Lord would have more concern about enslavement. *"He that oppresseth the poor to increase his riches shall surely come to want."* Is that not so, Mister Bridger?'

'Proverbs Twenty-Two, I believe,' Bridger replied as another manservant began to light the lanthorns around the courtyard walls.

'Yet,' said Veranna, 'are these not also the words of your Bible? *"Both thy bondmen and thy bondmaids, which thou shalt have of the heathen that are around you."* And is the Jew and the Greek, the slave and the free, the man and the woman, not all one in the eyes of Yesu Kiristu?'

'Leviticus Twenty-Five and Galatians Three,' said John Bridger cheerfully, yet earning himself a reproachful glance from my husband.

'And I am not a rich man, *sahib*,' Veranna protested. 'Indeed, with my wife now dead, I am the poorest man in Madras Patnam.'

His face set in a mask of misery, for he lost his wife less than a se'nnight ago. One of his wives, I should say. For there is a second, at Condore, near Masulipatnam, I collect. Perhaps others. And the death of his wife did not prevent him, immediately afterwards, from announcing the marriage of his daughter to an old family friend. The daughter is eleven. The friend is indeed old. Kasi Veranna may think himself the poorest man in Madras Patnam, but he certainly owns the finest mansion, out beyond the town itself. Besides, there is all this *palavra*, as Joseph would call it, about whether Mister Veranna may actually be a Mussulman, for Matthew has deduced that he trades among the Mahometans as Hasan Khan. It is all very strange. But that, of course, is India!

'We are, naturally,' said Joseph, 'sorry for your loss. Your wife, sirrah. But about San Thomé I can do absolutely nothing though I will report this conversation to Council when we meet on Monday. And you may, of course, raise the matter directly with Governor Master upon his return.'

I almost felt sorry for Veranna.

'Ah,' he smiled. '"*Master, give unto your servant that which is just and equal.*" I shall look forward to the Governor's judgement, *sahib*.' Tip for tap, it was a tolerably amusing clench.

There was an obsequious bow, and the fellow was gone, John Bridger murmuring about Colossians.

'You must allow that he is well-versed,' I said but, by then, Joseph had taken my arm and drawn me into the house, where Katherine Barker's celebrations seemed to have been overtaken by a singing competition between several of the menfolk.

'Here,' Mister Yale was shouting, 'I shall tip you a few new staves.' And he launched into a rendition of *Kentish Dick*, followed almost immediately by his own version of *The Wandering Jew's Chronicle*. At least, I assumed it was his own version, for the final stanzas, giving praise to the king, finished with lines praising the beauty of Sweet Catherine. A blessing upon her. A prayer for her fecundity. Catherine of Braganza, of course, so far as the context of the ballad was concerned, though Elihu carefully directed the words towards Miss Barker, bringing a flush of additional colour to her dark cheeks. Yet she entirely missed the fro'ward wink of his eye directed at me as the closing notes were played.

'Is there no end to the man's talents?' murmured my husband sarcastically.

'It seems he has provided an opening for the Cavaliers,' I said, while Vincent Seaton gave some instruction to the musicians. In the absence of Agent Master, with all hands now stepped up, Seaton has been given responsibility for the Mint, while both he and Mister Yale have assumed the responsibilities of Joseph and John Bridger as Justices within the Choultry Court, the sessions held as necessary within the Choultry itself, the open guildhall just within Black Town that serves also as an inn or *caravanserai*. 'And now we must tolerate this damnable tune once more!'

The opening strains of *When the King Enjoys His Own Again*. Popular enough for all those of their faction to participate, fuelled of course by the copious amounts of wines, Brunswick mum and cherry brandy they had imbibed. John Bridger had been boasting only yesterday that, this season, he has taken receipt of three hundred bottles of Canary and thirty-eight gallons of claret. And Joseph alone received ten cases from the *Bengal Merchant*.

Yet the final stanza, at last.

'*"Then fears avaunt, upon the hill*
My hope shall cast her anchor still,
Until I see some peaceful dove
Bring home the branch I dearly love."'

And I turned to my husband, some foolish comment upon my lips, yet stilled when I saw him sway, his features suddenly ashen.

'It's nothing,' he whispered. 'Just…'

'What?'

'I know not. Something in those words. A premonition, you might say. Yet nothing, my sweet. Nothing.'

Nobody else seemed to have noticed, however, and Seaton was shouting from where he stood, swaying with the effects of the wine splashing from his cup.

'Perhaps the Deputy Governor will lead us in a loyal toast,' he cried, lifting the goblet above his head.

'Of course,' Joseph replied, and took a glass of Canary from one of the Gentue servants. I did likewise. 'Ladies. Gentlemen. I give you the loyal toast to His Majesty the King.'

'The King,' we all repeated, but the words were hardly spoken before Seaton was proposing another, as we all knew he must.

'Queen Catherine,' he cried. 'The Duke of York. All other members of the royal family.'

I gritted my teeth, the response this time more ragged. A toast to those advocates of the Romish Church? To hell with the Papist Duke of York.

'The royal family,' muttered a few of the guests.

'And a plague,' yelled Seaton, 'upon the heads of all who plot against them. Damn their souls.' There it was. The inevitable chill that seemed so suddenly to waft from the *pankah* above our heads. The latest news from England. Mama had devoted several pages to it. A canting fanatic and former High Church priest, Titus Oates, along with his friend, Israel Tonge. Sworn depositions before the Privy Council. Allegations against numerous Jesuit and popish nobles. Evidence of a plot to assassinate the king, to hasten the succession of Catholic James, Duke of York. Then the murder of popular magistrate, Sir Edmund Berry Godfrey upon

Primrose Hill. Oates's claim that this was proof of his accusations. Five Catholic peers sent to the Tower. Powis, Stafford, Arundell, Petre and Belasyse. Each of them, of course, also a leading supporter of the Cavalier faction – the faction to which Oates has attributed a new name. An unfamiliar word suddenly on all our lips. A word that now implies much more than its previous description of Irish brigands. Tories. 'Damn all plotters' souls,' cried Seaton again, this time into an almost silent room.

Heavens! Is that not rich? That these "Tories", Cavaliers like Vincent Seaton, should feel themselves threatened, even here, half a world away from England. Well, it is not so strange. For the Restoration of the Monarchy, nineteen years ago now, which was supposed to fill the civil war chasms separating one half of our society from the other, has left us as deeply divided as ever. And those of us from the Independent faction, whose forebears have fought to free us from absolutism and idolatry, will not rest until the chasms are filled only by the faded and failed fantasies of Papist and Cavalier alike. For it is the Cavalier faction, the Crown party, entirely in control of Parliament, which has continued to persecute Dissenters of all shades for nineteen years now.

So I looked to my husband to step into that breach tonight. Some words of wisdom, perhaps. Yet he had merely set down his goblet again, nodding slowly as Mister Yale, instead, led Seaton aside, assumed the aspect of some jocose buffoon.

'Sirrah,' cried Elihu. 'Is that not the reason cobblers are always such good fellows? Because they set men upright, upon their feet. And are always mending soles.'

Katherine Barker bestowed a smile of great admiration upon him and most of the other guests laughed loudly. Too loudly. The tension broken. For now. Yet then Joseph, still grey about the gills, begged me to excuse him a moment while he went to exchange a word with Mister Dixon, our talented Master Gunner, chief engineer and church builder. So I drifted about the room as the dancing was resumed and I decided that, in the best spirit of diplomacy, as the Deputy Governor's wife, I should at least offer some two-faced congratulation to that chit of a girl. She was, of course, firmly attached to Mister Yale's arm once more. They were facing away from me, and I was about to touch her shoulder when I heard the fellow murmur to her.

'Indeed, my dear,' he was saying. 'A great shame. Hardly the right man to act the Governor's part. But with a Governor like Agent Master, which of us should be surprised that his Deputy is such a dull cove? A man is known by the power he wields, is he not? And I fear that Mister Hynmers brandishes little in that regard. I'm told he handles the Council meetings in a manner that is absurdly casual and unhurried. No, I fear the power in that household is wielded rather by the Mistress than the Master.'

Well, the arrogance of the man. The scrub! I retraced my steps as rapidly as I was able, almost collided with Joseph.

'There,' he said, before I could repeat Yale's nonsense. 'Some good news. Dixon has promised that he will allocate some men to start work on Monday.'

'On what?' I replied.

'I explained. Yesterday. On a new wall, to properly separate the burial ground from the guava gardens. Stabilise the terrain there. Ensure that baby Walter is never disturbed again.'

Oh, how I prayed today. In the Fort House mess hall, naturally, cleared once again to serve as our chapel since St. Mary's is not quite completed.

I prayed for Joseph Junior, almost beside myself with fear for the boy.

I prayed alone, and when I returned to the house, I barely regarded my husband upon his sick bed.

'You expect me to sympathise?' I said. 'When you have sent my child from me. Taken another of my sons.'

'We agreed,' he murmured through his calenture. 'When he was ten, we said.'

'A decision after he turned ten. That was our agreement. Not this arbitrary business. Throwing him aboard the first available ship the very instant he's seen his birthing day.'

'It was not that way, Catherine. You know it. The boy wished to sail. His great adventure.'

I tried to calm myself, to remember how it transpired. Governor Master back at Fort St. George two weeks ago. And Joseph Junior suddenly fixed upon the idea of England, two older boys of his acquaintance already with berths arranged aboard the *Golden Fleece*.

'Yet I cannot bear it,' I wept. 'Not knowing. For how long? A year, at the least.'

'With luck the *Fleece* will pass one of our outbound vessels and bring us news by July.'

'News? That the child has survived half the voyage? And that will be consolation, you collect?'

Yet I could not sustain my rage against him for long. He seems so very ill. And by the time I had looked in upon the other boys, each of them also still distressed by Joseph Junior's absence, my husband had received a visit from the Governor himself.

'Well, Mistress, how is your patient this evening?'

'As you see, sirrah. A little brighter than this morning, I believe. Is that not so, Joseph?'

'A little, yes.'

The *pankah* boy was working furiously to keep him cool.

'The good doctor has visited?'

'He prescribed mangoes,' I said. 'He seems to have great faith in mangoes.'

'But you have the flux?' said the Governor.

'Flux indeed,' Joseph replied. 'Mango is the least thing I should be able to keep within me. The very thought...'

He was already pale but has now assumed an even deathlier shade. And a troublesome sound to his breathing, an unwholesome smell clinging to his body.

'Do not distress yourself, my dear fellow.' I admired the Governor's ability to entirely ignore the foul odour. 'I simply came to tell you that I have now read your report of proceedings during my absence. Exemplary, sir.'

'And your own voyage,' said Joseph, as I mopped his brow and straightened his sheet. 'Beneficial?'

'More troublesome than beneficial, I believe. And the Directors will be less than pleased with the matters I have conveyed to them for their attention. But if they wish to make a success of our factories here, they must needs decide to invest more in the business. Though you should not concern yourself with that. John Bridger has taken up your duties admirably. Yet this fever has left us desperately short. And you are certain you would not be better out of the town? Several of our fellows are down at St. Thomas' Mount. Did you know?'

'Catherine told me. But I shall be fine here. Up and back at my work within the week.'

I doubt that Agent Master believed that any more than I did, but I forced myself to bite down on my tongue, on my concern.

'And apart from this mango for the flux, Doctor Fryer has treated your ague in the normal fashion, I suppose?'

'My husband has been bled twice each day,' I said. 'And a brew from powdered Jesuit's Bark.'

'Induced vomiting?'

'He has needed no inducement in that regards.'

'Well, I should not say so, but the Gentues are frequently more adept at dealing with our agues. Have you sought advice.'

'I have,' I replied. Sathiri, naturally, her infusions of cinnamon, honey, garlic and ginger. Though she frightens me each time she visits. Always bright in her prognosis. Yet something in those dark, unfathomable eyes. She fears for him, despite her outward assurances.

'Well, I should go,' the Governor whispered now, seeing that Joseph had drifted back into a slumber. 'If there is anything you should require, Mistress, you need only ask.' I led him out to the *veranda*, saw that we were about to receive another visitor, Mister Yale. 'Oh,' said the Governor, almost as an afterthought, but the words spoken rapidly, before Yale could join us. 'I suppose that your husband has a properly signed expression of his wishes? Yes,' he coughed, 'I imagine that he would have done so. A thorough fellow, Mister Hynmers.'

I wanted to stop him, correct his pessimism but, by then he had exchanged a curt greeting with Mister Yale, and the latter was standing before me, dressed in an elegant saffron tunic, a *kurta*, patterned. And a pair of loose-fitting *pai jamahs*, white, to match the simple turban he had taken to wearing at times in place of his periwig.

'I hear,' he said, 'that your husband can no longer complete the accomps. Might I offer my assistance, madam?'

I wanted to ask him whether he already had poor Joseph dead and buried, ready to fill his shoes, yet that felt as though it might be tempting fate.

'Mister Bridger has assumed those responsibilities. It has been my husband's only concern. To ensure that his duties are properly fulfilled.'

'A virtuous man, your husband. And glory, as they say, is the reward of virtue.' He touched his fingers to the saffron tunic as he spoke, regarding me as though something should signify.

'Yes, Mister Yale, I have heard that saying. Though I trust my husband is not bound for glory just yet.'

He laughed.

'No, sirrah,' he exclaimed. 'Merely my family's motto. *Praemium Virtutis Gloria*. You see?' I peered closely at the fabric, realised that the *kurta*'s pattern was, in practice, the repeated design of a tiny embroidered coat-of-arms – white shield, red saltire cross, some small creature above. 'And I am certain Mister Hynmers shall make a full recovery. Though no harm in seeking a little additional assurance. Is that not so? And with the chaplain back from his tour of the Bay, perhaps your husband might appreciate his blessing. It might be good for him.'

What was I missing? Joseph has escaped the grip of worse illness in the past. Though, of course, neither Mister Yale nor Governor Master would understand his resilience. I needed to lighten the mood – for my own sake as much as anything else.

'Ah, good for him,' I repeated. 'I am so frequently reminded today of old Aesop. You collect his fable? About the sick man questioned by his doctor and explaining that he perspires profusely. The doctor tells him that sweating is good for him. Next time the patient complains of constant shivering, and the doctor confirms that shivering is a good sign too. The third time, the sick man is suffering badly with the flux. And that also, the doctor says, is a good thing. After the doctor has gone, the patient's wife asks her husband how he fares...'

Mister Yale laughed uproariously, slapped his own thigh. It seemed so highly inappropriate and I turned quickly, back towards the house.

'And the fellow replies that he seems to be dying of very good symptoms. It is one of my favourite stories.' Then he recollected himself. 'Oh, God blind me! I fear I must apologise. I had not intended...'

It occurred to me that he might not have laughed so loudly had he known that I was familiar with the tale principally through one of Matthew Parrish's poems, *Old Aesop*. For some animosity seemed to have grown between them.

'Not intended?' I said. 'What, sirrah? To so despoil the end of my anecdote? To make such unseemly commotion outside a house of the sick? Or merely to imply that my husband might be at death's door?'

'None of those, Mistress. Or do I mean all of them? I am no longer certain. But please, let me send for the chaplain.'

'Evans?' I said, taking delight in having so deflated this bellows-bag. 'I doubt he would be able to spare time from his trading with the interlopers.' Joseph had been very fond of old Reverend Warner, but he has gone back to England now, taking with him the secret about baby Walt that he shares only with myself, with Joseph, and with Mister Yale. He has been replaced at Fort St. George by a younger man, Reverend Portman though, when the *Williamson* arrived, she brought with her a more senior chaplain, for the whole Bay of Bengal. A pretentious Oxford scholar, another Welshman, who seems more interested in turning a personal profit than saving our souls, and who manages to keep poor Portman very much in the shadows. 'I thank you, Mister Yale. But I fear the Reverend's presence would be more likely to cause my husband's relapse. All the same, I shall tell him you called.'

And there I left him, flouncing back indoors where I found Joseph awake once more.

'Yale,' he said.

'He wanted to send Reverend Evans to minister for you.'

'I heard you laughing together. Does my condition amuse you?'

'How can you say so? He believed the senior chaplain would be good for you. And I tried to snub him with Matthew's *Aesop*. You remember? It was the fable that amused him, though I intended more his wounding than his entertainment.'

'All the same. He pursues you, I fear. And in this place...'

'Regardless of our location, husband, I remain your faithful and adoring spouse, moral in all things. You know my belief, my dear. That morality will always triumph over any adversity.'

'I wish I could believe so.' It was little more than a whisper. 'But my dreams are so full of evil. The girl, Kalai, burning upon that pyre. The *sadhu* and his curse. The serpent. Poor Walter. And that reminds me, sweet girl. The boys. I made provision only for Joseph Junior, for Richard and for Elford. I need to make an addendum. To the schedule. For baby Benjamin.'

'Plenty of time for that once you are on your feet again. Oh, Joseph. You are a worry-pot.'

I tried to laugh, but no sound escaped my throat, it was so tightly restricted.

'I feel so wretched,' he said. 'Had I been strong enough, I should have gone in search of those Poison Nut seeds you collected.'

The *yettikottai* seeds? Surely he was jesting. I had indeed made a small excursion back to the Garden House last October, to see the pavilion completed and some visiting emissaries in temporary residence. While there, I had noticed those orange fruits again, only now they were all on the ground, withered and desiccated, the round lozenges of their seeds simple to extract. A remembrance, I had decided. Though I was careful to handle them only with my kerchief and to store them, upon my return, in a locked casket with my most precious pendants, rings and necklaces.

'I shall ask the *ayah* to brew you another of Sathiri's infusions,' I said. 'That should answer perfectly.'

'But the schedule, Catherine. I am serious. If anything should go awry, you must make sure that Benjamin is legally provided for.'

'This is the fever talking, husband. Get some rest and we will speak of this later.'

'No,' he insisted, though it was difficult for him to speak, and the words made him breathless. 'My mind is clear for the moment. And there is one more thing. An investment to be made. You remember? That I told you this time last year how we should have an exceptional return on our trade? Well, so we did. An additional four thousand pagodas, my dear. Sixteen hundred pounds. It is kept on deposit for us at the Mint and you will find the voucher in my writing box. You know the place?'

'I do.'

'Then you shall take the coin to the Jew, Antonio do Porto. You have met him. He will help. Tell him you wish to invest in his business. The diamonds.'

On the far side of Black Town lives the thriving Jewish community. The Paradesi, they call themselves. Matthew knows them well and has explained to me many times how they are the descendants of Jews expelled from Spain and Portugal – the lands that, in their own Hebrew tongue, they call Sefarad. But here, within the towns they have settled in India for more than a century, they call themselves the Paradesi. They are interlopers, of course, trading independently in their gems and corals, and much to the official annoyance of John Company. But our representatives in Fort St. George tolerate them – more than tolerate them – for the private fortunes they help to create.

'And then?' I said. 'Then I shall dispatch them carefully home to Mama, as we have done before. She will keep them safe until we, ourselves, can return to England. As we shall do, husband, as soon as you are recovered.'

I can barely write. Simply this. That, after three months in which he seemed so often on the verge of recovery, only to sink once more, I am finally left howling Joseph's name into the darkness of his passing. I see the light leaving his eyes, and in the eyes of the dead we see our own mortality reflected.

I hold on to my darlings, try to explain. Oh, how to explain when I do not understand myself? This emptiness after the tears. The impotent rage at the world, which I feel again, as I did after Walter. The questions that scream in my head. How? Why?

And those hateful feelings that have no place here, now. Guilt – my recollection of the times when I did not love him at all, before I had learned to do so. But the anger too – that bizarre blame I cast upon him for having deserted me, deserted the boys, left them fatherless. Yet, more than this, my scorn for Katherine Barker now fed and stoked by my memory of her birthday celebrations.

> '*"Then fears avaunt, upon the hill*
> *My hope shall cast her anchor still,*
> *Until I see some peaceful dove*
> *Bring home the branch I dearly love."*'

It goes around and around in my head and I keep seeing his face, suddenly ashen-grey.

'It's nothing,' he had said. 'Just… I know not. Something in those words. A premonition, you might say.'

Volume Two

Fort St. George, Madras Patnam

I had determined never to commence another volume, though now it seems fitting that I should do so. Perhaps, if nothing else, in Joseph's memory. For, today, we saw the monument unveiled, and my husband interred afresh, three months after his passing but the pain no less immediate.

A tall obelisk, its sections carved in the local Pallavaram by Dixon's stone-cutters. A tapering column, surmounted by an orb, and the column seated atop a square vault. The vault is commodious, an arched open doorway at each end, and the doorways joined by a short passage. Within, there is a vault set into one wall and into this vault Joseph's casket was laid with great reverence.

Then more blessings from that grasping priest, Reverend Evans, before the vault was closed and sealed with the tablet upon which Joseph's entirely inadequate obituary is carved.

> *Here lies interred the body of Joseph Hynmers who served the Right Honourable English East India Company several years as 2nd in Council of Fort St. George, in which station he departed this life on the 28th of May 1680.*

Across the passage, there is a further vault, ready to take the remains of baby Walter if I so choose. And I know that Joseph would relish the baby's comforting presence, yet I could not quite bring myself to make the decision. Not yet. Perhaps the melancholy, the madness, that has so often overtaken me these past months from this double loss. But something else, I fear, for which God cannot forgive me. Some insane jealousy that Joseph might be re-united with our child, but I should not. Besides, the monument itself had seemed such a good idea when I first perceived the notion, and there were many who wished to subscribe for its completion, Mister Yale most prominent among them. "For my friend," he had said. Yet I had never counted him a friend of Joseph's, and doubt that Joseph ever thought of him that way either. Liked him well enough, my husband had often said. But not a friend. Never that. So I rejected his and all other such offers, relying simply on the almost immediate profit gleaned from that new investment in Antonio do Porto's trade in diamonds. Literally, a brilliant dividend. At the time, it seemed fitting, both the profit and the obelisk it purchased.

But then, last month, the *Indian Trader* arrived. Among other things, she brought me news of Joseph Junior. The vessel had passed alongside the *Golden Fleece* in March, and been hailed by the skipper with his speaking horn.

'Tell Mistress Hynmers and her husband that their boy fares well,' he had cried, little knowing that, by the time the *Indian Trader* arrived at Fort St. George, my husband would be two months dead. And it was, in truth, only the smallest of mercies to know that my son had safely reached the shores of Africa, with the most hazardous portion of his journey still to face.

Yet the ship brought other things too. A crate of gifts from Mama, a missive with the latest news, and a book. A precious book, which must have cost a small fortune. Bunyan's tale of morality, delivered as he says under the similitude of a dream. *The Pilgrim's Progress*. *"Do you see yonder Wicket Gate?"* Evangelist asks Pilgrim, and when I read the words, I knew I had erred. Joseph himself would not have wanted this vainglorious obelisk but, by then, the structure was complete. There was no going back. Though at least I might not compound my error by committing Walter's soul to such vanity also.

Perhaps others saw the thing differently however.

'A fitting tribute to a great man.' Matthew Parrish at my side, after the obituary tablet was sealed in place and I had been left to pay my respects.

'You say so, Matthew? I am not now so certain. All that time a-dying.'

Sathiri tells me that it is *karma*, that Joseph's death must have been written. And now this from Matthew Parrish. Our ability to paint silver linings around sable clouds. For me, my one desire is to be far away from everything that is familiar, so I might not need to deal with all that has become meaningless to me.

'He was a fighter. Everybody knew that. Hence the military honours at his funeral.'

The day after he finally gave up the struggle. Three volleys fired at his temporary resting place. A forty-gun salute from the walls of the fort.

'He was fighting for his boys, I think. Determined not to abandon them. And now, what?'

'I understand, Catherine. But with the news from England…'

'You think I care – about the news from England? I still wake every morning thinking that I have had the worst of dreams, that when I turn over, Joseph will still be there. There is nothing that motivates me now – nothing, Matthew, except to honour his memory, to make sure his fight was not in vain. Nothing now except the protection of our sons' future.'

And only the words of Master Donne to comfort me. *"Death, be not proud."* For, so long as I live, Joseph shall never die.

Another month gone by, and I have a plan at last, for today I took the most difficult step of my life.

But, meanwhile, a further letter from Mama, life continuing as normal there in London and she blissfully unaware that here the world has fallen apart. In truth I could not bring myself to read it in the beginning, though last night I finally settled to some embroidery work – the first I have attempted for six months – and, afterwards, I took the letter from my needlework box.

And I do care. Of course I do. I am, after all, a part of all this.

She reminds me that the king's pro-French tendencies, his wars against the Dutch, have created a gulf between himself and his Cavalier Parliament and, thus he has dismissed them, only to fare little better with the three Parliaments that succeeded them in the course of just one year. The main reason? The Exclusion Crisis, as Mama styles it. Fuelled, in part, by the Catholic plots that Titus Oates and others had, whether in truth or deception, attempted to expose, the new Parliaments had tried to introduce legislation that would prevent the king's Catholic brother, James, Duke of York, from succeeding to the throne. Naturally, as soon as any of these Exclusion Bills showed any sign of progress, the king dissolved the Parliament.

She clings to some naïve hope that Monmouth might become king though, of course, I know he will not. The king's illegitimate son, even one as popular as the Duke of Monmouth, cannot succeed. And now in exile, it seems. It is a cruel delusion.

I have told Matthew that I am done with spying, that now it must all be about the boys. But I may still have some role to play – after I have got past today and that difficult encounter with Mister Yale. He sat directly across from me, the opposite side of my dining table. Just the two of us, apart from the *pankah* boy and the servants scrurrying about with morsels of light refreshment. I had consumed perhaps a little too much of Sathiri's *soma*, to help me cope with the meeting. And Mister Yale, too, had filled his own wine cup several times already. Joseph's favourite *Fondillón*.

'Excellent, Mistress,' he said, raising the goblet to his lips.

'Yet you seem ill at ease, Mister Yale.'

'I had expected...'

'Other guests, I collect. But this must be by way of a business encounter. Thus I thought it best to conduct that business in private.'

We were not entirely alone, of course. That would have been unseemly. But our company was restricted to the *pankah* boy and those other attendants.

'They tell me you have had some considerable success already. Trading in brilliants with the Jew, do Porto. It's an area in which I intend to develop some expertise of my own. Perhaps in partnership.'

'With the Barker girl? I hear she fancies herself something of the expert already.'

'Katherine? God's Hooks, no. She certainly spends a great deal of time in their company, learning the trade, as you might say. But that old rogue Veranna has expressed some interest. He seems somehow to have repaired his affairs with Lingappa Naik, and therefore with Golconda. And with Shivaji no longer a threat...'

The news had all but passed me by while I was caring for Joseph, but Chatrapati Shivaji Maharaj had also succumbed to a fever only a few weeks before my husband's own demise, the eldest of his wives, they say, committing *sati* by leaping upon his funeral pyre. And I finally understood that terrible compulsion. For, if Joseph's remains had been similarly cremated, I should have been sorely tempted, at the time, to throw myself upon his flames.

'With Shivaji no longer a problem,' I said, 'we may make our best efforts to prosper until the next threat appears.'

'Business then, Mistress?'

'Business, yes. A proposal of marriage, Mister Yale.'

'Marriage, between...?'

I believed, at first, it must be one of his absurd jests. But then I saw the genuine confusion upon his face. He had dressed more formally for the occasion, his finest English coat, but over a scarlet *kurta*, embroidered in gold thread. And a full peruke upon his head – a garish chestnut vallancy, forsooth – instead of his now more normal turban. He had come with some intent of his own – one that I now perceived.

'Lord,' I said, as apologetically as I was able, 'you thought I would make an announcement. To friends of the family. That I plan to return to England with the boys. And, therefore, the house to be sold. Or inherited. Quite wrong, sirrah. Yet you are correct in this regard. My boys are the core of my proposal. They need a father, Mister Yale. Or, at least, one who can serve as an example to them in their father's stead.'

I watched as the words slowly penetrated that bovine skull.

'Me, ma'am?'

'I can think of none to better fill the role.' The words almost stuck in my throat.

In truth, I have been able to think of nobody else at all. Every other acceptable candidate already wed. The rest all scrubs. I have had fantasies about Governor Master, of course. I believe he has some interest in me also, but I am not seeking any amorous association here. Far from it. A business transaction, no more. And Matthew has warned me that the fortunes of our good Agent may soon be in decline, Seaton and others preaching against him with the Directors in Leadenhall Street.

'Mistress, if this is about the secret we share, about the little one, I can assure me that you have nothing to fear. It shall go with me to the grave.'

Oh, Mister Yale, I thought, *by how far do you miss your mark! If only you knew how much I despise you for perhaps having the chance to save my child from his premature burial and then failing in your efforts.* No, I can think of no better retribution than inflicting upon him responsibility for my surviving boys.

'I have no such fear, sir. But you have been kind enough to show me attention at times, and then to have the grace to let me grieve in peace these past months.'

'Yet a proposal of marriage. Forgive me, Mistress. The last thing I should have expected. Not least because I have never heard of such a thing. From a lady. A fellow's position, is it not? To set such a proposition forward. And yes, I must confess that I might have come to that, in time.

Indeed I might. Considered it an honour to pose the question. In time, as I say. A respectful amount of time.'

He was floundering, and there was an uncomfortable moment of silence. In my house, that is a rare thing in any case. Always one or other of the boys clattering about the place, and the servants less than unobtrusive about their business. Yet today I ordered quiet, and into that embarrassing stillness I now found it necessary to press him.

'Time, I fear, Mister Yale, is a commodity I possess in only short supply. And yes, I accept that my proposal may not accord with normal ritual, but that might easily remain another confidence between us. I durst not think what would be said about my morality if this conversation should ever leave this room.'

'And I, ma'am, durst not think how my own reputation might be damaged if there should be any implication that I had preyed upon the vulnerability of Joseph's widow.'

'Then I note that you have not rejected the notion, sirrah.' There was a cautious nod of his head. Nothing more. And I knew he had assumed his *alter ego*. Elihu Yale, the merchant adventurer. 'And perhaps that should be our beginning. A form of words, to cover how we have arrived here. A preamble, perhaps, to potential agreement.'

'I could certainly give that some thought, Mistress. Sir William had the foresight to sell his collection of law books to Council before he sailed away. I would not boast but I have made some special study of them. Bacon, Bolton, Perkins and many others. I am certain to find guidance there. In general, of course.' He laughed, the mood lightened for the first time. 'I doubt anybody has ever drafted quite such a document before. But you said preamble, ma'am? You propose a marriage settlement when there is none to bring a dowry portion to the table. Or perhaps your father…?'

I saw the hunger in his eyes, and I fed it.

'That which I bring to the table, Mister Yale, is Joseph's own wealth. His quite considerable wealth.'

'Forgive me,' he smiled at me, a condescending smile, 'for I intend no lack of sensibility, but the husband's wealth passes to the widow, her children too, of course. And if she marries afresh, her own earthly goods become the property of her new husband. Is that not so?'

'Precisely the reason we need a settlement. For my proposal is based on one or two further breaks with convention.'

I explained them, while Akbar appeared to charge Mister Yale's glass. Joseph had already bequeathed one-third of his estate, in equal portions, to Joseph Junior, to Richard, and to Elford. But he had made no codicil to his will since Benjamin was born and, though he had talked about this during his illness, my own refusal to accept the inevitable had, I think, prevented him from taking the necessary action until it was far too late to do so. More guilt for me to bear – that I had somehow added that burden to his illness. So I had calculated the value of a fourth portion, roughly one-ninth of the total. Approximately eight hundred pounds. Thus, my first clause, that this sum should be assigned by Mister Yale to Benjamin, with interest to be taken until his coming of age, or until the payment may be discharged.

Agreed.

Then the hospital – or lack of one. Our sick still condemned to seek medical care only within the bleak confines of the Fort House fever room. As good as a sentence of death in itself. And Joseph had not suffered, I collect, from his treatment at home. I hoped not. Yet I had this doubt, that if he – others like him – had the benefit of constant nursing, chances of survival must be higher. So a proposal that Mister Yale might sponsor the concept of a dedicated hospital, subscribe generously to its completion from his new-found fortune.

Agreed.

Third, the boys to be treated as though they are his own. I was amazed they had observed the requirement for tranquility so long, yet I knew it could not last, and they chose that very moment to break the truce, to go thundering along the upstairs landing, screaming at the tops of their voices.

'Yet they shall be kept under control, I trust?' said Mister Yale, with a look of slight dismay. 'And there shall be children of our own, naturally.'

I had not thought so far ahead. Indeed, I had not!

'Perhaps we move too fast,' I said, but he laughed again.

'A marriage without children of my own, Mistress. Can you be serious?'

'There is another thing, Mister Yale. That I will not have Reverend Evans officiate at the ceremony.'

'He is the senior chaplain for the Company here. For the entire Bay of Bengal. And my friend.'

'I estimate, sirrah, that my proposition will enrich you to the tune of three thousand pounds in gold and a further five hundred in jewels. I believe that we might find some accommodation between us on this point.'

'Ah, accommodation. Of course, I shall move into the house?'

'Well, naturally.' I offered him my most conciliatory smile. 'We might have to consider the question of sleeping arrangements. For a while, at least. I shall think on an adequate provision. But you will most certainly be allowed to name me "wife." And, at times, perhaps even Catherine.'

My wedding day, forsooth. And my wedding night too.

There has been a great comet in the sky for a week now. Sathiri and Tanani claiming that this is a remarkable portent, a wonderful omen for my marriage. Yet, to me, something of a disappointment after all the tiresome negotiations with Mister Yale – God's Hooks! My husband, I must now become accustomed to naming him. But how long will that take? Each time I attempt the word, it cuts through me as though I have betrayed Joseph over and over again. Even the date. Too close for comfort. For it had been on the Sixth of November, just two days hence, though eleven years ago, that Joseph and I were married.

And this betrayal of Joseph, I am not the only one to think so, either. All the opprobrium from the fart-faced wives of the Cavalier faction. No decent widow of the High Church would ever have contemplated such a thing, they said. Mister Hynmers no more than four months in his grave and she has already cast aside her weeds. And for Elihu Yale, forsooth! Such a reputation with the ladies. My dear, do you think it might be possible? That there was a dalliance before – well, such things happen, do they not? She is, after all, more native than European. Born where, did you say? And those Gentue friends. Not quite the thing. It simply will not answer.

I supposed not.

We had been careful, Elihu Yale and myself, to keep our bartering between ourselves though, privately, I had sought the blessing of Matthew and Sathiri, and the advice of Governor Master.

'Mistress Hynmers,' he had said. 'Catherine. Are you certain about this? You know, my dear...'

'Please,' I had replied, and touched my hand to his arm, desperate to prevent him saying something we might each later regret. 'Better to confine our words to the matter in hand. I have thought about this carefully. About what may be best for my sons. Nothing more.'

He was crestfallen, caused me momentarily to doubt the efficacy of my decision.

'Have you told them? The boys.'

'I shall only do so once the terms of my agreement with Mister Yale are settled.'

'But Mister Yale, Catherine. Great heavens!'

'Our lives are nothing but a series of crossroads, Governor. You know that. And once we arrive there, choose our onwards route, there is neither turning back nor blaming others for whatever we find along the new path.'

'No turning back? Surely we can always retrace our steps to the crossroads.'

'By then,' I said, 'the better path is invariably overgrown or lost entirely.'

He had accepted all that with the best of grace and, when I subsequently confided in him that my bargain was struck, he had made a small announcement to Council, with our shared intention that this pebble would spread its ripples across our White Town pond and beyond.

'Is this the way it shall be?' Elihu had raged. 'An announcement without consulting me? From the Council, of all places.'

'Would I have needed your authority to inform my father, sirrah? And in the absence of my actual father, Governor Master must stand as his surrogate. To give me away. If my father had then turned chattermonger with the news, I could hardly be blamed, any more than I shall suffer your censure now.'

'And the Council. I am promoted to Fourth, yet still denied a seat at the table. God blind me, Catherine, what does your precious Governor Master have against me. Seaton is my junior now. Merely the Provisional Mintmaster. Yet even he has a place on the Council. But not me. Not me. Unmanned by your proposal. Unmanned by the Governor's denial of my Council membership. Unmanned by the reception I receive from your boys.'

'Simply from Richie,' I had explained. 'It will take time. He has lost his father and his older brother almost at a stroke. He is no less resentful towards me than he is to yourself. And he is eight years old, Elihu. Eight. But the others...'

'The others? Young Elford yells with fear each time I visit. And the babe – for little Benjamin I might as well not exist at all. Total indifference is the very best I ever receive from him.'

'Time,' I had urged. 'You must give them all time.'

I have been working on a letter to Mama, to explain all this. But each of them I have balled and discarded. I had sent a lengthy missive to her with Joseph Junior and, please God, she will now have received this as well as the small packet of brilliants I gave into his care. Of course, when her own annual correspondence had been drafted at Christmas, and arrived in July, she was still blissfully unaware of all this. I pray to Our Lord that my eldest is now safely in her care though he will know nothing of his father's death. How can I tell them? And how can I ever explain this about Elihu? It was all made worse, of course, because the *Indian Trader* in July also brought that crate of goods for my husband. More wine. More pipes and tobacco. All those homely fragrances I associate with him. How could Mama possibly imagine that she had dispatched these gifts for one son-in-law whereas, now, they were the property of an entirely different one.

The only thing about which I have been consistent in my discarded scribbling to her is the details I have given of Joseph's will, the amounts he has bequeathed to my two fractious brothers. Twenty pounds to each of them. And the last sketches he ever made of our boys. Beautiful sketches, light pen strokes upon the paper. In addition, I will send her another bag of diamonds from my own portion of the inheritance, plus gems to the value of eight hundred pounds for her to keep safe on Joseph Junior's behalf. Apart from all that, I hope she will enjoy my account of the seemingly endless preparation for the marriage.

This was made more complicated by Sathiri's insistence – and my ready compliance – that we should, so far as might be possible, follow the customs of her own people. After all, she had argued, I have lived here ten years now. The land in my blood. My own blood in the earth of Coromandel. So I had endured a session in which Sathiri had filled my withdrawing room with the sickly sweetness of burning incense, then performed the casting of horoscopes, her *Nakashtra Porutham* – all propitious, naturally, even the fact that Elihu and myself share the same birthday.

'An excellent month,' she had declared. '*Aippasi* is a good month. And the day you have chosen will this year be that on which we perform the *Annaabishekam*, the rice ceremony to Lord Shiva. It can absolve the bad *karma* of your previous births and purify the *karma* of your current life. You must have rice that day, Catherine. Make sure it is blessed. And *Aippasi* is also the month in which we will celebrate *Deepavali*, our Festival of Lights, to commemorate the defeat of evil Narakasura by our Lord Sri Krishna. If you had chosen *Aani*, *Aavani* or *Maargazhi*, I should have counselled against it. But early in your November, *Aippasi*, is a good month.'

She had shaken her head in dismay at the number of stages we were forced to forego, but she at least ensured that the Marriage Agreement was witnessed by a priest, albeit one of my own religion in the shape of Reverend Portman. And we made a decent attempt to arrange gifts and blessings for the women she described as my *Sumangalis*, the married women who might play a role in my wedding. We even persuaded these *Sumangalis* – Winifred Bridger, Mistress Crouch, the Widow Keeble and others – to help with the preparation of special grain and lentil pots, all the vibrant colours of the spice bazaar, which Sathiri seemed to think important. But she was at least satisfied that we were honouring some form of *Lagna Pathirikai*, the formal announcement and exchange of gifts.

It was the way in which Elihu and myself had resolved the form of words upon which we had settled. The Marriage Agreement was only known to the two of us plus Reverend Portman, but its broad terms we had decided to make public, and therefore explain the reasoning for our union, through a betrothal ceremony. At the beginning of October, when our dickering and bargaining was all done. A plighting of our troths, of course. Consents about the future.

'Do you pledge to be a shield, each for the other?'

'Do you pledge to always care for the children of this marriage, without grace or favour, one above the other?'

And so on. The spousals.

Then another concession to Sathiri. One that rang with our own traditions in any case. A hand-fasting to seal our pledges.

In the Gentue tradition, she tells me, this practice is called *hastaganthi*, their priests using an intricate network of interlacings to bind right hand to right hand, thumb to thumb, whereas Reverend Portman was simply required to wrap a red and gold cord about our wrists, one loop for each vow given.

After that, the banns. Each Sunday for the remaining three weeks of last month. No just impediment declared, much to my surprise, that might impair the wedding itself and thus, today, the ceremony itself.

Memorable, I suppose, simply for the venue. For this was the first significant event held in the recently completed grandeur of St. Mary's. Young Richard – Reverend Portman – had written to the Archbishop of Canterbury explaining the building schedule and its imminent completion and, this July, also aboard the *Indian Trader*, received a reply authorising him to officiate in the new church, and to consecrate it. He did so only last Thursday, a solemn occasion with thunderous, sulphur-stench volleys fired by the whole garrison and a salute from the Fort's cannons. Even then, there was controversy. No attendance from either the local Portuguese or French clergy. Papists, of course, but we all remembered the way in which Governor Langhorn had celebrated the consecration of St. Antony's. So, a particular surprise that Father Ephraim was notable by his absence.

'Oh, my dear,' said Reverend Portman when I passed comment to him on the fact. 'But the Senior Chaplain forbade me from sending him an invitation.'

That hypocrite, John Evans, of course!

But, by then, I had made my grand entrance, much to the dismay of many in attendance. It seemed perfectly reasonable to them, apparently, that Elihu should be waiting for me, attired in a mixture of his finest English and Gentue garments. He was even sporting that special head-dress that Sathiri calls a *thalaip*. Yet when the Fort's musicians and the new choristers struck the gentle opening strains of Byrd's *The Match That's Made* to announce my arrival, led by Elihu's bride-men with their sprigs of rosemary – he had chosen Henry Oxenden and John Willcox at my insistence, for they were the least objectionable of his friends – and myself on Governor Master's arm, all heads turned towards the entrance and there was a collective gasp of dismay. It could have been, I suppose, the presence of that chit, Katherine Barker, as my chief bridesmaid. But that was at Elihu's insistence. Some urge of his to placate her. For what, I had no idea. Yet I know that, in reality, it was my own garb.

It is a rarity, of course, for a new dress to be bought, simply for a wedding. And I possess that very fine gown of blue and gold satin brocade, the shining taffeta ribbons, the fine linen under-sleeves and lace cuffs – the gown that always turned Joseph's head so. Dizzied him, he used to say, by the feel of it beneath his fingers, and upon which he discourteously blamed each of my pregnancies – a risk that I did not wish to run this night. Yet I was less than certain about Sathiri's insistence on this alternative. An emerald *saree*, nine yards of Kanchi silk, threaded with gold. Flowers of white and orange blossoms around my hair, all my finest jewels, necklaces and gold bangles. Though I had entirely rejected her suggestion that I might also dress my head with the decoration she brought to me.

'But it is *jadainagam*, Catherine,' she had insisted. 'For luck. For fertility.'

'Fertility is not something I require this night,' I had replied. 'And besides, how could anything in the form of this serpent bring me luck?'

I had thrown the ugly thing across the table, perhaps more brutally than I had intended. But it has been difficult enough to cope with this day with Joseph always so present in my thoughts, without the added reminder of the way Walter perished. Yet perhaps that helped to steel me too, made me collect that this was, after all, entirely about my sons. Each of them.

So my only other concession to tradition has been that, beneath the *saree*'s folds, I had tied my blue garters above the knee. For I knew that here, at least, was a custom I could not avoid without risking my pact with Elihu himself.

The ceremony itself was unremarkable, mechanical. The ivory beauty of St. Mary's archways almost lost on me. The beeswax polish of its new pews a painful reminder of my lost domestic bliss. The white-draped altar with its gold trappings like a beckoning tomb. The consents we had already given at our hand-fasting now repeated in the present tense. There was the formality of a kiss, and my exit was made, now on Elihu's arm, to the rather more joyous second movement of the same song, *The Match That's Made*. And then there was the procession to the Governor's house. The food. Plenty of rice, naturally, to appease Lord Shiva. Copious amounts of drink. The bride pie pastry so lovingly prepared by my *Sumangalis* – and the glass ring within the pie's mutton and sweetbreads, discovered as we had hoped it would be in the portion served to Katherine Barker. Toasts, therefore, to the next bride. *And good luck*, I thought, *to the poor wretch who has to marry that one.*

And so, to the inevitable. I had rehearsed this part with Elihu several times, to ensure there should be no mistake. But, by the requisite time for going to our bed, he had consumed considerably more Brunswick mum than he could handle. I feared the worst. He was singing loudly – *Cherry Ripe*, how inappropriate – as this second, more raucous procession swayed and staggered across to the house. My house. The house I must now share with the fellow. They crowded onto my *veranda* as Tanani tried in vain to quieten them, the boys having gone more than willingly to their beds some time earlier, and that portentous comet no longer worthy of even a glance into the night sky. Yet it was a hopeless task, Tanani's attempts at order, and the two bride-men, despicable Vincent Seaton behind them, John Nicks and Katherine Barker too, caroused up the stairs and followed me into my tallow-lit bedchamber. There I had to display each leg in turn, lifting the *saree*'s green folds, so that Oxenden and Willcox could fumble at my thighs to remove the garters and fasten them to their hats. Except neither of them had remembered to bring such headgear with them, forcing the Barker girl to tie them instead – she found this hilariously amusing, for some reason – about the men's periwigs.

Then the undressing, at Katherine's less than tender hands. But thank the Lord there were no pins with which she could injure me. Simply the jewels to be removed – I watched carefully to ensure they were all accounted for – and the *saree* to be unwrapped, spinning me around, down to the simple shift I had ensured should remain in place. After that, I climbed beneath the sheets, as the room filled with other guests and my *Sumangalis*, at last, to stand guard over me. Until my husband should arrive. My husband, the borachio, with his sour breath, stumbling and crashing into my fine oak dresser as he stripped his own clothes down to his linen.

'In Scotland, they say,' he yelled, 'wives may be taken on trial for a whole year. What say you, wife?'

Then he collapsed on top of the bed beside me, while the guests drifted back to their celebrations and left us to our nuptials. Except, of course, they knew nothing about the clause I had made him accept. For three months at the least, separate beds. His own bedchamber. Yet, this first night, it happened differently than I had intended, myself slipping quietly along the corridor to the room appointed for my new husband – there, that word again – while he, for his part, was driving pigs, snoring fit to waken the dead. And I, for mine, have been left in peace to write these lines.

I have spent all this time trying to discover what happened. Nicks and the Barker girl. The banns only read once and everybody pretending that this was perfectly normal.

'You must surely think it strange?' I said to Elihu over breakfast. 'Nicks and Katherine.' He shrugged, pretending to be absorbed in his books. 'And must you do that? The books, I mean.'

Joseph never needed to work through his breakfast.

'Strange? I fear this is rather like the pot calling the kettle black, is it not? Was there ever anything more strange than our own coming together?'

'But the very next Thursday? One day she's following you around like a moon-struck calf at the wedding, the next – literally the next – she's betrothed to John Nicks. And then they too are wed. A se'nnight after our own.'

'I should have thought you would be pleased. It was Katherine who discovered the ring in the bride pie, after all.'

'True. Though I have never heard of anybody else discovering the bride pie ring one Thursday and being married the next. And I still do not understand your insistence that she should act as my chief bridesmaid.'

'How many times, Catherine? Simply an honour to her father. He is our Steward, when all is said and done. A significant role in providing so much of the wedding feast. It was the least I could do. She wanted it badly.'

'Or did you wish to display your harem? Flaunt your dalliance with her alongside your marriage to me. I hear you have often admired the practices among Moor and Gentue.'

'No dalliance. None. Though, at times, I am left to wonder— '

'Whether you might have chosen her instead? Oh, I do not flatter myself, sirrah. You simply followed the road to the safest speculation.'

'A trifle beneath you, I fear. But this imaginary dalliance hardly fits with her almost immediate marriage to Nicks.'

'No? Or perhaps her father was shocked to hear, in the aftermath, perhaps at the feast itself, that his daughter was the subject of such gossip among the White Town women over their scandal-broth.'

Shocked? Good gracious, he must be deaf to the world. I have been hearing stories of Katherine's lack of morals for longer than I can remember, though now it seems to have resonance across Fort St. George as a whole.

'You have a ripe imagination, my dear. But they are wed, and let that be an end to all this nonsense. Except to say that we should hold close to the new Mistress Nicks for I suspect she could soon buy and sell us all with her knowledge of the diamond market.'

I have to allow that he is correct. Since Kendal's drowning – either by tragic accident or at Vincent Seaton's hands – she has become very much our English expert on the subject. So much time spent among the Paradesi folk, a veritable apprenticeship. Personally, I avoided like the plague availing myself of those skills during my own transactions, but she possesses ability, that is certain.

'Such praise,' I sneered. 'You shall tell me next she has been named to replace Veranna.'

The Indian merchant had died just after Christmas and Agent Master had shown his mettle when the fellow's second wife – the one who lived near Masulipatnam – had arrived for his funeral, intent on throwing herself upon the pyre. The Governor forcibly arrested her and resisted all protests from Gentue and Mussulman alike at this supposed outrage. Extraordinary. Yet more so because many of those like Seaton and his friends in the Cavalier faction had also protested that this was a breach of Company policy against interference with local custom. None of them truly supported the practice of *sati*. Of course they did not. But the knives were out for Agent Master and we all knew it.

'Wherever do you derive such ideas, wife?' He stressed the word, curse him. 'And we shall not name a new native chief merchant until my return. There, forsooth! That, at least, has brought a smile to your face.'

A lapse in my performance, I fear. I try so hard to mask my emotions with him.

'I had forgotten. When do you leave?'

'A few days. Though I shall not be gone long. Still, an important mission. New Dutch Governor at Pulicat, and Agent Master has at least had the foresight to send me with our collective congratulations. Crucial, you understand? That we should forge better relations with the Dutch, now that we are friends again.'

Well, that may be one way to regard this diplomatic adventure but I understand very well that Governor Master is not undertaking the journey himself – merely dispatching one of his officials who does not even, to my new husband's constant chagrin, have a place at the Council table. A junior official, therefore, is all the new Dutch Governor might merit.'

'Oh, indeed,' I said, tasting the hypocrisy like honey on my tongue. 'And I trust you will remain safe and well in the process.'

'God blind me, my dear, but I have the constitution of an ox. As you shall see when I return. By then we shall have been three months wed. Do you collect? Separate beds no more, I say. Time to begin thinking about our own family.'

I am constantly astounded that he has honoured our agreement at all, but the idea of finally consummating our marriage makes me sick to the pit of my stomach. Yet I tried to make light of it. After all, Pulicat may be no more than twenty-five miles away, but much may go amiss in these lands on a return journey of thirteen or fourteen leagues.

'Shall you be more capable, do you think, than on our wedding night? Dead drunk, were you not?'

'Fie upon it, my dear. Have you not heard the story? A drunken fellow returns home one night to find his wife hard a-spinning. She accuses him of being a base borachio, but he reproves her for chiding him. After all, he says, *you* have spent all evening a-spinning and myself a-reeling. A-spinning, Catherine. Is that not what you do?'

Does he know? Or was this some chance remark? Perhaps some clench around the embroidery that had become my regular excuse for my late-night introspection and solitude. I raised the question later, with Matthew Parrish.

'How could he possibly?' Matthew replied.

He was in uniform today, a small contingent of his musketeers near at hand, with a loaded hand-cart, beneath the Caldera Point bastion, while I, and my own company – *ayah*, servants and children – marched hither and thither searching for fresh ingredients to replenish our grocery stores. I love it! The sing-song and ever-joyous cries of the traders, the flash of smiling teeth in those otherwise inscrutable faces; the reds, greens, yellows, tans and purples of their vegetable produce; the scent of cumin and garlic, of coriander and pepper in the sizzling *neyi* of their cooking pans; the laughing eyes and bright *sarees* of the fortune-tellers, garland-weavers, cloth-dealers and chicken-sellers surrounding the bazaar's stalls, which themselves spill out beyond Market Lane's swelling hordes and the Shambles to each of the adjoining streets. Untouchables? Well, not to me.

'He is no fool,' I replied. 'And our faction is hardly in the ascendancy here. Not so numerous that any of us might escape scrutiny.'

'Joseph's loss had even more repercussions than any of us could have foreseen, did it not? Governor Master and poor Bridger now so badly outnumbered on the Council, even without your new husband. Unless we are fortunate, they will each suffer the repercussions of their own success. Have you read Machiavelli? *The Prince?*'

'I have not.'

'We should all have this imprinted in our brains: *"It ought to be remembered that there is nothing more difficult to take in hand, more perilous to conduct, or more uncertain in its success, than to take the lead in the introduction of a new order of things. Because the innovator has for enemies all those who have done well under the old conditions, and lukewarm defenders in those who may do well under the new."* Is that not apposite?'

'Those who have done well under the old conditions? Here they are legion. And all of them enemies? I fear so. Yet the Governor is meticulous in his own records. He can surely have little to fear. But my husband? How he hates it. You are certain that keeping him from a Council seat is helpful? Despite everything, he is no Cavalier by disposition.'

'Nor one of us either, Catherine. But he has their ear. They will recruit him if they can. Manipulate him, certainly. For he is malleable, your Elihu Yale. So we need to know, my dear. You are well-placed, after all…'

'You want me to spy on my own husband?'

At first, it seemed preposterous.

'Why else would I have encouraged you to wed him? Of all things. The Governor as well. Yet we need intelligence. About how these Tories might proceed.'

'Concerned about your own position too, Matthew?'

'Me? I'm just a humble merchant captain. Even with all the promotions, still merely Senior Merchant. Where does that place me? On fifty pounds per annum, of course. A princely sum. But with no prospect of a seat in Council. Not that I should wish one. Equivalent to Eighth, I suppose, though not even in the lists. And they will always need those of us with a talent for soldiering, don't you think? Here we are, with Shivaji only just dead, and the Mughal Emperor moving to take back the territories he'd won. Gingee. Vellore. And Shivaji's son – the one they call Sambhaji – mobilising his warriors to halt him in his tracks. One way or the other we'll be caught in the middle again. Then they'll need me. Ah, here – you see?'

Caught in the middle? Yes, I supposed we must be. Our families at risk once more. Threatened. And here was the threat upon our very threshold, the reason he was waiting with his men. Along North Street, a great clamour, a *halla bol*, as Sathiri might have named it. A clashing of cymbals, drums, and then the trumpeting of an elephant, the clatter of horses' hooves just before a procession of armed warriors came into sight up the slope from the guava gardens, past the burial ground and Joseph's monument.

'Who are they?' I said.

'Lingappa's men. We picked up word this morning. You remember, the *Avaldar* who Veranna insulted so badly? It would be better, Catherine, if you took the boys back inside the walls.'

I had never before heard him sound so concerned – about anything. They were a fine sight, though, the *Avaldar's* warriors. Spears and shields, pointed helmets. Bowmen too. A few arquebusiers. Then the elephant, a *howdah* crowded with more spearmen. Behind the great beast, there seemed a few more riders, and then a cheering crowd pouring from the Mahometan quarter of Black Town.

'Please, Catherine. I mean it. We have no idea how this may play out.'

But in the middle of the procession, there was a palanquin, richly adorned in scarlet and gold, and it came to a halt immediately outside the doors of Father Ephraim's popish church, St. Antony's, fifty paces ahead of us. And there was the priest coming out to see what the commotion was all about.

'Stand right in your files!' Matthew yelled to his men, and they ran from around the bastion's base, as Lingappa's *Avaldar* climbed from the palanquin, his servants rushing to shade him with their roundels. 'Make even your ranks!' Matthew's second order, and his musketeers dressed their lines. He had worked hard with them, instilled far more discipline in his own fellows than that displayed by the drunken rabble of the second company.

'*Monsieur* Parrish,' said Father Ephraim. 'Perhaps the Governor?'

'I am here at the Governor's orders, Father. A visit from Lingappa Naik himself might, of course, warrant Agent Master's attention. But since Shakeel Ahmed is simply one of the *naik*'s military officers…' Matthew bowed graciously towards the *Avaldar*.

There was a brief exchange between the Mussulman Commander and Father Ephraim.

'The *Avaldar* says…' the priest began.

'I understood him well enough. Please thank him but tell him we have not yet replaced Kasi Veranna. That Governor Master very much regrets the disrespect shown towards the *Avaldar* on his previous visit, and I am authorised to make some modest reparation.' He lifted his hand and the cart was trundled forward. Bolts of broadcloth, several chests – doubtless filled with gold pagodas – and a collection of weapons. Yet the *Avaldar* simply laughed, spat a stream of Telugu invective at both Matthew and Father Ephraim.

'He cannot be serious,' said the priest.

'I fear so,' Matthew replied, then turned to me. 'Please, Catherine. It would be wise to go back now.' But despite myself, my inner apprehensions, I remained, simply instructing Tanani and Akbar to take the boys home, much to Richard's objections. 'And you, Father,' Matthew continued. 'Better stand aside.'

'But you cannot,' cried Father Ephraim. 'All these innocents. The women. The children.'

The *Avaldar* was screaming something but Matthew had assumed his normal composure.

'Father, what do you imagine might happen if we acceded to this demand? Surrender Fort St. George? He knows we will not agree. And I do not believe there will be bloodshed.'

'But you are outnumbered, *monsieur*.'

Matthew merely smiled.

'Sections!' he yelled and, to my astonishment, from the dwellings along each side of the street, more of his musketeers emerged, their weapons made ready. 'Present!' And with admirable precision, each of the men blew upon his match, opened the musket's pan and lifted the butt smoothly to the shoulder, each aiming straight at the *Avaldar*. The Mahometan warriors spun about in all directions, readied their own weapons, but their leader had understood the message. That he would undoubtedly be the first to die. He was shouting to them and, slowly, the tension eased. 'Now, Father,' said Matthew. 'I should not want to be misunderstood. And my Telugu is less adequate than I should like. Would you mind translating, therefore? Explain to him that his men may leave in peace. But the *Avaldar*, I fear, must be placed under arrest.'

Another siege. A month already. No respite even for Easter Sunday. And the start of another year in a few days. Yet I must wonder at the sad level of morality to which we have here descended. When we should all have been at our worship, praying to God Almighty for our deliverance, I was astonished to see the number of our young men playing at stool ball outside the church itself – and some of them plainly inebriated. Oblivious to the dangers that surround us.

The siege. Lingappa's revenge, of course, for Matthew's bold detention of his *Avaldar*. Our poor town blockaded, neither goods nor produce entering or leaving. No food, no fuel. The inhabitants of Black Town and White Town each suffering the effects – though this plainly strikes the Gentues, Moors and Jews far harder than our own community. Near to starvation.

Yet the siege has this advantage, that it delayed Mister Yale's return from his journey to Pulicat, from Jan Company's new Governor. Delayed him for a while, at least. But when he eventually broke through Lingappa's lines, he seemed changed.

'I wish us to be partners in this marriage, Catherine,' he had said on his first night back at the house. The children were settled in their beds and most of the servants dismissed, apart from the *pankah* boy, for it was especially humid, the sweat trickling down my back.

'Business partners?' I was genuinely uncertain of his meaning.

'A partnership of equals.'

'I recall an evening – young Katherine's birthday, I collect – when I accidentally overheard a conversation between you both. Something you said about the power in this household being wielded by the Mistress, not the Master. Not by Joseph. No, please do not trouble to deny, nor qualify. For, in part, you were correct. We each had our role to play. And yes, for the governance of the household, for the domestic arrangements, I reigned supreme. Yet on other matters, Joseph ruled with a rod of iron. You cannot have a marriage of absolute equals, Elihu. Not in all things. An equal partnership is one thing, a pairing of equals quite another. Perfect equals in a marriage simply become perfect rivals, neither giving ground to the other. Your Antony and Cleopatra are perhaps a case in point.'

He smiled at that – flattered, I think that I should have noted his penchant for Shakespeare. Then he conjured what he considered some appropriate lines from the play by way of response.

> '*"What, says the married woman you may go?*
> *Would she had never given you leave to come.*
> *Let her not say 'tis I that keep you here.*
> *I have no power upon you."'*

'You see, sirrah. She measures her affections only in terms of power.'

'Well,' he said, 'I have no intention of holding you to our agreement. You shall not be coerced into any act you feel may be precipitate. You follow my drift, I trust?'

Indeed, I did. And the offer did more to wound me, to shame me, than any attempt he might have made to force me to his bed. Thus, that night, I invited him to my own. It was not the same sharing of pleasures I had enjoyed with Joseph. More a gentle but one-sided rutting, the night's intolerable heat, a cramp in my feet, and a crack in the ceiling plaster, all more notable than the act itself. Not the worst experience therefore, though it left me with a dreadful fear. Might I be gotten with child again? For I was far from ready for that step with Mister Yale. Yet this past week Eve's Curse came upon me as usual and I was mightily relieved.

Then, today, he scolded me for my lack of tolerance towards those young players at stool ball.

'What?' I said. 'You hold with this foolishness that, after Palm Sunday and Holy Friday, more levity should be allowed on the day of Our Lord's Resurrection? Despite the siege?'

'We have no idea how long the siege may last. Whether we shall

all even survive it. So we should not begrudge those young men their moment in the sun. We share so many customs here, do we not? Being from all parts of the country. My own family still follows many of the traditions of Wales, for example. And those two young rascals from Preston have brought their pace-egging with them. Should your boys not enjoy that particular entertainment?'

And so it was that, to my utter astonishment, I later found him in the kitchen, instructing the servants and children alike in the art of wrapping eggs in onion skin and boiling them until they were quite solid, by which time they had also assumed those intricate patterns of gold mottle. Pace Eggs, he had explained to Rich. From the Latin word, *Pascha*. Easter.

Then, this evening, when the same pair of junior writers came a-merrymaking around the houses, each of them at horse play, outrageous costumes, one dressed as St. George, the other as some Mahometan they named Bold Slasher, Elihu led my boys out into the procession to join in singing their raucous piece of doggerel.

'You see, my dear?' he yelled. 'Is this not prime?'

By the end of April, the siege had been lifted. Though not without considerable grief for those within our charge. And in a manner not entirely to Elihu's liking.

'Parrish! Parrish! Parrish!' he cried. 'What in heaven's name do they see in the fellow? And where is my best periwig? Council tomorrow and I must prepare.'

The servants had picked up his mood, scurrying about the house, creating their own inimitable impression of industry to match his fuss and bother.

'I suppose it has something to do with him saving us. Matthew, I mean. And Akbar has taken the peruke for cleaning and curling.'

The commotion he has made all this time about being denied a seat. And now he has one – why, I could swear he is timid. And oh, how he rages about the house at times like this. His honeymoon with myself non-existent, of course. And, with the servants, little better. Thank goodness that it has lasted some while longer with the boys. But Matthew? Precisely as he had predicted. The day after Easter Sunday, and he was dispatched with a great many Gentue porters and his company of soldiers, marching those fifteen miles west to Poonamallee, to Lingappa's very heartland, raiding his territory and carrying off great quantities of the Company's goods that had been seized there, as well as some supplies for our relief. But not enough. Not nearly enough.

'It was not Parrish that saved us, but my strategic thinking. That half-hearted attack on Poonamallee was never going to be sufficient. We needed to show Lingappa we meant business. You have to be ruthless with these fellows, Catherine. Ruthless.'

'It was Council's decision, was it not? The raid on Poonamallee.'

'Indeed. But Parrish is our senior captain. A mediocre merchant but supposed to have expertise in military matters. Yet half-hearted, as I say. It was my suggestion, mine alone, that settled matters. Though who does the Council choose to reward?'

Two weeks later, after Poonamallee, and Matthew made another foray, this time all the way to Condore, almost as far as Masulipatnam, and there besieged the village. It was a daring act, an offensive against the Sultan of Golconda himself. Matthew steadfastly refused to talk about his adventure, but my husband informed me that he had given the villagers a choice – either to open our supply lines afresh or to suffer the consequences. I believe Elihu recited the tale in some attempt to diminish Matthew in my eyes, to highlight his ruthlessness. Well, he does not understand me very well, does he? And those villagers could not concede, of course. More afraid of their headman, their *polygar*, and of Lingappa Naik, than this few dozen white men from distant Fort St. George. We should always choose wisely, of course – or choose not at all. But that night Matthew took the village, inflicted many casualties, drove away the *polygar*. Then he seized many provisions and made his way back down the coast.

'It seems reasonable,' I said, defiantly. 'After Condore, it was only necessary to say that Parrish *sahib*, Parrish the Devil, was coming and other villages in the region fell into line.' And the siege was, to all intents and purposes, emasculated. 'Was it not thus that the deal was done?'

The *Avaldar* returned safely to his master, having been treated with the utmost courtesy throughout, and Lingappa agreeing to surrender his demand that we should abandon Fort St. George. In exchange, an exorbitant annual payment to him in pagodas. So, there we are, tribute now being paid not only to Golconda and Chingleput, but to Poonamallee also. The very thing we had tried to resist. But trade must flow, of course. And its wheels need constantly greasing.

'Well, we shall see how long it all holds.' He sounded so petulant. 'But this business of rewards. Really, I thought it should all change. New Governor. Myself at last on the Council.'

More than four months since Easter and I wish I could claim it as married bliss though, in truth, it was more truce than tryst. And the arrival early in July of the *Bengal Merchant* set much of that upon its head.

'Only a modest reward, husband. After all, he received no more than a silk scarf for his trouble at Poonamallee. A hogshead of arrack for his men and a few pagodas shared among the Gentue porters. Yet all that wealth they brought back.'

'All goods the Company had already purchased, my dear. You defend him too much, and I wonder why you should do so. To deliberately defy my views. Your absurd defence of Streynsham Master also.'

'Because I know Agent Master to be a scrupulous man. Honourable. As, I suspect, you believe him to be also.'

'It matters not one jot what I believe. There is the evidence to consider. I have not sat all this time in the Choultry Courts, nor studied our law books, without knowing that evidence is all. And Governor Gyfford has brought that evidence. No smoke without fire, my dear.'

William Gyfford had been the least expected item of the *Bengal Merchant*'s inventory. No stranger to Fort St. George, he had been posted here long before I arrived, though Joseph had experience of him – and dismissed him as something of a buffoon. Yet he carried written instructions from Leadenhall Street that he should immediately replace Mister Streynsham Master as Governor. Outrageous.

'A fire sparked more by those who have briefed against him, I fear. Seaton and his ilk. Master is a courageous man. Perhaps somewhat imperious. But only so much as his position requires. A tendency to plain speaking, of course.'

I recalled Matthew's words from Machiavelli. Streynsham Master had made no secret of his admonitions against the Directors for their own faults in the poor management of Fort St. George and, of course, the beneficiaries of that poor management here at Madras Patnam – the unscrupulous among our own officials, the independent interlopers and the Indian merchants alike – had all screamed from the remedial measures he had put in place.

'Regardless of your view, Catherine, the Council must present charges against him – and it is my role to prepare the case. How might it seem if my own wife was expressing such doubts outside these walls?'

'You think I have too much time on my hands, husband.'

'The truth is that – well, I had thought by now...'

'That I would be with child. Yes, you have made that clear.'

It stung his manhood. I knew it did. And I cared not.

'One more thing to trouble me,' he said. 'On top of all this. The

Company under even more scrutiny from the Crown. And His Majesty himself facing such tribulations.'

'The Crown, I believe, is simply playing John Company like a fish, Elihu. Threatening its trade for no better purpose than to increase the garnish given each year in making sure that license remains with the Honourable English East India Company. After all, is any other company in a position to deliver this enterprise? And the king? You know my views. The Exclusion Bill, to stop his popish brother succeeding to the throne. If he had any wit he would accept Parliament's proposal, rather than using his Lords to block it. Why, sirrah, would you see an agent of Rome back on the throne of England?'

'By preference, no, I should not. But the laws of succession are sacrosanct, conferred by God Almighty as surely as the divine right of the king himself to rule. For our governance, Catherine. All else, the Lord will resolve.'

It sounded simple enough here in my house on Middle Street, but I knew from Mama's latest missive that matters in London and elsewhere were now fever-hot. Every day one more Popish Plot story until none able any more to tell truth from fiction. Another Lord, William Howard, Viscount Stafford, condemned to death for conspiracy against the Crown.

'The Lord will resolve, as you say, husband. And what He may not, I suppose can be left to the Council.'

'Catherine, your tongue!'

'They tell me that one of the charges will centre upon the illicit sale of four elephants. I think you needs be careful of your reputation, Elihu. Such things tend to become the stuff of legend here in India.'

It was preposterous. Elephants, indeed!

'There are other charges. The handling of this entire business with Lingappa. And questions about some of his dealings with John Bridger too.'

The knives out.

'After Agent Master,' I protested, 'John Bridger is the best of men. For pity's sake, sirrah, how many times have he and Winifred eaten at our table? They are friends. And now this! Are you truly so greedy for advancement?'

'We are known by the power we wield. Or the way we carry out our duties, regardless of personal sentiment.'

'So you have said before. Well, you should make haste to draft that letter to your father's associate. Tell him that his congratulatory gift on your promotion to – let me see, this would hark back to your advancement merely to Eighth, would it not? Anyway, he should be advised that his expression of good fortune has been roundly overtaken by these latest glories you have gleaned. Through the assassination of our friends' characters.'

A somewhat belated gift, also unloaded from the *Bengal Merchant*. Four barrels of Sandpatch Ale. And my jibe seemed to wash over him like water from a duck's back.

'The gift from Edisbury?' said Elihu. 'I think I shall bide my time before thanking him. Perhaps a note to Pa, though. By repute, the place Edisbury plans to build will be even finer than Plas Grono. I should find out more.'

'Dreams of empire, husband?'

'Of course not. But Edisbury and his new hall will one day be *our* neighbours, Catherine. It would be well to know how that particular land lies. And empire, you say? It will be hard for us to build empire with the new directives. All this additional labour, and our chances of reward so shattered.'

Yet another consignment aboard the *Bengal Merchant*. Two hundred thousand pounds in gold and silver and a distinct change in policy. Sixty thousand to be invested in diamonds – and the Company to now take control of the local trade in brilliants. Total control.

'Is it so bad?' I said. 'Only the diamond trade, after all. Rubies, emeralds, pearls – we have them in abundance. Jade and sapphire. Coral even.'

'It is the diamonds though, Catherine.' He was exasperated, as though I were too foolish to grasp the significance. 'The trading values in London. Or Antwerp. Besides, it is the way the Company has expressed its wishes. All of us summarily prohibited from further private trade in them. No reasonable man can be aggrieved, they say.'

'I agree with them, husband. What reasonable man could complain when he has the rest of India's whole vast wealth at his fingertips?'

'It is still my right to feel aggrieved yet, even here, we are told that any who feel this way should simply seek employment elsewhere.'

'Isn't this where Katherine Nicks may play a part. The restriction cannot apply to private traders, and she seems to be establishing herself as such, does she not?'

I admired the harlot for very little. Yet there was this, at least. Dedication to this apprenticeship she had taken upon herself, a woman making her mark in this world of men.

'The Company would then class her as an interloper, deny her the ability to live within the Fort itself. Impact upon her husband too, of course. Likely bring charges upon his own head.'

Well, that was interesting.

'And the Black Town Jews,' I said. 'This restriction prevents the purchase of brilliants from the Golconda mines. Purchases only to be made here, within Fort St. George. There must be plenty of scope for private investment through Antonio do Porto and his colleagues.'

I did not tell him that I am still reaping the rewards of those pagodas I had invested with do Porto himself.

'Well, it might throw into question the possibility of a subscription to a new hospital, my dear.'

'That would be unfortunate, Elihu. Breaching our settlement so soon. Unfortunate indeed, if you cannot find a way round this obstacle.'

I left him to ponder his conundrum while I retired to my chamber, to read the rest of Mama's letter afresh. It made me weep, of course. That impossible lapse of time, between the happening of events and news of those events leaping the void that separates India from England, or back again.

Oh daughter, she writes. *If you could hear the tales with which your foolish father fills the head of young Joseph, it would make you wail. Those dread pirates, Sawkins and Essex, both killed. The seas now hopefully safer for honest travellers like yourself, should you choose to now send Richard home also.* She seems not to have taken account that these devils were both active in the Caribbean, and that our local pirates here are a different breed entirely. *And that rascal Thomas Blood dead too. Imagine, a Royal pardon, not a day spent in prison for his stealing of the Crown Jewels, then condemned, eight years later, for defaming the character of Buckingham. Only a short sentence but enough to inflict gaol fever upon him. And, even then, the authorities saw fit to dig up his body again lest his death be some further display of the fellow's trickery.*

But, apart from your father's influence, the boy is flourishing. He misses his own mama and papa, naturally, talks about you both often. And he is determined to follow in your husband's footsteps for no better reason, it seems, than to allow you all to be re-united at the earliest opportunity. For he is set upon John Company for his future. And so, as with Joseph Senior before him, he is enrolled at Turberville of Kensington with some of the gems you sent and has, to this date, applied himself diligently to his studies. I have attached a note, in his own hand, that you may judge his progress. Of course, I am teaching him that he will need strength and fortitude to attain his goal. That righteous ambition alone is not enough. He will learn!

And here it is, flown to me all those countless thousands of miles, stained by its journey and stained more by my tears. Joseph Junior's own words in his tidy, flowing hand that looks so readily like his father's. An account of his lessons at Turberville's. Mathematicks and music, those inseparable twin subjects. And languages, Latin and Greek, Italian and French. French, he says, according to Mister Turberville, will soon be the language of world trade.

I trust, he says, *that Papa will be proud of me.*

Oh, my poor son. This is cruel beyond belief. So I set the note aside, return to Mama's own letter. She seems, at least, to have suffered no further mis-births, though my brothers still give her cause for concern. No love lost between them, she says, and my father incapable of controlling them. But good news at least, for the diamonds I sent her with Joseph Junior – just Joseph now, I collect, the only Joseph – are safely on deposit and awaiting my further instructions. Well, I must think about our futures then. All the possible permutations.

They say, now, that perhaps fourteen thousand have died in the storms that struck Porto Novo last month, and the Dutch factory there all but destroyed.

'Well,' said Elihu, without any word of sympathy for the devastation, 'it may have delayed the start of my expedition, but it has certainly cleared the way for our success. And I have spoken with Bridger. He is happy to sell us this place. That will be a blessing for him, will it not?'

He was dressed tonight in his travelling clothes, loose cotton *kurta* for a dust coat and a turban in place of his peruke, a gold embroidered baldrick for the rapier at his side, all ready for the journey he was about to make yet elegant enough to grace this gathering in his honour to speed him on his way.

'You said that without any trace of irony, husband. My congratulations. You help the Council concoct these absurd allegations against Streynsham Master, force him to leave Fort St. George, then you make a virtue of offering to buy this beautiful house that Winifred loves so dearly.'

Their garden house. It stands on a small ridge, west of town, surrounded by citrus trees, and is blessed with a regular cooling breeze. Their pride and joy, valued more than, collectively, the several properties they also own in Scotch Street. But John Bridger can see the writing on the wall, I think. Whisperings and rumours that, after Master, he may be next to fall victim to the Cavalier faction's machinations. And, therefore, he has begun to convert some of his assets to capital. Not that such a thing could be discerned from the number of his servants. Good gracious, a virtual regiment of them scurrying about in their turbans. Some of them, at least, shall have to go!

'Simply business, my dear. They have no need to sell. The evidence we've prepared to send to the Directors barely mentions Bridger himself.'

That was hardly encouraging for I have it from the women's gossip that Vincent Seaton may have already sent incriminating stories back to Leadenhall Street by last year's ships. I have warned Matthew and he, in turn, has advised John Bridger to prepare himself, to begin gathering evidence and resource in his own defence.

'It seems,' I said, 'that these days it does not require any involvement of the Council itself to bring a witch-hunt down upon the heads of its senior officials.'

'Your obsession with poor Vincent Seaton again. He really does not deserve your scorn, Catherine.'

'"Yond Cassius,"' I quoted, '"has a lean and hungry look. He thinks too much: such men are dangerous."'

For there he was, Seaton himself, striding across the reception hall to join us, seemingly joined at the hip to our new Governor Gyfford. And after just a twelve-month with Elihu Yale I know *Julius Caesar* as though I wrote it myself.

'Here he is,' bellowed Gyfford. 'Man of the hour, yet skulking in this corner. Can't blame him though, Vincent, eh? The beguiling Mistress Yale to keep him engaged. Was you saying your farewells, sirrah?'

Gyfford, the very antithesis of his predecessor. In almost every way imaginable. He normally spends his days marching around with a drummer and a brace of standard bearers. Pompous fool. And regarding me now, as he usually did, with those pig-like eyes that seemed always endeavouring to prise apart my garments.

'A fine evening to set out, Elihu,' said Seaton. 'Have you decided on a first stop?'

'Only to Perumbur, I think,' replied my husband. 'On the road by nine and there long before midnight. An easy first march. But at least that puts us on the road south for an early start tomorrow. After that – well, four days perhaps before we cross into Bijapur. You see, my dear?' he turned to me. 'Strategic thinking.'

He is very proud of himself. The argument he has set before Council. That with the Gentue Marathas and the Golconda Mahometans at each other's throats again, it is foolishness to have all our eggs in Golconda's basket. That now is the time to seek a second alliance, with the new

Raja of Gingee, the Commander of Sambhaji's forces there in the wake of Shivaji's death.

'We was all struck by the simple elegance of your scheme, Mister Yale. Plenty of *pishcash* to pacify the Raja, perhaps bring us a new factory to the south. Porto Novo or thereabouts. And, at the same time, send a message to Lingappa Naik that we are no longer solely reliant on Fort St. George. Prime, sirrah. Prime.'

'Simply using the gifts granted me by God Almighty, Governor.'

'And this proposal for a hospital. The lives we may save. Black Town. Great Heavens, how it is grown since I were last here. Tripled in size, I collect. What do you say, Mistress Yale? Are you not proud to be his wife?'

I wanted to tell him that my only purpose or desire was to provide a father for my boys, a figure of authority in their lives. But proud to be his spouse? No, never that. How could that be when I still feel this contempt? My original doubts about baby Walter now turned to certainty with the passage of time. That the Lord Jesus had given my little one a second chance – his cries from the grave. But Elihu's actions too tardy, too inadequate to seize the proffered gift.

'I lost my first husband, Governor, to an illness that I believe could perhaps have been treated more efficiently in a dedicated hospital. How could I not be proud that we may now have such an asset within Fort St. George?'

I accepted a glass of *panch* from a passing manservant, also proud that I had avoided the question so well, neither the Governor nor Seaton seemingly aware that I had done so. But I caught the pain in Elihu's eyes.

'I should give much,' he said, when they had moved on, 'to win your admiration, Catherine.'

'We have a settlement, Elihu. Neither admiration nor affection were necessary elements in its drafting.'

He led me further away from the guests gathered here for his departure.

'For pity's sake, my dear, you sound as heartless as a saw-bones about to take my leg. In any case, there is risk in this journey I must now make. And we are bound to be disturbed again before too long.' There was a great deal of wine, Brunswick mum and arrack *panch* being consumed in the adjoining rooms.

'You have presumably written some final wishes?'

'Of course. The drawer in my desk. A copy to be sent home and letters for my family. Especially Thomas.'

Married a year and I have never met even one member of his family. This disturbs me. Joseph's father had died long before we were wed, and his mama passed away just before we sailed for India. But I liked her, his brother and sister too. Yet the Yales? We had discussed them, naturally, Elihu fond of recounting tales of how, though they had travelled to the Colonies in search of religious tolerance, they had found in Connecticut only Puritan dictatorship there. Boston merely marginally better. And thus the father and mother settled once more in Wrexham. Wales, of course. The north, that area known as the Marches. The string of uncles and aunts, brothers and sisters, some already prematurely deceased, several still living. Among these, none so precious as his younger brother, Thomas, eleven years his junior.

'It would be a great pity should Thomas succeed in following your footsteps, as he wishes, and come all the way here only to find you perished at Porto Novo.'

He was not amused. But then I did not entirely intend humour. Thomas has been serving his time in the counting house but now, it seems, he may well have found himself a place with John Company.

'Yes, a pity. So shall you at least ensure that, if our ships sail before my return, the documents are dispatched?'

I agreed, received a peck on the cheek by way of thanks, and then there was a great fanfare. Time for the finale and Elihu's setting forth. It was impressive, I must allow: a small army of native porters; two sections of the Second Company's pikes and muskets; carts and beasts of burden loaded with hundreds of yards of broadcloth in every quality or colour; crates of weapons – fine blades and firearms, both; casks stuffed with gold; panniers holding looking glasses, sandalwood and rose water. And, tethered to one of the carts, an exquisite Arab stallion, purest white. Close at hand, Elihu's palanquin, four bearers already shouldering the curved bamboo pole from which his carrying compartment was suspended – and the whole compartment decorated with that Yale coat-of-arms.

Elihu settled himself within the palanquin to some words of encouragement from the Governor and a round of applause from well-wishers – Council members, Schoolmaster Ord, Chirurgeon Heathfield, John and Katherine Nicks, John Barker, the Widow Keeble. And yes, the Bridgers, though their faces were set and stoney.

'Filthy business, this with the Bridgers.' Matthew Parrish at my shoulder.

'What will happen to them?'

'It's to be hoped that John has had the sense to make some decent investments. One thing for the Governors to be removed, the Company knowing that they have their own independent wealth. But men like Bridger? And on the word of a scrub like Seaton.'

'Certain?'

'As certain as I can be. But there goes the procession. Your husband waving from the window as though he is a king. How shall you cope without him? You may have to resort to Sathiri's mantras for warding off demons.'

'You say so? In truth, I recite them every day of my life. Since Walter. And then Joseph. Yet with Elihu gone I might at least not need such reliance on her *soma*.'

He laughed.

'And the Governor,' he said. 'Impressed with Elihu's initiative.'

'Of course. Thinks I should be proud of him. Though I still do not understand. You so carefully planted the seed for this expedition in my husband's mind, convinced him the idea was his own. The credit for this should be yours, Matthew, not Elihu's.'

His eyes grew cold again, as I have seen them do before.

'Consider it,' he said, 'simply an investment for the future.'

The somewhat stilted celebrations went on most of today, from the moment when Elihu's expeditionary force was first sighted, plodding back towards Black Town.

'Did the Governor share my reports with you, my dear?' he said, once it was all over and he had collapsed upon the *diwan*.

'He was more than generous with his time,' I replied. Governor Gyfford, his daily visits. To make sure I was cared for, he would say as, each afternoon, before *siesta*, I surrounded myself with more and more servants, made sure never to venture forth or be in the Governor's company alone.

'And more than receptive to my plans for a new fort. The place just beyond Tegnapatam. Such a site, Catherine. Commands the whole area. One day we shall have it. Name it afresh for St. David. In honour of Wales.'

'I imagine Gyfford must have been less than enthusiastic about those false rumours.'

'Great heavens, must you ruin everything? It was not my duty to check the veracity of the intelligence – simply to report it.'

He had done so. Intelligence gathered, it seems, from three Dutch merchants, each very much in his cups. News from England, they had claimed. One story that the Catholic Duke of York, heir to the throne, was in Scotland with an army of forty thousand, and engaged in yet another civil war at home. The second, that the Portuguese had mustered an enormous force at Goa and were just about to march upon us, murder us all in our beds.

'No,' I said. 'Checking the veracity was William Gyfford's duty. But he failed to do so. Instead, the first rumour had us almost at each other's throats. Civil war between whom? It seemed not to matter, for our bold Cavalier faction, your friends, Seaton at their head, simply came out swearing blind allegiance to popish James and demanding that all others did the same.'

'Seaton again! I am certain, Catherine, that it cannot have been as black as you paint it. Besides, I am part of no faction, as you well know. And I shall brook no criticism of the Governor. He is an able man. Trusted me with this expedition.'

'You did not see him when he thought us under threat from the Portuguese. I have never seen a man in such a state of perturbation. Orders. Counter-orders. Panic everywhere.'

'And you will now tell me it was Parrish who saved us from this confusion.'

'It took him a week, no more, to make sure we had the very latest news from Goa and from England too. There was no way your Hollander borachios could have been in possession of anything more recent.'

Matthew had merely smiled when I suggested he might have deliberately sown the rumours, for he had certainly risen once more in everybody's estimation by the speedy way he had brought sanity back to Fort St. George.

'Well, curse the fellow. Took some of the shine from my own success. And what a month, Catherine. You can hardly imagine.'

But I could, the tale already told to me several times over. His success, in the end, in finally meeting Shivaji's Commander for Gingee – Sambhaji's man, now – the Raja Harjee, despite the obfuscations by the Raja's Counsellor, his *pandit*, Gopal, Subidar of Porto Novo, himself fabulously wealthy. Endless negotiating ploys and delays, bartering for *pishcash*, Elihu eventually sent on to Trinomalee, accompanied by many horsemen.

'Trinomalee sounds like a great wonder,' I said.

'The houses in the town are mean enough. All thatched huts. Yet the setting, upon the Annamalai foothills. Astonishing. At a great crossroads too. Remarkable temples. But even there that fellow Gopal made great mischief. Caused delays. Until, in the end, there was a great procession. A week ago now. To the Raja's *durbar*, his state reception rooms. And there they made us wait half an hour in the intolerable heat of the audience hall. Incredible place, decorated throughout with verses of the Alcoran. Carved into the walls. And left there, even though the Mussulmen no longer rule in Gingee. Then the Raja's grand entrance. At the farther side of the room, three alcoves, each with gilded doors. A great fanfare as the central alcove opened, and there sat a figure upon some manner of throne. Yet only in silhouette. For behind him was a window, in the Moorish style, and beyond the window, the sun, its rays shining directly into my eyes.'

'The Gentues and Moors are very adept at these things.'

'Well, there was the problem. I had come to do business with the fellow, to trade honourably, yet he professed to need nothing from us. Why, the damn'd fellow all but accused me of arrogance. The poor interpreter had to explain it over and over again, the Raja insisting we possessed nothing of value. Except, he finally admitted, the horse.'

I could not bring myself to also remind him that the Arab stallion had been Matthew's suggestion, too.

'The beast must have looked very fine,' I said. 'Silver bridle, was it not?'

'And scarlet laced saddlecloth. He allowed the horse to be brought right into the audience hall, among all the other *pishcash*. The broadcloth. Those elegant scimitars and rapiers. All the gold.'

'Yet only the stallion had value. Perhaps there is some lesson for us here.'

'I don't follow you, my dear. Still, the very next day we had an agreement. John Company settlements, houses and godowns, at Porto Novo, Cuddalore and Conimere. Favourable customs arrangements for our merchants. Though I still needed my wits about me, for when the written document arrived, Gopal Pandit had tried to inveigle extra clauses into the deal. The rogue.'

'Inscrutable, perhaps,' I said. 'It would serve John Company well, at times, to remember that the people of these lands have been masters of trade and commerce for countless centuries. I suppose the Raja is correct, they need nothing from us.'

'Yet you would not believe the things I have seen on my travels, Catherine. In one village, a man impaled, the spike pushed up through his nether regions and emerging at his shoulder.' I shuddered at the cruel image. 'Ten days a-dying, they said. Left there as a warning against any others tempted to steal from their masters. In another village, when they received us, half the men in the room with their noses missing. Men taken captive, punished that way, after the recent battles between Shivaji and the Khan of Golconda.'

I could not be troubled to remind him of the stories we had all heard, as children, about atrocities committed during our own civil wars. Cautionary lessons about the barbarity of our enemies.

'Well, you are home again now. And all this acclaim. The agreement you brought back. A twenty-one gun salute in its honour, then eleven guns for Elihu Yale himself. All those speeches. And here you are, husband, just nine years from your arrival as a humble writer.'

Sarcasm, of course, though he seemed not to notice.

'The agreement is important. Breaks our dependency on Lingappa and the Golconda Mahometans. Gives us three excellent additional bases around Porto Novo. And the ships still here. The *Golden Fleece*, at least. No need to send that copy of my will now, I collect, and just time to amend my letter to Thomas.'

'Then perhaps you might furnish your family with one additional piece of news, Elihu. You can tell them, hopefully with equal pride, first, about your negotiating prowess and, second, that you are soon to be a father.'

'But the baby?' he said to me, wringing the periwig between his hands.

'Gone,' I whispered, and stared up at the ceiling of my bedchamber, felt the cool draft of the *pankah* wafting down upon the bed.

Tears began to pour across his cheeks, that florid face, to the corners of his mouth.

Another, I thought, *that you have failed to save or protect.*

'Yet everything so...'

'Clean?'

First Mistress Crouch, then Sathiri, and finally Tanani, had ensured that all trace of the filth, the mess, the stench was all scoured from the room, the straw all removed, along with the linen and the tiny bloodied ruin.

'It is not right,' the *ayah* had insisted, 'for the *sahib* to see such things.'

No, of course not. Perish the thought that my husband should be so incommoded, witness the evidence of my agonies.

'Yes, clean,' Elihu sobbed. 'But did you not know?'

'I had pains. Awful pains. I sent for Mistress Crouch. Hot poultice for my belly. But then the bleeding began. It would not stop.'

'A boy?'

'There was no way to know.'

'You sent for the Chaplain?'

'It all happened too soon.'

'Then not baptised.'

'Elihu, yesterday I inhabited one world. The world in which both myself and that half-Portuguese chit, Katherine Nicks, each shared the same gift of life. But now I am exiled from that world. Expelled. As my baby has been expelled.'

'But if the child was not baptised, has no name, what will happen to its soul now? Its body?'

'You would have rather it been baptised as happens to others untimely delivered? Miscarried? Listed simply as "Creature" in the parish records because no other name has been agreed?'

'There will be a burial though.'

'A burial, yes. But no stone, Elihu. I will have no stone that does not bear the infant's name.'

'Might it have been my fault? Somehow?'

'Weakness of seed?' I murmured. 'How shall we know?'

Sathiri certainly did not believe so. More likely an inadequacy of nourishment, she had said. Some other flaw. Yet it must all be part of God's plan, must it not?

'Oh, my dear. Such a grievous loss. And am I cursed? I still hear the cries of that other babe. In my head, at night. And I know you must do the same, for you sometimes call to him in the darkness. Do you hold me culpable perhaps? And for this loss also?'

'You have told nobody, about Walt?'

'With whom should I share such a thing? But do you? Blame me?'

I turned my head away, unable to respond, and my silence must have been a dreadful thing.

Yes, I thought. And worse because, to please Elihu, we had hurriedly arranged passage for little Rich to sail for England aboard the *Golden Fleece*, along with Elihu's letter to his brother Thomas. The same letter that will soon deliver the glad tidings to the Yales of my pregnancy, the expectation of that new family member – the infant none of us shall ever know.

I had the collection of Mama's letters scattered before me on the writing slope. So many of them stained with tears. That one, of course, which arrived in the summer of seventy-six, dated January that year. Her grief at hearing the news of Walt's birth and death both at the same time.

And now, this one.

My poor dear child, how this separation is itself an agony. And I think about all of us, in this community we share. English and Scot, Dutch and Portuguese, Swede and French. Merchant traders and our families, so many thousands, split asunder by the endless waters of the Atlantic, the Mediterranean, the Baltic, the Indian Ocean and the South China Seas, as we risk our own modest rewards and pay the price of our lonely tragedies while we smoothe the passage of commerce and create the wealth of our nations.

And such tragedies. Poor Joseph. How dearly I loved that young man and how cruel his death. You must know that I embrace your memory and pray each night and morning for God to bring you some peace. I have broken the news to the boy, of course, as you asked. But he has taken it badly, neglects his studies – though your Papa has endless patience with him and assures me it will pass. Yet I have not thus far told your son about Mister Yale. It seemed that this might be too much for him to digest just now. I penned the note to Joseph's brother and sister, however, as you requested. A few words only, promising that you will write to them yourself in due course. Again, no mention of Mister Yale. Though I believe you have made a wise decision. We have each made enquiries about the family and it seems a worthy match. Enterprising and generally steadfast are the words most bandied about the coffee house in their connection, even though Mister Yale himself would have been too young when he sailed for India to make much impression here. Still, I imagine there will be some among your acquaintances at Fort St. George who must have looked askance at the paucity of your mourning.

Some? Great heavens, if only she knew!

And normally a longer period of widows' weeds would, of course, have been proper. All the same, as I have told you many times, the right thing is rarely enough in itself.

There are more words of intended comfort, gentle news of the family and Papa's various shortcomings, some indication that he has the wander-lust once more. Dreams of a return to his business in Alicante. A longing for the sun and the palm orchards of neighbouring Elche. Then, inevitably, the latest political intelligence from England.

The pot still boils, she writes. *The Exclusion Bill rejected by the Lords and our poor country therefore one step closer to being ruled once more by the Church of Rome. But we went to Tyburn, your father and I, to see Plunkett hanged, drawn and quartered.*

'Elihu,' I shouted. 'Plunkett. You must remind me.'

'Oliver Plunkett?' he replied, from below. 'Does your Mama send word of him? I was talking to Seaton about it only yesterday. The Primate of All Ireland, my dear. And Seaton says falsely convicted of treason. More mischief from those that claim a Popish Plot.'

Well, Seaton would say so, would he not? But at least I no longer have to look upon his miserable face, for Matthew Parrish has once again used his considerable skills to our advantage. The factory at Masulipatnam has been in need of a new Chief and, though Seaton was not immediately the obvious candidate, Matthew had quietly persuaded Governor Gyfford that Vincent should be given the opportunity and, such being Matthew's standing here now, Council carried that very decision. There is the danger, of course, that Seaton has today simply taken his mischief north with him but, personally, I think it worth the risk to remove such a strong supporter of the Cavalier faction – the Tories, as Matthew is now wont to call them – from Fort St. George.

'Can we be certain?' I said. 'That the conviction was false?'

Yet I was thinking about the punishment. Hanged, drawn and quartered. That most barbaric form of execution. And recalling Elihu's horror at the impalement he had seen and wondering at our ability, Englishman and Gentue alike, to inflict such cruelties one upon the other.

'I could not,' my husband cried, 'be certain of anything that happens in England any more. But did you hear, my dear, that the king has issued a warrant for the building of a new Royal Hospital? Chelsea, they say. For the care of his wounded or retired soldiers and loyal servants. Great minds thinking alike, do you not collect?'

I set the letters aside and made my way down to the withdrawing room, where Elihu was busy with his own correspondence, a scarlet *banyan* hanging loose over his nightgown.

'Good heavens,' I said. 'This clutter.'

'A few items I brought back from Gingee. I will have them stored in the godown, but I thought you might like to see.' They were elegant enough: an ebony *escritoire* inlaid with ivory; a satin quilt wrought with gold threads; an elegant japanned screen; and a large silver-gilt trencher. 'I purchased the trencher from some Portuguese, down on his luck and selling off all he possessed. Poor fellow. Made in Lisbon though and worth a fortune, I think.'

'And they are for this house? Or for the garden house we so unscrupulously purchased from the Bridgers?'

When the *Resolution* arrived in July, inevitably it brought instructions for John Bridger's dismissal. Allegations of illicit trading in diamonds and pearls. Also of dealings with an interloper. Seaton's handiwork, naturally. And poor Matthew, dispatched with some of his men to sequester John's books, everything that might have been the Company's property. They are still here, of course, the Bridgers. But now almost the status of interlopers themselves.

'Neither, sirrah. And these accusations of unscrupulous dealings – they simply will not serve, Catherine. The screen there, I am sending to Edisbury's wife. You remember Edisbury? That fellow building the new hall neighbouring Plas Grono. He plans to name it Erddig House, or something of the kind. He gifted me the Sandpatch Ale. Yes, him. I am just penning a note of thanks. Somewhat belated, perhaps. But I shall send him a case of chutney too. Keep the neighbours sweet, don't you think?'

He smiled, amused as always by his own wit. Another clench to be proud of.

'You are become a collector of fine goods then?' I said.

'Another form of investment for our futures, my dear. Some better compensation for our efforts, our losses, if we are not able to trade in brilliants.'

'And who has put that thought in your head, Elihu? Mistress Nicks again?'

'She has a fine head for commerce.'

A fine figure for other forms of enterprise too, I decided. Though compensation for our losses? What did he intend? The loss of our little one?

'A fine head,' I sneered, 'for ways to spend the wealth left to us by poor Joseph.' I enjoyed reminding him, at times, how much he owed to that inheritance.

'There will be precious little of that wealth left in any case if we continue spending so much on dispatching your boys back to London.'

'Yet my mother has again sent us more in goods than the value of Richard's passage. So fear not, husband, your account is still in profit.'

'Goods? I suppose I should be grateful to her. Twelve pairs of silk stockings. Twenty yards of satin. Another forty pounds of tobacco. Three cases of Alicante. And an entire chest of reading pipes. Well, there is nothing else for it. If that is the extent of your ambition for profit, Catherine, I suppose I must needs take up smoking the weed.'

The babe was born on the fifteenth day of May. A Tuesday, and the easiest of births, the little fellow strong and healthy. We have named him David, for Elihu's father, though I have taken to calling him Dormouse, a foolish nickname though he reminds me so much of that creature – that high-pitched whistling noise he makes when he sleeps.

Soon afterwards, my husband was promoted to Second in Council and that, in turn, led to his appointment as Acting Governor when Agent Gyfford left Fort St. George to undertake a tour of inspection around our Bay of Bengal factories. We had been singularly honoured, Madras named as a Presidency, as it had once been before, for a short while during the fifties. So, shared sovereignty with the Crown – presumably a chance for the Crown to squeeze further garnish from John Company. And Gyfford our first President.

'You see how far we are come, Catherine,' Elihu had said upon the day Gyfford sallied forth. 'Acting Governor. Acting President too, therefore, I suppose. Just one short step from the top. And poor Gyfford's health far from robust. So much to be done. Everything here too lax. Duties to be levied at long last in Black Town. The heathens have all ridden too long upon our coat tails without paying their way. The sea walls to be repaired. The hospital to be completed. All a drain on the Company's coffers.'

All talk, of course. Or so says Matthew. Elihu outstanding at writing new rules but no Solomon in their implementation. Months of negotiations on tax levels with Black Town's Moors, Gentues and Jews while, at their end, a settlement that has brought no real income and serves only to anger and irritate those required to pay the few *fanams* in house duty each year. And the sea walls dangerously still little better than they have been this long while past.

It was this matter of taxes, too, which dominated much of the discussion over the food served at a grand reception held in the Company's Garden House a couple of weeks after Elihu became Deputy Governor. A celebration to welcome one of our recent new arrivals, the old Jewish Portuguese merchant, Jacques de Paiva. Portuguese descent, like all the other Paradesi but, according to Matthew, his family had followed the diamond trade back to Amsterdam where he had been born, adopted the name Jacques, Matthew surmised, when he began trading with London – at a time when a French first name would have been entirely more acceptable than Portuguese, Dutch or, heaven forfend, Hebrew.

'You must appreciate, *senhor*,' he said, 'that you will not persuade my people to assist you in this enterprise if we are to be heavily taxed as our reward.'

The Garden House has become the regular venue for our Fort St. George festivities – last November a peace agreement with the Sultan of Golconda, another to end hostilities with Lingappa Naik, or our gala days to mark the king's birthday, Christmas, Easter and St. George's Day. It continues to benefit from extension and improvement, almost unrecognisable in its grandeur since those early days, the earthquake, and my gathering of the *yettikottai* seeds.

'I fear, sirrah,' Elihu replied, 'that the Jews of Black Town have rarely paid any taxation for the privilege of trading and living here. And most of them interlopers too.'

The servants were moving among us, replenishing our copper eating bowls with fresh helpings of dumpoked antelope, hare and partridge, mango and *achar* or, in honour of the de Paivas, Portuguese salt cod, *bacalhau*, with tomato and peppers. The colours glorious, reds and greens, saffron yellow, and the smells of their spices, the cumin and garlic, the *neyi*-fried onion.

'A difficult concept, is it not?' de Paiva laughed. 'The Paradesi, after all, have been here more than a hundred years. Arrived here from Spain and Portugal, from our Sefardi homelands, to avoid the persecution of the Alhambra Decree. The Gentues and Moors welcome us here, value the trade we bring with Amsterdam, Paris and London. Then along come the English – and call *us* interlopers. Though, naturally, they tolerate our interloping because we help your Company's representatives make such attractive personal fortunes for themselves. Diamonds. Until, of course, John Company decides to keep the diamond trade for itself, prohibits private fortunes to be made that way. And then – ah, now the Jews must pay their taxes.'

'And you forget, *senhor* Yale,' said the fellow's wife, also Portuguese, also Jewish, naturally – so young that I had, at first, taken her for his daughter, 'that my husband has this authority from your Directors. To help promote the Company's official trade in brilliants. That promotion will be easier if my husband is accepted as leader of the Paradesi community here. Perhaps this question of taxes could be – reviewed, let us say. Through my husband's good offices?'

I watched as Katherine Nicks appraised *senhora* de Paiva, Jeronima. They are perhaps of similar age, their complexion similar too, though Jeronima as exotically elegant as Katherine is plain. And the drab's second pregnancy has added no bloom to her features. But there was one thing in which they were perfectly matched – the way in which they each hung upon Elihu's every word. Adoration. Something to do with his name, perhaps. Oh, I know its meaning well enough. Elihu. My God is He. His parents had named him thus and thus he saw himself endowed. It seems that Katherine Nicks and Jeronima de Paiva might see it also.

'I think you will find, *senhora*,' he said, barely able to contain the smile that, I knew, would herald another attempt at an amusing quibble, 'that we have turned Fort St. George into a veritable merchants' *paradesi* too.' He waited for a response but received none and hurried on. 'Our new and flourishing Madras Bank, for example.'

'And a curb on the slave trade,' Jacques de Paiva insisted. 'So import-ant, do you not think? It was good to hear that your Governor Gyfford has made the trade punishable at last.'

'Though its significance,' said John Nicks, now Acting Second, 'perhaps a little overstated. The trade, after all, only really affects those displaced or become prisoners in these endless conflicts between Mughal and Maratha.'

'All the same,' Matthew Parrish told him, 'an abominable practice. Such an honourable thing that President Gyfford has taken steps to prohibit its infamies.'

Neither of us with any real respect for Gyfford. But this, at least, was a progressive action. And difficult for him since no sooner was his new rule established than the Council received instruction from the Directors, from Josiah Childe in person, on behalf of the king. His Majesty required Fort St. George to send him one male and two female Blacks, Gentue or Moor, it did not seem to matter. But they must be dwarfs, very young, no more than children really, and in good looks as well as small of stature. In fact, as small as possible – as though we had a surfeit of young, dwarf Gentues from which to select. Still, Elihu had managed to comply with the instruction, seemed to relish the challenge, and had arranged passage for the diminutive and exotic replacements for the king's recently deceased Lord Minimus. We had argued about the morality of all this, Elihu and I, but I had been forced to accept that an edict from King Charles the Second could hardly be ignored, even if I had no time for Old Rowley himself – as the wags still style him – or his Stuart kin.

'Well there, it is done,' my husband snapped at Matthew. 'And myself responsible for the Court of Admiralty that will hear future allegations of slave-trading.'

'And the taxes?' Jacques de Paiva reminded him.

'Very well.' Elihu was exasperated now. 'We can discuss the taxes. Now, let me see if the *panch* is ready.'

He offered our guests a bow and wandered off to mingle around the room, while *senhor* de Paiva excused us both and took me gently by the arm, leading me out to the *veranda*.

'I understand,' he said, 'that you have more than a passing interest in the diamond trade yourself, Mistress Yale. Antonio is a colleague. The rough stones you purchased through him were processed by our joint syndicate. So you see, my dear, we are almost partners.'

'Particularly since my husband is now Deputy Governor, responsible for the Company's diamond trade, and yourself the expert they have sent to assist in that regards. I collect that, yes, you may be right.'

Jacques de Paiva laughed.

'You know,' he said, 'that I was allowed to bring with me only one manservant. One maid, too – though the Company insisted she must be a Christian. Simply one Jewish servant for Jeronima. No more. Even then I had to pay all those costs myself. So while I may be prepared to fulfill my obligations to the Company, it will not be without providing a dividend for my own efforts. And my efforts, I can assure you, will be extensive.'

'You must forgive me, but I do not understand why you feel it necessary to tell me this.'

'Only this, *senhora* Yale. That we have a mutual friend in Matthew Parrish.'

'What does he mean, Matthew?' I asked him later, while the Fort St. George musicians entertained the reception's other guests.

'Let me ask you, Catherine. What has this place felt like since the *Beaufort* brought us the dispatches?'

'Everybody at each other's throats, you mean? Even worse than usual. There have been times I thought it would spill over into real violence.'

Last year, the king and his Catholic brother, James, Duke of York, had been travelling from Westminster to Newmarket for the racing. But a fire had destroyed half the town, the races cancelled, and the royal party returned early to London. Just as well, since it seems that a bunch of assassins had planned to wait at Rye House, on the route, and there to kill both the king and his popish heir. Their early return had thwarted the plot and the repercussions would be terrible, Lord Russell already beheaded. Algernon Sidney too. And dozens more awaiting either trial or punishment. Anybody even vaguely associated as opponents of the Cavalier monarchist faction immediately under suspicion. It might have been a long way from Fort St. George but the madness spilling over here as soon as the royal declaration arrived with details of the plot's heinous nature.

'I read the account of Russell's execution. That creature, Ketch, hacked him about so badly, yet none of the blows ending the poor fellow's misery until the very end. Deliberate, they say. And so many caught up in this so-called plot. The Monmouth Cabal, they name it, all fingers pointing at Monmouth himself, blaming him in his exile for the conspiracy. But perhaps an excuse to dispose of any they consider dangerous Dissenters. Many merchants among the accused, my dear. Will your father be safe?'

It was a constant concern, for I knew how frequently my father's outspoken opinions had landed him in trouble.

'Mama makes only passing reference to it. As though she is fearful of what she writes.'

'You once said, Catherine, that you would now only plot for your boys. Does this not change things?'

'Far from it. I now have five of them to consider.'

'Has their number not helped assuage your melancholy?'

'If anything, it makes it worse. Sathiri's *soma* helps, of course. But Walter's death simply highlights the vulnerability of the others. Two of them now in London, beyond my daily protection.'

'And their futures, my dear. Does it not trouble you, the world in which they will grow?'

'You know that it must. But does any of this relate to Jacques de Paiva?'

He sighed, rubbed his hand across his forehead.

'He has been making careful approaches to the Sultan of Golconda. He intends to purchase several of the diamond mines for his own syndicate. But with the backing of several very prominent individuals in England. Prominent, Catherine. They are interested in an extremely long-term investment, a political investment. You follow my meaning?'

'They say that last winter in London was the coldest in living memory. The Thames frozen solid. The Frost Fair. It seems to me that our poor nation must now be facing a lengthy winter in its government too.'

'But you are also thinking that even the worst of winters must always turn to spring. You are correct, of course. Though, in this case, the climate shall only change if it receives some substantial assistance. Finance, my dear. Finance.'

'*Senhor* de Paiva will officially be working with Elihu, the diamond trade for the Company. But at the same time raising funds for the Monmouth Cabal? And you want me to spy upon my husband on behalf of the Duke of Monmouth?'

'I wish that life were so simple. But those to whom I answer are more important than Monmouth. You know as well as I do that the king's bastard son can never rule. But there are others who might. No, do not press the issue, it is a long story.'

'Do not press the issue, sirrah? I think you owe me better than that, Mister Parrish.'

'A long story and one about which I am less than certain myself. Perhaps clear in time. Though perhaps not. Yet there are men of great substance who believe your political spring is truly possible. And some of those men are also among the Company's shareholders. A minority for now, yet prominent all the same. They all have an interest in *senhor* de Paiva's success. Concerned that there are others here involving themselves in the diamond trade who might interfere with his business. They need to be watched, Catherine. And carefully.'

'Katherine Nicks?'

'Of course. And her husband. It seems that Nicks may not be quite the harmless little scrub after all. Seaton too, of course. He may be at Masulipatnam, but he is still a serious threat.'

The scaffold had been erected outside the Choultry Gate and, at the appointed hour on that September morning, the three guilty men were led out to their execution. Three Mahometans who had hacked to pieces a fourth, a man caught in adultery with a wife of their family. Nobody seemed to either know or care about the fate of the woman, though there were ugly rumours. Yet the killers of the adulterer had been arrested, tried by a jury of six fellows from White Town and six from Black Town's Mussulmen. A sentence of death by hanging, and Elihu insisting that the executions be overseen by Matthew Parrish.

'Damn'd fellow seems to think he should be above such things,' said my husband, when we were all gathered, at his instruction, the boys too, to see justice done. As always with these occasions, it had all the clamour of a feast day: the press of bodies; the mingled scents of garlic, sweat and cooking oils; the street vendor cries above the soldiers' drumming; and the rainbow hues of *sarees*, turbans and uniform coats.

'I believe,' I replied, 'that he simply understands the regulations to require that executions should be carried out under the auspices of the Governor's bodyguard. He is, after all, more merchant than soldier.'

'You would not think so from all his swagger. More braggadocio than merchant, rather. He barely understands the meaning of the word. I wonder that the Directors have never taken steps against him.'

The three murderers were being dragged up the scaffold's steps by Matthew's corporals, two of those about to die stoical and resigned to their fate but the third wailing pitifully. I could not understand all his words but, in the main, protestations about his innocence, exhortations to Allah for his safe deliverance.

'Tanani,' I said, 'please cover the boys' eyes. They should not see this.' But it was an impossible task. At the ages of eight and six respectively, Elford and Benjamin have insatiable curiosities, wriggled to escape the *ayah*'s grip, intent on seeing every detail.

'The young scoundrels.' Elihu laughed. 'But they need to understand the ways of the world, my dear.'

'The ways of the world? I imagine that Seaton and others must be truly frustrated that the poison they have spread about Matthew has brought such little reward.'

'This obsession with poor Vincent, Catherine. Preposterous. Such fancies, my dear. Oh, Lord, look at the jig that fellow's dancing.'

The noose about his neck and the drop from the scaffold had cut short his weeping, but he was choking slowly while his body thrashed violently at the end of the rope.

'Are you certain you judged him correctly?' I asked.

'There was less evidence against him than the other two, but I believed they were all equally culpable in the eyes of God.'

'Then this is a wicked cruelty if the evidence was weak. Whereas Vincent Seaton is a man whose guilt is established, I collect, beyond doubt. His false witness against Streynsham Master. Against John Bridger. And against Matthew?' Simply a sigh of frustration from Elihu by way of response. 'I dread to think what lies he may have told. Or have your duties as Deputy Governor closed your ears to the whisperings? The fingers being pointed at any with even imaginary links to the merchant families and others involved with this Rye House Plot. Sheppard, the wine merchant. My father was an associate of his. Katherine Nicks had the temerity to ask me about it only yesterday.'

'You are the wife of the Deputy Governor, Catherine. Caesar's wife. Above suspicion.'

'I note that your defence of Seaton did not last too long.'

The two stoical fellows were now motionless, presumed dead. But the third was still flailing about, the crowd jeering at his discomfort, and I saw Matthew walk towards him, wrap his arms around the jerking legs, pull them sharply down to end his suffering, despite the onlookers' protests.

'You see, my dear. A weak fellow, that Parrish. But Seaton? He is, as you have gathered, a political creature. Yet he will not trouble you.

While I, for my own part, am more concerned with our enterprise. Now, my own godown. The beginning of our fortune. Some fine furnishings that I mean to return to England for storage there. And our trade in diamonds may be restricted, but I have made some interesting purchases of sapphires, rubies, coral and pearl. Neck-cloths, naturally. Spices too. Cloves, cinnamon and nutmeg. Dried poppy seeds, once we have extracted the opium jelly. Great heavens, how indebted I am to Thomas for making that connection.'

'Your brother is an astute young man.' Thomas passed through here on his way to Siam last July, and then on his return journey to England in January, their mission to open up trade with the king of that country a total disaster, due to the hotheaded nature of the fool sent to lead the mission, one William Strang. 'Yet,' I said, 'is there truly a market in England for opium? I thought it only finds favour with Persians and among certain castes of the Gentues.'

'Apothecary Sydenham is apparently keen to purchase every ounce we can send him for his laudanum elixir. My dear, I shall soon be a merchant prince. As rich as Virji Vora. I met him once, you know? That first journey to Gingee.'

Another legend. Dead these past ten years but still renowned as the wealthiest merchant in India.

'That is a considerable ambition, husband.'

The crowd had begun to drift apart, a palpable sense of disappointment that their entertainment had been cut so short so soon. Elihu issued some final instructions to members of his bodyguard and led the children, the servants and myself back to the house.

'You were saying, my dear? Ah, ambition. Not ambition at all. God Almighty has given me this gift, to make great wealth – how could I not use it? But it is the pursuit of wealth, the chase, rather than its mere accumulation that counts.'

I know it, of course, for it is the very essence of the merchant adventurer's existence, this trade across the sea routes of the world. But I know also that it can be a perilous master.

'That pursuit, I think, may sometimes leave us eyeless in Gaza, sirrah, slaves to ambition whether we intend it or not, blind to our true needs.'

'The chase indeed may require us to steer a careful course between the Scylla of greed and the Charybdis of selfish envy. Though it is a course that the Almighty has mapped for me.'

'And that first journey to Gingee, that was part of the chase?'

'Why do you ask?'

'I recall that the old Khan, before Shivaji's Marathas conquered the place – well, they say he had a taste for young men. I always wondered, Elihu, whether...'

'Wait. Did Governor Langhorn have that in mind when he dispatched me there? He did. I can see it in your face. You knew about this?'

'My dear,' I said, 'everybody knew. Everybody from Mistress Bridger upwards.'

'Mistress Bridger? So I was the entire town's bubble.'

'That is a harsh way to put it.' Yet I recalled how amused we had all been, the knowing glances exchanged upon his return.

'Harsh? Did you not think it cruel to practise so upon a fellow?'

I gestured back towards the scaffold.

'The world is full of cruelties, Elihu. The way of the world, did you not say? And you seem to have survived your experience at Gingee without undue harm.'

'You think so? Then you do not understand me very well, my dear. I survived at Gingee because I learned my trade quickly here in India. Oh, Gopal Pandit may have polished my virtues. But I took with me a comprehension that this is the land of the *"no sahib, sorry sahib"* one day, the bobbing of the head to politely terminate the negotiations. Then, the next day, the excuse to meet again on some other pretext, waiting perhaps for better terms to be suggested. Regardless of the gossip, those were the talents I deployed at Gingee and no others. Sadly, however, I was not so skilled as a boy. At St. Paul's. It was common enough, but...'

'You mean – at your school? You were... How is that possible?'

'Every office and establishment has two faces, Catherine. Did you not know? The honest politician and the corrupt. The pure priest and the sullied. The teacher dedicated to learning and the other, the predator, dedicated only to lessons in his own lust.'

When I look back now at my earlier volume, I can see it, of course. When Elihu had first been a guest in my house. How he had mentioned his time at Dugard's School and then a shadow passing across his eyes when he mentioned later being sent to St. Paul's.

'I had no idea,' I murmured.

'Why should you? And best not to dwell upon these things.'

Yet it was impossible not to do so. The most awful images filled my mind, and I thought about the boys, Joseph and Richard, now at Turberville's. Not such an establishment, surely. And Schoolmaster Ord, here at Fort St. George. He has been a friend this long while, yet what do I know about him really? Not a great deal. An amiable fellow, though solitary. I shuddered. Surely...

'You are correct, husband. Best not to dwell upon the matter.'

Two days ago, and a great tempest fell upon us from the northwest without warning. First there had been the rising sea, the highest of tides, with the crash of huge waves thundering against the sea wall. Then the wind, building steadily, minute by minute, from the hills inland, the sky blackening, growing dark as night, in the wake of which came the first debris, the palm fronds, tree branches, roofing thatch, all blown in from Black Town beyond the northern wall. Finally, the drowning, driven rain, great gobbets of water that hammered upon our walls and window screens.

'Tanani!' I screamed. 'Gather the boys.'

I thanked heaven that Joseph had possessed the foresight to purchase one of the properties with a cellar. For his wines, of course, though we had frequently talked about how it might one day provide us with a sanctuary. But then Tanani ran from the back of the house, baby David tight in her arms.

'Memsahib,' she cried. 'They have gone with Akbar to see the boats come in.'

The fishing boats. I had forgotten, and panic gripped me.

'To the sea wall?' I could think of no worse place to be. They had required proper attention for several years but received only cosmetical repair. Each storm made them worse. 'If my husband comes back,' I shouted, 'tell him, Tanani.'

I was down the *veranda* steps in a trice though, in those few moments, the gale had ripped the cap from my head, the rain plastering skirts and bodice to my body. Difficult to run, and the ground already a swamp, sucking the slippers from my feet. But I pressed on, barefooted, to the Sea Gate, praying that the boys would be safe.

There! Upon the steps to the gatehouse battlements at the very place where the stonework was most damaged, Elford pressed into a recess within the wall but no sign of Benjamin. Though I could just discern Akbar atop the crumbling, windswept masonry and struggling with something just beyond view, for there was sea spray, the ravenous waves pounding every few seconds and sending fountains of foam high into the angry sky. I screamed and Akbar glanced back at me, fear burnished upon his face.

'Help, *memsahib*!' he mouthed. 'Bring help!'

But where were the sentries? Their posts abandoned. I was on the stairway now, turned frantically to see if there was help at hand, and then Elihu was pushing past, knocking me aside, racing to the rescue. Around me the hurricane howled, the downpour having soaked every inch of my skin, chunks of shattered timbers slamming against the walls, and the gale's violence carrying the stench of decay. Yet here came my husband, carrying Benjamin, bent against the wind while I gathered Elford from his refuge.

'Akbar?' I shouted, for I could not see him.

'I took the boy's arm,' Elihu yelled. 'Stopped him from falling. But Akbar slipped. Or washed away. I am not sure which, though gone, my dear. We will send a search party, as soon as we are able.'

Two days ago, and we still count the cost, yesterday's anniversary of my marriage to Elihu, four years ago, passing unnoticed. Akbar one of many whose lives were lost, and no time for recriminations. We have not found him, poor dear man, and I was only grateful to our Lord Jesus that he has spared my boys this time. And, suddenly, here we are. The fifth day of November. Gunpowder Treason Day. Fireworks. No burnings of pope effigies this year – Gyfford having imposed a prohibition on the practice – but the great guns fired. A supper to celebrate our deliverance both from the diabolical schemes of Guido Fawkes and from the hurricane too: despite the deaths; despite the destruction of so many dwellings in Black Town and White Town alike; despite the devastation of a dozen or more fishing boats and *musolas*; despite the demolition of two godowns and the loss of all their stock; and despite the ruin of every furnace and boiler employed in the cleaning or processing of our broadcloth. A value of many thousands of pagodas in damage. And the Company's coffers at Fort St. George almost empty. But Elihu stepping into this other breach, an offer to loan the necessary gold from his own accumulating fortune. Agreed rates of interest, naturally. But still, I wonder. Perhaps time to reconsider. Perhaps I may have misjudged Mister Yale, just as that poor Mussulman was misjudged by him.

'The King is dead! Long live the King!'

We could hear the young naval lieutenant bellowing above the roar of the breakers even as the *musola* surf boats brought his small party ashore to the wrack-strewn high water line, now almost at the foot of the sea wall. The masonry was substantially repaired, though there remained scores of peons laboring upon its upper levels – yet all work stopped as they leaned on mattock and pick, sweat gleaming on their dark, near-naked bodies, to watch the arrivals.

A frigate-built vessel of His Majesty's Royal Navy away in the distance. The advantage of Presidency, of course. Shared sovereignty between Crown and Company – that naval ships are now so frequently anchored in the roads of Madras Patnam, and lending us the illusion at least of added protection.

My own new arrival had just been fed and left in Tanani's care, though she has caused fresh difficulties between Elihu and myself. Born just ten days ago, and a difficult delivery, but she is well and I was churched this Sunday gone. Yet it is the naming that has aroused such passions between us and I did not feel sufficiently strong, finally, to resist him. Indeed, if I had known it would cause such problems, I should probably have resisted him on that same Gunpowder Treason Day last November when, in my new-found admiration for him, I allowed the conception. Still, it is done and my little girl is beautiful. But Katherine! He tried to insist that it is in my own honour, though he was very peculiar about the way it should be spelled. And there is no other in either of our families.

'In your honour,' he said, 'yet avoiding confusion. On legal documents and such.'

'In my honour, Elihu?' I retorted. 'Or that of your business partner? She may be married to Nicks, but a drab she remains. And I see the way she regards you whenever she attends your little gatherings.'

I must be honest here. For I have begun to feel some envy. And not only towards that harlot, Mistress Nicks, but also towards the pretty young wife of Jacques de Paiva. We invited them for Christmas dinner, despite some comments from certain elements among the other women, deriding them as Christ-killers. So the meal had lacked its normal significance for us but, worse, Jeronima had regarded Elihu with such open admiration throughout the whole affair.

Still, that is not the content I intended for this entry, for that young lieutenant came ashore several days ago, bringing his earth-shattering news. And bringing too a whole batch of copies of the *London Gazette*. The edition dated Monday 9th February 1684/5 and the bulletin on the front side, written the previous Friday.

On Monday last in the morning, our late Gracious Sovereign King Charles the Second was seized with a violent fit, by which his speech and senses were for some time taken from him, but upon the immediate application of fitting remedies he returned to such a condition as gave some hopes of his recovery till Wednesday night, at which time the disease returning upon him with greater violence. He expired this day about noon.

'Fitting remedies!' Elihu had smiled, despite himself, when we read it alone again, together, that evening. 'His Majesty has a violent fit, and they give him fitting remedies. Is that a clinch, do you think?'

'It is no laughing matter, surely. The consequence...'

The new monarch had been proclaimed that same afternoon, the sixth day of February, at Whitehall Gate, at Temple Bar and at the Royal Exchange.

God save King James the Second.

'The consequence, my dear, is that we must now organise a great celebration. We are required to do so, and the Governor is hardly in ample condition to perform the duty. So it shall fall to me. And a crowning glory, I trust, to all our achievements throughout the rest of the year.'

In January, Elihu – then still Deputy Governor – had concluded deals with ambassadors from Sumatra, a deal activated through our new principal native merchant, Chenna Vincatadry, though all credited to my husband, naturally. And a hugely successful arrangement. Indian calicoes in exchange for Sumatra pepper. The same week, the first major dividends for the Company from Jacques de Paiva's diamond endeavours. And then, at the end of January, Gyfford's return to us, his tour of the factories satisfactorily completed, despite his recurring ill-health, and his reports to Leadenhall Street including a glowing endorsement for Elihu's successes.

'A celebration?' I said. 'That we now have a Papist once more upon the throne of England.'

'Please, Catherine! It may have been acceptable to express such views before. But now...'

'Yes, now it is high treason. My point, I think. Did you not hear the other news brought by Lieutenant Apsley?'

First, that the canting fanatic, Titus Oates, had been arrested for perjury. His allegations of a Catholic plan against the now-dead king proved to be a lie.

'I never truly believed that nonsense anyway,' said Elihu. 'Popish Plot, indeed. And look, it turns out to have been quite the opposite. This Rye House scheme. The Papists suddenly become the victims in all this. Those of our own religious persuasion held, instead, to be traitors, seditionists.'

The trials continue, it seems. And I tremble at the thought. The executions. Those like Sir Thomas Armstrong, hanged, drawn and quartered under the sentence handed down by Judge George Jeffries. Or the Bristol merchant, Holloway, another acquaintance of my father, whose head and quarters were dispatched back to Bristol for public display there. Others simply beheaded, though usually with great butchery. So it is no longer simply the lords and gentlemen at whom the finger of death is pointed, but at simple merchants too. Merchants like Papa.

'And now, husband, we must bow the knee to the Papists even more, simply to show our innocence. Is that it?'

'Just a celebration, Catherine. Nothing else. And think how the children shall enjoy it.'

But I was thinking about Matthew Parrish, the words he had spoken about *senhor* de Paiva's clandestine activities apart from his official duties.

His sponsors back in England, those prominent individuals interested in a long-term political investment. It was the only salvation to which I could cling – that, somewhere, somebody was planning intelligently to deliver us from the evil of this Catholic succession. It is the reason, of course, that I must tolerate Jeronima's admiration for my husband. For now, at least.

So, over the next few days Elihu busied himself with plans for the celebration while I was occupied with my little Dormouse's first steps and suckling the baby to whom we had agreed to refer, by mutual consent, my husband and I, as Kate. Baptised Katherine but, at home, Kate. And, during those days, I both amused myself with the other gossip and, equally, broke my heart with the plans to send my two darling boys, Elford and Benjamin, back to England.

First, the gossip.

About the king's death, naturally. The Widow Keeble has been enjoying a dalliance, it seems, with that naval lieutenant, and she swears he has shared the tales abroad on London's streets. Those "fitting remedies" that had amused Elihu so much. Bled until he was bloodless. Fed an elixir made from extract of human skull. Hellebore root stuffed up his nostrils. Opium and wine – hopefully not my husband's opium! Forced to eat the gallstone of an East Indian goat. One of ours? And some attendant at the postmortem claiming evidence of poisoning. Good gracious, they sounded precisely like the symptoms attributed to powder of the *yettikottai*. So I could not help thinking. Those dwarf Gentues we sent him for the royal entertainment. Could it be? Some revenge for their enslavement?

But where does this leave us? How will the succession of this Catholic king change our lives here? How will my life in particular be affected?

And then the boys. They are much younger than I should have liked, Elford nine and Benjamin only seven. But my fear for them now surpasses all reason. My nightmares about Walter have begun afresh and I will not risk them. Besides, Elihu believes our marriage will prosper if we have some time to focus ourselves around Davy and Kate. Well, we shall see.

Finally, it seems that we are once again at war. And, again, I tremble at the prospect. The Company's negotiations with the Mughal Emperor had broken down and, in a fit of anger, Josiah Childe and the Company's Directors had dispatched a fleet of twelve warships to attack Aurangzeb's own vessels at Hoogli and elsewhere. Many of our own soldiers have been dispatched to strengthen our forces. The latest we hear is that our ships have fired the town there, destroyed five hundred houses. I fear – we all fear – that there shall be retribution.

Meanwhile, I had no choice but to endure the celebration. The proclamation read at each of the gates in turn, the procession led by Governor Gyfford, doing his best to maintain his composure on a prancing pony. Then his bodyguard, fifes and drums. Behind him, all the native merchants and a dozen elephants, each bearing the Company's colours, the red and white horizontal stripes. Cymbals and horns. After the elephants, our depleted companies of soldiers, all pipe clay and polish. Finally, the entourages of the visiting ambassadors from Persia and Siam, with Elihu at the head of the Fort's remaining officials.

The procession wound its way to the Garden House, where no expense had been spared with bonfire, feasting and fireworks.

Magnificent! Or it would have been if I had not been experiencing this awful sense of foreboding.

The boys have been gone more than two months, sailed early in October with Captain Goldsborough on board the *Bengal Merchant*. And Tanani gone with them. God speed them all and hasten the day when I hear they are safe in England. I could have wished they had shown at least a little distress at our parting but nothing was going to dampen their excitement and, in truth, they had been so very low for several weeks simply because their original date of departure, in September, had been delayed.

So I attempt to find solace with little David and baby Kate – each of them like miniature portraits of their father – while, at the same time, trying to instill some sense of discipline in our new *ayah*, a cousin of Sathiri's. She is simply one of the many new servants within our household since Elihu determined that his status, as an aspiring merchant prince in addition to his position as Second-in-Council, must warrant a greater complement than Joseph and myself had enjoyed. And that is without the additional numbers employed at the garden house. It takes such time to oversee their work, forty of them now. In fact I wonder whether this is his intention for he has oft-times declared that I should not trouble myself so much about the factory's politics if I did not have a surfeit of time on my hands.

Well, I could have told him that I had picked up rumours of today's riotous assemblies several weeks ago. Through Sathiri, among others. But I knew he would have ignored my warnings, admonished me for listening to gossip.

Gossip almost turned to gunfire.

It began at dawn. A great tumult carried to us on the fever-laden breeze. Chanting and singing. A cacophony of pounding percussion.

Cries of alarm from within the Fort. A bell rung in the temporary tower outside the church. Our soldiers pounding across the square. And Elihu in his nightshirt with a brace of pistols in his hands.

'What?' he shouted. 'We are under attack?'

It was a reasonable concern, given our continuing war with the Mughal Emperor. Though it is not the Aurangzeb's Mahometans that afflict our forces. For at our soldiers' camp in the Hoogli swamps, half of them have died from fever in the past three months.

'A protest about taxation, I think.'

'How can you be certain, woman?'

'I thought you must know. Matthew had intelligence of its planning days ago. Did he not tell you? I assume it is the reason his men are so readily at their posts.'

'Ah, he may have mentioned something. But the fellow is always seeing conspiracy around every corner.'

'This sounds like more than a rumour, I think.'

And so it was.

By midday there were enormous crowds baying outside each of the gates, and the gates themselves had been secured. Outside the walls, the bazaar merchants in the Shambles and all along Market Street had refused to open their stalls or to sell any produce to residents of White Town. Here, in Middle Street, I was alarmed to see a section of musketeers had thrown up a barricade against the possibility of the walls being scaled and, outside the house, Governor Gyfford had come to inspect our defences, accompanied both by Elihu and Matthew Parrish.

'My dear,' shouted my husband, 'you should really remain inside and bar all the doors and shutters.' But I smiled politely and remained on the *veranda* as he turned to the section's corporal. 'If a single black face,' he ordered, 'appears above the walls, you will open fire on the devils. You understand? Here, of all places. My wife and children within.'

'Governor,' Matthew tried to reason with Gyfford, 'firing on unarmed protestors, I fear, will not serve. It would take little to stir them into an angry swarm. We would be badly outnumbered.'

'Perhaps it would be better to concede a little,' said Gyfford. 'These taxes bring so little to our coffers, after all. It cannot hurt, surely. What say you, Mister Yale?'

'What I say, Governor, is that a quick sally through the Choultry Gate with an enthusiastically commanded push of pikes, a close quarters volley, and we could clear this rebellious bunch in moments.'

'Or trigger a massacre?' Matthew sneered.

'Was we to get this wrong, sirrah,' said the Governor, 'there would be the devil to pay among the Directors. With this, and the Emperor Aurangzeb threatening to take back Gingee from the Marathas, and Bijapur from the Sultan Sikandar Adil, we would have enemies on all fronts.'

'Our credit with the Directors is strong,' Elihu insisted. 'The new trade with the King of Siam, Governor. Great heavens, strong indeed.'

He was pleased with himself again. A prince's ransom in jeweled pieces. Rubies, diamonds and emeralds, all procured with the assistance of Mistress Nicks and dispatched in September to King Narai's representatives in Ayutthaya. Many hundreds of pounds in gold. And elephants. Siamese elephants.

'Sadly,' said Matthew, 'we are not so strong in arms or men. Use of force should be our strategy of last resort, Governor.'

'You have a better plan, Mister Parrish?' Elihu asked. 'Well, of course you must. You always do, sirrah.'

'It seems to me,' Matthew told them, 'that, at this stage, the mere threat of action might suffice. Test their resolve. Invite the headmen to come and parley, remind them that their taxes are modest, and bring their own rewards. But if they do not abandon this foolishness by sundown it will cost them their fine houses. Not those of Black Town's honest yet misguided citizens but just the dwellings of the headmen. Moor, Jew and Gentue. The same with the stallholders.'

'Exactly as I said myself,' said Elihu. 'A show of force.'

The stratagem worked, of course, and my husband claimed credit for its success, in its entirety.

Such a year, this has become. The taxation disturbances. Then the outbreaks of fatal fevers, agues and scrofula, such that the Council agreed to send urgently to the king that he may bless some Touch-Pieces for us – little good though they may do us, first, by the time they arrive and, second, from the hands of a Papist.

Next, the return of Elihu's brother Thomas from Siam. Another failed mission and, worse, his bringing of bad news. Those pieces of jewelry my husband supplied to King Narai, adorned with precious gems, and for which Elihu had been paid so handsomely. But the French have been winning favour with Siam, scuppered Thomas's mission and, besides, persuaded old Narai that the jewels are inferior, over-priced, could have been made cheaper and better in Paris. The pieces sent back. Gyfford has protested on Elihu's behalf and a reply received just this week. An irate reply, threats of retaliation, demands for reimbursement of the gold paid to Fort St. George.

But how to find the necessary funds to reimburse them even if the Council were so inclined. For the coffers are empty again. Thus, another loan from Elihu's private wealth – *our* private wealth, I should say. Five thousand pagodas, with interest charged at ten per cent per annum.

Meanwhile, war all around us, the Mughal Emperor conquering Bijapur from the Sultan Adil – no longer content to hold suzerainty over the Shia Mussulmen of the Deccan Plateau but presently desiring to take them entirely into an expanded empire. Next will be Golconda. We all know it. The Sultan Abdul Hasan's days are numbered and with him, perhaps, also our own. For our own war with Aurangzeb drags on, back and forth, though mercifully still distant from us here in Madras Patnam.

Then news from England. More executions arising from the so-called Rye House Plot, including Anabaptist, Elizabeth Gaunt, burned alive at the stake, apparently for no other crime than giving shelter to one of the plotters – everybody knowing that this was simply a message for Dissenters in general.

Worse, open rebellion in the West Country. Charles's bastard son, James Scott, Duke of Monmouth, determined to overthrow Catholic James, his uncle. A landing at Lyme Regis, battle at Sedgemoor and Monmouth's army defeated. A similar rising, in Scotland, also suppressed. Treason trials under the presidency of Judge George Jeffreys. Bloody assizes. Monmouth and so many of his supporters executed. Yet the worst thing, Mama has written, is that the whole episode has been the subject of such indifference, even the gibbets attracting little attention in that England where gibbets are commonplace. She is scathing, talks about the will of the people, how it changes with the weather-vane of history. *Karma*, I suppose Sathiri would say.

And now this famine that has swept across so many regions of India. We have seen famine before. Of course we have. Yet this one is terrible in its extremes and shows no sign of abating. All around the Bay of Bengal.

I saw its worst effects today, as I went with Mistress Bridger and a whole tail of our respective servants to the burial ground. An accidental encounter, in truth, for she has been noticeably more distant since we purchased the garden house. Yet we were each headed in the same direction, through the town now fallen almost silent, to pay my respects to Joseph and to make sure no further damage had occurred to Walt's fractured headstone. I have been concerned, since some of the older stones are now being removed and sited afresh around St. Mary's. There was an opportunity, of course, for Walter's headstone to be among them, though I think he will rest more soundly there, near his father. But as we made our way around the edge of Black Town, all seemed very different.

'My goodness,' I said. 'How many more can we take?'

Everywhere the ragged, downcast processions of those seeking refuge, those shambling away from the ravages of war, from the south in Bijapur, and from starvation everywhere else, west and north. A suppressed wailing filled the space where empty-handed higglers wait for trade goods and produce that never comes.

'May God console them,' she murmured, and then she spoke a word I did not understand. '*Ha'makom*,' I think it was. I had asked her once, about her name, Winifred seeming unlikely for a Portuguese. But she had simply told me that, when she met John, she had been Winfriede and Winifred had simply been easier for his friends and family. Yet there was something about her that reminded me so much of Black Town's Jews, many of them now suffering the effects of the famine along with all others. For, in today's Black Town, even rich men are reduced to beggary. And everywhere there are hands stretching out to us for alms, for succour.

'May Almighty Jesus bring an end to the flooding, restore their crops, Winifred. For consolation will not feed them.' We found ourselves turning a corner and there, ahead of us, the corpse of a young woman, little more than a skeleton even before her death and now surrounded by flapping, strutting vultures that had already begun to peck at her eyes. Several of the servants chased them away and I looked around for anybody who might come to take care of her. 'And we have all become so horribly accustomed to seeing this every day.'

I caught sight of the Gentue headman for the district, scolded him in my own inadequate Tamil, and only moved on when he had arranged a detail of peons to cover and remove the body.

'The Council, it give so little to ease the suffering,' said Winifred, with a certain superiority. And she was correct. One hundred pagodas only, for the purchase of rice in quantities that will assuage few of the distended bellies nor pacify those empty food bowl eyes.

'Though many have given generously to the subscription. Yet not enough, of course.' I am still not certain why I felt it necessary to act the apologist for the Council members.

'John has give what he can,' she said, as though she needed to highlight his independent success alongside his generosity. Since his dismissal by the Directors, John Bridger has continued to trade independently, now himself an interloper, and seems to have flourished, purchased more properties on Scotch Street with the proceeds of their selling the garden house to us – the garden house that seems to only serve the entertainment needs of Elihu and his friends.

'I cannot pretend, Winifred, any love towards his latest fortunes, but I have to admit that he has given generously to offset this tragedy.'

The worst irony of all. That there, below us, stood some of the new pens, the enclosures recently built to house the growing numbers of slaves here, the former prohibitions against the trade now forgotten.

'They are *infelizes*,' said Winifred. Unfortunates. 'But, most of them, they have choose the path of – how do you say, *servidão*?

'Servitude.'

'Yes, servitude – happily enough.'

We passed two more funeral parties, the evil stench that has filled our nostrils for so many weeks far worse in that place and, overhead, even more of those brutish vultures, circling and waiting.

'As an alternative to starvation? I suppose I understand. Though my Dissenter beliefs scream against the entire concept. But if it was a clear choice, between selling my children into slavery against seeing them starve and die in such agony, perhaps I might be persuaded.'

Indeed I might. For is that not the secret of life? To keep open as many of our options as possible for as long as we may dare. And if my only remaining option to keep them alive...

'Give you joy of your boys' escape to England, Catherine,' Winifred was saying. 'You have news of them?'

'Of Elford and Benjamin nothing. Too soon yet.' I keep persuading myself that this is nothing unusual though, in my heart, I pray each day that some inbound ship will have brought word of them, passed their own vessel somewhere on the high seas. Though nothing. And there have been those storms. What if some harm has befallen them? I cannot bring myself to think of it, nor the consequences for Elihu Yale if sending them home has put them in harm's way. Yet I collected myself, remembered Mama's letter. 'But Joseph and Richard?' I said. 'Yes, word from my mother. Joseph will be sixteen this year, Richie fourteen, his studies completed and due to begin an apprenticeship. Joseph, however, is bound for your homeland. The Douro, Hardwicke's godowns within Porto's English Factory House. A good beginning for the boy, though his heart is set on John Company, like his father.' And there it was, before us. Joseph's mausoleum, the shadow of its tall pyramid stretched out like a finger to caress Walter's own broken memorial. 'Yet I hope that, by the time his ambition is met, we shall be entirely rid of this abomination, these slave pens in Fort St. George.'

She shrugged. And little wonder. The Portuguese, of course, are famous for their trade in this human misery, at Hoogli and elsewhere.

'Are those who work the land in England any better than slaves, Catherine? In Portugal certainly they are not. *Verdade?*'

At that moment, my little Dormouse broke free from the *ayah* and waddled towards me on those unsteady legs, so that I swept him into the air, into my arms.

'I am accustomed to the arguments,' I said, 'but here the barbarism of the practice is overwhelming.' In districts principally controlled by the Gentues, there is a great profusion of peons taken as prisoners of war. In Mahometan regions, such slaves are at least often able to raise themselves from this lowly status by embracing Islam. And, in general, the Mahometan Mughals deplore the whole concept of slavery – except, again, for those taken as trophies of their wars. Yet this famine has led to a substantial increase in availability.

'*Tal excesso.*' Such a glut. 'All those more mouths to feed or, as John, he says, see our *investimentos* just wither and vanish before they can ship abroad.'

Gyfford's solution. To speed the transit of slaves as far as may be possible. His insistence – the Council's decision, enthusiastically supported by Elihu – that every outbound vessel westward-bound for our English colony at St. Helena must carry at least ten slaves or, if travelling east, the same number to feed the insatiable appetites of Sumatra. Or perhaps the Company's new Factory House at Canton. Yet where is Canton, exactly? China, of course, but beyond that I do not know.

'Well, at least I am spared the indignity of Elihu himself participating in the damnable trade.' It gave me a sense of self-righteous satisfaction, for he must be one of the few among our Company officials who does not profit from the slave trade. Yet Winifred simply smiled, regarded me incredulously.

'Do you say so, *senhora* Yale?'

'Is this not your opportunity, Elihu?' I hissed at him, as our servants scurried about our garden house, serving chicken meatballs, pickled herrings and fowl sausage, filling the rooms with their heady aromas. 'Rid us of this abhorrent trade. Now you are Governor and President at last?'

Gyfford had received the instructions displacing him from his post some weeks ago. He had received them with great equanimity, almost relief. His health deteriorating rapidly now. And though Elihu's letter of appointment to replace him had also been received, there were no clear orders about how or when this should be implemented. Not a summary dismissal, as Streynsham Master's had been. Yet today the Council decided to take matters into their own hands, with Gyfford's own agreement, and the transition has taken place. So tonight a celebration. Out in the torch-lit garden itself, our Fort St. George musicians performing enthusiastically and, in the adjoining entertaining room a score of couples dancing the moderate steps of an *allemande*.

Little enough, however, to rejoice about, apart from this. The famine still with us. Yet more seeking refuge from the wars, the Mughal Emperor Aurangzeb having fulfilled his threat of removing the Shia Abdul Hassan from the Sultanate of Golconda, our whole territory, the Coromandel Coast, now directly part of the Mughal domain. So it will not be long, we fear, until he turns his full attention to Madras Patnam, the Company's war with Aurangzeb dragging on. And the trade in slaves grown great from Fort St. George by reason of the great plenty of poor folk seeking escape from starvation, or war, as well as their cheapness as a commodity. Abominable!

'What would you have me do, my dear – leave all those poor devils to starve rather than take them into servitude as they demand?'

As if upon a cue, one of our Gentue retainers passed with a *parota*-laden platter.

'Perhaps we might simply feed them? A modicum of Christian charity without, just this once, expecting a return on investment. And the children, Elihu. Have those children expressed this desire to become slaves?'

'Ah, I understand. The little one playing upon your mind.' He cast a proprietorial glance at my belly. Another month yet before this latest addition sees the light of day but already enormous. 'Besides, this is not really the time or place. I should get back to our guests. For here comes Parrish,' he whispered. 'Been trying to avoid the fellow all evening.'

And he was gone, pushing himself into a knot of the Cavalier faction that was wound about Vincent Seaton, here from Masulipatnam.

'The new Governor is proving especially elusive this evening,' Matthew smiled and kissed my hand. 'But, my goodness, how finely attired he is.' From Matthew Parrish this was compliment indeed, for his own scarlet *kurta*, uniform scarlet, drew admiring glances from all quarters, as did the bejewelled sabre, a curved *talwar*, that so often hung at his side on such ceremonial occasions.

'His clothes, he says, make him the man he aspires to be.'

And the man he aspired to be, this evening, was not the merchant prince but, rather, the very image of English, or perhaps Welsh, nobility.

'I have rarely seen a periwig of such length or quality,' said Matthew, in the voice he normally reserved for reciting his poetry.

'The wages of his enterprise, my friend. I could simply wish that so much of it did not emanate from the slave pens. He keeps reminding me that the Book of Exodus speaks of the Israelites as slaves and that the Book of Genesis makes clear they accepted that slavery willingly to escape their own great famine. Therefore, he reasons, this similar situation must be acceptable in the eyes of God. Worse, he regularly recalls those biblical verses that seem to make slavery itself seem unobjectionable. I cannot believe that so few see the trade with such innocence. I keep thinking of my own children.'

'The boys all safe, at least.'

'So I am constantly reminded.' It was a couple of months ago. An inbound ship brought word that the boys were safely within sight of

England. I had been confused, for it transpired that the vessels passed each other in May last year. They had then been at sea seven months and still not ashore. And I was obliged to wait for Mama's most recent letter, which came to me in the charge of Tanani – her duties fulfilled, and now returned to Madras – before I knew for certain that Elford and Benjamin were in her care. Twenty-one months after they sailed. Tanani gave me a full account. A tedious voyage. Terrible storms and the ship suffering awful damage, needing repairs before they could reach the Channel. 'Oh, Matthew, I will never again commit my children to such a voyage without me there to care for them.'

'Hopefully the need shall not arise for many years. Let us drink to that, at least.'

Another of the younger servants, this time with a tray of arrack *panch*. We each took a glass, toasted each other's health.

'Yet I wish I could be so certain,' I said. 'You have seen Elihu's letter of appointment?'

'You think he would have shared that with me? But I assume from your manner that it may have been crafted with as much sensitivity as that which dismissed Gyfford – I have rarely seen such offensiveness. I care no more for the fellow than you do, but the missive is an insult to all of us. Gyfford – each person at Fort St. George, it seems – guilty of profiteering and impertinence. Great heaven, I wish that Gyfford possessed sufficient wit for profiteering but the best I could say about him is simply that he does not.'

'My husband's instructions are little better. They spell out clearly their mistrust of all here, Elihu included, implying that he has many faults. Yet they require him to turn the stream of his good parts into a better channel. Their phrase, and lyrical for the Directors. Clear that they even doubt his loyalty.'

'You would hardly know from his demeanour.'

There was a great deal of raucous laughter and backslapping from Seaton's little group.

'Elihu chooses to ignore such things, to read no further than the appointment itself. And always ready with excuses for Josiah Childe.'

'The appointment conditional?'

'On tighter control of the coffers. Demands that those in Madras not paying taxes be considered seditious, this now being a Presidency, and put to death. Put to death, sirrah. So it is to be a rent paid on every property, a poll tax on every head.'

'And thus you believe Elihu's tenure as President may be short-lived, perhaps requiring you to return to England sooner rather than later.'

As though he had heard his name mentioned, my husband turned, caught my eye and waved.

'I almost hope it might be true,' I said. 'Yet that is the least of it. But this constant threat of war. It makes me so low.'

Aurangzeb, his armies now within a few miles of Masulipatnam. Presumably the reason for Seaton's return here, seeking reinforcements perhaps. Or maybe just escaping from the rumours of atrocity. And in the south too, ten thousand of the Mughal Emperor's wild horsemen rampaging around Gingee.

'We shall be protected,' said Matthew, 'never fear. Three more companies to be raised, trained bands from among the Gentues and Moors. Perhaps a Portuguese company too. And every writer or factor to be instructed in serving the great guns. We shall be safe enough.'

I dabbed a kerchief at my brow, wiped away a line of perspiration that even the efforts of our best *pankah* boys were incapable of preventing.

'From this awful heat? From the termites? From the famine? From the storms, Matthew?' Only last week, another wicked tempest that sank and destroyed each of the recently arrived supply ships for which we had prayed so long, yet sunk out there before their cargoes of rice and grain could even be brought ashore. 'And from the sickness,' I went on. 'You know the balance sheet even better than I. Last year, sixty-eight dead. One in five of us here within White Town alone. One in five. Well, the Lord has already written Walt onto my debit column. My own one in five among the boys. And now the counting has begun afresh with little Kate. This other that I carry. How long, Matthew, before another is taken? For heaven's sake, I convinced myself that Elford and Benjamin were gone too. All that time and no word. I fear it has added greatly to the imbalance of my mind also.'

There are times when I find myself entirely lost, voices inside my head, drowning in terrors to which I can give no name. And when they strike, all I can do is run for Sathiri. Her mantras, her *soma*, her instruction in the ways of *karma*.

'A harsh year for you, Catherine. And in Black Town nobody

even troubles to count any more. Each of the burial grounds full to overflowing. It is a charnel house.'

I had not noticed Seaton break away from his companions, and it startled me to hear his wheedling voice at my side. Unlike Elihu, his garb was all native, though worn without elegance.

'Charnel house?' he said. 'Why, Parrish, you exaggerate surely. Do you not think so, Catherine?' The worm would never have dared such familiarity while Joseph was alive, yet now he regarded me with a predatory eye. 'After all, you are now the President's wife. A little more circumspection, perhaps, about the images we portray to the outside world. The Mughal Emperor must believe we are strong, resourceful, too dangerous for conquest. Do you not agree, Parrish?'

'Is that your purpose, sirrah?' Matthew smiled. 'Here, so far from your post – convincing Aurangzeb of the danger we pose to his ambitions.'

'You are impertinent, Mister Parrish. I should have a care, if I were you.'

The climate had never succeeded in adding colour to Vincent Seaton's features, though they now brought to mind that pallid evil of the cobra's head, his eyes equally reptilian. Yet Matthew seemed unmoved.

'I care enough to know, Mister Seaton, that the Mughal Emperor is already aware of our condition. And Gyfford was a fool not to send a diplomatic mission as soon as the Emperor took Bijapur. The French and the Dutch have already done so and now they have his ear. It will take far more than false images to keep him at bay.'

'And you, I suppose, have heard what he wants from us?'

'I heard that he talks about fifty thousand gold pagodas simply that we may maintain the concession for Madras alone. But Masulipatnam? The proposed new Factory House at Porto Novo? Perhaps you must needs gather your own intelligence on those.'

'Oh, I fear Masulipatnam may be doomed. A shame. Such a long history. The Greeks. Ptolemy. They say its name gives us the word muslin. Did you know, Catherine?'

'Fifty thousand pagodas.' I laughed, sipping at my *panch*. 'And the coffers all empty again.'

'But the slave pens full, my dear,' Seaton sneered. 'We must all be grateful to the slaves, eh?'

'I realise now,' I said, 'that Mama may be right. Morality alone is sometimes not enough to triumph over evil but it is often the only weapon we possess. That old adage, that if you resist evil you may not always triumph, but if you do not resist it shall surely drown you.'

In the entertaining room, the *allemande* was over, new couples now taken up an elegant *correre*.

'God's Hooks.' Seaton pretended to be taken aback. 'Yet the trade has given you all this.' He turned a half-circle himself, in time to the music, raised his hands dramatically to the ceilings. 'This opulence. Your husband now with his own first ship. And the intention, he tells me, of levying a duty upon each slave sent off from this shore. One gold pagoda per head. An admirable concept. Your husband, each of us who are company officials, all the interlopers too, enrich ourselves through this honest trade – and, at the same time, employ that trade as a revenue source for the Company itself. I think we shall all benefit greatly from Elihu's tenure as President.' *Each of us*, I thought. And I remembered what a fool I had been. That discussion with Winifred Bridger when I had believed Elihu's involvement in the trade to be without personal profit. *'Do you say so, senhora Yale?'* But Seaton was not yet done. 'God blind me,' he said. 'Do you have any idea how many were shipped from here just last month?' Of course I knew. More than six hundred. A single month. 'Yet there is this, too. That John Company now being so rich in Presidencies, the king himself has turned his eyes our way. The new Crown expects great things from us.'

'Like bending the knee to Rome, you mean?' I said, and he shook his head, almost unraveling his gem-studded turban.

'Mistress Yale, it will never be thus. You need look no further than those who are the king's most trusted advisors. William Penn – a Quaker, like your father.' I was about to correct him but he had barely drawn breath. 'Pepys, his Secretary of the Navy, the absolute epitome of the Protestant High Church. All of us here. Barely a Catholic among us. Why, think you, that so few share your fears?'

'Perhaps,' said Matthew, 'it is the story of these past four years, since the succession has been so much on everybody's minds. And all those, individuals or corporations, suspected of lacking sympathy with the concept of a Catholic monarch have been purged, lost charters or personal possessions. It is not a matter of so few sharing our fears but so many fearful of expressing them.'

Fear. Oh, I know fear. I smell it in every ounce of milk I feed my babies.

'Fear, Mister Parrish,' said Seaton. 'Of what? King James is simply imposing toleration upon England. Ensuring that all faiths should have the ability to worship freely. Is that not what you would both desire? For Quakers? For our Nonconformists, our Dissenters? Our Jews? And yes, for our Catholics too. The king's coronation oath, regardless of his private beliefs, is still to protect the established Church of England.'

Our Catholics? I saw again the swaying head of the serpent.

'And for how long?' I sneered. 'Long enough to slowly put his fellow-Papists into high office? To further extend his poxed standing army of Irishmen with Catholic captains? Indulgences and exemptions from the Test Act. And then – what? He takes a leaf from the book of French Louis, his persecution and expulsion of all the Protestant Huguenots?'

Seaton gestured to the tobacco rack on the wall behind Matthew.

'May I?' he said and, without waiting for my permission, he took one of the long reading pipes, began filling it from my husband's best Dutch weed. 'Yet even were that true, Mistress Yale,' he continued, 'everything you have conjured, we are still faced with the dilemma that all kings are directly descended from Adam, a direct and divine line of accession that can ever be broken by any kind of intervention less than that of God Almighty.'

It was an ancient argument, largely rejected by Dissenters, more attuned to Locke's teachings, to my family's deeply held beliefs.

'Then God be praised,' said Matthew, 'that the Almighty will rid us of the iniquity of a Catholic monarch when he finally enters the Kingdom of Heaven and the line of succession passes to the Princess Mary.'

'That sounds dangerously close to sedition, Mister Parrish. Willing the premature demise of His Majesty, perhaps?' Seaton turned to me, a sinister smile creasing his equally sinister features and tobacco smoke writhing from his teeth. 'And that is a subject we should discuss in private, Mistress. Sedition. Though, for the nonce, I must needs speak with Reverend Evans.'

Sedition. These days the word itself can make one feel as though we already face the executioner's axe. But before I could respond, he had left us, shouting across the room to that scoundrel, our senior chaplain who,

I knew, was profiting as much from the trade in human bondage as any other man there. The hypocrite. Yet it was Seaton's parting words, of course, that stayed with me, chilled me.

'Sedition?' I said aloud. 'Why in heaven's name should he wish to speak with me about sedition?'

I am certain that Matthew must have been able to discern the consternation that caused me so to quiver.

'Impossible to know what transpires in the mind of one such as Seaton. But be careful, my dear. I have said before that he is a dangerous creature.'

Sedition. It has been a night for sedition, and I allowed myself to be caught up in its heady embrace, the giddiness of its intricate revolutions, as surely as my husband and Jeronima de Paiva were swept up by the stamping, spinning steps of their dance.

'They make a fine couple,' said her husband, as we watched from the table at which he had seated himself to ease his limbs, his hands resting upon the gem-encrusted handle of his walking cane.

'Seaton.' Matthew stood at his side, a fixed smile upon his lips, and the word spoken as though it were some simple pleasantry, to mask our conspiracy. 'He spoke of sedition. Have you any idea what he intends, *senhor*?'

'He has spent considerable time in my company,' he replied, playing the same game as Matthew, his tone light. An innocent admiration for the music, perhaps. 'Mistress Nicks too. Questions, questions. About the profitability of the mines. About the returns for the Company's coffers. Seaton suspects there may be more to our enterprise than meets his weasel's eye.'

'And Katherine Nicks?' I said. 'What is her part in all this, apart from the obvious?'

She had taken Reverend Evans for her partner, while John Nicks looked on, fingers drumming on his own table as the chaplain gripped her ever more tightly and Katherine allowed herself to brush against Elihu's body with increasing frequency. I suppose I should have felt the same annoyance as Nicks but I was simply embarrassed that the spectacle afforded such clear discomfort to *senhor* de Paiva.

'If, as we suspect, *senhora* Yale,' he said, 'Seaton is an agent for the

Cavalier faction within the Company, it would surprise none of us if he has recruited the Nicks woman to serve him here while Seaton himself is engaged at Masulipatnam. And they will know how things move in England as much as we do.'

'Which is?'

'Rumour only, my dear,' said Matthew. 'Rumour that the king has sent William Penn to The Hague. To Mary. Clever move, sending a Quaker. To seek agreement that his indulgences and exemptions for Papists may continue after his daughter's succession. It seems that Mary may have been amenable, but her husband certainly not.'

Strange that William of Orange, who masterminded so many of our defeats in the last Dutch war, may now end up on the throne of England. William and Mary.

'Where else,' I said, 'might we now look for salvation but the Prince of Protestants? And no surprise that the champion of Europe's Protestants cannot be seen to offer concessions to popery.'

'It will not be a simple matter,' said *senhor* de Paiva. 'There are many among the Tories who find no favour with the Church of Rome, yet may fear Protestant William even more. Dutch, that is one thing. But he has a reputation as another Cromwell. Among some, at least. And then all those others. Quakers. Those of my own faith all too ready to heed the king's promises about religious freedom for all. Nonsense, naturally. But he plays a clever game.'

'Though gentlemen in England, Catherine, now active to bring about that glorious spring you spoke about. Henry Sydney and others.'

Henry Sydney's brother, Algernon, had been executed for this alleged part in the Rye House Plot.

'With finance provided through *senhor* de Paiva,' I said.

'We all must play our modest parts, Mistress.'

The jig was done, Elihu escorting Jeronima back to her husband. He was perspiring profusely, though de Paiva's young wife seemed as cool as a cucumber.

'Great heavens, *senhor*,' he said, 'your wife shall be the death of me, I swear. And I am greatly in your debt. The letter you wrote on my behalf to the Directors.' Elihu turned to me. 'You collect, my dear? Those jewels that Thomas brought back from the King of Siam. Ungrateful wretch! But thanks to *senhor* de Paiva's confirmation of their value, I am exonerated.'

'For that, at least, we should be grateful.'

He seemed oblivious to the fact that his exoneration struck almost the only positive note in the entire letter apart from the actual appointment.

'Indeed. And now, if these good folk will excuse us, I would dance with my wife. Ah, a *gavotte*, I think, is it not? Just the thing, my dear, for one in your commodious condition.' I could think of few things I wished to do less but, heedless of my reluctance, he drew me onto the dance floor. 'And I have a scheme, good wife,' he said, as we took up the steps. 'To win back some favour from the Directors. Not that I need it, you understand. I shall be known by the gains I bring them. Though some minor demonstrations of my loyalty to Crown and Company shall not go amiss, I think.'

'You intrigue me, sirrah. Crown and Company both, you say. And why should we need to demonstrate our loyalty to the Crown.'

Lifting steps to left and right, *double à gauche* and *double à droite*, the gavotte's little leaps performed as diligently as I was able.

'For the very reason you needs must ask the question, Catherine. It does not go unnoticed, your open antagonism towards King James.'

There it was again. Like Seaton, this implication of treasonous intent.

'He is like to be as dissolute as his brother,' I said, regardless. 'Hypocrisy again. News from England that he is in bed with his mistresses one moment, then at Mass the next.'

'News? My dear, that is nothing more than the gossip of the White Town women over their chatter-broth. But, that aside, my scheme stands on its own two feet for the good of Madras in general. Time for a new beginning, perhaps. So many of our street names that now mean so little. French Street, for example. Now that we have St. Mary's we should honour the fact, as we would in England. Name it Church Street instead. And Scotch Street. Does anybody now recall why we styled it so? And what better way to acknowledge the passing of our deceased king than to have Charles Street instead.'

'I think I see where this is leading, Elihu. So which is it to be?'

I was uncertain whether he had heard me for his attention seemed fixed on Katherine Nicks, now sporting a new partner.

'What do you mean, my dear?'

'With which of our thoroughfares, exactly, do you intend to pay homage to Catholic James?'

'Ah, I rather thought Points Street. After all, with our extensions to the walls, it really no longer *points* anywhere at all.' He roared with laughter at his own witticism. 'And then, my dear, we must write to your mama. Thank her for these further gifts she has sent, repay her with a small packet of gems. God blind me, I should very much like to meet her. She seems a fine woman. Your father too, I imagine.'

Mama would be delighted, of course. She has this great thirst for family about her, yet finds herself left with only fractious sons and a distant daughter. That is why my boys matter so much to her. Far more, I imagine than does my careless Papa.

'If you think I am antagonistic towards the Church of Rome, husband, you should not wish to hear my father's words. He sees Catholic hands behind his long imprisonment at Smyrna.'

'All the same, I should relish the chance to discourse with him. When my duties here are done, and we are settled once again, wealthy, in London.'

'Wealthy from trafficking in human misery.'

Double à gauche. Double à droite. And the baby kicking in my belly.

'Oh, my dear,' said Elihu, 'I shall not allow you to despoil my good humour. There is too much at stake. For the Company, far more than for myself. But I have given the matter some thought. I believe you should deserve a gift also, for all you have given me. The blessing of young David. And Kate, of course. This new babe too. Suffer the little children, Catherine. Is that not your counsel to me? So there shall be an order through Council at our very next gathering. We shall prohibit the bondage of any child under the age of ten!'

I was bidding farewell to some of our guests, still astonished at Elihu's words, wondering at this small but inadequate mercy, when Seaton appeared once more beside me. He was clutching a bundle of documents.

'A successful evening, Mistress?'

'For my husband, yes.' He took me not too gently by the arm, ignoring my protest, steered me towards the garden and onto the lanthorn-lit path between our acacia hedges. 'What, in heaven's name...'

'And for your Whiggamor friends too, I collect. Oh, I witnessed your little gathering, ma'am. Parrish and yourself with that damn'd Jew. Though the wife is comely enough, I suppose. Elihu certainly seems to think so. But her husband? Too old to care perhaps. Or glad to have some younger fellow satisfy her needs.'

I pulled my arm free of his grip, though the force of his fingers, the smell of his tobacco, the sibilance of his tongue, seemed rooted in my flesh. Yet I found myself drawn along, desperate to know where his talk of sedition might lead me, fearing that I already knew the answer.

'Do you dare, Mister Seaton? In my own house, to voice such calumnies. Shall I call my husband, sirrah? Have you repeat them to his face?'

'You must do as you think fit, Mistress Yale. Yet there are several things you might consider. First, these.' He unfolded the bundle, showed me a collection of broadsides. 'They tell me that these are now commonplace on the streets of London. Broadsides and ballads galore. Satires. Seditious publications, circulated among soldiers of the army, sailors of the fleet. Within coffee houses and among street peddlars.' He flashed a few before my eyes. One entitled *The Converts* and plainly displaying the likeness of many in high places already turned to popery. Another, in the same vein, with the bold heading, *England's Betrayers*. A third, exhibiting the scourges and instruments of torture that, it claimed, were so common within the convents of our country.

'And why should I consider these?'

'I found them in your own withdrawing room, Mistress. What else is there to say? Published in Amsterdam, naturally. The Dutch again. And then imported clandestinely to England for distribution. From the coffee houses and similar locations, as I have said. Coffee houses like that run by your father, of course. Breeding grounds for treason.'

'My father is simply an honest merchant, Mister Seaton. And those broadsides are not mine. Nor did he send them to me.'

Somewhere, back towards the house, I heard Elihu call my name.

'We have found copies elsewhere, of course,' said Seaton. 'And some agent of the Dutch must have ensured their passage to Fort St. George. Yet honest merchant? Your father? All that time he served in prison. For sedition too, was it not?'

'Wrongly accused and later exonerated.'

'Though still mingling with his treacherous friends. Winstanley, I have heard. Holloway of Bristol, naturally. Well, both of them dead now and good riddance to such filth.'

The night was filled with the sound of insects, hidden in the blackness beyond the flames.

'My father always had interesting friends. But none of that changes the fact. Those broadsheets are not mine.'

I kept my voice level, I think. Steady and assured, though my insides were churning. He had found no such thing in my house, of that I was certain. But had they originated in Papa's coffee house? Was there some evidence to implicate him?

'I suppose your marriage to Elihu does provide you some immunity. But not enough to protect you from accusations of regicide, I fear.'

I laughed openly just then, now fallen more easily into my part.

'A fie upon it, sirrah! My husband believes that he is jocose, yet you easily exceed him in that talent. Regicide, you say?'

'Nonsense, of course. But does that matter? Say a thing often enough, whisper it in the right ears, to those willing to listen, and it becomes greater than truth. Have we not seen that? Oates and his Popish Plot. Then all those implicated in the Rye House conspiracy who, in fact, had so little to do with its inception. Elizabeth Gaunt, a good example. Oh, how brightly she burned, they say.'

The firmament above burned also, though the stars served now only to diminish me, to punctuate my own insignificance, my vulnerability.

'I do not fear you, Seaton.' I lied, knowing it could not sound convincing, and barely able to restrain myself from trembling before the terror he engendered. The image of that horrendous death. And he sneered at me.

'Did you know, Mistress Yale, that there are now, in the Tower of London, two young Gentues? They are dwarfs. You may recall them. One boy and one girl.'

'Three,' I said. 'There were three of them.' I remembered the disgust I had felt at Elihu's lack of feeling about taking them.

'The second of the girls died at sea, on their journey from Fort St. George.' I sobbed, despite myself, both for those little ones and the blessing that none of my own had suffered the same fate on that perilous voyage. 'But the other two,' he went on, 'lived to entertain our late monarch, as they had been intended.'

'You think that is any consolation to me?'

He looked at me as though I had lost my mind.

'Why, do you think, I should wish to console you, madam? No, I simply wished to illustrate that the two who survived were present at the king's last evening. An evening of debauchery and dissolution, some may say. Luxury without parallel except, perhaps, here at the Court of the Mughal Emperor. Profane sycophants practising every sort of sin. A Sunday evening, yet God forgotten.'

'Then I hope he burns in hell.'

'The king may sometimes forget God, my dear, but the Almighty would never abandon his anointed to the fires of hell. Yet there he was, the king, toying at the same time, for all to see, with two of his harlot concubines. A pretty French boy, a catamite, sweetly singing bawdy ballads. Twenty of England's greatest nobles gaming at Basset with more gold than most of us will see in a lifetime.'

It sickened me, that image, to the very pit of my soul.

'This is the corruption that your Crown party, your Cavalier faction seeks to prolong?'

'Of course. Directly descended from Adam. The succession dictated by the will of God Almighty. It is all that we have. The only thing that stands between us and the anarchy of the mob.'

'And the Gentues? Those dwarf youngsters?'

I was suddenly very afraid for them.

'Their quarters searched after the king's death. And there they found – well, can you guess? No, perhaps not. Yet apparently they had hidden seeds of the Poison Nut, brought with them all the way from Madras.'

Elihu called my name again, fainter now. I had forgotten, his amusement at news of those "fitting remedies" and then word of the attendant present at the postmortem, the rumours of poisoning that we had dismissed so readily. Yet now I recalled how I had thought about those dwarf Gentues even then. The *yettikottai*. In jest. Of course, in jest. Though it seemed like no jest to me now.

'It is absurd. The accusation against those poor children, let alone that there should be any connection to myself.'

'Yet they were selected by Elihu. Not too difficult to persuade those with ears to listen that you would have influenced his choice. Then we mix in some witnesses to your outspoken Dissenter views. Your family history. Your father's links to enemies of the state. His time in prison.

These broadsides. You see, Catherine, how easy that would be?'

Curtains of threatening clouds closed slowly across the heavens, across the horizon of my own future.

'What do you want, Mister Seaton?'

I was genuinely curious, though I tried my best to sound haughty, dismissive. And I was fearful of his possible response. The look in his eye was almost lecherous.

'Little more than that which you already provide to the traitor Parrish. He has lived a charmed life, madam. But now it is time to clean the stable.'

'That which I provide for Matthew? Forgive me, but...'

Did he imagine some immoral liaison between myself and Matthew? I was reasonably certain there must be gossip of the sort around White Town. And, somehow, his foolishness gave me new confidence against him.

'Coy. And almost convincing. But you are betrayed, I fear. By your friend, Mistress Bridger.'

'I do not believe you.'

'Yet you must ask yourself how she and her disgraced husband have managed to remain here so long, in such comfort. And she a Jew, of course. You knew?'

'I did not.' It was obviously a lie, for I had certainly suspected as much.

'Naturally, you knew. They may not be required to wear a Jew mark, yet that does not mask them. So easy for one in her position to fall from grace, drag her family down with her. The only one of her kind, apart from your friends, de Paiva and his wife, still permitted within the walls, rather than in Jew Town.'

Of course, I was thinking about the distance that had grown between us since Elihu purchased the garden house that she had loved so much. But surely...

'How could Winifred Bridger possibly betray me?' I laughed at him.

'Oh, she has been our eyes and ears this long while, listened to your confidences, watched your liaisons. Enough for me to gather considerable evidence against you, Catherine. The secrets you garnered from the other wives. The tittle-tattle that Parrish employed to see so many of our faction dismissed, to seek control of the Council here. Yet

190

we quickly enough learned to play the same game. You see?'

'All I see, sirrah, is the disreputable rogue who helped to bring down decent men like Streynsham Master. And John Bridger himself, of course. Or did you not share that snippet with his wife?'

'Of course I shared it. Do you take me for a fool? My poor confession to her. About how sickened I have been at working under Elihu's instruction, directed by him to damage poor John. So, in the end you lost. And now we also have enough to bring you down too. Your family as well. All this I have laid before you. So think carefully upon your children, Mistress Yale. How easily those in London – or here, at Fort St. George – could fall within our reach. Or, at the least, think about how they will survive with their mother in prison, or worse.'

The children. Suffer the little children. The baby's kick once more, yet one less painful than this apparent betrayal by Winifred Bridger. But what Seaton had said was all too plausible. He would have stoked the fires of revenge in Winifred. But betrayal is still betrayal. And that brief sense of confidence had vanished again as quickly as it had come to me. I could hear the quaking in my own voice now.

'Elihu would never allow you to harm our children.'

'No? I suppose not. But he cannot defend the indefensible. A seditious wife with a seditious family? A wife who has helped her associate, Parrish, to plan sedition? De Paiva's Jewish conspiracy to raise funds for those who would plot against God's appointed king, seek to bring down the anointed House of Stuart.'

'You would have me act the spy upon my own friends.'

I hoped the words would properly convey my outrage, and that my outrage would still my own self-doubt.

'Perhaps a simple affidavit may suffice. But yet intelligence, madam. Intelligence that will provide irrefutable evidence against the king's enemies. The last of them. Evidence provided by Caesar's wife.'

I laughed in his face, of course. Yet, as I wandered back alone through the flickering shadows, the faces of my surviving children floated before me. Joseph Junior and Richard – how much they must be grown by now. Or Elford and Benjamin. David and Kate. This new burden that makes my steps so awkward – and yes, I could imagine those tiny features, even though those of baby Walt have become little more than a blur.

I thought too about how tenuous is our hold on life, saw images of the many families broken and destroyed both here and back in England by the turmoil of these troubled years. Matthew was right. The purges. The persecutions.

And I knew, though I already despised myself for it, that I would comply, for he had left me nothing but the excrement of choice.

God has punished me.

I find myself trapped in that passage within Joseph's mausoleum, the weight of the obelisk above crushing down upon me, and I cannot escape.

Visions that cut through the voices around me, seeking to offer condolence. Visions that drown out the echoes of the tomb. Visions of the baby's birth, her baptism and my latest churching. Anne. We named her Anne, for my mother. Though, Lord Jesus help me, I cannot bear to regard her. Visions of the moment when, immediately she drew her first breath, little Davy – my darling Dormouse – gave that mewling cry, the beginning of so many that would fill his final four months, day and night until, yesterday, he finally succumbed, perished in my arms.

Not yet four. Not yet four.

Oh, sweet Lord Almighty, I offered up *senhor* de Paiva as that creature Seaton had demanded, and then he was dead. The very day before David fell ill.

So here I am, trapped. Joseph at my back within his cold cave and there, just across the arched tunnel beneath the Pallavaram pyramid, the yawning vault into which they push my child's casket.

Husband, I whisper to Joseph in my mind. *My one true love. Watch over this little one. You know him not, but he is my flesh too. And therefore somehow your own. Perhaps intercede on my behalf with the Lord our God, that He might forgive the wickedness I have done.*

Yet I remain trapped, as the vault is closed, seeing the words that may one day be written as his epitaph. *Here lies David, son of the Honourable Elihu Yale, born on the fifteenth day of May 1684 and died on the twenty-fifth of January 1687/8.* Something of that order. And no, of course his mother shall not be named there, for she does not deserve even that measure of mention. All so cold, so final, as I fight to bring back every memory, every moment of Davy's short life, to fill this screaming in my brain, and to store those memories and moments there, to cement the pictures in place as securely as the vault's headstone. The contentment he brought me each time he nestled against my breast; the joy he gave as he tried to form his first sounds; the way he brought a lump to my throat whenever he grew excited to see me; his first tentative steps. Oh, Davy, how shall I survive without you in my life?

And worse, there is this. The question. No, not a question. The knowledge. That all those moments, those countless moments of pure joy, priceless to me, the mother, are those that leave not the slightest mark upon the child when he or she has grown. Lost. No single vestige or recollection of those early years unless I myself retain them. But I know the little one does not possess them.

So, Joseph my love, watch over him if you are able. Teach him about his mama, for I know there will be no vestige of my being left for him to recall, wherever his infant soul may wander.

This climate, this place, rots all. It turns everything to rust or corruption.

'Seriously?' I said, as we stood on the *veranda*, watching Katherine Nicks, her brood of children and her servants snaking back towards her home on Choultry Street. 'You intend to allow her the contract in replacement of *senhor* de Paiva?'

'Whyever not?' said Elihu. 'She has more acumen in that regard than anybody else in White Town and I am not authorised to employ anybody for the Company's diamond transactions who does not reside within the walls.'

'And your private business partner too. How convenient.'

'Why should that trouble you, Catherine, for pity's sake? I have told you before. God Almighty gave me this great gift, to create wealth. It would be sacrilege to waste it.'

The sun was an uncut gem, disappearing beyond the ragged skyline in a setting of deepest copper, to the strains of monkeys screeching in the guava plantations and the noisy abundance of Black Town's late evening.

'It was the Lord who gave the gift? Truly? Strange, I believed it was my marriage portion, Joseph's fortune, which made this possible for you. Yet I should have seen this coming, I suppose. We had only a business arrangement, after all, you and I. Joseph's fortune on one side, protection for my children on the other.'

I had married him because I wanted an equal, a genuine partnership, though all I now have is a rival. A fine line between those two cousins. Elihu an antagonist. This was my money, Joseph's money, when all is said and done. Money with which he has become so free.

'And do I not provide for them – the children?' he said.

I sniffed at the air, some stench of rotten vegetation carried on the light breeze. Some dead thing. Some other thing dead beyond that, from my heart.

'You have forgotten? It has slipped your busy mind?'

'My golden boy, you mean? What? You were about to scold me that I have not remembered little Davy's birthing day? We must all grieve in our own way, wife.'

'He was barely cold in his tomb before you were back in Council. Next day. The very next day!'

'As you remind me each week. Though I fail to understand why you should think it necessary. My son and heir, Catherine. My only son. And if this marriage disappoints you so much, I wonder that you should have suggested it so readily. Ah, but you needed a father to figure in your boys' lives, did you not? No matter that this might be seen to diminish me, to stimulate the Fort's gossips. But sadly life is rarely simple and, with Davy buried, there were duties to attend. Or would you rather I had left the rest of our children to the ravages of Sambhaji's hordes?'

The funeral barely finished when the news arrived. Sambhaji's Maratha warriors, two thousand wild horsemen, plundering a town barely a dozen miles distant, five hundred massacred, and Sambhaji determined that Madras Patnam should be next to suffer.

'Then our Lord Jesus be praised for Matthew Parrish,' I snapped.

'Parrish? My dear, it was my raising of the new levies, the daily practice of the great guns that deterred the rogue.'

And there they were, marching across the open ground towards the Fort House, a trained band of native militia with their tatterdemalion uniforms and strange array of weapons.

'Oh, what a fool I am. I had imagined it was Matthew's mission to the Mughal Emperor.'

There had been a deal struck, the Emperor Aurangzeb persuaded to dispatch his general, Sadeek, with a huge force to drive off Sambhaji. It seems his hatred for the Marathas far exceeds his loathing for John Company. And, in return, several conditions: those fifty thousand gold pagodas to be paid for the concession here; all the Mughal Emperor's subjects who had previously taken refuge in Black Town during the Marathas' advance to be forcibly returned into his territories; and the port's trade in slaves to be abolished. Yes, abolished.

'That mission has cost us a great deal,' Elihu snapped.

'Yet saved our skins. Perhaps our souls too.'

The trade in human bondage has taken a strange but welcome turn. Divine intervention, surely. First, Elihu's indulgence that no children should be exported had been cursed as a foolishness by Father Ephraim, of all people – because it had left unprecedented numbers of abandoned children in Black Town, their enslaved parents not being beneficiaries of my husband's half-hearted generosity. At times we should be careful what we wish for. But, second, Aurangzeb's demands for his own subjects to leave Madras Patnam, return to the villages from whence they had come, brought some immediate relief in our famine crisis. Fewer mouths to feed. Third, the famine was further alleviated by the arrival of the *Royal James* and other vessels loaded with grain to fill our warehouses. And, fourth, this enforced abolition of the trade entirely, at Aurangzeb's command.

Elihu picked up a small bag of brilliants from the *veranda* table, samples that the Nicks woman had left for his assessment, and he tossed the thing upon his palm as though weighing the contents.

'It hits our purses,' he said, 'yet I thought it would warm your heart – that we passed the order through Council yesterday. As close to Davy's birthing day as I could manage. There will be fines now, significant fines, for those who continue to trade illegally. Perhaps that will help to offset some of the Company's losses.'

It did, indeed, help to ease the aching inside me, but I would not let him see that.

'So long as the Company does not suffer,' I sneered. 'How pleased I am. Yet I should have felt more satisfied without the knowledge that such strict enforcement stems more from Aurangzeb's threat of his wrath should we not entirely comply. In any case, Elihu, the world knows that with the famine relieved, the surfeit of potential slaves has dried up. Hypocrisy. What? You shake your head? Deny that the trade has become more trouble than it was previously worth. You know how much this offended me. Still offends me. Will always offend me, taint me because it makes me a hypocrite too.'

'For good or ill, it is over.'

'Over? For our purse it may be over. Yet for those thousands already sold as chattel, how many generations of their children will continue to wear our chains? And warm my heart? How could that be? Do we not have *senhor* de Paiva on our conscience?'

'De Paiva? That was months ago. Went to Golconda in the line of duty. To check on his diamond mines. Hardly our fault that he fell ill. Hardly unusual, my dear.'

One in five, I thought. But ill? By the time he was brought back there was not a person who believed other than that he had been poisoned. His manservant's lurid description of his early symptoms. I, perhaps better than anybody, knew the truth of this. Seaton had demanded that I sign an affidavit, confirming that I had been told, by *senhor* de Paiva himself that, besides his responsibility to the Company, he had involvement in procuring funds, through the same diamond trade, for the benefit of the Monmouth Cabal and other covert groups dedicated to the fall of His Majesty. With the affidavit, Seaton had told me, nobody would question whatever accident might befall him. After all, he had said, who will concern themselves about one Jew, more or less? And he had been correct.

'But Seaton...' I began, almost convinced that I should tell him the truth. But he refused to listen.

'Seaton!' he said, taking up his best pipe from the table and beginning to fill it from the tobacco jar. 'Always this obsession with poor Vincent. You will malign him once too often, madam. And *senhor* de Paiva? We have at least taken care of his widow.'

Oh yes, this is true. With almost unseemly haste, Elihu insisted that, given Jeronima's need to now vacate their fine dwelling on Gloucester Street, she should immediately take up residence, along with her Jewish maid, in our own garden house – the house we had purchased from the Bridgers, and I cannot help seeing some dreadful link between Winifred Bridger's betrayal of me to Seaton, my own betrayal of Jacques de Paiva, and Jeronima's residency. The garden house and betrayal.

'Take care of her?' I said. 'Can you imagine the way this has been received around the Fort?'

'I am the President, Catherine. Do I truly need to trouble myself with foolish rumour? Ah, but here comes Tanani with the children.'

'Children?'

I remember touching my fingers to the locket at my throat, which now concealed within those tiny miniatures of both Walt and Davy.

198

'*Memsahib*, your daughters. Ready for their beds.'

Kate ran forward and threw herself in my arms, and I planted a kiss upon her forehead before passing her to Elihu. But the other? I could not even bear to look upon her face. There has been a wet nurse for her since David died and, before that, I had watched the way in which Anne had slowly sucked the life out of the boy, strengthening with each day that he weakened. Or that was how it seemed to me, still seems that way, and I cannot shake it. I try, but the image persists.

'Catherine,' Elihu snapped. 'Your daughter, our child – for heaven's sake! Little Annie, God bless her.' He set Kate down and handed her back to the *ayah*, made some clumsy effort to stroke the baby's face. 'You cannot surely wish her ill,' he said. 'What troubles you, wife?'

I had no idea. It is usual for me to suffer rapid changes in my humours after birthing, a certain tendency towards tears and irritability. But those things soon pass. Yet this? One moment I can look out upon the green hills and feel that I am mistress of all I survey, the next I am buried by an all-consuming terror that the creatures dwelling in those hills must surely come to devour me. One instant I pace the floor, as skittish as a mongoose and then, moments later, I cower in corners, barely able to remember my own name, my limbs like lead. Today I may find myself rushing about White Town, talking nonsense to anybody who will listen, though those grow fewer by the day. And now I do not even have Winifred Bridger for company. I have not confronted her, of course, for I know not how without risking exposure of my own sin, my betrayal of *senhor* de Paiva. So I merely shun her. She knows, though. I see it in her eyes. And tomorrow I will see each of the other women as enemies also, keeping secrets from me, plotting my downfall. Hateful women. Later, I will know that little Annie is possessed by the Devil, by some distortion of Davy's soul. Thus, there will be serpents. Fearsome serpents straight from my nightmares of Walt's death. Oh, how they bring back my terrors. Crawling upon my floors, creeping inside my clothes. Though always, always, this resentment: that Elihu might have saved Walter, yet failed; or that he could have procured better treatment for Davy, but had not done so. His fault, both of their deaths. His fault.

'To bed, Tanani,' I said, and the *ayah* took the girls with nothing but that slight affirmative swaying of her head. I was still struggling to find a reason that might satisfy Elihu's question. 'The boys,' I finally told him. 'In England. I fear for them and it defies my logic. Tell me, husband – that thing of which you spoke, the way you were so used at St. Paul's school… Is that true?'

'Do you taunt me, wife? What would you wish to hear? Some admission that it could not be other than the truth? A monstrous truth. Buried so deep within me and shared with not a single living soul except yourself because – well, do I need to explain? Yet you cannot believe that your boys face that same nightmare, Catherine. Can you?'

The monkey madness again, that jarring jungle screech that split the gloom. I think it was the monkeys anyway, and I looked into Elihu's face, saw the pain there, the hope for some crumb of comfort, despite his anger, his bluster. Yet I felt nothing but repugnance.

Yes, here everything turns to rot, rust or corruption.

I read afresh my previous entry and it shocks me, shames me, yet it makes a strange prelude to all that has befallen me this month gone. For the *Royal James* may have brought us grain, alleviated the famine, but it also brought us piracy. Pillage. And great danger.

Dear Sathiri helped me through the worst of my black humours, though they are never far from my door. These days they tend to take the form of retrospection, my looking back upon those paths I have trodden, searching for the forks and crossroads at which, had I chosen a different route, some of my tragedies might have been avoided: kept Joseph at my side; averted Walter's awful end; made my bed with other men, more admirable men, just in the event that I had missed that better turning with Joseph; taken Davy from here while there was still time; or perhaps not made the error of this latest babe I have been carrying these past couple of months.

These illogical humours have been little helped by the other evil news all around. The Mughal Emperor's forces may have put Sambhaji's savages to flight but they are far from defeated, the garrison left on alert and Fort St. George to all intents and purposes living under siege conditions yet again. And then the news that Aurangzeb's fury against John Company has been kindled afresh. Despite the truce and payments negotiated through Matthew's diplomacy, the Directors have sent an entirely new fleet to blockade the Mughal ports on the west coast, have attacked pilgrim vessels on their way to Mecca. As a result, Aurangzeb has threatened to drive every Englishman into the sea.

It has all taken its toll on our people. Half a world away from home. Oppressive, choking heat, month after month. Illness as the monsoon's skirmish line. Surgeon Heathfield one of the first fatalities, dozens more in the ensuing weeks. Elihu's insistence that the situation called for all hands to man the proverbial pumps. Hard work, he said. Noses to the grindstone – that was the best remedy. Business as usual. The trained bands, the native levies, the Portuguese recruits, all set the task of strengthening our defences, of preventing potential dangers, stripping thatch from Black Town's roofing lest it become a fire hazard either through accident or invaders' intent. Many of the ruinous dwellings demolished too. Discipline. Rules. The factors and writers all given double duty. And oh, how it was despised, the resentment towards my husband among officials and levies alike almost matching my own.

Was there a positive side to all this? Of course. For the state of alert, the continued though diminished threat from Sambhaji, the growing threat from Aurangzeb, had at least provided Elihu with all the excuse he needed to delay rounding up the leaders of those reluctant to pay their taxes and executing them, as he had been instructed by the Directors. Yet even that temporary delay could not last forever and last month another ship arrived, this time carrying additional John Company soldiers, more than a hundred of them. These were hard-drinking men, rough, sharp-edged as our Golconda diamonds, encamped beyond the walls, their purpose clear – orders that they must be used to finally eradicate the taxation rebels.

'Well, shall you do it?' I demanded to know one morning as Elihu and I sat at our respective distant ends of the dining table, the *salmagundi* and rice porridge cooked to break our fast untouched and growing cold upon the side board.

'This instruction bears the stamp of both Company and Crown.' He slammed his hand down hard upon the polished mahogany. 'It cannot be ignored. As President I cannot simply disregard the thing. In any case, the headmen have had their warning. Every chance. We have reduced the amount they must pay to little more than a token. Yet they defy me. Despite the protection we afford them – have afforded them for forty years. Kept them free.'

'Free to suffer starvation, you mean. Free to be taken into slavery. Free from piratical acts?'

'"*Aye, there's the rub,*"' he quoted. 'These pirates, I must deal with them, of course. My duty as President and Governor. And who better to set them by their heels than these new fellows.'

'Little better than buccaneers themselves, are they not?'

'"*There is nothing either good or bad, but thinking makes it so.*" If you see evil in those men, Catherine, I am sure you will find it. Yet I see no fault in setting one pirate to catch another.'

It was nothing new, piracy along the Coromandel Coast. Occasionally our vessels would arrive in the roads bearing tales of some daring but usually thwarted attack upon them by desperate Moorish corsairs in their deep-sea *dhows*. Yet, three years ago, that all changed. Roundsmen. Those who had previously been content to plunder the Caribbean, then found even more lucrative hunting grounds by rounding the Cape of Good Hope to raid rich Mughal ships in the Arabian Sea. Much, indeed, as John Company's own vessels have done. But the Roundsmen had now brought their audacious business around the southern tip of India and into the Bay of Bengal. And if there were fortunes to be made plying trade for the Honourable English East India Company, they were a pittance compared to those that could be garnered through more open piracy. So, whenever there was news of Roundsmen along our shorelines, it was commonplace for Company sailors to mutinously abandon their own ships, set out on a new and lawless career.

'Your particular concern about these rogues, I suppose, has nothing to do with your own vessels?'

Elihu's personal enterprise has grown so large that, in addition to his first ship, the *Diamond*, he has now purchased a second – and, perhaps predictably, this he has named the *David*.

He looked at me as though I were a fool.

'A threat to one is a threat to us all. The Company too.'

'Then how many are they?' I asked, determined to ignore the slight.

'The last report told us there were the six who mutinied from the *Royal James*, as well as the survivors of that Roundsmen's brigantine, the *Devil's Pearl* – the one sunk beyond Pulicat. So, another dozen, we think. And then a ragged bunch of local villains. They are thirty or forty in total, according to – well, our reports.'

'From Matthew, you mean?'

'From Parrish, yes. Must we even have him over the breakfast table?'

'Perhaps you would prefer to have Mistress de Paiva over it instead. Or is that something you reserve for the garden house?'

'By God, Catherine, I shall not have this! These damn'd suspicions.' He was shouting, as he often does now, and it pleases me to enrage him so, to see him storm from the table as he did that morning. 'Very well,' he bellowed, grasping the sword, scabbard and shoulder strap, more ceremonial than functional. 'I shall lead this expedition myself, see if you shall think better of me, less of Parrish, upon my return.'

A week ago, the day after Elihu had gone off in the Governor's palanquin at the head of his new ruffians – as well as much of our original garrison and the Black Town levies – I managed to find some peace. Elihu's forces had marched north, towards Masulipatnam. For Matthew's reports placed the pirates in a camp around the shores of the Pulicat Lakes.

So it was uncommonly quiet. Another Sunday afternoon. Tanani had settled the two children for their *siesta* and I was contemplating that same temptation, for this latest pregnancy tires me so. I had returned to the second part of *The Pilgrim's Progress* that Mama had sent me with her other gifts, both for myself and Elihu. Those gifts are a well-established ritual now and, for every inch that the gulf between my husband and me widens, the tighter he seems to stitch close the distance between himself and my mother.

She had been on my mind, therefore: the glowing references in her latest letter to my good fortune in finding Elihu; the book, and that section about Christiana leading her four sons and their neighbour, Mercy, forth upon their journey – which has struck such a chord with me; and, finally, Mama's assurances about the continued well-being of Joseph Junior, Richard, Elford and Benjamin, my own dear boys – though it is a sadness to me that only Benjamin, the youngest, should have penned a personal note, a ten year old's careful scrawl, to accompany Mama's missive. Still, I could see him in that moment, bent across the writing slope in my parents' withdrawing room, quill in hand and tongue protruding from between his teeth in concentration. It made me weep pitifully.

Then that moment when the shots rang out.

At first it barely disturbed my sojourn. Common enough, after all, this past year, for the great guns to be practised, or the garrison and its levies drilled in musketry. Yet then it struck me that this was a Sunday, the garrison stripped, only a section or two at most left in the Fort

House under Matthew's frustrated command. And, as I carried the book out onto the *veranda* to ascertain the cause of this untimely disturbance – though, so far, without any perception of possible danger – I could see some of those men stumbling out of their quarters between the northern bastions, racing for the pike racks or fumbling with their matchlocks.

Then, to my horror, there was the crackle of more muskets. Men fell, and a haze of gun smoke drifted across the scene.

A drum within the fort began to beat out a tattoo, a call to arms, though muffled and somehow impotent. More dead and wounded and, now, many heavily armed bravos sprinting into view around each of the Fort House corners I could see.

There was a tug at my sleeve, the chief *pankah* boy, other servants crowding the door behind him.

'*Memsahib*,' he pleaded. 'We must close door. Inside, *memsahib*.'

Screams away to our right. And there, on the outer ramparts, two sentries were being butchered with clubs and axes.

'In a moment,' I gasped, biting back the bile rising in my gorge. 'The rest of you, go. The Sea Gate, quickly!'

How many servants were still within? I had no idea. Some lived in the narrow barracks behind the house, others within Black Town, and it was the duty of Tanani, as *ayah*, or Geerthan as *khansama* – head steward since Akbar's death – to regulate how many we needed in service on any given day. '*Jao!*' I shouted Go! And they reluctantly obeyed, though I knew that Tanani would stay with the little ones regardless of any orders I might give.

Bullets whistled in all directions and I knew the *pankah* boy was right. I should join Tanani, bar the doors and windows. But then I saw Matthew.

He was outside that north door of the blockhouse, a horse pistol in each fist, yelling to his men to get back, heaving a wounded fellow onto his shoulders. It was, after all, the purpose of this strongpoint, to provide a refuge of last resort for the three hundred family members of Fort St. George, its two companies of regulars and its resident writers, the other single men. Yet our families were not inside its protective shell, its jutting corner bastions. We were trapped out here, at the mercy of wild animals.

Those of the raiders with muskets had found shelter, behind carts or bales left – contrary to regulations – in the open ground between the Fort House and its surrounding streets. From there they exchanged fire with Matthew's defenders at their loopholes or now high upon the battlements.

But there were others, fearless of the risk, running from the far side of the square, arms full of loot, vestments and altar chalices from the church, overflowing jewelry boxes and fine satins from the houses of whatever unfortunates they had already ransacked.

The crackle of guns. More smoke. And from the eastern wall, another bunch of outlaws, a towering, ugly brute at their head, a brute with the features of a ravenous wolf and swinging a long, curved scimitar. Behind him he dragged a woman by her jet-dark hair. Sathiri.

I glanced quickly towards the Fort House, terrified for my friend, seeking any sign of Matthew in the desperate hope he might rescue her, but I could not see him.

Something clawed at me through my fears. A wakening suspicion that, deadly as this attack might be under any circumstances, there was direction to this. Motive beyond the obvious. But whatever that direction it was hidden, far beyond my fear for Sathiri, my fear for my children, the fear for our home.

What to do? I was helpless to save my friend from here and, so it appeared, was Matthew. Useless. My fists clenched in frustration.

A stray ball splintered the *veranda*'s rail near my hand, and I recoiled as a sliver of wood sliced a gash in my arm. I cried out, dropped the precious book, caught the eye of that wolf-faced devil who had Sathiri in his grip, and I saw him point his sabre in my direction.

It was all the spur I needed and, clasping my dripping arm with my good hand, I finally hurtled back inside the house, rattled home the bolts behind the front door and ran from room to room, as though the devil himself was at my heels, slamming closed the shutters as best I could on my downstairs windows, my anguish at being unable to help Sathiri swelling with each and every action. Shutting her out too, I silently screamed.

Shots and shouts outside. I could hear Tanani even above all this, keening in fear, though I had no doubt she would defend the girls albeit at the cost of her own life.

Yet those shutters would not hold long against a determined attack. And were there arms in the house? Elihu had accumulated some fine weapons over the years, but these were trade goods, I recalled, stored in his godowns. Fine duelling pistols, swords and other collectors' pieces. But real weapons?

I raced for the stairs – clumsy with my damaged arm, my skirts not raised enough to prevent me stumbling, suddenly aware of the babe in my belly – at the same instant as the whole house seemed to quake, the front door almost sundered when somebody threw their weight against it. The crash of the impact, the cursing and roaring from the terrace walk. Then the splintering of a window shutter.

At the top of the staircase, with my heart racing so much I was certain it must fail, I turned along the gallery, barged past my own chamber and past Elihu's, until I reached the larger of the children's rooms, and there I found Tanani, her eyes wide with fear, holding the babe. But not alone for, in defiance of my orders, there too were the *pankah* boy, holding little Kate, and Geerthan, the latter with his protective hand upon the *ayah*'s shoulder.

Oh, praise be! I thought. *Such loyalty.*

And then I cursed myself for a fool, stopped dead in my tracks. It was not a protective hand at all. It held a narrow, wicked blade that he pressed to Tanani's throat.

'I am sorry, *memsahib*,' he said. 'Truly, Geerthan is sorry.'

Motive beyond the obvious. Betrayal. How? For what purpose? And how far did it reach? I ignored Geerthan's pitiful apology and looked instead to the *pankah* boy, to poor Katie in his arms, while below there was the crash of crockery, the clatter of ransacked drawers and coffer chests, the roar of drunken voices. Geerthan's gaze turned swiftly to the door and the *pankah* boy seized the moment, stared into my eyes, the merest shake of his head to confirm that he was no part of that. But was he being honest? Did it matter? Because, by then, they were coming up the stairs, heavy steps upon the treads, and a voice, coarse accent – Irish, I decided.

'Struggle any more, you black-hearted jade, an' I'll pull out every inch of your heathen's hair.'

I stared around the room, desperate to find some weapon, some way of setting Tanani free, but there was nothing. Just the thickening of the already threatening mood, a chill fallen upon us that had nothing to do with the *pankah* boy, for the ceiling fan hung motionless, its hempen ropes dangling around his knees where he was still nursing Kate, trying to calm her distress.

No, nothing to do with the *pankah* boy, that chill. And I forced myself to avert my eyes from its true source, tried to close my ears as well, though that was impossible. Kate's whimpering. The *pankah* boy's soothing croon. Geerthan's continued pathetic pleas for forgiveness. Tanani's keening. And now the noise of brutish struggle as those evil creatures forced themselves into the inviolability of my children's sanctuary. Cursing. Sathiri's quiet agonies. The stink of those cruel men – their leather, their sweat, their iron, their rum. The ring of their steel. My horror made me want to vomit. Cold sweat upon my brow.

'What were you promised?' I spat at Geerthan, into the midst of this chaos.

'My life, *memsahib*.'

I turned to face my attackers, my knees like liquid and my stomach heaving.

'And you!' I stammered. 'Release my friend or, I swear, you will feel my husband's wrath.'

I have to admit that this wolf-faced fellow was not as ugly as I had first imagined. His features were long, certainly. Canine, that was true. Much grey in his wiry beard, his matted hair. But there was sharp intelligence also in his deerhound eyes. Intelligence – and humour. It surprised me as he laughed at my intended threat. Not cynical laughter, merely amusement.

'A pity, lady, he's not here. He'd be the Governor, I'm guessing.'

He had sheathed his sabre, I saw, though his fingers were still entwined in Sathiri's long hair. My glance met hers and I saw that there was no fear in her eyes, simply pain and indignation.

'Governor and President,' I said. 'And I will thank you once more to unhand both my friend and my property.'

For I had seen that, in his free hand, he was holding my book, the one I had dropped from the *veranda*. Yet I realised I had misspoken when he turned towards Sathiri.

'This heathen?' he said. 'Is it possible to be both friend and property?'

'I intended the book, sirrah, as I am sure you must know.'

I took accompt of the sword, set in its scabbard hanging from his broad and buckled shoulder belt, the four pocket pistols holstered

208

beneath each shoulder. And I counted into the rogue's stock his two companions: one of them cruelly scarred – face like a spiked fish – sporting a cudgel; and the other, wiry as a monkey, hefting a spontoon, a half-pike. There was something familiar about him.

'Ah, the book,' said wolf-face. He finally released Sathiri. Or rather he pushed her to the floor. 'This? I read Part One. He has a certain wit, your Mister Bunyan, don't you reckon? It's what this world needs, more instruction in morality.'

'Men like you? Only capable of learning finally at the end of a rope.'

'"*By Laws and Ordinances you will not be saved,*"' he said, waving the book at me, even though the quotation comes from Part One, '"*since you came not in by the door.*"' But his gaze was elsewhere and I followed it, to where the *pankah* boy was rolling little Kate away from him across the polished floor while, in one other fluid movement, he looped the bitter end of the pulley ropes around Geerthan's ankles, pulled sharply and brought the wretch crashing down upon the baby's crib.

I was upon that treacherous *khansama* without thought, my nails raking at his eyes.

'Then see what your life shall be worth when my husband returns!' I spat.

He screamed, dropped the knife, sent it skittering across the boards, and I was dimly aware of the *pankah* boy seizing Tanani's arm, pulling both her and baby Annie to the same corner where Kate was howling.

It is difficult to recall now precisely how the thing played out. Something of a blur. For our recollections are so often questionable, doubtful, in the sense of leaving us in two minds, undecided between one image of events and another. But these are the things I remember – or think that I do.

The wolf-faced man's hands upon me, the book falling open to the floor. He dragged me away from Geerthan, rending the fabric of my sleeve, knocking my cap askew, scattering my curls across my face like a curtain to block my view still further.

'Enough!' he cried. 'If you want to see those children again, enough.'

Deep within me I screamed, for his menace had conjured an image of Katie's face. Only Katie. Of the baby, Anne, there was nothing. And even now, as I write this, the horror of my indifference repels me.

Yet then my inward howl seemed to manifest itself outwardly also, thundering in my ear, a bellow of pain from wolf-face and I saw that Sathiri had seized the knife, leapt upon the pirate's back and buried the blade deep into his shoulder.

'Jade!' he cried, and shook her off, still held me but reached with his left hand to the knife's hilt.

There was a sickening crack of shattered bone, Sathiri crashing to the floorboards beside me, her skull a mess of blood and that devil with his cudgel standing over her.

'What say you, skipper?' he cackled. 'Will that serve? For a message to Parrish?'

'Shut your stupid mouth,' shouted wolf-face. But he need have no worry, for that bravo would never speak again. The third pirate had driven his half-pike through the rogue's neck, released a fountain of gore that sprayed across my face as he pulled it free.

'Mistress...' he began, but got no further. One of those pocket pistols in the pirate captain's hand sparked, flamed and barked, filled the room with the sulphur stench of gun smoke.

'These days, mistress,' said the pirate, 'you can trust nobody.'

I looked into the dead man's eyes, wondered why he should look so familiar. Though by then wolf-face had tossed the weapon aside, drawn a second pistol and employed it to also still Geerthan's whimpering forever. I thought for a terrible instant that the slaughter might continue but, after a moment's hesitation, he only cursed, holstered the discharged firearm and, after briefly and vainly attempting once more to reach the knife, to dislodge it, he grabbed my arm.

'God dammit,' he said. 'It wasn't supposed to be like this.'

And then he was hauling me back towards the gallery.

'Look after them,' I called to the *pankah* boy. 'Tell my husband...'

But it was all lost in the chaos. Down the stairs, through the ruin of my reception hall, the damaged front door, more shouting beyond, yet no shooting. Had we lost the battle then? Was Fort St. George taken? Would Elihu find somebody to care for the girls? Jeronima de Paiva, of course. And thank our Lord Jesus that the boys were safe with Mama.

I felt no more fear then, as though it had exhausted itself, even out there on the terrace walk. More death. The piteous moaning of the wounded. But a cordon of Matthew's soldiers, their muskets at the ready, lined up before the house. Matthew was with them.

'Sathiri,' he shouted, 'is she safe, Catherine?'

'Stand down your men, mister,' said wolf-face, 'or it'll go worse for the Governor's pretty wife.'

'Release that lady,' Matthew told him. 'And the rest of your prisoners. If you do, there may be some chance to save your hide.'

'We need safe passage. A ship to take off the rest of my men. And a thousand gold pagodas. Then we'll see.'

'The rest of your men are either dead or taken. Those left are too few to crew anything bigger than a surf boat.'

'Safe passage and the gold then.'

'Matthew,' I sobbed. 'Sathiri...'

'Stow it!' said wolf-face.

Matthew was silent for such a time, it seemed an eternity. Yet he read my eyes and I saw his features freeze as he realised the truth. And me? I could think of nothing but Sathiri, her poor shattered head.

'You now have a simple choice,' said Matthew at last. 'The fate you deserve, fastened alive within a gibbet's frame and left to suffer a long and painful death, drowned in the incoming tide, your body become food for the creatures of the deep. Or a swift and merciful execution.'

Wolf-face looked past the dead and wounded in the square, and along the street to where a silent Black Town crowd had gathered. Then he glanced up to the sky, the wheeling vultures also silent. Peaceful. And he released me, fumbled with that one still functioning hand to unsheathe his sword, to drop it on the *veranda*, followed by the two pistols below his useless right shoulder. But the third pistol he could not manage.

'Mistress?' he said, and I was happy to assist, though I almost stumbled, the relief at my rescue making my head swim, fighting with that memory of Sathiri's murder, rubbing at the bruising where wolf-face had gripped me so harshly. I was filled with a lust for revenge, thought briefly that I should use the pistol. But then he shouted to Matthew. 'You're Parrish?' he said.

'You know me, sirrah?'

'Only this, Parrish. That it wasn't supposed to be like this.'

No, I thought. It was the *pankah* boy. Perhaps if he had not taken that valiant action with the rope. And, as Matthew stepped forward to secure the pirate's surrender, I realised that I did not even know my own *pankah* boy's name.

So, the *Royal James* has brought us so much: the grain to relieve our famine; the correspondence and gifts from Mama; the pirates and their rapine; and, one final thing, instruction from the Crown that the Fort St. George Presidency is now authorised – required indeed – to fly the royal standard alongside the Company's own flag. Thus we must hoist our loyalty to Catholic King James upon the wind for all to see. Though what better way to honour that new royal standard than to raise it first, four days ago, to celebrate the punishment meted out to the few surviving pirates and those mutineers from the *Royal James* who had joined them. Examples to be made. My husband's authority to be restored.

Their wolf-faced captain had been put to the hot iron in an effort to discover the truth behind his claim that it was not supposed to end as it had done. And the other rogue's words – a message to Parrish. Yet wolf-face stubbornly refused to say more, simply to give his name, Samuel Bembridge, and finally he was shot – as he had been promised – at the Sea Gate by firing squad.

But first there had been Sathiri's funeral. The Gentue burial ground and all the surrounding area, the entire guava garden and beyond, thronged with mourners. Her body had been cleansed at the home she shared as Matthew's *bibi*, and dressed in her finest *saree*, then laid out facing south, where the Lord of Death awaited her. An oil lamp at her head and a small coin placed at her temples. I had been there throughout, remembering her wisdom, her mantras, my tears cascading down my cheeks, but lost in the verses recited by the old face-painted holy women in their red and saffron robes. The smell of incense. The tinkling of finger bells. The whole sadness repeated again when all Sathiri's friends and relatives, scores of them, gathered to sing their lamentations.

Some time later, a group of exquisitely attired musicians arrived, drums beating and cymbals crashing outside while the women set about the task of building Sathiri's funeral palanquin, a *paadai*, bamboo poles, coconut tree leaves, garlands of flowers. More rituals. And then the noisy procession through the streets of Fort St. George, permission graciously given by my husband, the *paadai* borne on the shoulders of my friend's male relatives. A notable absence of our White Town neighbours, of course, but in Black Town the procession assumed almost a carnival atmosphere, dancers spinning and cavorting among the crowd. But at the boundaries of the burial ground, we women were prevented from going any further. Matthew told me later that it was the custom, lest the women related to the deceased should be so overcome by our grief at sight of the funeral itself that we might throw ourselves on the pyre. And he described the final ceremonies for me, the lighting of the fire. He described them with difficulty, barely able to force the words through the barrier of his pain and loss.

So I was able to see her consumed by the flames only from a distance, my own body raked with sorrow too, a profound emptiness within me at the realisation that it has been Sathiri's friendship – more than friendship – which has made so many of my trials and tribulations more tolerable here in Madras Patnam.

The following day, Matthew and Sathiri's nephews returned to the burial ground, collected her ashes within a sealed jar, and the processions began again, this time to the shoreline where the ashes were scattered upon the waves. Later, the feasting, tributes paid to this woman who had been, after all, the most renowned *dai* in the whole region – and my truest friend.

By then, the executions had begun, the shooting of wolf-face almost an extension of the funeral arrangements. Next evening, one of the mutineers from the *Royal James* was given the drop from the yardarm of his former vessel. Another was hanged at the Black Town gibbet, his body riveted into the iron frame, that it might not fall apart too quickly as its flesh rotted or was slowly devoured by vermin and vulture. And, two days ago, we gathered at the Choultry Gate to see the three remaining mutineers punished. A small scaffold had been erected and, upon it, Herrold the Blacksmith's brazier burned brightly, while Elihu made a speech about crime and punishment that was so clearly directed, not only towards the three mutineers but also at the Black Town headmen who had been summoned to stand at the front of the crowd. And they were required to remain in the full glare of the sun, only those of us with the appropriate status within White Town afforded the privilege of our own roundel parasols or, in the case of the Council, their own shaded seating.

'Those three,' I said to Matthew Parrish at my side, still dressed in mourning white, 'are they truly more innocent than the rest?'

'Hardly innocent, though played no part in the raid, it seems. Deserted their fellows before it began. So, traitors even to their fellow-mutineers. But your husband has come to some agreement with their master, the captain of the *Royal James*. Punishment that will serve both their ends. For myself, I would gladly have put them to the sword. Their mutiny attracted others to their cause, fanned the flames that ended...'

In flames, yes. Sathiri's murder.

'Oh, Matthew, what shall we do without her?'

'I cannot speak of it, Catherine. She would hate me for it, but there is revenge to be had, and I shall not begin to know peace until I feed upon it, sate myself. To still the famine within me.'

I had told him, naturally. About the words of the wretch who killed her. A message for Parrish. And he had sworn he would extract the truth from that wolf-faced Roundsman, Samuel Bembridge, before he died – though in that he had been unsuccessful.

'A message,' I said, 'what does it mean? Did the fellow reveal nothing when the irons seared him?'

'Nothing,' Matthew replied. 'I have turned it over and over again. There can be no logic here. But, if there were any, I could only assume they must have known my man had infiltrated their camp, wished to take some revenge.'

'The fellow with the half-pike was one of your own?'

'Though plainly failed to forewarn us of the attack. And that makes me wonder whether their original plan did not intend quite so much mayhem. He must have believed there would be time to raise the alarm.'

'It had gone awry long before the *pankah* boy's intervention, then.'

I knew his name by then. Naturally I did.

'Of course, Catherine. And you? The baby?'

'We seem to have suffered no ill effects. Though how I will fare, birthing this one without Sathiri to ward away the evils, I have no idea. My ninth. Sweet Jesus, my ninth. My tenth if I include, as I must, the mite I lost from my womb. And in my thirty-eighth year, heaven help me.'

I received no answer, however. Elihu's speech was finished and he had summoned Matthew forward to preside over the punishments, while the same drums and cymbals that had danced Sathiri to her funeral now raised today's heat among the crowd almost to fever pitch. Oh, how humanity's humours race at the prospect of some self-righteous cruelty in the name of justice.

'My pleasure,' Matthew cried, and climbed the scaffold at the same time as my husband descended, the two men passing without exchanging even a word. But I saw Elihu whisper an instruction to one of the guards before taking his seat in the shade reserved for the President. A moment later, the soldier had found me.

'The Governor has requested that you join him, mistress.'

I could have ignored this "request" but I had already seen the Portuguese Cabal off to my left – Katherine Nicks and Jeronima de Paiva, with their new associate, Winifred Bridger – surrounded by servants and sheltering beneath their roundels. Between them they now had almost total control of the Company's official diamond trade and a great deal of White Town's private trade in gems too. And thus they were in almost daily liaison with Elihu. Liaison in its many disparate ways, I was certain. Jeronima still resident in the garden house, naturally, and Elihu – a man of strong passions – has not been near my own bed since we discovered that I was, once more, with child.

Of Winifred's role I can only speculate, but her peculiar betrayal rankles in an entirely other way. It calls for a different form of revenge than the one I plan for Jeronima and Katherine. Well, I have been working on it. Though, for now, I would take my chair alongside my husband, demonstrate to the world that I am still the President's wife, the still fecund mother of his children.

'I am glad you see fit to attend,' he said, as I received the barely courteous and begrudged greetings of the Council members. Tories to a man now, of course. The Cavalier faction. And I make no secret of my own loyalties. How I despise them. 'These punishments,' he continued, 'are intended in part, after all, to deal with these rogues' affront to the Governor's wife.'

'I should prefer, husband, that you might not pretend to punish them on my account. Those fellows may be guilty of a great deal but we both know they played no part in the abomination suffered by our household. Besides, it seems to me more profitable to seek out those responsible for the raid. For Sathiri's murder.'

'This again? They are pirates, woman. And Parrish's *bibi*? Really!'

Yes, pirates. Mutineers. The first of them now being dragged by three brawny soldiers in shirtsleeves, towards the brazier, our new surgeon on hand. The soldiers pinned the miscreant's arms, forced him to his knees, an arm tight around his neck and a fistful of hair to haul back his head while the fort's farrier, with wrapped hands, pulled the iron from the coals and applied it, sizzling and smoking, to the mutineer's left cheek. The scream must have been heard a mile away, the stink appalling from both seared flesh and singed hair. The surgeon dutifully performed his medical duties, splashed a sponge from a pail of water laced with strong vinegar and slapped it against the wound as the fellow swooned upon the platform, the large letter 'P' now embossed forever into his face.

'Pirates,' I said, 'who had apparently found some way to penetrate our home in advance and threaten Geerthan into betraying us. Geerthan, for pity's sake!'

'There were enough local rogues among the number of the dead. Both here and at their camp. A hundred possibilities.'

'And their capture of Sathiri? This supposed message for Matthew? Their clear aim of attacking our house in particular. Looking for me, Elihu. For me.'

'If we had moved into the Governor's official residence as I suggested, this would not have happened. Your own stubborn nature to blame. The Governor's house has its own guards. You know that.'

He gave a signal for the second mutineer to be brought before the farrier.

'It misses the point,' I snapped. 'We were targets, myself and Sathiri. Her capture or her killing some revenge for actions undertaken by one of your own merchant captains. Your misdirected jealousies are not important here.'

Another scream, even louder than the first. More stink of roasting skin and scorched flesh.

'You will accuse me next of deliberately leaving the place unguarded,' Elihu sneered. And, to be honest, the thought has crossed my mind more than once, though I know it is a foolishness. 'God blind me, Catherine,' he went on, 'your imaginings will be the death of you. Better if you devoted your efforts to the babe you carry, or to showing a little more affection for poor Nan.'

'The girl wants for nothing. Nothing. And the Governor's residence? Now I think of it, have you not given John Bridger and his shrew of a wife the run of the place. Katherine Nicks the use of the Governor's private office too? How convenient.'

'Bridger finds himself in dire straits since his dismissal. Was it not you who lectured me about them being friends? But now – Winifred a shrew? My dear, how fickle you are become. And Katherine? She holds the commission to conduct our diamond trade. A significant role that merits a prestigious office. Ah, here comes the last of them.'

The third mutineer, weasel-thin, though he seemed entirely unconcerned, casual about his punishment.

'A bluff cove, this one,' I said, and watched as he shrugged himself free of his guards, marched alone towards the brazier. Yet he was studying the crowd, as though he might find salvation there. Or a friend. And then he smiled, a quick nod of acknowledgement towards the Council members' seating and sunshade. I turned to see for myself. They were chatting among themselves, our bold senior officials, presumably already bored with the proceedings – their trade deals, their private profits and the day's business their only concern. But one among them, just one, who was not engaged in conversation. 'Seaton,' I said. 'I should have known it would be Seaton.'

He had been here more than a month, ever since Masulipatnam was lost to us, exactly as he had predicted. Our futile little war with the Mughal Emperor. Indeed, Aurangzeb had now driven us from everywhere except our factories on the Bombay islands or here at Madras Patnam. In a short while, Josiah Childe's war with the Mughals will have cost the Company all of India. But this concern was far from my own thoughts when I saw Seaton. He had approached me not long after his return, the same veiled threats, demanded an affidavit against Matthew. Yet this time I had refused and, since then, I had seen nothing of him.

'Seaton?' Elihu groaned. 'Oh, Lord save us from another conspiracy theory about Vincent Seaton.'

'He knows him. Look!'

The mutineer's bravado seemed to have deserted him, his previously implacable façade now turned to fear.

'Mister!' he began to shout, but at that instant one of the soldiers, a veritable ox, leapt forward, threw one arm around the rogue's throat, clamped the fingers of the other hand around the prisoner's mouth, kicked the legs from under him and, at the same time, hauled the fellow's head to one side, making it easier for the farrier to apply his iron.

No scream this time, but the mutineer struggling so that the branding rod seared down the man's face and onto the soldier's arm, the sleeve of his uniform shirt. The thin cotton was insufficient to protect its wearer, who bellowed in rage.

'Oh, Christ Almighty!' the mutineer sobbed, tears blinding him as the other two soldiers jumped on him. But he managed to turn once again towards Seaton. 'You...'

He managed no more, for the fellow with the burned arm had seized the mutineer's head, twisted it savagely to one side until the neck snapped.

Elihu had steadfastly refused to acknowledge my interpretation of the events, naturally. Dismissed my delusions. And turned directly to having the two survivors of his punishment lashed to poles, borne away by a small escort to banishment in India's wilderness. Besides, the spectacle had earned him an additional reward – those Black Town headmen having experienced an epiphany, suddenly realising the importance of promptly paying their outstanding taxes and ground rents.

So I later found myself alone, in that short tunnel within Joseph's mausoleum, my roundel bearer waiting outside. Something scuttled out into the sunlight at the farther end. A lizard or rat, perhaps. A distinct animal smell about the place now, despite the flowers I often leave there.

'My darling man,' I remember saying, as I touched my dead husband's name upon the stone with one hand, the other going to the locket at my throat. 'And my two little soldiers.' Davy just six feet from me, across the passageway, and Walt out there in the sunshine, beneath his own broken memorial. 'You know what I must do, of course, do you not?'

I prayed they were together, though sometimes in my darkest hours I was afflicted by the heresy that Heaven might be other than we imagined. I thought of all those souls, those millions upon countless millions of souls, all those who had died since the dawn of time, scattered across some infinite and featureless plain upon which it was simply impossible to find our already departed loved ones. How many writers must the Almighty employ to try and keep track of his charges in that unimaginably vast godown?

'And what, precisely, might that be, Catherine?' It startled me, made me clutch at my heart, at my belly. For an instant, it sounded so much like Joseph. Though it was not, of course. Merely Seaton, silhouetted in the arched entrance behind me. 'What must you do, mistress?'

'He thought he would be saved, did he not, Mister Seaton? That last fellow?'

'It must seem like vapid trickery, I suppose, but I had promised that he would be released. An act of mercy upon the scaffold. Sergeant Naylor had a simple instruction to release him in a particular way. Though it was, in the end, all more clumsy than I intended.'

'And Sathiri, the same?'

'You did not answer my question. About what you must do.'

What was he doing there? It seemed like a sacrilege, a desecration of this sacred place. And I was searching for a lie, any lie, that might hide my true intentions.

'Walter's gravestone,' I said. 'Have a fresh one carved.'

Seaton had taken a step towards me along the passage and, instinctively, I moved backwards too, anxious to maintain the distance between us. I could see him better though, his cropped hair, the loose *kurta*.

'Only those who lie for a living,' he said, 'ever truly master the art.'

'Then I have known some exceptionally gifted amateurs in my time, sirrah. Or do you tell me that your true occupation lies elsewhere than in John Company's employ?'

'Tell me, were you afraid? When Samuel Bembridge and his crew came to visit. Or did you show the same pretense of bravado that I see in you now? You tremble, my dear.'

Did I? If so, I was not aware of it, though it was always cool inside that tomb. He moved still closer, brushing his fingers along the wall, and I almost stumbled over some rubble in my efforts to keep away from him.

'You must,' I said, 'have had some hold over Bembridge, that he would not betray you, nor your intentions, even when he was put to the irons.'

Seaton had taken advantage of my lurch to advance along the tunnel. He was close now, and there was a hunger in his eyes.

'I feel sorry for them,' he said, 'these Roundsmen. Do you not? Forced to ply their trade here, a world away from Port Royal where so many of them have made their homes, left their families. Oh, they have families, Catherine. And the promise of a pension for wife and brood of by-blows is a powerful incentive.'

I edged back still further, knowing that I should simply run, but I was desperate to solve this conundrum, though he had extended his left arm, ready to seize me if I tried to escape.

'A pension? Well, now at least I can discount John Company as your paymaster. Josiah Childe and our Directors would be too tight-fisted to contemplate such a thing.'

'The Company?'

He was now directly opposite, sunlight at that end of the tunnel dazzling him. Just that arm's length away. Yet I still sought the truth. I had contrived this scenario. That the Company was beholden to the Crown for its licence to trade. That the Company paid huge amounts to the Crown to preserve that licence. This much I knew for fact. Yet the Crown must be aware of those within the Company's employ who were staunchly Parliamentarian, those they might believe to be part of the Monmouth Cabal, or similar – and therefore apply pressure to the Company to rid itself of those undesirables. Simple dismissals in the first instance. Men like Streynsham Master. Even John Bridger. And then, later, more drastic measures. *Senhor* de Paiva. But now...

'I collect,' I said, 'that I may have applied an excessively simple analysis. The Crown would shed no tears to see displaced or eradicated those who share little love for its depravities, its injustices. Yet I sense little about you of the Crown agent. So, the alternatives – well, there can be very few.'

'No time for children's games, Catherine.' He stepped towards me, reached for my face. But I lifted my hand, so that he grasped my wrist. 'And I hate to be repetitive,' he said, 'but we must return to our original scheme. An affidavit from you that we can use against Parrish. Discredit him.'

'And see him dead, like Jacques de Paiva?'

'One Jew more or less. Does it matter?'

I could smell his breath now, and he was holding me tight. I knew that I had left any attempt at flight far too late.

'It matters to me,' I snarled, 'for I should never have betrayed him. Yet I am thinking of the news my Mama has sent me from England, the new king's suspension of the laws against Papists.'

'And Dissenters, my dear. Your own will benefit too.'

He lifted his free hand towards my cheek. I tried to push it away, but he was strong – so strong that he left the hand there, palm open before my face, menacing me. Something more than menace. Almost soporific, like the swaying hood of the cobra.

'Not for long, sirrah,' I gasped, tried to free my pinned hand again, pushed with the other against his hypnotising right hand. 'Has he not already tried to expel the Fellows of Magdalen College for their refusal to turn their institution Catholic? And you, Seaton – are you one of those happy to swing with the winds of change, like Fitton, Dryden and the rest, rushing to convert to the Church of Rome?'

'*Memsahib?*' It was the young roundel bearer, poking his head into the tunnel.

'You can go, Aadesh. All is good here.'

'All very good, *memsahib*,' the boy replied, and the head disappeared from view.

'As he says, my dear, *very good*.' It was a poor imitation of the Tamil accent, but he quickly continued. 'As it happens, there are many of us who never renounced our faith at all. The one true faith. Though now, Our Lady be praised, we no longer need to hide it.'

Seaton a Papist. I should have known. Perhaps I always have known it. Yet I knew I was simply playing for time now.

'And a new papal nuncio to London, is there not? Mama tells me that our king, the King of England, prostrated himself on the ground before this mouth of the Pope. So, not an agent of the Crown, sirrah – but of the papal nuncio perhaps?'

'We waste time, Catherine. I will have that affidavit. Or who knows how your next lesson might play out?'

'Perhaps it may be more simple if I just tell Matthew Parrish how this pirate raid was supposed to frighten us both into subservience. Until it ran out of control, of course. And my friend, Sathiri, paid the price.'

'Jews on the one hand,' he sneered, 'heathen harlots on the other.'

There was a roar. Such a combination of pain and rage, rebounding around the tunnel as Matthew Parrish crashed into us, a blur of white, broke the miscreant's hold upon me and slammed him against the passage-way's wall, against Joseph's epitaph.

'Scum!' Matthew yelled, his hands around Seaton's throat and lifting him bodily from the ground, Seaton using both his own fists in an effort to break the grip. Matthew would kill him, I knew he would. But

I wanted something else – to have the wretch brought before Elihu to wring the confession from him once more, and then to see him swing for his involvement with the pirates, with Sathiri's death. So I ran to them, took a hold on Matthew's arm and shook it.

'No, Matthew, not like this.'

But, to my surprise, he swept his arm back, retaining his grip on Seaton's windpipe with just one hand and knocking me to the ground.

'Get away,' he cried. 'You're no damn'd better than him.'

How much had he heard? I had no idea, but enough to turn him against me, plainly. Then I saw Seaton reach down with his right hand, fumble with the skirts of his *kurta* to reveal an oriental dagger sheathed at his waist.

'Matthew!' I shouted, and began to clamber to my feet, though he needed no warning. He must have sensed the movement, pinned Seaton's hand to the wall before the fellow could unsheathe his blade. But Seaton lashed out with his feet, caught Matthew a wicked blow to the groin that sent him reeling back, releasing Seaton to regain his footing, choking and spitting, cursing, no longer impeded from drawing the dagger, leaping forward, putting the evil point to Matthew's neck.

'I'd love to finish you, Parrish,' he snarled. 'But I might have trouble explaining this. Though a story about how I discovered you both in a moment of passion, here in her first husband's tomb – what say you, Catherine?' He spun towards me before I could react or answer, had his arm around my waist and the blade now to my own throat. 'Of course,' he said, 'in the struggle…'

'*Memsahib*! Oh, *memsahib*!' Aadesh the parasol bearer, still here, standing in the tunnel's mouth. Bless him. For it distracted Seaton. He turned his head and I bit down hard upon the thumb that gripped the knife's hilt.

'Christ above!' he screamed, and tried to shake his hand free, but I bit even harder, like a terrier, until I tasted the iron of his blood.

Matthew was up, rushing towards us, and Seaton almost wrenched the teeth from my jaw as he finally let go of my waist and raked the knife across Matthew's chest and midriff.

I watched in horror as a line of blood spread across the white fabric and Matthew sank to his knees before me, while Seaton ran down the passage, knocked Aadesh aside and was gone.

Today I received a message that Matthew would see me after all. I had feared him dead, for he had collapsed unconscious into my arms. The roundel bearer had run to fetch Doctor Browne, his chirurgeon's mate, and his assistant but, by the time they arrived, Matthew had regained his senses though refused to speak even a word to me.

So it was with great trepidation that, this morning, I stepped across to the hospital. I am rather proud of the place, built in the Tuscan style along from St. Mary's at a substantial cost, much of which had been advanced by Elihu. That portion of my marriage settlement, of course.

For the rest, however, I have been less than satisfied with the outcome of that negotiation. The sum of eight hundred pounds to be allocated for Benjamin still not discharged. Elihu says that this will serve my son well, for the sum is gathering interest so long as it remains within my husband's coffers. Yet it still troubles me, for it could as easily be accruing interest in Mama's London bank. So many things to concern me. Matthew, naturally. But my fears for him wrapped about all the rest.

Then there is the question of the boys in general. To be protected, nurtured as though they were his own when, in truth, they had been shipped off to England, facing the horrendous perils of the voyage, when they were still little more than infants. And yes, I know that, in part, I had my own justifications for sending them but he never once made any attempt to persuade me differently or offer any paternal guidance to them. And David? Well, what can I say? Protection for my sons? It is risible.

Yet the hospital? This is my crowning glory. It serves now not only the folk of Fort St. George but, on many occasions, also the denizens of Black Town. My return on the three thousand pounds in gold and the five hundred pounds in gems that Elihu had gained from marrying me, and through which he has increased the value of his good fortune many, many times over.

I thank heaven, all the same, that my marriage has procured this, at least. A place of care for Parrish in his hour of need. I found him on the upper storey, in the main dormitory with its shutters all thrown wide to admit the healing sea breeze so that, from his cot, he had a limited view of the ocean, the ships out there in the roads.

'I dread to think what this place must be like when the windows are closed,' I said, hoping to break the silence between us with a modicum of wit. For, despite the refreshing wind, the Italianate décor, the dormitory was still overpowered by that hospital stench of vomit, faeces and foul food. I thought of another couplet he had written, about being healed of the illness but killed by the treatment. 'Matthew,' I went on, at last. 'You asked to see me.'

Finally he looked into my eyes, making no effort to hide the contempt.

'I had wondered so many times,' he murmured, 'whether Seaton could truly have been responsible for de Paiva's death. But I kept hitting the same obstacle. If so, how could he possibly have known?'

He was weak and pale, the bandages wrapped around his otherwise naked torso stained black with his blood. Doctor Browne told me yesterday that the wound is serious, deep, though not deep enough to have penetrated any of Matthew's vitals. No venom either, Lord Jesus be praised. So the cut across his stomach has been sutured and that across his breast bound tight, the doctor's own agglutinative applied to help seal the flesh, the whole length of it soaked in a balsam to nutrify the injury.

'That balsam,' I said, 'must contain a healthy helping of turpentine.' At close quarters, the resinous aroma was almost enough to cut through the hospital's other smells.

'So, how did he threaten you, Catherine?'

'The scent of resin always reminds me of that time when we opened the Company's Garden House. You remember? When Sathiri told us about the fruit of the Poison Nut? The *yettikottai*. Did you know, Matthew, that those children, those dwarf Gentues sent by Elihu for the king's entertainment – that some of those same seeds were found in their possession after he died? That they were imprisoned?'

'You betrayed de Paiva to protect your husband from allegations of regicide. You seriously believed that Seaton could deliver such a threat. Or was there more?'

I should have told him, about that threat I had taken to be more credible. Against my father and mother. Seaton's long arm to London. The ease with which, these days, all that was needed was a pointed finger at a Dissenter, mention of the Monmouth Cabal. But I knew that nothing I could say would neither assuage Matthew's grief, nor excuse what I had done.

'Nothing more,' I said.

'And you think Yale deserves your protection. Do you choose not to hear the things that are spoken, about his dalliance with Katherine Nicks, now that her husband is out of the way, down in Conimere?'

'Choose, Matthew? You think I have free will in this? There is no free will to choose unless there are true options before us.'

'Then his more than mere dalliance with de Paiva's young widow. How much of all this was contrived between your husband and Seaton – to help pave Elihu's way to Jeronima. Ah, you have not thought of that. Or do you simply shut your eyes to the inconvenient truth?'

'Seaton is gone,' I said.

'You helped him, Catherine. In Joseph's tomb. If I still possessed a shadow of doubt after all that I overheard, it disappeared when you tried to pull me away from him. That one moment. It gave him just the edge he needed. His escape. This.'

He touched the blood-soaked bandages, winced with the pain.

'I wanted the wretch to be brought before the court.'

'Truly? Doctor Browne tells me that your husband has reported some private feud between Seaton and myself. An unfortunate accident. Seaton transferred to Bombay with immediate effect. Really, how much evidence do you need? And I cannot shake off the suspicion that it was more than convenient for Elihu to have stripped the garrison in time for the pirates' raid. That Seaton arranged the thing I have no doubt at all. Perhaps merely to set loose terror upon us. To frighten us from our beliefs. Or frighten us away entirely. But the depth of your husband's knowledge – of that I cannot be certain. Yet you see where that leaves me, Catherine? If I doubt the husband, must I not also doubt the wife?'

There must have been a dozen ways I could have responded, a score of assurances I might have offered him. Yet now I could think of nothing else but the obvious.

'I know not even how you came to be there. I know not what would have transpired had I not been there.'

'I saw Seaton leave the compound. I did not even trouble to collect my rapier. Followed him. But I rather wish I had not.'

It was my turn to gaze deep into Matthew Parrish's eyes, and I saw there nothing but that same cold contempt, the friendship we had once shared entirely dead, along with the love of his life. And there was just this, the recollection of two lines from one of his poems that I particularly admired.

No matter how distant the true villain's shame,
'Tis always those closest we suffer to blame.

Christmas has all but come and gone – and I am heartily glad to see the back of it. The house has been decked with green, as always, though this year the colours are jaded and weak. A redundant kissing bush has hung from the ceiling too. Christmas Eve brought us mummers and wassailers, all of them strangely out of tune. And the midnight service – well, how could that be taken seriously when it was conducted by that venal paunch-bellied Tory charlatan, Reverend Evans?

Then came the Feast of the Nativity itself, joyless carols and raucous music upon the streets, with Elihu appropriately serving as our Lord of Misrule, he and others all garbed in vomit yellows and venom greens, going about the town with annoying pipes and drums, jingling bells, kerchiefs waving and badly painted hobby-horses a-prancing.

A perfect pretense at gaiety – though, for me, a torture. The truth is that I am lonely, friendless. Instead of the company I would normally have enjoyed at our Christmas Day feast, this year it was simply the most senior Council members and a couple of their shrewish wives – Higginson, Briggs, Littleton and that Scots braggart, Fraser. Cavalier faction, each of them, their discussion all tales of woe.

With the brawn pudding and souse, speculation that, Bombay now being blockaded by the Mughal Emperor, Fort St. George must surely be next in line for imminent destruction. A silver lining for me, of course – Seaton trapped in Bombay too, and though I wish no ill upon their garrison, it would be true justice if he should perish there.

Then, to accompany the boar's head – its mouth stuffed with lemons – and the shred pies, there was a heated exchange about an issue that had, of late, come to dominate Council meetings and to vex Elihu considerably. His honeymoon as Governor over. Accountancy issues about whether my husband has been paying the correct level of taxes upon his own private trade goods, as well as bickering over the way he has been collecting those poll taxes and ground rents. Favouritism, apparently, in their application. Surprise! And I feel not an ounce of pity for him.

Finally, with the plum puddings and spiced ales, the wives' complaints about the Gentues' recent celebration of *Karthikai Deepam*, their Festival of the Six Stars, a carnival of lights, with its squibs, sky rockets and other pyrotechnical contrivances. How this had been allowed to disturb their sleep for several nights in succession but, worse, seemed to have attracted far greater attention and attendance from our writers, factors and soldiers than the previous evening's midnight service. Outrageous, they said. The whole community turning native!

I was pleased to see them all leave, though that simply deepened the darkness of my humours, Elihu and myself forced into uncomfortable companionship with little or nothing to say, one to the other for some time. I was making some show of instructing the manservants in clearing the table, more from boredom than necessity. But he had taken Nan – as he has taken to calling her – upon his knee, and she was wailing, as was her wont. Never content, that child. But Elihu seemed oblivious to her cries, jiggling her up and down while looking frequently from Katie romping about on the floor, to the windows.

'Have you decided?' I said. 'What we should call this one?'

It sounded harsh, more so than I had intended, simply my weariness. Just a few weeks to go, however, my belly enormous.

'If it is a girl, as you seem so certain, then Ursula. For my mother.'

Yaj, the *pankah* boy, was working hard to keep the room cool. He has become somewhat renowned since the attack but now seemed to be taking Elihu's obsession with the windows as a gauge that he was too warm.

'Is there something outside to distract you?'

'A stool-ball match due to take place in the gardens,' he replied. 'I should officiate.'

'Who is it this afternoon, husband? Who has the honour on Christmas Day – the Nicks strumpet or Jeronima the harlot?'

'Please!' he snapped. 'The children.' And he waved for Tanani to come and take them away.

'It was convenient, I suppose, her husband dying when he did. Were you already rutting with her? Before?'

228

Matthew's words have been eating away at me all these months.

'You mean while you and Parrish were carrying on your own filthy little tryst? Oh, that injured look again. You think I don't know? Poor Seaton told me how he came upon you both. How he was attacked by Parrish and had to defend himself. I only wonder at his kindness and honour in keeping the whole thing to himself.'

'He did so because he is an inveterate liar. I told you what happened.' I slammed one of the serving dishes upon the table for emphasis.

'Have you forgotten? How you sobbed all those days after Parrish was shipped out? Like some love-struck loon.'

There had been not even a farewell, simply a casual remark from Doctor Browne that Matthew had gone. For his own good, it seemed. Some poison in the wound that was unlikely to heal in our local climate.

'I miss him,' I said. 'But not in the way you intend. I miss both of them. Matthew and Sathiri. But you would not understand. I overheard you once, Elihu. Many years ago, telling Katherine Barker as she then was, that the power in my household was not wielded by Joseph but by me. It was a foolish remark. But here I am now, feeling as though I possess no power at all. None.'

'Do you not, my dear? Well, let me count the ways. The bags of diamonds you have so often dispatched to your mother. It was clever of Joseph, before he died, to deposit so much with the Jew do Porto. Did he know, Catherine – that you would marry again so soon? Did you plan it together? Never mind. You know the worth of all those brilliants, year after year. And now? Accumulated to nine thousand guineas.'

'You have been studying my accompts?' I tried to keep the concern from my voice, for my private accompts I guard carefully, along with these journals. And heaven forbid that he should ever read them.

'Your mama keeps me well informed about her investments on your own behalf, and those of the boys. It is right and proper. Or, at least, it would be in any normal marriage.'

'It is all honest wealth, at least. Have you not schooled me in that? About how a talent for creating wealth is a gift from God. Whereas your own…'

'This nonsense of slaves again?'

'It is an irony, is it not? The Mughal Emperor threatens retribution

229

unless the trade is stopped. But then we find ourselves at war with him anyway. Does the trade resume? It does not. At least, not in its previous form. The supply no longer so readily available. Besides, it would have been dishonourable. So dishonourable. You had given your word, albeit to our enemy. Yet when our people upon Sumatra send to tell us they have desperate need of slaves, that compulsion to chase wealth takes you once again in its grip. As surely as those with an addiction to gaming cannot help themselves. So, what to do? To maintain your honour but also to quench your thirst for fortune. Ah, of course! Send your ships to Madagascar, so that African souls, instead of Indians, can be taken in their hundreds, dispatched to Bengkulu.'

'God blind me, Catherine, if I am honest I must tell you it surprises me that you are still here. You seem to have little love for poor Nan. No respect for me as your husband. No association with the other women here in White Town – why, you treated them over dinner with scant courtesy. And Parrish is gone. Or are you waiting for word – whether he has survived the voyage or not?'

Well, all of those things and more have been on my mind a long while, though there was another question that Matthew Parrish had planted in my brain.

'Tell me,' I said. 'The ships you sent to Madagascar. Your slave-catchers. Were they, by any chance, the pirate Roundsmen there?'

The first day of January, the first of the new calendar year, must also be the first New Year's Day in all my married life, the first in almost twenty years, that no gift, no token of affection, has been exchanged between myself and one or other of my two husbands.

Yet, this Twelfth Day, Elihu has been happy enough to lavish beneficence on the other women in his life. So he had arranged an elaborate procession to our garden house. And what more fitting, on this day, than he, Higginson and Briggs dressed as the Magi, mounted on camels, leading our caravan of palanquins out to carry gold, Arabian frankincense and myrrh to each of his drabs. It seemed to me something of a blasphemy, though nothing surprises me any longer.

The feast was elaborate, suckling pig and spitted goat, chicken and all manner of vegetables in a variety of *kari* sauces. And I mingled dutifully, the perfect hostess, chatting to all and sundry because there was work to be done. Dressed in my finest green damask, the one with the ample pockets beneath the skirts, and sporting my scented Persian fan. Yet always the same opening remarks.

'My dear,' said Katherine Nicks, wiping a dribble of dressing from her ugly chin. 'How long is it now, until the baby's here?'

'Three weeks,' I replied curtly. 'Though your own children, they must all be a joy to you both. And you are so in looks, Katherine. But the latest? Gracious, you named him Elihu. My husband was deeply honoured. To be the boy's godfather too.'

Godfather, indeed! Did he think us all fools? Lacking in basic mathematicks? I can count the months as well as anybody else, know that the drab's husband could have been nowhere in the vicinity when this one was conceived.

'Too kind,' she said, her face a mask of innocence. I could have slapped her. 'And yes, Elihu. But tell me, this new mine...'

I scowled at John Nicks himself, wondered how he could remain so passive. Elihu had last year appointed him Chief at our factory in Conimere, though unalluring Katherine had remained here – her work too important, naturally, for her to accompany her husband in his lonely outpost. He had been fortunate in the appointment, for there remained a cloud over his head from back in Governor Langhorn's day. Was that what sealed his lips? Those convenient gaps within the Company's books that hid such a multitude of sins. Yes, fortunate. For Elihu too. But now John Nicks was back, the factories at Conimere and Cuddalore closed temporarily, due to the war with the Mughals.

'John,' I said, 'it was foolish of me to mention the thing. It was a confidence that Antonio do Porto shared with me.'

'But a new mine,' Katherine smiled. 'Not something you can simply reserve to yourself. And surely you didn't expect John to keep this from me.'

'No? Are there no secrets between you then?'

She smiled, those dark eyes daring me to pursue the matter.

'John tells me,' she said, 'that the quality of the stones is exceptional.'

I had met him before Christmas, just after his return to Fort St. George, on my way back from meeting with Antonio, still excited by the samples I had purchased from him as part of our joint investment in a wholly new venture.

'Well,' I replied, 'with the greatest of respect to him, John does not have quite your own eye for the quality of brilliants.' I knew that the compliment would sound begrudged but, today, that did not matter.

'Oh, I would never trust my husband's judgement on such important issues. No, my dear, I visited the mine myself, two days ago.'

'Did Antonio give you leave to do so?'

'Do Porto's guards were reluctant to allow me access, and it cost me more than I should have liked but, in the end, I was able to look inside. If the little I saw is anything by which to judge, it must be one of the richest seams in Golconda.'

'I could not comment,' I said, tersely.

'Come, Catherine,' she said, 'this could be crucial for the Company. And for many of us with private interest in the trade too. Word spreads, you know? We have investors keen to be part of this. Hardly Christian to deny them, don't you think?'

'You should speak with Antonio.'

'We did. He told us to talk with you. Equal partners, he tells me.'

'For my own part, I am not looking for additional partners, Katherine. And – well, do I need to say more?'

'You may not like me, Mistress Yale, but I do represent the Company in this. And besides, I understand you may be considering a return to England.'

'Am I?'

'According to Elihu, yes.'

I was not surprised that he shared our private conversations with her. Pillow talk. I was simply surprised that her scrub of a husband should disregard the implication. Or did he know about her liaison with Elihu and not care? Besides I had as yet made no firm decision. Simply a consideration. Just one possibility among many.

'And if that were true?'

'It would make sense to make capital of your assets. Allow us to purchase your half of the partnership. At a reasonable profit, naturally.'

'I think not,' I said, and moved on, went to find the Bridgers.

'Ah, Catherine,' said Winifred, though her manner was stiff, formal. 'How long is it – until the *nenê* is born?'

'Three weeks,' I replied, trying not to sound too bored, nor to give away my new-found contempt for her. Traitor. 'And you, John, how are you faring?'

'We still have a roof over our heads. Not as fine as this one, of course. But the Governor's residence is very far from a hovel. And our houses on Scotch Street generate an income. It still rankles, my dismissal, though Winifred's now receiving some dividend from her work with Katherine Nicks. Is that not so, dear one?'

She gave the slightest nod of her head by way of acknowledgement, but she could not meet my eye.

'I greatly admire your dress, Winifred.'

She said nothing in reply, though it must have cost a pretty penny. Winifred Bridger had plainly made a tidy profit from her betrayal of my confidences. Could I blame her? Husband dismissed, his honour ruined, she a Jewess, each of them so open to banishment from our society. This house, that she had loved, taken from her. And by the man she must blame for her husband's fall from grace? So could I? Blame her, I mean. Oh yes, certainly.

'You know the other thing that rankles?' John asked me. 'That day when I was dismissed. Parrish came to our home with a file of his soldiers, to sequester my books. As though I were some common criminal.'

There. One more thing to add to their grievances against us.

'Doing his duty, surely,' I said. 'At the Governor's command.'

'Is that not what they always say?' Winifred snapped, at last. 'The *inquisidores*, the men with power – who now cast us out.'

'Cast out, Winifred?' I said. 'Surely your friend Seaton at least ensured you did not suffer that fate.' I saw her pale at mention of Seaton's name. And what – guilt? 'But I forget myself. Might I be allowed to have your drinks charged afresh? The *panch* is excellent, is it not?'

Seaton. If I had wished him dead before, the way he had manipulated me, the self-loathing he had engendered in me, it was nothing compared to how I felt after his desecration of little Davy's tomb. Yet he was not here. Not in person. Just Winifred as his surrogate. So I forced my hands to steadiness as I carried their drinking glasses to the table where the beverages were displayed and there I filled them, casually looking about me and reaching inside my pocket for the twist of paper I had hidden there – a twist of paper into which I had so carefully poured powdered seed of the *yettikottai*, the Poison Nut. It seemed appropriate.

Then I returned their drinks to them, making sure I presented

Winifred with the venom-laced glass, told the Bridgers I would try to find them again later, and went in search of Jeronima de Paiva. My third task of the afternoon. I waited until Elihu left her side and moved in quickly, deciding to deal with the predictable query under my own initiative.

'Ah, Jeronima,' I said. 'How pleasant to see you. And, before you ask, the babe, it is due in three weeks.'

'Yes,' she replied, 'I know.' Of course she did. 'But is it true – you plan to return to England?'

'It seems the decision must already have been made for me.'

'But how will you find things there? You have no love for this new king, I think.'

'As dissolute as his brother before him. But he cannot live forever. And when he dies, with no son and heir, it will be Protestant Mary who succeeds him. God will provide. It will be difficult, meanwhile, with a Catholic on the throne, but why should it trouble you?'

'The Church of Rome is no friend to those of my race, Catherine. You know that, I think. Yet I do not take this king's own faith too seriously. From what we hear he sleeps with his mistress one moment, then attends Mass the next. More hypocrite than fanatic, is he not?'

'That remains to be seen,' I said. It was an interesting discussion and, if it had been anybody but this harlot, I might have enjoyed it. Besides, I was somewhat distracted by my own doubts about the efficacy of the *yettikottai*. Those Poison Nut seeds have been languishing in my jewelry chest all these years. Did they lose their potency after all this time? And, if so, what effect might they now have on treacherous Winifred Bridger? On the other hand, if the powder remained potent, how long before her demise? And could her death somehow be traced to me?

'I suppose so,' Jeronima de Paiva was saying.

'What?' Her reply startled me.

'I agree. It remains to be seen – whether your King James chooses to rule intelligently, through some consensus with the people and faiths of your country, or whether he is driven by the Pope to turn back the clocks, force the Church of Rome down all your throats.'

'It seems he has not so chosen though,' I said. 'To rule intelligently. His new troops. His Declaration of Indulgence. His attack upon the bishops.'

This much news had reached us with the ships arriving latest in the roads. James had drafted in new Irish troops, all with Catholic officers, to almost double the size of his standing army. Then he had attempted to force through reversals of anti-Catholic legislation – in the name of freedom of worship, naturally – but had then imprisoned seven notable bishops because they had refused to punish preachers sermonizing against the Catholic threat.

So I knew the answer already. If Seaton is any example, there will be a thousand other Catholic agents, everywhere across England and its interests overseas, undermining or eradicating those who would stand against Papist domination.

'It certainly looks ill for your country,' she said. 'Dangerous. Perhaps for all of Europe.'

'This was not precisely the conversation I had hoped to have with you, Jeronima.'

'I imagine not.'

'My husband seems,' I said, 'to have almost fulfilled the first of his life's ambitions.'

'To exceed his father, and all others in his family, in the accumulation of wealth. Yes, it drives him.'

'He could not have even begun had it not been for the marriage portion he gained through my first husband's death.'

'By all accounts he was a fine man.'

'We found our level. Some equilibrium between us. Whereas, with Elihu, we have become almost competitors.'

'I admire your honesty, *senhora* Yale.'

'Then please allow me to be honest about his second ambition.'

'He seeks an heir.'

'And I am now too old to give him a son. This child I carry, it is a girl. I know it.'

'He grieves so greatly for the loss of David.'

'And I for them both, David and Walter. I have such nightmares, such evil humours.'

'You tell me this because it will add to the guilt I already feel. About your husband.'

'Of course. A little salt in the wounds.' To add, I thought, to having to share him with Katherine Nicks. And I often wonder precisely how that sharing works in practice.

'Catherine, I must tell you this,' she said. 'You are the only woman of any substance in all this White Town. I admire you greatly and, if you say the word, I will be gone. Out of your life. Your husband's too.'

That was courteous. But, then, she did not know about the *yettikottai*.

'There is no need. It seems that I will, after all, now be going back to England. Alone, except for the children. Besides, how will he now beget an heir unless with you, Jeronima?' I saw her face crumple at the thought, and I knew then it was the worst curse I could possibly conjure. And I could think of no better revenge for this Portuguese drab than to inflict Elihu Yale upon her. But I gave her my most engaging smile. 'So, let us say no more about it and part as friends, my dear. Besides, I have some other unfinished business to conclude with Mistress Nicks. Though I assume you already know about that. Antonio do Porto's latest mining acquisition. To make capital of my investments and assets.'

We should have sailed a week ago, but the winds have been against us and there has been great delay in loading the *Rochester*'s casks of fresh water. But now, at last, the sailors are straining at the capstan bars, weighing the anchor with their stamp and go, stamp and go, their lusty singing.

The captain has kindly surrendered his cabin for my purpose, as well as the adjacent smaller cabin reserved for any occasion when he is required to carry some dignitary or other. But it is little enough space, all of it combined, for my own cot and that of Katie, now almost four, of course. Then we have one crib swinging on gimbals for my latest angel – Ursula, indeed, at Elihu's insistence – born on the last day of January, and also accommodated in here, with me. But the second swinging crib, for Annie, at eighteen months, I thought best to leave in that neighbouring space with Tanani, who must now face this awful trial again for the second time.

How will our *ayah* take to England? I have no idea, but I have promised her she will be allowed to come home to Madras whenever she chooses. But as I write this, my gaze turning anxiously and often to the stern windows, I know that Tanani's possible return trip is the very least of our concerns. First, we must survive the journey back to England. And, even before that, we must succeed in getting under way without further impediment.

Yes, perhaps one of my last nostalgic views of the Coromandel Coast, my home these past twenty years, but my anxieties more driven by the chance that, even at this eleventh hour, my wicked sins might still catch up with me.

First, the Bridgers. What can have gone wrong? Winifred still in perfect health but her husband John struck down with such a flux, immediately after Twelfth Day, they were convinced he must die. And his torment has continued ever since. How? I had been so careful to make sure they took the correct glasses. Some twist of fate in Winifred's favour. Too late to do anything more about it, but Doctor Browne immediately began to express suspicions relating to Bridger's symptoms and I have lived in fear from that very day, that those suspicions could somehow point in my direction. I have expected, ever since boarding, that a *masula* boat might follow us out, carrying soldiers or a thief-taker to detain me.

Then, second, there is the new venture I had established with Antonio do Porto. He has been angered for some time that the syndicate in which he and Jacques de Paiva were partners had been so badly diminished by Katherine Nicks and her contract for the Company's diamond trade. The fact that Jeronima de Paiva was part of Katherine's little cabal seemed to make things even worse for him. So he had been more than happy with our arrangement. Indeed, he had instigated several refinements. Besides, he had plans of his own. Retirement among India's other major community of Paradesi Jews, on the western coast, the Malabar Coast, at Cochin, while most of his interests in Madras Patnam would be managed by another partner, Pedro Pereira.

So, this new diamond mine. Worthless, of course. I had arranged that accidental meeting with John Nicks before Christmas, sworn him to secrecy about the mine's exceptional value knowing that this would be the best way to spread the word. There is nothing, I have found, quite like swearing somebody to secrecy to ensure a rumour's rapid dissemination. And we had invested in a modest quantity of uncut diamonds between us so we could seed the mine in readiness for the visit that Katherine Nicks would inevitably make. Beyond that, it was simply that matter of feigning reluctance to accept other investors, which helped honey the trap. Allowing myself to be persuaded to return to England enabled me to change my mind, accept offers to buy out my share – though only these past few days – and since then the gold has simply flowed in, more than enough to enrich both Antonio and myself.

Today, Katherine Nicks will have discovered that the mine has no value at all and she must now, I imagine, be chasing back from Golconda in the hope of having me arrested. If she had been less tardy, she might have succeeded. Yet, as things stand, my nine thousand pounds invested with Mama will be doubled. The gold, and two purses of uncut brilliants, are here among my travelling cases while Katherine Nicks will have to explain to private investors like Fraser, Littleton, Briggs and Higginson, many others, where their peculation has led. More difficult, Katherine will need to confess to the Council, and to the Directors at Leadenhall Street, how the Company's more official investment in a new mine has gone so disastrously wrong. I doubt she can survive.

Will she attempt to have me charged with criminal deception, fraudulent illegality? Of course. But I shall hopefully be back in London long before any report can reach Leadenhall Street. And I have my own plans for how matters might proceed from there.

All of which brings me to Elihu himself. I wish I could claim some credit for his brother's opportune return to Madras Patnam just in time to bid me farewell, but in truth this was mere serendipity. However, I was at least able to arrange a surprise visit for him to the garden house and catch Elihu in a moment of intimacy with Jeronima. Thomas was, naturally, appalled by his lack of morality.

'But a Jewess!' he said to me later. 'How is that possible?'

It was certain that the next correspondence would convey the news to Elihu's family and I imagined the furore with which it would be received.

In addition, Thomas returned with news that the Council's speculative expedition to China, in which Elihu had personally invested a thousand guineas, was something of a disaster. The Governor would, undoubtedly, attempt to put some positive twist to the tale, but I carry with me evidence of this fiduciary impropriety. Evidence too about his avoidance of correct taxation on his private trade goods. Or the favouritism he has displayed in the collection of those poll taxes. Other information about the running of the Company's operations here at Fort St. George, which may be of interest to old friends like Streynsham Master.

It seems the least I can do as repayment, given so many grievances against him. The payment plus interest still outstanding to poor Benjamin. The risible level of protection he has afforded to my boys – and especially David. His failure to save Walt. The way he has paved his own future upon the foundation of Joseph's own hard work. The way that Jacques de Paiva's death opened the way for him to Jeronima – regardless of whether or not he was actually complicit in the thing. The depth of Elihu's involvement, if any, with Seaton and the raid – and therefore with Sathiri's death. Elihu's white liming of Seaton's attack on Matthew as a feud. Not one concubine, but two. My suspicion, just a suspicion, that Elihu may have had involvement with the Roundsmen in Madagascar.

And then, if any further reason for me to escape is required, there is my need to get away with the gold before anybody finds out about the mine. I have right on my side and, more important, I have taken the steps I need to ensure that right prevails.

Beyond all these issues, there still remains the imperative to survive this voyage. Six months at least. My treasure to be protected from our own light-fingered sailors, or from any number of piracy hazards. The drinking water, which decays so frequently in the tropics. Food full of weevils. Food so plain and unappetising that weevils might seem like an exotic ingredient. My own hampers of wine, hams and luxuries will be exhausted within weeks. The threat of violent storms, disease, the amorous inclinations of drunken crewmen. The vulnerability of the girls. Keeping them nourished. So many things stand in my way. But my rewards if we survive this? To see my boys again, of course. Reunited with Mama and Pa. To employ my modest fortune – wickedly procured or not – in a way that, for the first time in my thirty-eight years, I may determine entirely of my own accord. To raise my daughters far from the perils of the Coromandel Coast. And, God willing, to heal my breach with Matthew Parrish.

Of course, Vincent Seaton also has his reward. Matthew out of the way. Me too. We are defeated. Nobody left at Fort St. George who might now undermine the ascendancy of the Tory and Cavalier faction. It eats away at me, despite the new opportunities, the fresh beginnings that lie ahead. But who knows? Perhaps I might yet strike a blow at them from London itself. And I have not entirely given up the hope that we might eventually be revenged on Seaton himself.

For now there is simply this. The crack of wind in canvas as the anchor breaks free and the *Rochester*'s bow comes about when she catches the breeze. The vessel pitches gently with the sea's murmur repeating itself, over and over along her waterline, like one of Sathiri's mantras. *May there be well-being for all. May there be peace for all. May there be wholeness for all. May there be happiness for all.* She had once instructed me in the meaning of *karma* and, if I have it right, she meant that which is within our lives and remains indelibly written – that we are today merely whatever our *karma* etched for us in a previous life. Our actions in this life, therefore – and only our actions – can shape the *karma* of our future existence. Our mantras are not actions in themselves, but they can help us understand the true nature of things and therefore bring us to act accordingly. Can such philosophy sit alongside the teachings of our Lord Jesus? I think so.

Sathiri, I remind myself, means 'beautiful one' and that, in turn, conjures the ode that Matthew penned in her honour:

In Memoriam

Beautiful One, I must now say farewell,
In dreary darkling halls some while to dwell.
Though certain I shall be to hear your voice,
Reminding me oft-times: 'Rejoice! Rejoice!'
For we who Cupid lov'd, for lovers' gain,
Shared with this world more honest joy than pain,
Should grieve, of course, for one so dear we lost,
Though lose no single memory as cost.
And therefore keep those sweeter days alive,
In memory eternal to survive.

Through the cabin windows I can see not only the palm-fringed strand but now Fort St. George itself, beyond the line of breakers, slowly falling away astern and I hear Joseph laughing, as he did that day we first encountered Elihu Yale. Joseph laughs, and there is my chief regret, my deepest doubt. That I leave behind the final resting places of my beloved Joseph. Walter and David too. The *Rochester* surges forward, and so must I. To seek those actions that may set my *karma* in a life to come. For new voices beckon me and I know I shall never return here again.

The End

Historical Notes and Acknowledgements

I stumbled into this particular story through a chance discussion with our excellent Member of Parliament, Ian Lucas, early in 2018. He had developed a fascination with one of our Wrexham (North Wales) constituency historical celebrities, Elihu Yale, whose elaborate tomb stands in the old burial ground of St. Giles Church in the town's centre. Ian's fascination was infectious, though I soon became even more intrigued by Yale's wife.

There are frequent references in Elihu Yale biographies and online articles to Catherine, incorrectly claiming that she was at least part Indian. But a cursory glance at records of her wedding lead us to understand that she was born in 1651, location unknown, but possibly in Alicante, probably the third of four or five children. Her parents were certainly Walter and Ann Elford – the latter being the daughter of Richard Chambers, a former alderman of London. In 1669, Catherine married Joseph Hynmers and sailed with him the following year to the East India Company post at Fort St. George, in modern Chennai. During the following decade she gave birth to four sons, Joseph, Richard, Elford and Benjamin – though, from reading husband Joseph's last will and testament, not necessarily in that order. The fifth child, Walter, is purely fictional, although it is very possible that she had, or lost, an additional infant around the year 1674. Otherwise, the background I have given for Catherine's family is accurate, though it required a lengthy period of research since, sadly, Catherine appears mostly only as a footnote in Elihu Yale's story. Yet their lives were entwined for almost fifty years. And there is that mysterious reference in his own will: *"To my wicked wife..."*

I believed, therefore, that there was a part to be played here for historical fiction. The traditional and best role for historical fiction, I suppose. To fill the gaps in our knowledge with some plausible possibilities, and to 'bring to life' a previously untold aspect of a more familiar chapter in recorded history. In this case, bringing the lesser-known portions of Elihu Yale's life to a wider public but, perhaps more importantly, bringing Catherine out of the shadows.

The most common source for Elihu Yale's life – and those few rare references to Catherine – is Hiram Bingham's 1939 biography of the man. Bingham, of course, achieved fame as the fellow generally credited with the 'discovery' of Machu Picchu. Given the resources available at the time, Bingham's biography is reasonable, though as I began to study some of the other works available, both then and now – most of them relying on the original records of the Honourable English East India Companies – I began to notice discrepancies, particularly in relation to place names. And his list of acknowledgements lacks any mention of a single Indian source. In addition, the biography takes no account of the turbulent political backgrounds, both in India and at home in England, which so plainly would have shaped so many of the incidents simply recorded by Bingham as though they happened entirely without cause. Yet it was Bingham's almost unquestioning loyalty to the mythical image of Yale simply as the philanthropist *nabob* and collector that I found most difficult.

This is unashamedly a work of fiction. So, events in Madras have been composited and so have some of the characters. The fictional Matthew Parrish is based in part on a certain Lieutenant Richardson, and in part on the poet and adventurer Matthew Prior, as well as others. And the fictional Vincent Seaton is based in part, though very loosely, on Yale's associate Vincent Sayon and, in part, on various Jacobite plotters.

However, perhaps a word is needed on the subject of Yale's involvement in slavery. Here I have stuck rigidly to the events record-ed in the English East India Company's own official records, the Consultation Book for Fort St. George, particularly for the years 1687 through 1688. We see, for example, in the minutes for 17th January 1687, under Governor Gyfford, that each vessel bound for the English colony on St. Helena must carry ten slaves, for there was then a great demand for slaves in that colony. Then with Elihu Yale presiding over the Company's meetings in Madras, his note that, given the growing number of slaves traded through the port, a customs duty of one gold pagoda should be paid to the Company for each slave shipped out. In October 1687, confirmation that the duty is still being paid and the trade continuing. In February 1688, reaffirmation of the rule that every outbound Company ship should carry ten slaves. Finally, on Monday 14th May 1688, the trade abolished, with penalties to be paid by those continuing the practice but significant exemptions for those already possessing slaves but not yet having shipped them abroad.

A man of his times involved in an accepted trade of the times? Yes, of course. Though there were already significant voices in several nations raised against the abhorrence of slavery, even in 1688, and perhaps the greatest shame is that abolition of the trade at Fort St. George did not arise through some new-found enlightenment but, more likely, through the demands of the Muslim Mughal Emperor. Yale clearly had no scruples about the trade when, very late in his tenure as Governor, he responded positively to a demand for slaves from the Company's factory at Sumatra by sending to Madagascar for a great many African slaves to be purchased there – though I have brought that incident forward in the novel.

So far as Catherine herself is concerned, we know that, in 1680, her first husband Joseph Hynmers died, and she very quickly married again, pretty much in the circumstances of the novel, to Elihu Yale. We also know from an entry in the Fort St. George diary, for 28th May 1680, and recording the death that day of Joseph Hynmers, that Joseph Junior, then aged ten, had been sent home "by the last ships" – presumably in January of the same year.

As I have said, the birth and death of baby Walter is pure invention, though it is at least possible that Catherine gave birth to an additional child, possibly still-born, around 1674. Similarly, there is no record of Catherine miscarrying early in her marriage to Yale, but it's another real possibility. Yet the births, travels, marriage and deaths of her other children – Joseph Junior, Richard, Elford, Benjamin, David, Kate, Anne and Ursula – would all have been very much as they appear in the novel. They form a moving, tragic and entirely forgotten saga in themselves.

The pirate attack on Fort St. George is just one more invention, though the records show the number of times that the Council had to deal with piracy incidents, and the punishment meted out to mutineers from the *Royal James* is certainly factual.

Catherine finally left Madras on board the *Rochester* on 23rd January 1689 with her three children and her Indian *ayah*. It was a terrible voyage back to England. But that, as they say, is another story.

Otherwise, I owe a great deal to the main sources I used for the research and, if anybody wants to pursue the detail further, they were as follows:

For Madras and Fort St. George: *Sources for the History of British India in The Seventeenth Century* by Sir Shafaat Ahmad Khan; *Vestiges of Old Madras, 1640-1800*, East India Company Records, by Henry Davison Love; *The Diaries of Streynsham Master, 1675–80*, from the Indian Records Series and digitised from an original in the University of Minnesota; Fanny Emily Penny's *Fort St. George, Madras*; the essay *The English and Dutch East India Companies and the Glorious Revolution of 1688-89*, by K.N. Chaudhuri and Jonathan I. Israel; *Sati: Historical and Phenomenological Essays* by Arvind Sharma; *Madras in the Olden Times* by J. Talboys Wheeler; the Honourable English East India Company's *Masulipatam Consultation Book, 1682-83*: A.K. Raychaudhuri's *Jan Company in Coromandel, 1605–1690*; and Hiram Bingham's *Elihu Yale* for the American Antiquarian Society, 1937, and his 1939 biography of the same name.

For the politics in the period leading up to the Glorious Revolution, Simon Schama's superb *History of Britain, Part Two: 1603–1776*; and the *Journals of the House of Commons: Volume 5*.

For Piracy in the Indian Ocean, 1680-1710, *The Pirate Round*, on the website of author Richard Platt.

For additional background to the lives of Catherine and Elihu Yale, *Elihu Yale: Merchant, Collector & Patron* by Diana Scarisbrick and Benjamin Zucker; Anne Elford's *Last Will and Testament*, from the England and Wales Prerogative Court, April 1697; *London Marriage Licenses*, page 447, for the wedding of Walter Elford of St. Mary, Aldenbury (merchant and bachelor, about 36) and Ann Chambers (of same, spinster, 17, daughter of Richard Chambers, Alderman of London); *Parish Register*, St. Giles Church, Wrexham; Brown's *Cases in Parliament*, Volume VI, 1803; *The Midwives of Seventeenth Century London* by Doreen Evenden; *Mercaderes ingleses en Alicante en el siglo*

XVII by José Ignacio Martínez Ruiz; and *Yale: A History* by Brooks Mather Kelley.

My personal thanks to fellow-author Vaseem Khan for the work he undertook in reading through an early version of the novel; to my excellent editor, Nicky Galliers; to the superlative Cathy Helms at Avalon Graphics for her work on the cover concepts; to Helen Hart's brilliant publishing team at SilverWood Books and especially to Catherine Blom-Smith; and to my hugely supportive beta-reader, Ann McCall.

Finally, a particular acknowledgement here to those subscribers who pre-ordered copies and thus contributed to the crowd-funding project and promotional work that made this publication possible. Thanks to all of you!

Joan Roberts; Steph Wyeth; Annette Gardner; John Isherwood; Jed Smith; Beverly O'Sullivan; Chris Remington; Sheila Browne; Jean Coates; Gary and Charo Titley; Bernice Daly; Deborah Swift; John Haywood; Monika and Paul Evans; Norah and Ian Lucas; Paul Jones; Abi Davies and Mila-Rose Ince; Liz Davies; Sarah Payne; Julie Tift; Judy and Bob Jones; Mary Greening; Heidi Chapman; Bill Fairhall; Peter Booth; Ann McCall; the Creative Team; Sharon Powell and Kim Pimlott; Paul Jeorrett; and Tony Evans.

Glossary

ACCOMPT – An old spelling for *account*.

AGAINST – In addition to its modern meanings, *against* could mean *before*.

ALCORAN – The Koran. See also *Mussulman* and *Mahometan*.

A-NIDGETING – see Nidgeting.

AVALDAR – Here, a senior commander of either the Mughal Empire or the Marathas.

AYAH – A maidservant and/or nursemaid employed by Europeans in India.

BANDITTI – Common phrase for Jacobite rabble.

BANYAN – Dressing gown.

BETTY – The woman's name was often used for any maidservant, something like the way "Jeeves" can now stand for any butler.

BIBI – Here, the Asian mistress of Europeans in India; thus, the *bibikhana*, the house or dwelling normally allocated to such women. Politely referred to as "gentlewomen."

BIT – *Deceived*, *duped*, taken in, *tricked*.

BOHEA – A variety of tea, pronounced *bo-hay*.

BRAVO – A hired *assassin*; sometimes used loosely for any *ruffian*.

BRILLIANT – As a noun, a *diamond*.

BUBBLE – As a noun, a *dupe*; as a verb, to dupe or trick.

BUMPER – A (toasting) cup.

CALENTURE – A fever or illness, especially in tropical regions.

CANDLE BOX – Wooden or more ornate container, usually hung on the wall near fireplace or set on the mantle.

CANIONS – Close-fitting usually ornamental kneepieces joining the upper and lower parts of the leg covering and worn by men especially in Elizabethan and Jacobean England.

CAPUCHIN (CLOAK) – A cloak with a hood.

CAUDLE – A warm drink given to sick persons or invalids.

CAUNCE – An alcoholic, herbal cordial.

CHATTER-BROTH – *Tea*, or sometimes scandal-broth.

CHURCHING – The religious ceremony required to purify women after childbirth.

CLENCH – A *pun*; also spelled *clinch*. See also *Quibble*.

COLLECT – *Gather* as in "I collect that…" means "I gather that…"

COMING TO THE PARISH – Claiming poor relief.

CONVERSATION – Any social interaction. *Criminal conversation* was adultery.

COROMANDEL – A lengthy stretch of coast in southeast India.

CUP – A *cupping-glass* was a vessel used to draw blood; to *cup* a patient, therefore, meant to bleed him or her, a very common medical procedure.

CUT A CAPER – To lead somebody on a dance, either literally or figuratively.

DAI – An Indian midwife.

DEVIL'S TATTOO – Drumming fingers on a table.

DICKER – Barter.

DISSENTER – English Protestant rejecting the doctrines of the established Church of England. Those opposed to state interference in religious matters and members of independent, non-conformist faiths – such as Anabaptists, Puritans, Quakers, Ranters and others.

DRESS ONE'S HEAD – To 'do' one's hair, particularly women, but might also apply to men's preparations of their wigs. Women of any status would not be seen in public without their hair dressed and would never receive a gentleman without dressed hair AND a cap.

DRIVING PIGS – Snoring.

ELIHU – A biblical name, of course, normally translated as meaning *My God is He* and pronounced like those similar names Elijah and Elisha so, in this case, Ee-LYE-hyoo. It would not have been uncommon to shorten this name to Eli, but I can find no recorded instance of this having happened, in correspondence or anywhere else, in the case of Elihu Yale.

FACTORY – A trading post from which factors purchased, received, stored and delivered their merchandise. See *godown*.

FAMILY – In large households, the *family* often included the domestic servants.

FANAM – A small Madras coin worth a few pennies.

FANCY – The word is derived from *fantasy. Mind. Imagination.*

FLAMBEAU – A flaming *torch.*

GARNISH – Fees a prisoner paid a jailer to gain better treatment. *Bribe.*

GENTUE – European term for non-Muslim Indians before the word Hindu became common.

GODOWN – A warehouse. See *factory.*

HIGGLERS – Itinerant dealers in small goods.

HOITY! TOITY! – Riotous behaviour; flighty; frolicsome, e.g. "Such frolicsome behaviour!" but also sometimes an adjective "Hoity toity behaviour."

IDIOT – *Idiot* didn't always have the same insulting tones it has today. An idiot was more usually someone with impaired mental ability.

INTERLOPERS – Independent traders and merchants.

JAKES – A privy or latrine.

JILT – A harlot, *whore*, or kept mistress.

JOCOSE – Humorous, witty.

KHANSAMA – A chief steward employed by Europeans in India.

KIT-CAT – A mutton pie.

LINE – The equator.

LINK – A *torch* (see Sedan Chair).

LINSEY-WOOLSEY – Inferior mix of linen and wool/cotton; therefore "cheap."

LIST – As a verb, *list* could mean *enlist*, i.e., to join up with a military organisation.

MAHOMETAN – The standard spelling for a Muslim. See also *Alcoran* and *Mussulman.*

MARGENT – The *bank of a river.* Sometimes spelled *margin.*

MASULA – Surf-boat. Sometimes *masoola* or other spellings.

MINT – Most obviously, a place where money and coins are manufactured. But also that area within the parish of St. George the Martyr in Southwark, where Henry VIII had once had a mint but now a squalid area of London. In the Middle Ages, the "Liberty of the Mint" provided sanctuary for debtors and criminals who lived within the district.

MOBILE VULGUS – Our word *mob* is just a shortened version of the Latin phrase. Swift resented the clipping, and preferred the longer form.

MUM – Ale.

MUMCHANCE – Silent, mute.

MURTHER – An old spelling of *murder*.

MUSSULMAN – A Muslim. See also *Alcoran* and *Mahometan*.

NEYI – *Ghee*, clarified butter.

NIDGETING – Summoning a midwife and other women to assist at a birth. To go a-nidgeting.

NIGHT DEMON – A nightmare.

OLIVER – (Slang) Chamber pot, or the Oliver's Skull.

ORDINARY – As a noun, an *ordinary* was the chaplain at a prison.

PAGODA – Either a temple or, more usually here, a gold coin minted by the English East India Company with a figure of the god Vishnu on one side, and each coin worth eight shillings (twenty shillings to the pound).

PANKAH – A large fan, usually ceiling-mounted, and operated by a servant.

PARADESI – Jews in India, their origins in Spain and Portugal, Sephardi in modern Hebrew.

PATNAM – Here, denotes town or city.

PECKSNIFF – A hypocrite.

PECULATION – Like the worst form of *speculation* means personal enrichment, embezzlement.

PERUKE – Another word for a wig, or periwig.

PETTY-FOGGER – Contemptuous term for unscrupulous lawyer.

PLAIN-WORK – Basic sewing.

POESY – An obsolete word for *poetry*.

POSSE COMITATUS – A *posse*. The "force of the country."

POUNCE POT – The shaker containing pounce, the fine powder used for drying ink.

PROTEST – *To declare* as in "I protest!" means "I declare!"

QUIBBLE – A *pun*. See also *Clench*.

RAIN-NAPPER – An umbrella (*umbrello*).

RANTER – Somebody who talks foolishly, raves, from the Antinomian Sect of 1645.

RECEIPT – *Recipe*.

RELICT – Something that survives; a *widow*.

RENCOUNTER – A meeting (or, as a verb, to meet). Early form of *encounter*, of coure.

ROUNDEL – A parasol.

RUB – An obstacle, rough ground, as in "there's the rub."

SATI – The practice among upper caste Hindu women of burning themselves on their husband's funeral pyres.

SCIENCE – *Science* was often used to mean learning or knowledge of any sort, not just the "natural sciences" and "social sciences" now covered by the term.

SCRUB – A mean, insignificant fellow (from shrub, a stunted tree).

SIMKIN – (Slang) A fool.

SE'NNIGHT – A week.

SOMA – A semi-mythical Vedic ritual drink, an intoxicating and addictive elixir, its ingredients disputed but possibly derived from hallucinogenic mushrooms and/or the climbing milkweed, Moon Plant, Somlata (Hindi) or Somamum (Tamil).

SPONGING HOUSE – A house kept by a bailiff or justice of the peace to detain debtors before their removal to debtor's prison. Also spelled *spunging house.*

STAY – To "stay" one means to satisfy, e.g. "Will this hock stay you until supper, sir?"

TARTER – A stick to beat carpets etc.

TATTERDEMALLION – Untidy, scruffy, ragamuffin-ish.

TINKER'S DAMN – Tinkers swear continuously therefore their curses are worthless.

TIP A STAVE – Literally to arrest somebody (with a tipstaff) but used figuratively to mean "do a bit" as perhaps in "I'll tip you a stave" – I'll sing you a verse.

TORY – Originally a term applied to Irish outlaws of various sorts, and then, after 1678, to the Cavalier faction – Royalists, High Church Anglicans, Catholic sympathisers, etc – remaining after the civil wars and conflicts of the 1640s and 1650s. Those who supported the hereditary rights of the monarchy, the absolute and divine rights of kings. Later identified with Anglicanism and the Squirearchy.

TOUCH-PIECE – A coin pierced for suspension around the neck as an amulet, often presented by a monarch to the recipient or purchased from the king or queen. This arose from the belief that monarchs could cure certain diseases including scrofula. The coin would normally bear the portrait of the monarch so that the piece could take the place of the monarch.

TRAINED BAND – Militia.

TURK – It sometimes meant natives of Turkey, but it could often be used to refer to anyone from the East, especially any Muslim. As a slang term, it referred to any man who was particularly hard, as in "He was a real Turk."

TURKEY MERCHANT – Not a seller of large flightless birds, but a trader with contact with the Turks. Cloth was the most common item traded.

UMBRELLO – An early version of *umbrella*. See also *rain-napper*.

WHIG – Originally a term (*Whiggamor*, or *horse thieves*) applied to various groups of Scottish Presbyterian/Protestant/Covenanter (anti-Royalist) factions during the civil wars and conflicts of the 1640s and 1650s. Later applied to those in the 1680s opposed to the Catholic Succession of James II. Non-conformists committed to limiting the power of monarchy. Later identified with landowning families and the wealthy middle classes.

WONT – Accustomed OR habit, e.g. "He was wont to…" or "It was her wont to…"

YALE – Anglicised form of the Welsh Iâl, meaning *fertile uplands*. In medieval Wales, Iâl was a commote (a hundred) within the Kingdom of Powys, its capital at Llanarmon-yn- Iâl (The Church of Garmon in the Fertile Uplands). The Lords of Iâl ruled the area from their castle at Dinas Bran. The yale, on the other hand, is a mythical and heraldic beast, a vicious horse-sized goat – probably from the Hebrew *yael*, a mountain goat – sometimes spelled *jail* and, in Latin, *eale*, but unrelated to Yale/Iâl except that the coat of arms for Yale University carries the mythical creature as one of its elements.

Catherine's trials and tribulations continue in the second part of her journals, Wicked Mistress Yale, The Glorious Return. *Here is the first entry:*

Monday 20th May 1689

The ship was sinking. That much was plain, and the sight of our own sails, coming up over the horizon, should have been as wondrous to them as the descent of God's angels from Heaven on the Day of Judgement. No trumpet fanfare though, simply a single shot from one of the *Rochester*'s guns to alert them of our proximity, should their lookouts somehow now be more focused on survival than their duties.

They were fortunate to be in such peril in that precise spot, though a piece of fortune, it later transpired, entirely due to the skills and tenacity of her navigators in bringing her there. One of the few places where outbound vessels from the European ports and destined for the Cape of Good Hope and beyond – after following the trade winds across the Atlantic from the coast of Brazil – cross paths with those inbound and driving north up the west coast of Africa. Yet, when the *Rochester* sighted them they were many hundreds of miles from land and in heavy seas.

By the time we were hove-to and within hailing distance – and Captain Sutton able to satisfy himself that they posed no piratical danger – the Dutch seamen had taken to their boats and their vessel, the *Johane*, was down by the bow, listing to starboard, her decks almost entirely awash, bails of cargo rising and falling on the swell.

They wanted to be taken into Cape Town, of course, though Captain Sutton would have none of it. We had already been delayed in that port longer than he would have liked, taking on water, fruit and other fresh supplies. But mainly the foul weather blowing in from the northwest. And the news. Oh, that astonishing news. News that now made it even more imperative for us to reach England with all possible speed.

Yet his decision causes great unrest among our crew. Some of them are veterans of our own recent wars with the Hollanders, and suffered horribly in one or other of the defeats inflicted upon our navy.

Besides, we are a John Company ship and they our bitter rivals from the Dutch East India Company – Jan Company, as we disparagingly name them. Anyway, so many additional bodies make the *Rochester* badly overcrowded, seriously increases the number of mouths to be fed. Our nearest landfall now will be the Azores, still more than a month distant.

'I could put you and your men ashore there, sirrah,' our captain told the Dutch skipper as, this evening, we shared supper together in the cabin Sutton had taken for himself after surrendering his own, and a neighbouring cabin, for the use of myself, my three baby girls, and our Gentue *ayah*, Tanani, when we left Madras Patnam.

'*Nee*, my friend,' said Captain De Groet. 'If more supplies you take at Ponta Delgada, we can sail to London. Our new big city, *ja*? Our capital too now.' He slapped his meaty hand down on the table with unbounded joy, considering how close he had come to disaster. A rogue wave in hurricane conditions and the *Johane* had begun to founder, taking on water faster than the crew could pump her clear. They had tried, fought a valiant battle to get her to Cape Town but, in the end, it had been a matter of simple mathematicks, of scientific certainty.

'England conquered,' said Captain Sutton. 'I can scarce believe it.'

Conquered? Liberated, more like, though Sutton's weather-beaten officers obediently shook their heads in shared dismay. De Groet's sailing master, however, a normally taciturn fellow with a strangely nobbled pate, could barely contain his excitement.

'Conquer?' he said, with an irony in his voice that echoed my own thoughts. 'We are one now. *Goede vrienden*. Good friend.'

The news we had picked up in Cape Town, though Captain Sutton had almost refused to believe it. Yet here it was again, confirmed by the *Johane*. There had been a revolution in England. To my ears, a glorious one. In June, Mary of Modena, the Catholic Queen of Catholic King James, had borne him a Catholic babe, also named James. Or had she? The news told how rumours quickly spread, soon became accepted as fact, that the infant was not truly the King's son, and had been substituted for a child still-born.

In any case, much of England had hoped that having a Catholic monarchy again after one hundred and fifty years – with the exception of Bloody Mary's brief interlude, of course – would be a temporary aberration, would disappear with James's death, the succession of his Protestant daughter, another Mary. And suddenly that hope was dashed.

'I can scarce believe it,' I said, unable to restrain my enthusiasm any further. 'There we were, all Christmas at Fort St. George, continuing with our normal round while, in England, the world was being turned upside down. Heavens! It takes so long, the back and forth of news, we might as well have been on the moon.'

It was something of an exaggeration, that thing about our normal social round. It was over Christmas, after all, that I had finally determined to seek some revenge: to leave my husband Elihu to his avarice and licentiousness at Fort St. George; to poison the woman who had betrayed my secrets to that popish agent, Vincent Seaton – though sadly I seem only to have succeeded in poisoning the creature's husband; and to cheat Elihu's two harlot concubines, as well as John Company itself, from a small fortune, and thus enhance my own.

'Good friends we may be.' Sutton paused with a piece of salted cod halfway to his mouth. 'And I am no adherent to the Church of Rome. Far from it. But the king? He is anointed by God. And none but God should set him aside.'

Oh, how bored I am with that foolish opinion.

Within a week of the baby's supposed birth, a group of senior figures had written to Mary's husband, James's son-in-law, the staunchly Protestant Hollander William of Orange, and invited him to force James, through military intervention if necessary, to confirm Mary as his heir. Word of the letter had spread rapidly and James, it was said, had been horrified by the level of popular support surrounding it.

'And was this true – about William landing at Torbay?' I asked De Groet. 'It seemed such an unlikely story when we heard it. The details so confused.'

'True, *ja*.'

Torbay, with an army of twenty thousand Dutchmen at his back. It seems he had quickly marched on London, but halted his advance outside the city, making a declaration that the sovereign English Parliament should decide what might happen next. Oh, joy! Parliament. The word alone makes my heart sing. But that much was all the news we had at Cape Town, and the uncertainty, the way that England's future hung in the balance, had gnawed at me ever since. So I thank God for this encounter with the *Johane*, and word of what has been happening, at least until just after Christmas.

'It seems, sir,' I said to Captain Sutton, 'that the king has rather set himself aside, has he not?'

'That is what we hear, *mevrouw* Yale,' said De Groet. 'Your King James, he run away. He throws away your *Grote Zegel* – how you say?'

'The Great Seal,' I replied, thankful that all my years of close proximity to the merchant communities of Portugal, Holland, Spain and India have gifted me at least a working knowledge of several other tongues. 'You heard that he threw it in the Thames?'

'Ja, in the *Theems*. Then run to France. He come back. Then go again. *Stadhouder Willem* – William – now is in London. December, that was. He is there. Our soldiers in London too. Your Westminster.'

'But the people,' said Sutton. 'They shall not accept it, surely. A Dutchman on the throne of England. A Dutch army of occupation in London.'

'Perhaps a *republiek* you shall be. Like us.'

'Could that be possible?' I wondered.

'We tried that, sirrah,' Captain Sutton smiled. 'Cromwell, you know? It turned out very badly.'

'The English,' I said, 'fear uncertainty more than the devil himself. If the throne is empty, I can see no reason why they should not accept Stadholder William as King, if Mary rules as Queen. After all, it is little more than eighty years since we brought James's grandfather from Scotland to reign over us after the death of Queen Bess.'

'Different kettle of fish entirely, mistress,' Sutton laughed. 'Between a Scotsman, and a Dutchie – begging your pardon, De Groet.'

Captain De Groet shrugged.

'Ja, different. You English at war with Scotland five hundred years. With *Nederland* just fifty. And your husband, *mevrouw* Yale. Big man, him. *Nederlandse* king, he will like?'

Elihu will likely to be too occupied with his infidelities, his concubines – *senhor* de Paiva's Jewish widow, Jeronima, and that drab,

Katherine Nicks, with her brood of children and several of them, it seems, his by-blows. But that would not suffice for answer here.

'My husband is the Governor of the Honourable English East India Company's post at Madras. At Fort St. George, Captain De Groet, as you must know. But he is also President there. Do you collect?' I spoke slowly. 'The English Crown has seen fit to also declare Fort St. George a Presidency. That means Madras Patnam is an official colony under the protection of the English throne. As such, Elihu has a responsibility to whoever sits upon that throne. He was required to serve King James loyally and he can do no other than to serve whoever might now succeed him.'

Of course he would. How could he not? These were the things that drove Elihu. First, the imperative for a male heir – an imperative destroyed with the death of our dear son, Davy, now entombed with my first husband, sweet Joseph, and alongside the shattered headstone of the third among five sons into whom Joseph and myself breathed life. Tragic deaths that still caused me to swoon often into the darkest humours, the worst of nightmares.

'And others at Fort St. George, *mevrouw* – they will see same way?'

'England has been divided, Captain, for the past fifty years. Fort St. George is no different. When I arrived there, we were divided too. The Cavalier faction, those we now call Tories, on one side. Dissenters, Parliamentarians, those opposed to a Catholic succession, those dedicated to limiting the monarchy's power – those the Tories now call Whigs – on the other. I fear I might over-simplify. But two opposing factions anyway. Yet, slowly, the Cavalier faction has worked studiously to rid itself of the most vociferous among its opponents. Dismissals. And perhaps worse. Now, my husband governs a Presidency where that same faction entirely holds sway. Men who will remain loyal to Catholic King James for as long as their purses allow them.'

Elihu's second imperative. The accumulation of wealth. He sees it as a gift from God, a sin if he fails to ignore that flair.

'Dismissals – and perhaps worse?' said Sutton, and I saw that his officers were all poised over the plates, hanging upon my words. But this was neither the time nor the place to discuss the possible murders in which Vincent Seaton is implicated – Major Puckle, that poor cove Sawcer, *senhor* de Paiva and my dear friend, Sathiri.

'I fear my tongue ran away with me, Captain. Dismissals, certainly. Each of the Governors before Elihu, in fact. Streynsham Master, for example. An exemplary fellow but driven out through those same political machinations. But my husband will do his duty, as I say.'

Of course he will. His third imperative, blind loyalty to John Company – after he has fulfilled imperatives numbers one and two.

Yet I shall do my duty too. I thought about Matthew Parrish, wounded in a fight with that scrub Seaton – mouthpiece for the Cavalier faction and an agent for the papal nuncio in London. Matthew was shipped home last year but not before his discovery that Seaton had forced me to betray our associate, Jewish diamond trader Jacques de Paiva – a betrayal that led to de Paiva's murder. The revelation has ruptured the trust between Matthew and myself, but I know that, if he has survived the journey back to England, he will now be in the thick of things.

Given the chance, I will play my part too. Salve my conscience. Compensate for any wickedness I may have done in the eyes of God. Strike a blow against my own enemies and those of England. Gather my family about me – Mama and Pa, the boys already in London, the three girls asleep here on the *Rochester*, safe in their cots. And perhaps even find some modicum of happiness.

Lightning Source UK Ltd.
Milton Keynes UK
UKHW041840190319
339472UK00001B/45/P

9 781781 328552